A WILD CARDS MOSAIC NOVEL

DEUCES DOWN

The Wild Cards Universe

The Original Triad
Wild Cards
Aces High
Jokers Wild

The Puppetman Quartet
Aces Abroad
Down and Dirty
Ace in the Hole
Dead Man's Hand

The Rox Triad
One-Eyed Jacks
Jokertown Shuffle
Dealer's Choice

Solo Novels
Double Solitaire
Turn of the Cards

The Card Sharks Triad
Card Sharks
Marked Cards
Black Trump

Deuces Down
Death Draws Five

The Committee Triad
Inside Straight
Busted Flush
Suicide Kings

American Hero (e-original)

The Mean Streets Triad
Fort Freak
Lowball
High Stakes

The American Triad
Mississippi Roll
Low Chicago
Texas Hold'em

Knaves Over Queens

A WILD CARDS MOSAIC NOVEL

DEUCES DOWN

Edited by
George R. R. Martin

Assistant Editor
Melinda M. Snodgrass

And written by

Michael Cassutt	*Stephen Leigh*
John Jos. Miller	*Kevin Andrew Murphy*
Melinda M. Snodgrass	*Carrie Vaughn*
Walton Simons	*Mary Anne Mohanraj*
Daniel Abraham	*Caroline Spector*

Illustrations by

Timothy Truman

TOR

A TOM DOHERTY ASSOCIATES BOOK

New York

DEUCES DOWN

Copyright © 2002 by George R. R. Martin and the Wild Cards Trust
Expanded edition © 2020 by George R. R. Martin and the Wild Cards Trust

Illustrations © 2002 by J. Boylston & Company Publishers

A Tor Book
Published by Tom Doherty Associates
120 Broadway
New York, NY 10271

www.tor-forge.com

Tor® is a registered trademark of Macmillan Publishing Group, LLC.

The Library of Congress Cataloging-in-Publication Data is available upon request.

ISBN 978-1-250-22720-1 (hardcover)
ISBN 978-1-250-22722-5 (ebook)

Our books may be purchased in bulk for promotional, educational, or business use. Please contact your local bookseller or the Macmillan Corporate and Premium Sales Department at 1-800-221-7945, extension 5442, or by email at MacmillanSpecialMarkets@macmillan.com.

First published in the United States by iPicturebooks

First Tor Edition: January 2021

Printed in the United States of America

0   9   8   7   6   5   4   3   2   1

To Len Wein and Chris Valada, my four-color friends

Introduction

That the Wild Cards series is still alive and kicking after over 15 years might be a surprise to some, but not to me. Then again, I'm the creator of James Spector, aka Demise, who died from the Wild Card virus but still managed to stay alive long enough to wreak havoc through several volumes of the series. The book you're getting ready to read, *Deuces Down,* is not only the first new Wild Card opus in quite some time but also proof that the story ideas and concepts nurtured by the series' writers have a way of coming to fruition eventually.

Let me digress for a moment to explain how I was lucky enough to become a Wild Cards author in the first place, since it bears to some degree on *Deuces Down.* When George R. R. Martin, Melinda Snodgrass, and the rest of the New Mexico writers and gamers were creating the foundation for the series, George cleverly decided to expand his group of participating writers beyond the borders of the Land of Enchantment. Being either incredibly insightful or a masochist, depending on how you look at it, one of the first people George turned to was his long-time buddy Howard Waldrop, who wrote "Thirty Minutes Over Broadway!" the lead story in *Wild Cards.* To know Howard is to love him, but his artistic temperament can best be described as inflexible, so it doesn't make him ideal for team projects. Howard's plan was to write his one story and jump ship, which he did. Master agreements and consortium points weren't part of his game plan.

At that time, Howard lived in Austin (of which I'm a native and current resident) and was one of the Turkey City writers. Turkey City was, and is, a writers conference where friends sit around reading and then dismembering each other's stories in turn. Given its Texas location, Turkey City was a bit more of a rock-em, sock-em affair than some of the more genteel writers conferences, but to date no fatalities have been reported among even the more brutalized participants. Another then–Austinite and Turkey Citizen was Lew Shiner, who George also quickly got on board for Wild Cards. Lew loved comic books and was an up-and-comer on the science fiction scene, being (with Bruce Sterling, also an Austinite and a Turkey City writer, I'm sure you're getting the general drift of this by now) one of the core group in the newly formed cyberpunk movement. Lew's character Fortunato, along with his antagonist, the Astronomer, was an integral part of the first Wild Cards triad. Lew, Howard, and I hung out a lot, including going on a weekly comic-buying run. Since I was also a Turkey City regular, Lew knew I could write, and sold George on giving me a shot at Wild Cards. How hard a sell he had to give George, I'm not sure. George had met me several times, read one of my early (unpublished and unpublishable) stories, and agreed to see what I could do. I wasn't entirely without credentials, having done some work for DC Comics that eventually showed up in *World's Finest* and *House of Mystery* as well as having a short story or two published.

Incidentally, I did the comic book writing under the name Bud Simons, which is what everyone calls me, although I'd been using Walton Simons for my fiction. This created mistaken assumptions about my true identity later on, but how was I to know? In any case, I was completely psyched to be on the Wild Cards team. The notion of being in the same book as Roger Zelazny filled me with glee, but I was going to have to earn it. The first book *Wild Cards* was already full, so I went to work on a Demise story for *Aces High* that I cleverly tied into Lew's Fortunato yarn. George bought it and I've been lucky enough to be a Wild Carder ever since.

Now in those days, if you got a couple of Wild Cards writers together, sooner or later (usually sooner) the conversation would drift to aces, jokers, and upcoming story ideas. The exception, as always, was Howard, who was far too busy for all this folderol, other than to explain (in consummate Waldropian logic) how his piece of the Wild Cards pie would keep getting bigger over time. Lew and I, on the other hand, spent a lot of time bouncing ideas off each other. In the process, we came up with Kid Dinosaur and most of the Astronomer's ace cronies.

During one of the early sessions, I went off on an absurd tangent and made up characters like Sign Girl, who could stand up in front of a neon sign or billboard, look like one of the letters, and disappear, Grow-Grip Man, whose hands became enormous when he grabbed someone, and Puddle-Man. Puddle-Man looks like . . . well if you've read Bradbury's "Skeleton" you know what he looks like. If you want to find out how that might actually be useful, read "Walking the Floor Over You" later in this book.

Which brings us back to *Deuces Down*. As writers, we've been talking about doing this particular book in the Wild Cards canon for a long time. After all, for every alpha ace power like those of Fortunato, the Turtle, and Golden Boy, there has to be an omega. Might not the effect on those lives be as dramatic as those fortunate enough to receive more profound abilities? We always thought so, and you hold the result of that notion in your hands. *Deuces Down* has another advantage in that its stories aren't all contemporary. The first book covered the history of the Wild Cards universe during its first forty years or so, but since that time the stories had remained firmly in the here and now. With *Deuces Down* those first four decades are

opened up again to the possibilities of the storytellers herein. We hope you
enjoy the results.

Just for the record. Walton Simons is not a pseudonym for the wonder-
fully talented comic book artist/writer Walt Simonson. Not that I wouldn't
give a lot to be able to draw as well as he does. "A lot" doesn't include being a
Wild Cards writer, which I don't think I'd trade for much of anything short
of world peace.

Walton Simons, February 22, 2002

Age of Wonders

by Carrie Vaughn

If I'm an ace, I'd hate to see a deuce.
—Timothy Wiggins, congressional testimony in 1953

ONE

June 2003

RALEIGH JACKSON SET HER alarm and planned on leaving the apartment early, grabbing coffee and a bagel on the way to the *Aces!* magazine office, so she wouldn't have to talk to her mother. But when she stepped into the kitchen to grab her bag and coat, Aurora was sitting there wrapped in her silk robe, two mugs of hot coffee placed in front of her, beaming with a thousand-watt smile. Even this early, a shimmer of light haloed her head, to match the bright smile.

How had her mother managed to be awake before eight? She was an actress, theater people were never up before noon. "Good morning!" Aurora gushed at her.

Raleigh sagged. "Hi, Mom." She climbed onto the stool at the breakfast bar, took the offered mug with a wan smile, and waited for the lecture.

At least Aurora let her take a first sip before launching in. "So. You're really going to do it."

Raleigh gritted her teeth. She loved her mother, she did . . . "Yes. I'm really going to do it."

"Raleigh, I love you, and I wish you wouldn't take this job."

"Mom—"

"*Aces!* is a rag! A gossip-mongering rag!"

But it was a gossip-mongering rag that everyone read. "It's a first step. A big first step. I get a few professional bylines, I break a few stories of my own—this is a really big deal. I gotta start somewhere."

Her mother might have been bitter that *Aces!* hadn't published anything about her in a decade. Raleigh knew she kept a scrapbook of clippings from back in the day, when Aurora had been at her peak during the seventies, when she'd been in her twenties, beautiful and glowing—literally—and starring opposite Robert Redford.

Aurora was pushing sixty now, and still beautiful and glowing. Just not young anymore. The rainbow of light and colors that she could make ripple around her had taken on a silver sheen, a hint of diamond sparkle among the reds and oranges. She couldn't dye that color away like she could the gray in her hair. Raleigh loved the silver lights; they were like a crown over her mother's head. Aurora was maybe learning to love them. She still turned heads, anyway.

But she wanted to work, and good acting gigs for aging actresses were few and far between. She'd done some TV guest spots over the last few years, and she never complained. But it wasn't the same.

Her mother hadn't taken a sip of the coffee yet; she just held on to the mug like she wanted to strangle it and glanced out the window over the Upper West Side skyline. "Do you have to start at all? Can't you work someplace . . . quiet? Journalism isn't quiet." She made it a declaration, forceful. "I just want you to be safe."

Quiet. Raleigh's whole life had been about keeping quiet, keeping calm. They'd had this same fight when she wanted to go away to college. To summer camp. When she wanted to take riding lessons.

Maybe Aurora wouldn't have looked so constantly fearful and unhappy at all the unquiet things she wanted to do if Raleigh hadn't been positive for xenovirus Takis-A—a latent, just waiting for her card to turn. And when it turned, she would probably die. She'd survived puberty, when many latents' cards turned. The other most common trigger was stress. That constant hum of anxiety had run under everything, her whole life. She almost didn't notice it anymore. Or, she pretended she didn't. Absently, she adjusted the chain of the MedicAlert bracelet on her left wrist, with her name and "*XT-A+: unexpressed*" engraved on it. "I could get hit by a truck crossing the street and then how would we all feel for worrying so much?" Raleigh said.

Aurora looked stricken. "Maybe you should just stay home forever."

"Mom . . ."

"I know I know, I'm sorry. You're all grown up and have to make your way in the world, I get it. I just . . ." Tears welled in her eyes, and at moments like these Raleigh could never quite tell if they were genuine or if she had summoned them, on cue. Everything with Aurora had to have a little drama in it.

Fine, she wanted drama? "I'll tell you what, Mom. I'll make you a deal. I won't take the job. I'll call *Aces!* up right now and tell them I won't be there. *If* you tell me who my father is."

Aurora stammered a bit. Then her expression went to panic, eyes widening, face draining of color.

Raleigh gasped. "Oh my God, you don't know, do you? All this time I thought you were just being stubborn but you *don't actually know!*" Look at that, not even on the job yet and she'd gotten her first big scoop. She wanted to scream.

"Oh, honey, it was the seventies," Aurora said, shrugging a little.

"I was born in 1980!"

"There was some spillover."

"No wonder you won't take me to see *Mamma Mia!*"

"Well, that's mostly because I don't know anyone on the production who can get us comps."

Raleigh had to get out of here, somehow, right now. She leaned forward on the counter, and wrapped her hands around her mother's, still on the coffee mug. Her skin was deep tan, teak-colored, against her mother's pale. That told her a little something about who her father was, at any rate. Her deep brown eyes to Aurora's blue, her curly black hair to her mother's red-gold, which would be going to roan if she let the color grow out. Still striking in either case.

Still didn't narrow it down much. The thing that did narrow it down? Her father had the wild card virus, too. "Mom. I love you. And I'm taking this job. Who knows, maybe I can bring some respectable journalism to the place."

Aurora huffed a laugh. "You're worth a million of whoever they've got over there."

Raleigh drank down the coffee and let her mother see her off at the door, giving her a big hug. At least she wasn't arguing anymore. "I'll tell you all about it when I get home."

"Looking forward to it," Aurora said. As Raleigh headed for the elevator down the hall, she called out, "And watch out for Digger Downs, he's a creep."

Thomas "Digger" Downs, *Aces!* senior reporter for going on three decades, met her at reception. He was of average height, nondescript, trending toward paunch in middle age. His brown hair was thinning. He looked her up and down. She couldn't tell if he was sizing her up or checking her out. She had dressed as professionally as she knew how, her dark hair in a bun, wearing a muted blouse and neat slacks.

His gaze narrowed thoughtfully, an expression she couldn't interpret. "Raleigh Jackson? Digger Downs, nice to meet you." His handshake was professional enough, at least. Then he asked, "And how's your mother?"

She had known her relationship with Aurora would come up and was relieved to get it out of the way as soon as possible. "She said you're a creep." Held her breath, waiting for the reaction.

Downs laughed, and Raleigh let the breath out. "You'll get along just fine here. Come on back."

The magazine's offices were in Midtown, in an older building down a side street. Not a prestige address but still in the middle of everything. The lobby had a wide desk at reception, a couple of seating areas and coffee tables filled with back issues of the magazine. Blown-up, framed covers hung on the walls, a timeline from the start on up to the present. Iconic images. A view of the Great and Powerful Turtle's first shell, the original tricked-out VW Beetle flying overhead, with the Empire State Building as a backdrop. One of superstar Peregrine's early covers, the young model glancing over her shoulder, hair brushing her cheeks, her astonishing wings draped around her body, raising the question of whether she was wearing anything under them. Jumpin' Jack Flash, arms spread and cloaked in flames, laughing as he flew over Central Park.

And there was the famous picture of her mother, a young ingénue perched on a grand piano, holding a champagne glass, while her ace power flickered a rainbow cascade around her.

Downs caught her staring at it. "That's a great picture of her."

"Yeah. She's got a print of it framed in the living room. If you haven't seen her lately, the lights have gotten some sparkles in them. Like diamonds." Not white or gray, certainly not. "You might think about doing a photo shoot, getting an updated version of that. It'd look great."

He gave a crooked smile. "Already hustling. Bring it up with Margot, okay?"

It wasn't a no, at least. Margot Dempsey was the magazine's editor in chief. Raleigh wasn't sure she'd ever get to meet the woman at all, and was suddenly nervous all over again.

Next came an open room with rows of desks and computers, ringing phones, filing cabinets along the walls, whiteboards with lists of names. Stark lights, a row of windows looking out over another row of windows, and *bustle*. A charge in the air, like everyone had a mission, and you couldn't help but walk a little faster and talk a little louder to keep up with them. Being out in the world and making things happen. This was exactly where she wanted to be.

"Everyone, our new junior reporter, Raleigh Jackson. Raleigh, this is everyone. Suzy's the department editor, Jim's got the Hollywood beat, Eddie's on fact checking—"

"You guys check facts?!" voices answered in chorus, followed by laughter, like this was an old, beloved joke. Eddie held up two middle fingers.

Downs made a half dozen more introductions, features writers and beat reporters. Already overwhelmed, Raleigh missed names and would have to check the magazine's masthead to remind her.

Eddie, a young white guy with glasses who couldn't have been much older than her, called out as they passed through on their tour. "Question, New Girl, and this is very important: should Jack Braun only date women close to his actual age, even though he still looks twenty-two?"

Serious journalism, Raleigh murmured to herself. *Serious journalism.*

"You do know who Jack Braun is, don't you?" Downs asked darkly, as if this were a test.

"Golden Boy," Raleigh answered. "One of the Four Aces. Hasn't aged a day since 1946."

"Okay, good. We get some interns in here who think the Four Aces was a British rock band."

Eddie asked again, "Well, how about it?"

Raleigh answered, "That's a pretty intense ethical question. Like, let's flip the genders. What if Golden Boy had been Golden Girl? What if the strongest ace in the world had been a woman who never aged? Would you be asking me the same question? Or what if Braun had been twelve when his card turned? An eighty-year-old who looks twelve. What then?" Yeah, that made the question pretty icky, didn't it?

Eddie turned to Downs. "She's too serious for this place."

"We're trying to class up the joint," Downs said, shrugging like it was out of his hands.

Raleigh already loved it here.

Downs led her on, through a door to a hallway with a tiled floor. "Didn't Braun date your mom once?" he asked.

Probably. Aurora had dated everyone, it seemed like. So had Braun, for that matter. Jack Braun was definitely not her father. Probably definitely not her father. "I'd have to check the Rolodex," she said.

"You might get a kick going through the files for tidbits about her. Stuff she might not have told you." He winked.

Like who she'd been dating nine months before Raleigh's birth. . . . Plenty of time for that later. "Anything you can think of off the top of your head?"

"Well, it was a bit of a scandal when she showed up pregnant and refused to say who the father was. You, ah, want to share that bit of gossip? Not that anyone cares now, mind you. Just for my own interest."

"I'm sworn to secrecy," she said, lying.

"Right. Anyway. Moving on. Ms. Jackson, meet the archives."

The door at the end of the hall opened to reveal a side room. Downs pulled on a string—the light was actually for real a bare bulb turned on with a dangling string, and she wasn't sure she'd ever seen such a thing outside of the movies. But then this whole building looked like it should be in some independent auteur film from the seventies.

The room was . . . astonishing. Dozens of banker's boxes, book boxes, post-office bins filled with paper, along with hundreds of manila folders accumulated in archaeological layers, probably for as long as the magazine had been operating. Dust on some of the boxes was thick; Raleigh smelled ancient rotting cardboard. Anything the magazine hadn't thrown away, but hadn't been of immediate use, must have ended up here. She was afraid to touch anything lest it disintegrate from age and neglect, so she merely stepped forward, staring.

"We've always had more material than we can use, you know? You plan a big human-interest story, but then Peregrine gets knocked up and the baby-bump watch clears out your features schedule for the next six months. You think you've got enough material for one thing, you just need one more interview, and for whatever reason it never happens. But we can't throw anything away, so it ends up here. It might all be garbage, but there might be some big scoops hidden away. We've been wanting someone to go through it for a while now."

She couldn't even get her eyes to focus to read labels, there was so much to look at. Typewritten labels, handwritten notes, files rubber-banded together, some with paper-clipped addenda. The newer boxes and files had sticky notes on them. "This is amazing."

Downs smiled wryly. "I thought you'd say that. It's why we hired you. That series of restaurant reviews you did for your college paper? 'The New Food Scene in Jokertown'? Those pieces were great. You didn't go for the sensationalist angle. Just about everyone who writes about Jokertown who isn't from Jokertown acts like they're a tourist, someone at a carnival sideshow. But you—you wrote about the place like a local. You made your reader feel like a local. Maybe you can take that outlook and do something with this mess. It'll probably be pretty thankless, but who knows."

It was either a mountain of trash or a gold mine. She wouldn't know which until she started digging. She couldn't wait. "Where do I even start?" she breathed.

She expected him to say something trite, like *at the beginning,* or to walk away laughing. Instead, he went to the back of the room, to what might have been the oldest box there, its cardboard sagging. Coughing, he dug through it and came out with a single folder.

"Try this," he said, handing it over. Coughed. "You might want to go outside to read it. We probably ought to issue respirators to come in here."

She'd stopped paying attention, completely enthralled by what she held in her hands. The handwritten label on the edge of the folder read, *Fidel Castro.*

Four Days in October

by John Jos. Miller

Monday, October 13th, 1969: OFF DAY

TOMMY DOWNS KEPT A straight face as he showed Sister Aquilonia the Ebbets Field press pass his father had obtained for him. It was hard not to smile, but he knew the Sister would deem him insufficiently serious if he did, and deny him leave from school.

Sister Aquilonia, his ninth grade English teacher at Sanguis Christi and the faculty advisor to the school newspaper, *The Weekly Gospel,* was obviously impressed by the pass, but still needed some convincing to sign him out of school for the day. Tommy didn't know how he knew that, he just did. He was, he frequently told himself, a good judge of character. It helped when he was hot on a story.

"Well . . ." Sister Aquilonia stroked her vermillion chin. She used to be a Negro, until the wild card virus had turned her a striking orangey-reddish. Some of the boys said that it had changed her body in other interesting ways, but it was impossible to tell for certain because of her voluminous habit. She did, Tommy noted, smell rather sweet, but he wasn't sure if that was her actual odor, or some kind of perfume. Nuns, he knew, generally didn't use perfume, but neither did he remember her smelling so nice before. He thought of complimenting her on it, but something told him not to.

"I gotta get to Ebbets today, Sister," Tommy pressed his case. "I gotta take advantage of this opportunity. My Dad went through a lot of trouble to get me the pass."

Tommy's father was a salesman for a Cadillac dealership over in Manhattan. He was a real wheeler dealer. He knew how to get a little sugar for himself when he closed the deal, or in this case, for his son. Even though Tommy was only in the ninth grade there was no doubt that he was going to be a reporter when he grew up, and he was already working hard to establish his credentials. *The Weekly Gospel* was only his first step, as he saw it, on his way to journalistic immortality.

"No doubt," Sister Aquilonia agreed.

Tommy knew he almost had her. "Think of it. I bet I'm the only reporter on a high school paper with a Series press pass. The *Gospel* will have an exclusive: Inside the World Series through the eyes of Thomas Downs."

The idea of covering the Series appealed to him largely because it meant four days away from school, four days of freedom untrammeled by nuns and uniforms and kids mostly bigger than himself. Not that Tommy wasn't a Dodger fan. There was hardly a boy breathing in the city who wasn't a Dodger fan that summer. Cellar dwellers for as long as Tommy could remember, the Dodgers had somehow catapulted themselves out of the basement and had taken the National League East Division crown. Then they'd beaten the vaunted Milwaukee Braves in the first ever Divisional Series, and, as National League champions, were facing the heavily favored American League champs, the Orioles, in the World Series. They'd already split the first two games in Baltimore. The next three were scheduled Tuesday, Wednesday, and Thursday for the Dodgers old park in Flatbush, a thirty minute subway ride from Sanguis Christi, in Queens.

"Well . . ." The nun considered options with agonizing deliberation. "Okay." Tommy suppressed any signs of glee as Sister Aquilonia scribbled on a release form, tore it off the pad, and handed it to him. "Here's a pass for the day—good for noon. That should give you plenty of time to get over to Brooklyn and run down your story."

Tommy hid his disappointment. Only noon? He'd miss less than half the day? *Well,* he philosophized, *that was better than nothing.* Knowing he had to stay on the nun's good side, he pasted a smile on his face. "Thanks, Sister. I'll get a good story, you'll see."

"I'm counting on it."

"I won't let you down," Tommy said, as he pushed open the classroom door and went into the corridor beyond. *Let's see,* he thought, *first period study hall. The penguin's note will let me report late. No need to hurry.*

Study hall was in the cafeteria. He didn't hate it, but it was boring. You had to sit there for almost an hour, being quiet, at least pretending you were doing something. He went down the silent, empty corridor, his footsteps echoing loudly. At the intersection he showed his pass to the hall monitor, almost contemptuously. There was no lower form of life at Sanguis Christi than hall monitors. They were all brown noses.

The monitor checked his pass, waved him on. He went down the hall, past the second floor boy's bathroom. Dare he go in, he wondered? Sometimes you could kill some time with the guys, but sometimes it wasn't the best place to be, all depending on who was hanging. A sudden urge to pee decided him, and he pushed open the heavy door and ducked inside.

Almost immediately, he knew he'd made a mistake. By then it was too late to back away. That would only have compounded his mistake, making him look like a scaredy-cat, and he couldn't afford to look like that.

The air was redolent with cigarette smoke, and something else. Tommy couldn't define it, but he could smell the wrongness in the air, hidden in the cigarette smoke. He couldn't define that smell, though the familiar odor had been popping up lately in unexpected, unexplained times and places. It was subtle. He couldn't figure out where it came from. It was just sometimes there, tickling his nose and prodding his consciousness, as it was doing now.

"Hey, look," one of the three said, "it's Tommy boy."

Tommy recognized him from around Christi. He was known to all, even the nuns, as Butch. The kids also called him Butch the Bully, but not to his face. He was a senior, much older than Tommy, who having skipped a year in grade school, was young for a freshman. If rumors were to be believed, Butch was older than anyone else in school. From what Tommy knew about him, he was dumb enough to have been held back a year, or even two. Dumb but big. And mean.

That was a bad combination.

"C'mere, Tommy boy."

Tommy approached the three reluctantly. Butch was looking pseudo-serious. His sycophants were grinning. *Not a good sign*. Tommy knew that anything from a verbal hazing to a lunch money shakedown to a serious beating was in store. He also knew that it'd be worse if he ran and they had to chase him.

Butch straightened up from the sink he was leaning against. He expelled a long stream of smoke from his nostrils. It didn't smell like smoke from a real cigarette. Maybe that was where the sweet smell was coming from.

"How come you're not in class, Tommy boy?"

He had six inches and fifty pounds on Tommy. He was as menacing as any monster out of myth or movie, and much more frightening because he was there, he was real, and Tommy knew he could kick the shit out of him without breaking a sweat. That sudden, sweet order was strong around him. It was coming off him in waves. Not from the hand-rolled cigarette he was sucking on, pulling the smoke deep into his lungs, but from him. None of the others seemed to notice it. Somewhere in a corner of his frightened mind, Tommy wondered why.

"How come, Tommy?" Butch the Bully repeated, a harder edge in his already edgy voice.

"I have to pee," Tommy said.

Butch looked at his sycophants. "He has to pee," he repeated in an almost apt imitation of Tommy's higher, lighter voice. He looked back at Tommy. "I hope you don't pee your pants little boy."

His voice was lilting, mocking. The other two laughed. "Yeah, pee your pants," one of them said.

Tommy gulped, started to move backward, and Butch came towards him, his sycophants right at his heels. He had a bright, weird look in his too-focused eyes. Some bullies, Tommy knew, liked to have their henchmen deliver beatings for them. Butch looked like he liked to hand them out himself. "Do you need a diaper, little boy?" he said, grinning slow and lazy. "Only babies need diapers."

I hate this place, Tommy thought, closing his eyes.

Butch towered over him. Backed up against the row of sinks, Tommy had nowhere to go. Butch grabbed Tommy's shirt and pulled him up onto his toes with little effort. Tommy closed his eyes against the tears that suddenly sprang up in them. Would he rather take the humiliation of a pants-wetting, or the pain of a beating? Considering, though, that they'd probably kick his ass no matter what. . . .

You bastard, he thought, *you big dumb ugly bastard.*

Butch put his face close down almost against Tommy's. Tommy's eyes were still shut, but he could feel Butch's hot breath against his cheeks. "Piss your pants, boy," the bully said, his breath oddly sweet as a field of flowers in May. "Pisssssssss—"

Butch's final word was elongated, like a reptilian hiss, and it concluded with a strange, funny sound like a whispered, gagging, choke. Tommy opened his eyes. Butch's suddenly stricken face was changing contours.

His features slackened, then seemed to stiffen and tighten. He screamed into Tommy's face as his head grew narrower, more elongated. His hair fell out in clumps, down upon his shoulders and chest. Butch screamed again and his tongue flopped out of his mouth. It was long and bifurcated. It caressed Tommy's face like gentle fingers.

"Clarence—" one of his sycophants said, "Uh, I mean, Butch?"

Everyone stared at Butch as he started to twitch all over. Tommy got it first.

"He's turning a card!" Tommy pulled away from the bully's suddenly slack grip and started to back away fast. It took the other two a moment, then they backpedaled as Butch sank to his knees.

"Whu-whut's happening to me?" Butch asked plaintively, barely able to shape the words with his suddenly lolling tongue and elongated jaw. He shook like a dog trying to throw off droplets of invisible water, but no one answered him.

The boys ran from the bathroom, Butch's companions screaming like they were on fire. Tommy lost himself in the ensuing excitement, blending in as just another ordinary kid in a group of ordinary, if excited, kids. Eventually Butch was taken away by emergency medics. Tommy, watching safely from the crowd as they wheeled him past, saw that he was tied down to the dolly with all but his head covered with a sheet. He was still alive, at least. He twisted frantically against his bonds, almost as sinuous as a snake or lizard, hissing all the time.

Everyone was talking about it. Tommy, after getting back to the bathroom and unburdening his frightfully over-strained bladder, kept silent about his participation in the affair. He wondered about the strange smell Butch had exuded like a night-blooming orchid. As the morning progressed he managed to get next to Sister Aquilonia for a moment, and took a deep sniff. She gave off the same smell, but not as strongly. A couple others around Christi had it, too. Tommy made careful inquiries among his classmates, and nobody seemed aware of Sister Aquilonia's perfume, or that of the strange girl in eleventh grade who was quite pretty but had feathers instead of hair. As he checked out of Sanguis to take the subway to Ebbets Field over in Brooklyn, Tommy began to wonder. Began to think if maybe detecting that odor was an ability he had alone. It made him feel queasy and excited at the same time.

Was he a wild carder? If so, he was one of the lucky ones. He wasn't one of those pathetic misfit jokers, but more like Golden Boy, and that Eagle guy, and Cyclone who had that cool uniform. And the Turtle, of course, but no one knew what he looked like. Maybe he was a creepy joker hiding in his shell, but he, Tommy, was a normal kid, maybe just a little smarter than the others.

Tommy was running over the possibilities in his head as he arrived at Ebbets Field and asked directions to the locker room. The gate attendants were skeptical that he was a reporter, but all he had to do was show his magic pass and they let him through.

As he walked through the bowels of Ebbets Field, heading to the locker room, his mind wasn't on baseball. It was whirling with notions of him, Tommy Downs, actually being a wild carder, being—let's face it—an ace, with the secret power to ferret out those infected with the virus.

God, he thought as he entered the locker room, *that would be great. I wonder if I should get a cool uniform of some kind, like Cyclone's?*

He stood on the threshold of the locker room, looking over the scene of ball players undressing. They were legends, too. Some of them, anyway. Don Drysdale, Tom Seaver, Ed Kranepool. Others were just faces to Tommy, who was just a casual fan. Reporters wove in among them, chattering, asking questions, laughing, taking notes. Real reporters, from real newspapers. Not rags like *The Weekly Gospel.*

Tommy swelled with a sudden pride. He could do something the real reporters couldn't. He could sniff out wild carders. *Maybe.* He took a deep breath, almost unconsciously, and, almost unconsciously, focused his nascent power. And in among the locker room odors of dirty uniforms and sweaty athletes and ointments and balms of a hundred acrid scents, he caught a weak whiff of what he thought of as the wild card smell, and stood there stunned as someone went by and said, "Hey, kid, don't block the doorway."

But he hardly heard him, hardly felt the man brush by. He didn't even recognize him as Pete Reiser, Dodger manager.

All he was thinking was, *There's a secret ace on the Brooklyn Dodgers! Gee, what a story!*

It had been quite a year for Pete Reiser. He'd received the call from Cooperstown in January telling him he'd been elected to the Hall of Fame in his first year of eligibility. It wasn't unexpected because when he'd retired he'd had the most hits, most runs scored, and highest batting average in baseball history, but it was still a stunning achievement for a poor boy from the midwest who'd wanted nothing more from life than to be a ball-player, who, throughout his twenty-one season career, played like his pants were on fire in every inning of every game, no matter the score, unafraid of opposing players, head-hunting pitchers, or outfield walls.

What was unexpected was that as the first-year manager of a team that hadn't been out of the cellar since '62 he was still managing in October, his team tied at one game apiece in the World Series. He could hardly hope for things to get any better, but he did. He longed with all his heart to win the Series, to bring the Dodgers back to the heights of glory that he knew with them in the 1950s.

And it just seemed possible that they might do it.

He stood inside the doorway to the clubhouse, watching his team unwind after a light workout. They were a loose bunch, mainly kids with a sprinkling of veterans, built around a solid core of young pitching and little else. Seaver, Koosman, Ryan, Gates, and Drysdale, the glowering veteran brought in to solidify the staff and, not incidentally, to teach how and when to throw inside, a lesson that Seaver, the young superstar, had learned quickly and well . . . Jerry Grote, great at handling a staff and calling a game, not so great at hitting . . . Tommy Agee, a gifted defensive center fielder . . . Ron Swoboda, a lousy defensive right fielder with occasional binges of power . . . Cleon Jones, their only .300 hitter . . . Al Weiss, the hundred and sixty five pound infielder who couldn't hit his weight . . . Donn Clendenon, bought from the expansion Expos to spell the grizzled Ed Kranepool (he was only twenty-five but had been with the Dodgers for eight seasons; that was enough to grizzle anyone) and provide some pop from the right side of the plate . . . Ed "The Glider" Charles, their oldest everyday player who could still pick it at third but whose bat had left him two seasons ago . . . they were an odd and motley crew, but they managed to win, somehow, with great but inconsistent pitching, timely hitting, and an often suspect defense.

And excellent coaching, of course, Reiser thought.

One of the excellent coaches, the pitching coach, was conversing with rookie Jeff Gates at the youngster's locker. Gates and most of the pitchers called him "Sir," Drysdale and Reiser and a few of the older players still called him *El Hacon,* The Hawk. He'd gotten the name as a youngster, partly for the great blade of his nose, partly for his sharp, black eyes. Campy had hung it on him in the spring of 1950 when he'd been traded to the Dodgers from the Washington Senators. He'd pitched for the Dodgers for fifteen seasons, many of them great, some of them awful, and finished his career with four years with the powerhouse Washington Senators. Reiser had watched him save the last game of the '68 Series for the Senators, throwing with guile and guts and nothing else. He could see that there was nothing left in the Hawk's arm but pain. Reiser knew that if he was going to make anything out of the mess that had become the Dodgers, he needed El Hacon. Not for his arm anymore, but for his sharp brain which had absorbed so much knowledge over his twenty-year major league career. The one thing the Dodgers had was some good young throwers. He needed a pitching coach who could turn them into pitchers, and he knew that Fidel Castro was the man for the job.

He caught Castro's eye across the room, and Castro acknowledged him with a slight nod, offered a few more words of wisdom to the young rookie, patted him on the ass, and made his way slowly across the room, dropping a word here and there for Seaver and Drysdale and Grote.

"What's your thoughts about tomorrow, *amigo?*" Reiser asked his pitching coach in a low voice.

Castro's eyes were dark and earnest. His voice was that of a prophet supplying wisdom to his high priest. "We're one and one. Plenty of games left to play. Go with the Drysdale tomorrow, then, we can come back with Seaver on three day's rest for Wednesday. Keep Gates in the bullpen, with Ryan, just in case. But Drysdale, he is ready."

Reiser nodded thoughtfully. "I believe you're right, Hawk." His gaze suddenly narrowed as he looked across the locker room. "Who's that kid talking to Agee? Should he be here?"

Castro looked, shrugged. "Who knows, *jefe?* Maybe a new clubhouse boy."

Reiser shrugged as well. He had more important things to do than worry about stray clubhouse boys. He had a World Series to win.

Tuesday, October 14th, 1969: GAME 3

THE NEXT DAY TOMMY decided to forego school entirely. If he didn't show up they couldn't stop him from leaving early, and he had something more important to do than waste his time on phys. ed., algebra, and *Great Expectations.* He was on the trail of a real honest-to-Jesus story. An exclusive about the Dodgers' secret ace. This was a story a real paper would be glad to print, and maybe even pay big bucks for.

He arrived at Ebbets Field early, and his press pass again got him past skeptical security guards at the gate. The stadium was empty and eerily quiet. Tommy thought it downright spooky as he wandered around, trying to find the manager's office. He got lost almost immediately, and probably would have stayed lost until game time if he hadn't run into a clubhouse attendant wheeling a cart of freshly washed uniforms to the home locker room. The attendant dropped Tommy off at the door of the manager's office while on his way to the adjacent locker room, and left him there standing nervously in front of the closed door.

Tommy was not a huge baseball fan, but every boy who grew up in New York and had an atom of interest knew who Pete Reiser was. Besides Babe Ruth, maybe, he was simply the greatest player ever. Ruth held the career home run record, but Reiser had set marks in many other offensive categories while playing a stellar center field. He'd done most of that with the Dodgers, though his last four years he'd spent with the Yankees as a part-time outfield and pinch-hitter. He was a baseball god, and Tommy was reluctant to disturb him in his sanctuary.

But, Tommy thought, *disturbing a god was a small price to pay for a good story.* He made himself knock on the door. There was an instantaneous reply of "Come in," and Tommy did.

The office was a lot smaller than he'd imagined. The walls were covered with black-and-white photos of old Dodgers, going back to the real old days. There was a rickety bookcase across the back wall crammed with note-books and thick manilla folders and across the opposite wall an old leather sofa with cracked upholstery. The room needed painting. Reiser was seated behind his desk, pen in hand, scowling down at a blank line-up card on his neat desktop. He transferred the scowl to Tommy. "No autographs now, son. I'm busy," he said, then looked back down at the card.

"I—" Tommy's voice caught, then he took a deep breath, trying to calm himself. "I'm not looking for an autograph. I'm on a story."

"What?" Reiser asked, looking up again.

Tommy took a step into the room, suddenly confident. "Yeah, I'm a re-porter. See."

He took the press pass from the pocket of his Sanguis Christi uniform jacket and held it out for Reiser to see.

Reiser frowned. "Christ, I can't read that from here. Come on in."

Tommy advanced into the room until he stood across Reiser's desk. Reiser studied the pass, frowning. "You sure you didn't steal that from your father?"

"No, sir. I'm Tommy Downs. I represent *The Weekly Gospel.*"

Reiser grunted. He seemed to notice Tommy's Sanguis Christi uniform for the first time. "Catholic boy, huh?"

Actually, he wasn't. Tommy's father just didn't want him in public school, and the really private private schools were just a little too pricey. Sanguis Christi fit the family budget, barely. But Tommy saw no sense into going into all that. He could discern approval radiating from Reiser when he eyed the uniform. He simply nodded vigorously to Reiser's question.

"Well, I guess I can spare you a couple of minutes. Sit down."

Tommy took the chair across the desk, and slipped the notebook out of his pocket. He opened it and poised his pen over the first page, and said, "Ummmm." He realized that he didn't know what to ask Reiser. He couldn't just *ask* him if there was a secret ace on the Dodgers. Tommy suddenly had an awful thought. *What if Pete Reiser were the secret ace?*

What if all season long he'd been manipulating a lousy Dodger team, nudging things here and there with the awesome power of his mind, making a ball go through the infield here, making a batter strike out there, clouding a base runner's mind so that he tried to go on to third where he was easily thrown out?

Tommy surreptitiously took a long, shallow breath.

He smelled nothing unusual, discounting the stale odors seeping from the locker room next door. Still, he was uncertain in this ability. It was new to him. He wasn't sure how reliable—

Suddenly he realized that Reiser was frowning.

"Have I seen you before?" Reiser asked.

"I was in the locker room yesterday," Tommy said, "getting background for my story."

"Yeah, I remember you now," Reiser said. "So, what's this story you're talking about?"

"Story?" Tommy repeated. "Sure. I was just wondering. Wondering if, ummm, anything strange has happened this season? Anything unusual?"

Reiser laughed. "Unusual? Hell, son, the Dodgers were in last place last year. This year we won the pennant. I'd say the whole damned season was pretty damned unusual. Um—" Reiser hesitated. "Don't say 'damned' in your article. Say 'darned.'"

"Yes, I understand. But what I'm getting at . . . what I mean . . ." Reiser waited patiently. Tommy realized that the only way he could think of saying it, was just by saying it. "What I wonder is if you suspect that maybe someone on the team has some kind of power or ability that he used to help win ball games, like, maybe a secret ace or something?"

Reiser stared at him. "A secret ace? You think someone on the Dodgers is an ace?"

Tommy nodded. Reiser suddenly turned cold.

"Using an unnatural ability to win a ball game would be cheating," Reiser said flatly. "What makes you think someone on my team would cheat like that?"

"I can—" Tommy shut his mouth. He was about to say, "I can smell him," and then he realized how unbelievably dorky that sounded. *Smell* him.

Reiser just looked at him.

"I can—I can read their minds."

"Really?" Reiser asked, apparently unconvinced. "Can you read my mind?"

Tommy shook his head. "No. Only the minds of wild carders. I can tell that they're different than normal people. But, I'm, uh, I'm kind of new at it. I'm just learning how, so, especially in crowds, it's hard to tell who's who." That much, anyway, was true.

Reiser nodded. "Okay. Well. I'll tell you what. You've got your press pass. Hang around. Check things out. And come back to me *first thing*," he emphasized, "when you discover who the secret ace is. Because I want to know, first thing, when you uncover him. All right?"

"Okay." Tommy stood. There was no sense in questioning Reiser any longer. Reiser didn't know anything, and couldn't help the investigation. Tommy was sure of that.

"Remember," Reiser told him. "You come to me first with the name."

"I will."

"Fine. Good luck, Tommy."

"Thanks."

Tommy trudged from the office, half-discouraged, half-angry. Not only hadn't he advanced his investigation, he'd made himself look like a fool. Because he could tell, he just knew, that Reiser was patronizing him. He didn't believe Tommy for one second. He didn't believe there was a secret ace on the Dodgers, not at all.

Just another day in the dugout, Reiser thought, but of course, it wasn't. Ebbets hadn't seen a day like this since 1957.

The old park was jammed to over-flowing and the fans had cheered themselves hoarse before the first pitch was thrown. All the regular Dodger fanatics were present; the five-piece band known as the Dodger Symphony that played loud but almost unrecognizable tunes as they marched around the park, the guy on the third base line known as Sign Man, who could cause letters to appear on his blank piece of white cardboard, and all the thousands of normal (and abnormal) fans who'd experienced one of the great rides in baseball history as the '69 Dodgers fought their way to the National League pennant.

Reiser, returned from the pre-game conference at home plate with the umpires and Baltimore manager Earl Weaver, plopped down next to Fidel Castro in the Dodger dugout. "How'd he look warming up?"

"Drysdale? *Caliente,* boss."

"He better be *Caliente,*" Reiser said. "We need this one."

Drysdale was one of the old Dodgers come home, probably to finish his career. He had started with the Dodgers in 1956 and put up some decent numbers for a fading team, as well as garnering a reputation as one of the meanest sons of bitches to toe the rubber. In one of the disastrous trades that marked the end of his general managerialship, Branch Rickey had traded him in 1960 to the Yankees for Marv Throneberry, Jerry Lumpe, and pitching legend Don Larsen who had thrown a perfect game in the 1956 World Series, then squandered his career on booze and broads. Drysdale had put up near Hall of Fame numbers with the Yankees, while only Throneberry had proved marginally useful to the Dodgers. When the Yankees disintegrated in the mid-1960s, Drysdale went on to have some good years for the Cardinals. The Dodgers had bought him back in '69 to help anchor the fine young pitching staff they were assembling.

He sauntered in from the bullpen, a towel wrapped around his neck to soak up the sweat he'd already broken. He was a tall, lean, big-jawed man with a ruthless disposition and will to win. He was one of Reiser's favorites. Reiser knew better than to pep talk him or pat his ass. That would just annoy him, take him out of the zone he carefully crafted where every ounce of concentration, every erg of energy, was geared toward one thing: throwing the ball where he wanted to throw it. That done, everything else would simply take care of itself.

Drysdale sat off to one side in his own world. The rest of the dugout was full of chatter, young men pretending they believed they belonged in the Series, veterans just enjoying their Christmas in October and hoping that it would last a few more days. Their energy was nearly palpable. Reiser thought that if you'd stick wires in their asses they'd light up the whole city.

"LADIES AND GENTLEMEN," the P.A. system blared, "please direct your attention to right field, where the first pitch will be thrown by a very unusual special guest. It will be caught by our own Roy Campanella, first base coach and Hall of Fame catcher from Dodger glory days!"

The cheers started again as Campy, gone from stocky to just plain plump, strode out to a position midway between home and the pitcher's mound. The fans' ovation dwindled into murmured puzzlement as Campy, wearing his old, battered catcher's mitt, faced the outfield wall.

An armored shell swooped over the rightfield bleachers into the outfield and came to rest over the pitcher's mound. "Ladies and gentlemen," the P.A. announcer blared again, "we present *The Great and Powerful Turtle!*"

There was a murmur of surprise that quickly grew into an appreciative outpouring of welcome as the Dodger faithful greeted the city's great new, unknown hero. All over the stands people turned to one another and said, "I knew he was a Dodger fan. I just knew it."

A small porthole opened in the fore of the shell, and a baseball dropped, hovered, and performed a series of swoops, turns, and arabesques, eventually settling down soft as a feather into Campy's outstretched glove.

"LET'S GO DODGERS!" the Turtle blared from his own set of loudspeakers. His shell rose majestically and moved off to a spot right above the rightfield bleachers where it stayed for the duration of the game.

Drysdale rose, took off his warm up jacket. "Enough of this shit," he said. "Let's go."

He stepped out of the dugout, and the rest of the team ran out onto the field after him. *Castro,* Reiser thought as Drysdale hummed his eight warm-up pitches, *was right. D has his stuff today.* He retired the Orioles one-two-three in the top of the first.

Jim Palmer was pitching for the Orioles, the youngest of their three twenty game winners, and he looked good, too, as he warmed up in the bottom of the first inning.

Then Tommie Agee stepped up to the plate and lined a homer into the lower deck of the center field bleachers, and Reiser thought, *Here we go again. This team is amazing.*

But is it? a small voice in the back of Reiser's head suddenly asked. *Is it the team, or was that kid right? Is it someone just manipulating things, jerking puppet strings, with some kind of power given them by the wild card?*

Reiser would never had thought of it, if it wasn't for that kid. Sure, it's crazy to think that the kid was right, but the world was crazy, had been since September 1946 when the wild card virus had rained down out of the skies of New York City.

Wild carders were banned from pro sports. A guy like Golden Boy would make a mockery of the game. But what if others were subtle, even sly, in the use of their powers?

Reiser looked down the bench. The Hawk sat in his usual spot next to him. Beyond him were the men who had fought so hard over the long summer to bring pride and faith back to Brooklyn. Was one of them secretly manipulating events behind the backs of all the others, stacking the deck so that the Dodgers would win?

Reiser snorted aloud. *Bullshit.* He knew these men. He'd gone to war with them all summer long. They won and they lost, and it was their skill, determination, and, yes, sometimes their luck that bought them their victories. That was baseball. Sometimes luck was on your side and the little pop up off the end of your bat fell in for a double down the line; sometimes it wasn't and your screaming line drive sought out the third baseman's glove like a leather-seeking missile.

Castro caught his eye. "What?"

Reiser shook his head. *"De nada."*

But, somehow, he couldn't shake the kid's question from his mind.

Tommy Downs could tell that the Ebbets Field press box attendant was a wild carder, and not only because of his sweet smell. The guy was about five and a half feet tall and he was shaped like a snail without a shell. His hands were tiny, his arms almost stick-like in their frailty. He had neither legs nor feet, but his body tapered down to a slug-like tail. He even had snail-like feelers on the top of his head and a mucous coating on his exposed skin. His features were doughy, but good natured

"Hi ya, kid," he said cheerfully as Tommy approached the press box. "I'm Slug Maligne, ex-Yankee, press box attendant."

"Tommy Downs," Tommy said routinely, holding out his press pass, *"The Weekly Gospel."* He paused as the joker's words sunk in. "Ex-Yankee? You mean, the New York Yankees?"

Slug nodded cheerfully, as if this were a subject he never tired of discussing. "That's right. I was with them for twelve days in the spring of '59. Even got into a game. Yogi and Ellie Howard were both hurt. That was why I was on the roster. I was playing for the Joker Giant Kings—you know, the barnstorming team; I played for them off'n'on for over twenty years—and we were in town when Yogi and Ellie went down on consecutive days. Maybe I wasn't the greatest hitter, but I was terrific defensively. Nobody could block the plate like me," Slug said proudly. "Game I played was the second game of a doubleheader. Johnny Blanchard caught the first game; we were winning the second twelve to two and I caught Duke Maas for the last two innings."

"Wow," Tommy said. There was a story there, too—The Forgotten Joker of Baseball—but he couldn't lose sight of the story he was chasing. In fact, maybe here was somebody who could help him, if he played his cards right. "That's really interesting. Say, do you think you could spot another wild carder, if they were on the Dodgers?"

Slug frowned. "An ace, do you mean? Because anyone could spot a joker like me—and as far as I know I'm the only one who made it to the majors, even for a single game."

"Yeah," Tommy said. "An ace. Haven't some funny things been happening on the Dodgers this year?"

Slug's upper body shimmered, as if he'd shrugged tiny shoulders. "Kid, you hang around any team for a year, you'll see a lot of funny things. Why, I remember back in '56 when I was playing with the Joker Giant Kings—"

A sudden roar again shattered the air.

"Man," Tommy said. "I've really gotta follow what's going on with the game. Can we talk later?"

"Sure, kid," Slug smiled, and Tommy made his way into the crowded press box where rows of reporters were banging away at their portables.

"What'd I miss?" Tommy asked.

"Drysdale doubled two in," one of the scribes said laconically, shifting his cigar from one side of his mouth to the other. "Dodgers lead three to nothing."

Reiser didn't have to even think about managing until the fourth when Drysdale showed his first sign of weakness. He gave up a walk and a single. With two outs Ellie Hendricks, the big, hard-hitting Oriole catcher, scorched a line drive into left center. It looked like a certain two-run double, but Tommie Agee came out of nowhere with his smooth center-fielder glide that ate up the ground under his feet, reached his glove back-handed across his body, and snow-coned the ball in the webbing, robbing the stunned Orioles of two runs.

Sign Man held up his sheet of cardboard and the word "SENSATIONAL" appeared upon it in thick, black, sans serif letters. The Symphony broke into a spirited rendition of . . . something . . . as Agee trotted smilingly into the dugout and the Ebbets faithful shouted themselves hoarse all over again.

"What do you think?" Reiser asked Castro as Drysdale came into the dugout, put on his warm-up jacket, and sat down on his end of the bench.

Castro shook his head. "Don't worry, yet. He's throwing smooth. His motion is loose. He's got a couple more innings in him."

Once again, the prophet was right. It was the seventh before Drysdale ran out of gas. He retired the first two batters, but then walked three in a row. Reiser hardly needed Castro's confirmation. It was time for the veteran to come out.

Reiser strolled out to the mound, and signaled for the right-hander, the twenty-two-year-old flamethrower out of Alvin, Texas, a tall angular kid named Nolan Ryan. Ryan could throw harder than anyone since Bob Feller. The only problem was, he didn't have much of an idea where the ball was going once he released it. He struck out more than a batter per inning pitched, but walked nearly that many, and with the bases loaded and a three run Dodger lead, there was no room for error.

"We need one out," Reiser told Ryan as he handed him the ball. Ryan nodded calmly, like he always did, and started his warm-ups as Reiser headed back to the dugout.

"It had to be Blair up next," Reiser said as he sat down next to Castro. The Hawk, understanding what Reiser meant, only shrugged.

Paul Blair was a veteran, a patient hitter. He'd know Ryan was prone to wildness, and test him by taking a pitch or two. But today the kid seemed to have his control. He poured over two fastballs for strikes as Reiser, watching, gripped the bench, trying to squcczc sawdust out of it.

Castro muttered, "Waste one now, *hermano*. Make him go fishing. Waste one . . ."

But Ryan, perhaps overly confident in his stuff, came with heat right down the middle. Blair jumped it. He connected solidly, driving the ball on a line to right center, and Reiser knew that this one was going into the gap and would clear the bases for sure.

But Agee didn't. He ran to his left with the effortless stride of the born center fielder. Reiser, watching, seemed to see the years fall away and it was as if he himself was out there again, running down the ball. Agee, mindless of the outfield wall as Reiser ever was, dove, skidded, and bounced on the warning track, and somehow managed to spear the ball right before it hit the ground, turning an inside the park home run into an out, and the end of the inning.

If Ebbets had gone crazy before, now it became totally delirious. Sign Man's sign read "DID I SAY SENSATIONAL?" and the Symphony's percussionist dropped his base drum and it rolled down the bleacher's concrete steps rumbling like thunder. In the sky above The Turtle's speakers blared *"Happy Days Are Here Again."* The fans deluged Agee with applause. Reiser and Castro just looked at each other and shook their heads as Ryan strolled calmly off the mound.

The inning was over, and so for all intents and purposes was the game. Ed Kranepool hit a homer in the eighth, making it four to nothing. Ryan went two and a third innings, giving up only one hit and striking out four, and the Dodgers were up two games to one.

As the team charged the mound at the end of the ninth, engulfing Ryan in a swarming mass of laughing, jumping, hugging bodies, Reiser sat in the dugout and smiled.

Just another day, he thought, *at the ballyard.*

Wednesday, October 15th, 1969: GAME 4

THE PRESS BOX WAS oddly quiet as the game started. Tom Seaver, who in only his third year with the Dodgers was already known as "The Franchise," had taken the mound against the veteran screwballer, Mike Cuellar, another of the Orioles' plethora of twenty-game winners. Reporters were

mostly sitting before their portables wondering what would be the next im-
probable turn of event, who would be the next unlikely hero.

Tommy found Slug in his favorite perch in the back of the press box,
where the joker could see the action on the field below, the action in the
box, and the action at the buffet where management fed the reporters hot-
dogs, burgers, fries, pretzels, and soda. "Hi, Slug."

"Hiya, kid," the joker replied with a jolly smile. "Want a hot dog?"

"Sure."

"Help yourself."

Tommy fixed himself a dog from the covered serving tray and took a bite,
savoring for a moment his favored status as a member of the fifth estate. For
the paying customers dogs were fifty cents each. And he could have as many
as he wanted. For free.

"Take a coke to wash it down with," Slug said.

"Thanks."

But being a reporter wasn't all free dogs and cokes, clearly. He was getting
nowhere with his story. He had managed to strike maybe about ten names
off his list of possible aces, and even then he couldn't be sure he was right.
He didn't trust his nascent power. It seemed to be working pretty well now,
standing next to Slug. He could smell the wild card odor come off him in
waves, dampened only a little by the mucous layer which covered his body.
But in the locker room it was confusing. Today he'd only managed to get
close enough to Jerry Grote, Tommy Agee, and Al Weiss to cross them off
his list. If he had the time, maybe he'd eventually be able to eliminate all
the innocent Dodgers. But he had only the rest of today and tomorrow. If he
couldn't find the culprit by then, bye bye story.

He needed help. He needed a strategy, a way to approach the hunt that
might lead him to the more likely suspects. There must be some way to eliminate some of them. If anybody knew, Slug, who had seen all their home
games, might.

"I looked you up in *The Baseball Encyclopedia* this morning," Tommy said.
It wasn't much of an entry. One game for the 1959 Yankees, zero at bats,
four putouts. But somehow Tommy knew that Slug would be pleased if he
mentioned it.

And he was. The joker nodded happily. "That's right. It wasn't much of
a career, but it's more than any of those joes had," he said, waving his frail-
looking arm at the legion of reporters before them. He looked at Tommy.
"You know, some people think the Yankees put me in a game as sort of a
joke. You know, 'Look at the joker, ain't he something?'" Slug shook his
head. "But, if they did, the joke was on them. Me, I get to say I was a major
leaguer. I'm in the *Encyclopedia*. I still have my Yankee hat. Out of all the
millions and millions of kids who grew up playing and loving baseball, I
could say I made it. I was a big leaguer."

Tommy nodded. This was exactly the mood he wanted Slug to be in. "And
you know a lot about baseball."

"It's been my life," Slug said simply. "I played it for over twenty years. Wasn't a greatly remunerative life, barnstorming around the country with the Joker Giant Kings. Sometimes we barely got out of town with a nickel between us all . . . but the places we seen, the things we did, the boys we played against . . ."

"What about the Dodgers?" Tommy asked, steering the conversation back at least to basic relevancy. "What happened to them? They were so great in the fifties, then they got bad . . . real bad. How come?"

Slug shrugged nearly non-existent shoulders. "Nature of the game, Tommy. Branch Rickey bought the team when Walter O'Malley turned into a pile of ooze back on that first Wild Card Day in 1946." Slug shuddered. He looked remarkably like a bowl of sentient jello. "Every time I feel sorry for myself, I think of what could have happened, and I feel grateful. Anyway—Rickey was a great man. A great thinker. They called him the Mahatma because he was so clever. He brought the colored man back into the major leagues. Jackie and Campy and Don Newcombe and the rest. Other teams followed him quickly, but he was there first and he got the best. It gave him a couple of years where he was ahead of everybody. He made some great trades. He kept the Dodgers together.

"But nothing lasts forever in baseball, kid. The Dodgers won their last pennant in '57. They came close in '58. Finished second to Milwaukee, who they'd just beaten the year before. But after that it just went bad. All of a sudden the team seemed to get old, all at once. Jackie was gone, retired after '57. Campanella battled age and injury. He hung on for a few years, but he was just a shadow of himself. Pee Wee, Newk, Carl Furillo, all faded. Only Reiser played on, but one man can't carry a team. Their only decent pitchers were Drysdale and Castro, and Rickey traded Drysdale. In a last attempt to capture past glory, Rickey traded Duke Snider for five prospects, none of whom panned out. Rickey was in his seventies then, and not as sharp as he used to be. His son, who they called The Twig (but not to his face), took over more and more of the operation, but he was never as sharp as the Mahatma. When Rickey died in 1962 the Dodgers started their long stretch on the bottom of the league."

"But what was special about *this* year? How come they won the pennant?" Tommy asked.

Slug laughed. "Hell, kid, if I knew for sure I'd write it down in a book and somebody'd pay me ten thousand dollars for it."

"Do you think," Tommy said carefully, "someone could be, well, manipulating things . . . using some kind of power to change the outcome of the games?"

"What, like an ace or something?"

Tommy nodded. "Or something."

Slug laughed again, giggling like a bowlful of jelly. "If they were, kid, they're doing a hell of a job. Listen, I've watched them all season. They win games every way imaginable. Why, one night Carlton struck out twenty

men! Twenty! That's a record. But he lost four to two because Ron Swoboda
hit two two-run homers—"

"Then Swoboda—" Tommy interrupted eagerly.

"Swoboda hit .237 with nine home runs for the season. Does he sound
like a secret ace to you?"

"No . . ."

"Another time they had a doubleheader. They won both games one to
nothing. In both games the pitcher knocked in the run, Jerry Koosman and
Don Drysdale."

"Then—"

Slug shook his head. "All I'm saying, kid, is that these guys win by every
means imaginable. By pitching, by clutch hitting, by hustling on every play.
It isn't one man." Slug gestured down to the field, where Seaver had retired
title Orioles one-two-three again and was running off the mound. "Not
even him. And he's great. He's terrific. But the Dodgers didn't win in '67 or
'68 when they had him. And this year he's still their greatest player, their
only great player. Nope. Nobody's pulling any strings behind the scenes."

"What about Reiser?" Tommy said quietly.

Slug frowned momentarily. "Reiser? Well, no one was greater than him.
No one wanted to win more than him. I don't know, kid. What kind of
power would he have? The will to win? How would that work?"

Tommy shrugged. As it happened, Tommy knew that Reiser couldn't be
the secret ace. He smelled totally normal. *Unless.* Tommy thought, *somehow
he, Reiser was clouding his Tommy 's mind.* Tommy sighed. *Best not start thinking like that,* he thought. *That way lay craziness.*

"Uh-oh," Slug said with some concern. "Looks like Seaver could be getting into trouble."

In the ninth inning the Dodgers were up one to nothing. Seaver needed only
three more outs to nail down the Dodgers' third win. He retired lead-off
man Don Buford, but then Blair got only his second hit of the Series. Frank
Robinson followed with another single, putting men on first and third.

"He's tiring," Reiser said.

Castro nodded. "Let him gut it out."

Reiser blew out a deep breath. "I'm going to go talk to him. We can't let
this one go."

Castro nodded, and Reiser sauntered out to the mound, taking his time.
The bullpen was up and working. Given a few more minutes and Gates and
McGraw would both be ready, but Reiser didn't want to take Seaver out. You
had to show faith in the youngsters. You had to let them work out of their
own trouble, or else they'd never learn how to do it. He'd learned that lesson under Leo Durocher, his first Dodger manager, and it was a lesson he'd
never forgotten.

When he got to the mound the look in Seaver's eyes told him everything he wanted to know. Very few pitchers would actually ask to be taken out. Their eyes told the real story, whether they were tired, hurt, or scared. Seaver's eyes told Reiser that he was just impatient to get back to work. Reiser nodded.

"Right," Reiser said. "I just wanted to make sure you were okay, and I'm sure. Remember—Boog Powell is up. Jam him, jam him, and jam him again, but if the pitch catches any of the plate on the inside he'll hit it out. If you want to waste one, waste it outside, far outside. Don't let the big son of a bitch get his arms extended. If you do, he'll hit it out."

Out of the corner of his eye he saw the umpire hustling up to the mound to break up the conversation. He looked at Seaver, who still had that some-what far-away look of glassy-eyed concentration. He looked at Grote, who snapped off a nod and a wink. Grote couldn't hit much, but he was a great defensive catcher and called the finest game in the majors. He'd make sure Seaver kept his wits about him.

"Okay," Reiser said. He turned and strolled back to the dugout as Powell approached the plate.

Boog settled into the batters box and pumped the bat twice, three times at the mound. Seaver stared into his catcher's glove like an automaton, then went into his windup and unleashed his arm like an arbalest blasting a rock at a castle wall. The ball whistled out of his hand, fastball, inside, on the black.

Boog cut at it, unleashing his long, furious swing, and the bottom of the ball sliced off the top of the bat handle, backward, foul, whistling just over Grote's shoulder and by the umpire's head.

Boog half-stepped out of the box, swinging the bat loosely in his hands. "That boy sure is fast. Give me another of those."

Grote smiled. "Okay."

He put a single finger down, hidden between his thighs, and the runners took off from first and third. Seaver wound up and pumped another fastball to the same spot, maybe a little lower, maybe a little more inside.

Boog swung again, one of the fastest bats in the league, and caught it square, but the ball was right where Seaver wanted it to be, inside, off the black, and Powell hit it right off the handle. The bat shattered, the end heli-coptering out somewhere near second, the handle still in his hand as he started to run to first.

Boog was strong. If anyone else had hit that ball it was just a little pop-up to the second baseman, infield fly and two out, but Boog was *strong*. Weiss, playing second, knew the ball was over his head, knew he had no chance to get it, but ran out into right field anyway, legs pumping desperately. He glanced into the outfield and saw Ron Swoboda running right at him, furi-ously, eyes clenched on the ball as it floated softly up and out. Swoboda was a solid two-ten, a one-time ballyhooed slugger who didn't quite make it. He was one of the three or four rotating Dodger right fielders. He was by far the worst fielder. Weiss was a slightly less robust one-sixty-five, a utility infielder who had a very light stick but a great glove. He figured if anyone would catch it, it would have to be him, so he kept going, though Swoboda was thundering at him like an avalanche of doom and the ball was dying out there in no-man's land beyond second base but hardly into the outfield, kind of in center but Agee was nowhere in the picture and kind of in right but there was no way Rocky was going to reach it, no way in hell, and suddenly Swoboda was diving, was springing forward parallel to the ground as the ball was coming down so softly it would barely dent the grass when it hit but it didn't hit the grass as just an inch or two from the ground Swoboda stabbed it, reaching out back-handed, hit hard, tumbled over, and held on.

For a second there was silence in the stadium. No one seemed to believe what had happened. Blair, on third, had kept his presence of mind, and as Swoboda caught the ball and bounced along the turf, came in to score on the sacrifice fly, cursing all the way. Frank Robinson, on first, had gone half-way to second, then turned and went back when he was sure Swoboda had held onto the ball, cursing all the way. Boog, standing near first with the handle-half of the broken bat still in his right hand, stopped, and cursed.

Castro, in that one calm, utterly quiet moment, turned to Reiser and said, "Even the man with hands of stone can flash leather when you need it most," like he was quoting from some forgotten book of the Bible.

Then, as Swoboda stood and tossed the ball back into second, Ebbets Field erupted into unbelieving applause, the fans pouring their hearts out to the man who stood in right, the front of his uniform stained with grass and dirt.

It was like Mays' over the shoulder catch against Wertz in '54, Reiser against Mantle in '56 among the monuments in center, Agee's the previous day. But, hell, those guys were *fielders*. They could catch the ball. Swoboda, for all his lovable determination, was a butcher. He couldn't catch measles if you put him in a hospital ward full of spotted children.

Sign Man flashed "MIRACLE IN FLATBUSH," the band played something, nobody was quite sure what, and the fans yelled themselves hoarse. Again. Brooks Robinson came to the plate, and had to step out because the noise still surged over Ebbets like an unanswerable tide, until Swoboda, hands planted firmly on hips, touched his cap in acknowledgment. There was one last crescendo of approval, and then the noise dulled to a muted background rumble that peaked again when Seaver dispensed with B. Robby with three pitches and the Dodgers trotted back to the dugout.

"All right," Reiser shouted. "We'll get it back, we'll get it back," but the Dodgers didn't. They went down in the ninth, and, the score one to one, the fourth game of the 1969 World Series went into extra innings.

"You okay," Castro said to Seaver in the dugout as he took off his warm-up jacket, and the young pitcher nodded at the tone Castro used, which was more statement than question. He went out into the field and disposed of the O's with no problems in the tenth.

Grote led off the bottom of the tenth for the Dodgers, the seventh man in the batting order. Reiser wondered how much longer the game would go—likely longer than ten since this was the weakest part of a rather weak Dodger batting order, and the O's had a strong, well-rested pen.

Grote hit an easy fly ball to left, and Reiser was thinking that maybe Seaver could go another inning, maybe not. Then he realized that Buford, normally a fine outfielder, was standing rooted to the spot. When he finally started after Grote's fly-ball, he didn't have a chance to catch it, and it dropped in front of him. The "II" in the Schaefer Beer sign on the top of the right centerfield scoreboard flashed to signify "hit," but Reiser knew that base runner was a gift.

Grote didn't hit very well and couldn't run very fast but he hustled on every play, so by the time the ball got back into the infield he was standing on second base.

"Hayes," Reiser shouted. Milton Hayes, defensive replacement and pinch runner, went out to second for Grote. "We need this run, we need it," Reiser said tensely to Castro.

"We'll get it."

Weiss, hitting eighth, was intentionally walked, bringing up the pitcher's spot in the batting order. Seaver was out in the on-deck circle.

"We've got to get that run," Reiser called Seaver back.

"You could leave him in to bunt," Castro said, but Reiser shook his head.

"We'll create more doubt if we put in a pinch-hitter to do the bunting." He looked down the bench. The Dodgers had a weak bench, but there was one man who might be able to do the job, and, at the same time, plant the maximum amount of doubt in the Orioles' mind. Reiser called to Don Drysdale. "You're hitting. I want you to get the bunt down. Ignore whatever the signs say, just get the bunt down. We need those men moved over."

"Yes sir," Drysdale said.

He marched out of the dugout and took his place in the batter's box. The O's brought in a right-hander to pitch to the righty-hitting Drysdale who promptly plopped the first pitch down the first base line. He took off as fast as he could. Ellie Hendricks sprang out from behind the plate, quicker than seemed possible for a man his size, pounced on the ball, and threw it to first. Drysdale's arms were pumping like a sprinter's but his feet were moving with somewhat less speed. His left arm pumped downwards just as Hendricks released the ball, and his throw hit Drysdale on the wrist. Hendricks watched unbelievingly as the ball trickled towards second base. Davy Johnson and Boog Powell scampered after it, but Hayes, clapping his hands like a madman, crossed the plate by the time Johnson picked up the ball. There was no one even covering the plate, and the Dodgers had won two to one.

Ebbets Field went insane. The words flashed on Sign Man's cards, "AMAZING, AMAZING, AMAZING," as the Dodgers celebrated in a mass dance around home plate.

Thursday, October 15th, 1969: Game 5

TOMMY KNEW THIS WAS his last chance to uncover the identity of the secret ace, to get the story of a lifetime and start himself on the pathway of fame and fortune.

The game had already begun. Koosman was pitching against McNally, Tommy thought. He didn't really know. He was losing track of the unimportant stuff and focusing in on the big picture: the identity of the secret ace.

Slug Maligne seemed like a nice guy for a joker, and he sure knew his baseball. He didn't believe that a secret ace was molding events for the Dodgers. But maybe he was being just a little naive. Even though he was young, Tommy figured he had a pretty well-developed detective sense, and he knew a scam when he smelled one. And he could smell one at Ebbets, all right.

Only he couldn't pin the smell down to a specific individual. There were always too many people around. The scent itself was rather weak, but it had to stick to the clothes and belongings of whoever it came from. If he could check out the lockers on the quiet, take a whiff of the equipment, the players' street clothes, maybe he could finally track down the ace who'd been manipulating things behind the scenes.

He'd come to believe that Slug was right about one thing, though. It probably wasn't one of the big name players. He'd managed to eliminate some of the names conclusively. Some he wasn't sure of. But it had to be, he figured, one of the little guys, one of the newcomers to the Dodgers. Otherwise, why hadn't they played their cards before? Why hadn't they built success for them and their team in the past? Swoboda, for example, or Ed Charles. Why would they wait for this year to start pulling their tricks?

He had a couple of people in mind. He waited his chance and slipped behind a laundry hamper in the corner of the trainer's room while no one was looking; then it was a matter of quiet patience until the locker room cleared out right before game time. He had to be careful. He had to be quiet and subtle because occasionally a player would pop into the locker room to go to the bathroom or something, but Tommy had good ears. He could hear them coming down the hall and he was quick to hide. The lockers themselves presented no obstacles. They were stalls rather than real lockers, made of boards and wire fencing, totally open in the front. Some were messy enough to briefly hide in if someone came into the room.

It was nerve wracking, but Tommy thought you needed nerves to be a good reporter, and he had plenty.

He'd checked the first two guys on his list—Nathan Bright, the third string catcher, and Steve Garvey, a young third baseman the Dodgers had called up late in the season mainly for pinch-hitting duty—and found nothing out of the ordinary, except that Garvey seemed to get an inordinate amount of fan mail from girls who liked to include their photos with their autograph requests. He found himself lingering over a couple of the photos, almost tempted to pocket one or two—Garvey'd never miss them—until a sudden roar from the crowd outside wrenched his mind back to his quest.

He put the photos back. There was one more name on his list of suspects, Milt Hayes. He'd been in the majors for a couple of years, and was a fringe talent. The Dodgers mainly used him as a pinch-runner and defensive specialist in the outfield. *Maybe,* Tommy thought, *he figured his time in the big leagues was limited. Maybe he saw the Dodgers had a chance this year and he figured to get that one championship ring in his career. Maybe—*

"Can I help you, kid?"

Tommy straightened up from Hayes' locker, a startled, guilty look on his face. He turned to see Don Drysdale staring down at him, a look of concern compounded with wonder on his stern features. Drysdale was big, raw-boned and said to be downright nasty. *He must move quieter than a snake, too, otherwise he wouldn't have caught me.* He stared at Tommy with a hard glare that had intimidated more than a few major league batters.

"Uh, gee, no, Mr. Drysdale," Tommy said, "I was, uh, I was—I have a press pass!" Tommy held it out like a magic talisman in front of him.

Drysdale nodded uncertainly. "Uh-huh. Well kid, I suggest you get your butt back up to the press box, then with the other pervs and drunks. I don't think you're going to get much of a story out of sniffing somebody's street pants."

If only I could tell you, Tommy said to himself. But he knew he couldn't.

"Yes sir, yes sir," he said, sidling past the player, who turned to keep an eye on him as he scuttled for the locker room door.

He was almost there, when suddenly it hit him.

The smell. What he'd been looking for. There was no doubt about it whatsoever. He looked at the name over the locker, and was stunned.

He was sure Drysdale thought he was nuts when he started to laugh.

Tommy heard another roar from the crowd before he could make his way up to the press box, but it had a sort of downcast, moaning note to it, so Tommy knew that whatever had happened was bad for the Dodgers.

What happened?" he asked Slug Maligne, who was perched in his spot in the box.

Where you been, Tommy?" Slug asked. "You've missed half the game."

"Working on my story," Tommy said.

Slug shook his head. "You're missing the story, Tommy. The *game* is the story, kid. If you want to be a reporter you have to remember that, first and foremost. What happens down there on the field, where men give their hearts, where sometimes they leave pieces of themselves, all in search of that moment of perfection, whether it's a throw or a catch or wing of the bat, that's the story kid. Everything else is just lipstick on a pretty girl."

Tommy was pretty sure he didn't believe that. The story, to him, was a secret found and exposed, but he didn't feel like discussing the philosophy of journalism with Slug, who wasn't a journalist, so couldn't be expected to understand such things. "Well," Tommy said, "what'd I miss?"

"First, McNally hit a two-run homer for the Orioles."

"McNally?"

"Yeah. McNally. You know, the Orioles pitcher?"

"Um, yeah."

"Now Frank Robinson just hit another one. It's three to nothing for the Orioles."

Tommy wanted to shake his head and laugh, but he didn't. That would upset Slug, and he did sort of like the guy.

"Don't worry," he said. "The Dodgers are going to win."

Slug smiled at him. "I like a fan with faith in their team."

Sure, they're going to win, Tommy thought. *The secret ace will take control any time now.* He settled back to watch and wait.

As the game wore on, McNally looked invincible. Koosman found his groove and gave up nothing more. But McNally was still in total command as Cleon Jones, who hit .349 during the season but was having a poor Series, stepped up to lead-off the sixth. McNally threw one of his sharp-breaking curves and it bounced in the dirt at Jones' feet. Play halted as the ball rolled towards the Dodger dugout, and Jones got into a discussion with the plate umpire.

"What's going on?" Tommy asked.

"Looks like he's claiming the pitch hit him," Slug said.

Suddenly Pete Reiser bounced out of the dugout and showed the ball to the plate umpire. The umpire looked at, and waved Jones to first. Earl Weaver ran out of the Orioles dugout, his face already red, but turned back without a word as the umpire silently showed him the ball.

"What—" Tommy began, and Slug shrugged.

"You got me, kid. The ball probably hit Jones on the foot. Maybe it got shoe polish on it. Must have. It'd take something like that to shut Weaver up so suddenly."

Donn Clendenon, the on-deck batter who'd been watching with interest, stepped to the plate and immediately jacked a two-run shot into the stands.

Slug shook his head, as if in disbelief. "Can you believe this shi—stuff? My God, has this been scripted?"

The next inning Al Weiss, the utility infielder who'd hit two home runs all season, hit another one out, and Tommy suddenly knew it was all over but for the question of the final score.

"It's like they're blessed," Slug said.

Tommy smiled to himself. *That's one way of putting it,* he thought.

The Dodgers settled it in the eighth with two runs. Like most of their scoring that season, it was a team effort with a Jones double, a Clendenon ground out, bloop singles, and ground ball errors on the part of the Orioles.

The Dodgers took the field in the ninth leading five to three. The tension was so great that the stadium was virtually silent. Frank Robinson led off the inning with a walk, and Boog Powell came up as the tying run.

It always seemed to be the way of the game. The big man came to bat with the game on the line. If Powell was feeling the pressure, he didn't show it. He took a mighty swing at Koosman's first offering. He hit the ball hard, but on the ground, up the middle. Weiss, ranging far to his right at second base, dove, stopped it, got up and threw to Harrelson covering the bag. Robinson barreled down and Harrelson had to leap over him as he hit the bag in a hard slide. He couldn't make the relay throw to first. One out, Powell safe at first.

The game wasn't over yet, but Tommy knew that, really, it was. The secret ace wouldn't let the Dodgers lose.

Brooks Robinson, a tough hitter with decent power, lifted an easy fly to Ron Swoboda, who circled under it (Tommy held his breath, as did every Dodger fan in the stands) and caught it with a smile.

Davy Johnson followed Brooks to the plate. He was a tough hitter with decent power for a middle infielder, but he, too, managed only an easy fly to medium left field. Cleon Jones went right to the spot where the ball would come down, camped under it, caught it, and touched his knee to the ground as if in prayer. Grote ran out to the mound where the Dodgers' senior citizen third baseman Ed "The Glider" Charles was already doing a dance of inexpressible joy, and it was as if suddenly someone threw a switch and turned the sound on and the stadium erupted with an out-pouring of cheers and screams and shouts that Brooklyn hadn't heard in years and years. On the third base line Sign Man held up his sign and it said, "THERE ARE NO WORDS," and, indeed, there were none.

The locker room was like some scene out of a madcap version of hell, or at least pandemonium. Half-naked players ran around whooping and shouting like little boys, spraying themselves with champagne and beer and shaving cream. The utter joy of the moment almost over-whelmed Tommy. He snuck a bottle of champagne for himself, and swallowed a bit, but it was cheap stuff, rather stinging and bitter, not at all how Tommy imagined it would taste, and he ended up surreptitiously spraying it all over the locker room.

He wanted to join in the celebration openly, but the other reporters were at least trying to keep themselves somewhat aloof from the partisan festivities. They were wandering around the room (most surreptitiously swigging beers) asking what Tommy thought were mostly inane questions of the players. Slug's shoe polish theory was confirmed, but Tommy heard nothing else of importance.

Tommy was determined to keep the surprise to himself, not to let anyone else in on his secret. He wanted to confront Reiser with his certain knowledge, and get the manager's reaction. Then, *The Weekly Gospel* would get their exclusive, and what an exclusive it would be: *Miracle Dodger Victory Engineered by Secret Ace!*

Well, perhaps he would have to work on shortening that headline.

In the end, it was surprisingly easy. Tommy hung around in the rear of the room, in the shadows, watching as the celebration wound down without really ending as the players showered, dressed, and left the locker room still clearly high on emotion and crazed energy. It took awhile, but the locker room emptied of players and reporters and finally the only ones left in the clubhouse were those who also usually arrived first at the ballpark. Tommy found them in the manager's office, sipping beer and smoking thick, fragrant Cuban cigars.

"I know who the secret ace is," Tommy said in a dramatic, almost accusatory voice.

Reiser, lounging behind his desk with his feet up and a cigar in his mouth, groaned and sat up straight. "You, again? Jesus, kid, there ain't no secret ace. I've been over it in my head, I've watched everyone. There just ain't no secret ace."

"Really?" Tommy said archly as he came into the room. "How do you account for all the strange things that happened during the Series? The spectacular catches, the bad throws and Oriole errors, the unexpected home runs, *the shoe polish incident?*"

Reiser shrugged. "It's *baseball,* kid. It's the nature of the game. Strange things happen. Sometimes players rise to the occasion. Sometimes occasions rise to the players. You can't explain it. No one can."

"Then how do you explain the way he smells?" Tommy asked dramatically, pointing at Fidel Castro, who was sitting across the desk from Reiser, cigar in one hand, champagne bottle in the other.

"The way he smells?" Reiser asked.

Shit, Tommy thought, *I blew it.* "I mean—" He realized there was no sense in lying now. It was better to stick to the truth. "Yeah. I should have told you before. I can smell people who are affected by the wild card—"

"That's ridiculous—" Reiser began, but Castro interrupted him. "No. He's right."

Reiser turned to his old friend. "What?"

"I am a wild carder."

Tommy couldn't restrain himself from saying, "See? I told you, I told you!" He could barely restrain himself from doing a little dance of joy. Visions of headlines ran in his head. Screw *The Weekly Gospel.* He'd take this to *The Daily News.* And he was only in the ninth grade! Visions of future Pulitzers danced in his head.

"But I am not an ace."

"What?" Tommy's face fell. "I don't believe you."

Castro shrugged. "It's true. I never knew I'd been infected with the virus until last winter. I went to see the doctors about my arm. They did tests and discovered I had the wild card. They discovered my 'power' when examining my arm."

"What is it?" Reiser asked.

Castro shrugged again. "My tendons and ligaments are maybe twice as flexible as an ordinary man's." He illustrated by bending back the fingers in his right hand. They bent back pretty far. "But, more flexible or not, they were finished in my pitching arm. My arm was dead, useless for pitching. So, I retired."

"Flexible fingers?" Tommy asked weakly. "That's your power?"

"My elbow, too," Castro said, taking a reflective puff of his cigar.

"Hmmm. That's not much of a story," Reiser said.

"Still . . ." Tommy said, but hope was fading even as he tried to grasp it.

Reiser looked at him thoughtfully. "Look, maybe we can, uh, make this up to you if you keep it our own little secret."

"How?" Tommy asked.

Reiser shrugged. "I don't know. How about a season's ticket for next year?"

"Well . . ." Tommy wasn't much of a baseball fan, but his father was. And other people were. With the Dodgers being world champs, tickets would be tough to come by next year. They'd be hot items. People might be willing to tell him things, to do things for him, if he had tickets for important games. "How about two season tickets?"

Reiser shrugged. "All right."

"Okay," Tommy nodded, absorbing the notion that he could just as easily be paid for not revealing something, as for revealing it. "I guess I should go write my story now."

"Your story with no secret aces," Reiser said.

"My story with no secret aces," Tommy agreed. Flexible tendons weren't a footnote, let alone a whole story. Also, he suddenly realized, he'd have had to reveal how he discovered Castro was a wilder carder—by smelling him. Maybe he shouldn't tell the whole wide world about his talent.

Tommy smiled to himself. *As it turns out,* he thought, *there is a secret ace in the story after all. Me.*

He left the two men in the manager's office, celebrating their victory. He had his story, to write, his own victory to celebrate. Maybe it wasn't as glorious as he'd hoped it would be. There'd be no blazing headlines, no by-line in a real newspaper, but *Dodgers World Champs* wasn't exactly chopped liver, and it was a more manageable headline.

It's so cool, Tommy Downs thought, *being a reporter.*

He strolled down the corridors of Ebbets Field, dreaming of the thousands of stories to come.

Age of Wonders

TWO
July 2003

THE TROUBLE WITH MANY of these archived stories was finding independent verification. Rumors abounded about who might be a secret ace, who was hiding powers and what they might have done. People could talk about it all they wanted, but unless they had proof, some concrete way to demonstrate what they could do? No story. Conversely, there were examples of people who claimed to have powers, to be able to read minds or change the weather, who didn't have the wild card virus at all.

Still, Raleigh was happy to have a project to distract her from the sticky New York summer. Uncovering the truth about Fidel Castro was certainly giving her a good education in research and evidence. He'd been a great pitcher during his time with the Washington Senators, but not unbelievably good. Not ace power good. He'd probably been an even better pitching coach for the Dodgers, but that didn't have anything to do with whatever extra ability his ultra-flexible arm gave him. The guy was still alive, retired on the outskirts of Miami. She hadn't been able to get an interview with him. *Yet.* The man seemed to have an army of very nice managers and agents standing between him and the world. Maybe he was sick? She made notes.

Meanwhile, she'd been spending a lot of time at the New York Public Library looking for analysis, speculation, and information about wild cards in sports in general, for context. If it came out that Castro had wild card abilities related to his arm . . . would it put his Hall of Fame status in question? Did she want to be the one to bring that up?

The reference librarians were getting to know her, but the guy at the desk today was new. Late twenties, tall, with brown hair that was just a little too curly to ever be neat. His eyes lit up when she approached, like he couldn't wait to help. "What can I do for you?" His accent was native New York.

"Hi, yeah, I'm trying to dig up anything I can find on the 1969 World Series."

"Dodgers-Orioles, right?"

"You must be a fan," she said. "I've been through the *Times* and the *Post* but I wondered what kind of local weeklies or sports publications might have slipped through the cracks. Or if you maybe even have a stack of newspapers in the archives that never made it to microfilm."

He made a couple of notes on scrap paper. "That's a deep dive. What's the story?"

"I'm a journalist. Well, I'm trying to be a journalist." No, she really was a journalist. She winced a little and charged ahead. "I work for *Aces!*, I'm doing research for a story." She waited for the punch line—*they actually do research over there?*

Instead, he asked, "Wow, cool. Let me see what comes up on a quick search, if you don't mind waiting a couple minutes." He flashed a smile.

"I don't mind at all." She was suddenly self-conscious about her thrown-together appearance, a loose tank top over a peasant skirt, her curly hair pulled back with a scrap of cloth turned into a makeshift headband. She'd learned not to dress too fancy when she was going to be digging through the dusty archives, and no one in the library generally cared. Until she found herself talking to a cute guy . . .

She made sure her MedicAlert tag was turned engraved side down. It was a habit; she hardly realized she was doing it.

He tapped on his computer and made small talk. "It must be pretty glamorous over there. Celebrities, aces—"

"You'd be surprised. It's all nerds in the office. Only the cool people get the expense accounts and are allowed outdoors."

"And you're over here doing the actual work. Isn't that always the way?" That smile again. Raleigh was starting to get distracted. "You meet anyone famous?"

Besides her own mother? She didn't want to get into that. "A few. I'm not so interested in the flashy aces, though. They get written about enough, don't you think? I'm more interested in the not-flashy. The people with powers just trying to make a living. The ones keeping their powers secret for some reason. If they look like a nat, how would you ever know? That's maybe the biggest thing I'm learning on this job—all the secrets people keep about this stuff. I mean, you might be an ace and I'd never know unless you told me."

At this, he looked stricken, brow furrowed and lips frozen in a tense fake smile. "Ah . . . yeah."

She stared. "Wait a minute. *Are* you an ace?"

He winced, his finger tapping nervously on the desk. "I don't know that I'd go that far . . . and it's not that I'm trying to keep anything secret, really. But . . . okay. Here."

He picked up a bookmark printed with the library's contact information. Showed her both sides, like he was about to do a magic trick. Then he pressed the bookmark between his palms. Just for a second. When he showed her the bookmark again, it was blank. The print had vanished, just like that. He let the card fall to the counter. Raleigh picked it up, ran her fingers over it. It just felt like card stock, like it had never been printed on.

"You erase things?" she asked, still a bit skeptical.

"Printed matter, handwriting. I can do a whole book at once if I really concentrate."

"And you work in a library? Living dangerously, isn't it?"

"Keeps me on my toes," he said with a lopsided grin. "But I wouldn't call it an ace."

"I'm Raleigh," she said.

"Gavin," he said, taking the hand she offered.

"Maybe I could do a little write-up on you for the magazine. The New York Public Library's daredevil ace." She was mostly joking. Really, she wanted to keep talking with him.

"I'm not sure about that. It's not that I'm keeping it secret from work or anything . . . but it's not that great a party trick, it turns out."

"Oh, I don't know about that. 'What parking ticket, Officer?'"

He laughed. "When everything goes electronic, I'm screwed."

Someone stepped behind her, starting a line. Gavin glanced at the newcomer over her shoulder, and some of the brightness in his expression dimmed. "Microfilm publications. '69 World Series. Give me a couple of days and I'll see what I can come up with. How does that sound?"

"Thanks, I really appreciate it." The bookmark he'd erased still lay right in front of her, and in a fit of inspiration she grabbed a pen and wrote her name and phone number on it. Gave him a look, felt her smile turn goofy. Handed him the card. "Don't erase this."

"Never."

Raleigh got her next story by accident. She was gathering info for one of the regular *Aces!* columns about news from around the country, quirky stories about aces who didn't live in New York City and what they could possibly be doing in their benighted parts of the world. A freelancer had sent in photos from a comedy club in St. Louis of all places, a joint called Laughing Jack's. An up-and-coming ace comic had just filmed a special there. Jerry Hart was a human tape recorder, and his act involved slice-of-life stories with a soundtrack, along with samples direct from the audience.

In one of the photos, taken from stage right, Hart gestured with the microphone, a dynamic image that showed him haloed by stage lights with his audience as the backdrop, a Middle America crowd, mid-laugh. An older woman sat off to the side, looking over the crowd, not at the stage, with a proud and pleased smile. The freelancer's notes said this was Alice Smith, the club's co-owner along with her husband, Ralph.

The thing was, Raleigh recognized Alice from one of Digger's files, and that wasn't her name. She'd been a lot younger—her file had been put away in the archives in 1977, over twenty-five years ago. But it was her. Back then she'd been Carlotta DeSoto, and had a short-lived career as a comedian at a comedy club called the Village Idiot. The file had included a handful of publicity photos, and the woman had the same face, the same vivacious smile. And according to the file, she was an ace.

Carlotta DeSoto had vanished in 1977. The interview Digger Downs had tried to get with her had never happened. So what had she been doing all those years, and how did she end up in St. Louis?

Laughing Jack's was easy enough to track down—it had a website. So Raleigh called. A young female voice answered on the second ring. Maybe a box office clerk or someone who worked at the club. "Laughing Jack's, can I help you?"

"Yes, my name is Raleigh Jackson, may I speak to Alice Smith? It's about a booking."

"Just a minute."

Raleigh's heart raced. What if she was wrong about Alice/Carlotta? What if it wasn't her, if she didn't have the story straight? Worst that could happen, the woman would just hang up. Raleigh didn't have a thing to lose. Didn't tamp down on the adrenaline at all, though.

"Hi, Alice here." She sounded friendly, kind.

Raleigh's breath caught; she plowed ahead. She had her script all written out. "My name is Raleigh Jackson and I'm a reporter for *Aces!* magazine. I'd like to ask you a few questions about a comedy club here in Manhattan back in the seventies, the Village Idiot?"

There was a pause. Raleigh expected that. "Why do you think I'd know anything about that?"

"You are Carlotta DeSoto, aren't you?" The woman's short gasp in response gave her the answer. "Please don't hang up. Your ex-husband is dead, nobody's looking for you anymore. I'm a features reporter, I do human-interest stories. I would love to talk to you about why you wanted to be a comedian, especially back when it was really tough for women in the business—" Another breath, another bombshell. "—and if it had anything to do with any ace power you might have."

If the click of the line cutting off was going to happen, it would be now. But she didn't hang up. Raleigh could still hear soft breathing. Then, Alice—Carlotta—gave an exhausted laugh. "Seriously, I didn't think anybody remembered Carlotta. Don't you have better things to write about? The sad plight of professional dog walkers in Manhattan maybe?"

That was funny. An honest-to-goodness joke. Raleigh offered a thanks to the ceiling. "I'm interested in *your* story, Ms. Smith. I'd love to ask you a few questions. Just a half an hour of your time. If now isn't good I can call back."

"If I don't like your questions I'm not answering."

"That's totally fair."

"God. Okay. I'll do it. Just give me a minute to get a drink. And I think I may need to sit down."

Raleigh put the phone on speaker and pulled over her keyboard, ready to write.

Walking the Floor
Over You

by Walton Simons

THE CLUB WAS CROWDED, but a little less boisterous than usual. Audience members whispered to each other or played with their drinks, but they weren't giving the girl at the microphone the kind of attention she needed.

A lot of the customers were smoking, but Carlotta's routine was doing the opposite. It wasn't the material, and her delivery was spot on. *Well, as good as it ever was, anyway.*

She was gorgeous, though. Carlotta had creamy skin, delicate features, and a body that, as the joke went "would make a bishop kick out a stained-glass window." Her honey-blonde hair was cut in a Louise Brooks pageboy, framing her face to ideal effect. Bob leaned back into the polished bar rail and sighed. If he didn't have a personal interest in her, it would be easy enough to fire her. *Not much chance of that, though.*

In every crowd there was somebody who looked like they didn't belong. Tonight it was a pair of guys sitting together to the left of the stage, just away from the light's edge. They were young and looked like FBI agents dressed in particularly loud disco garb. One had a face with a hound-like quality and his companion was taller and thinner. Mentally, Bob dubbed them Mutt and Jeff. Neither man was laughing or even smiling at Carlotta's material, although they were certainly keeping their eyes on her. Bob decided to pay them a visit.

He navigated the floor over to their table. "Enjoying the show, gentlemen?"

The tall thin man looked up at him, expressionless. "Great," he said.

Bob cleared his throat. "It's traditional to laugh at the jokes."

"My friend has a medical condition that keeps him from laughing." The thin man smiled. It wasn't pleasant. "So I don't either, just to keep him from feeling bad."

"That explains why you're patronizing a comedy club." Bob wasn't sure what he wanted from these two, but knew he wasn't going to get it if they had their way. "Pay attention." He gestured to Carlotta. "You might just enjoy yourselves."

"I'm sure most of you can tell I'm not from around here." Carlotta

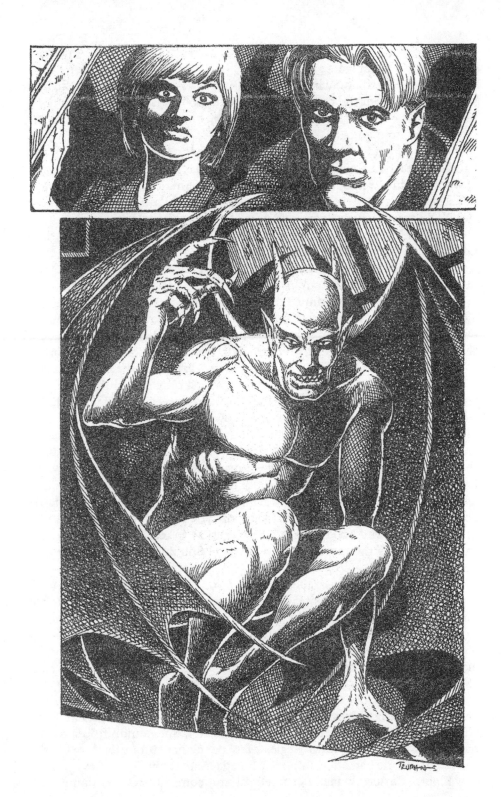

looked down ashamedly from her mike. "The truth is, I'm from America's heartland, the great state of Iowa."

"That would explain why you smell like pigs." A deep male voice, slightly slurred, came from the back of the audience. Bob walked in the general direction of the heckler. He'd done this plenty of times and would have the creep pinpointed quickly.

Carlotta tried to work the interruption to her advantage. "If there's one thing I've learned since being in the Big Apple, it's that no one can survive very long with a well developed sense of smell." Small laugh. "Getting back to Iowa. This is the truth, I swear to god. They held a contest in my home state for a new tourism slogan and asked Iowans to help them out."

"You suck, you corn-fed bitch." The heckler was even louder this time around. Bob picked out a large sandy-haired man in a tank top and faux leather pants sitting by himself a couple of tables away on the left. Bob pulled a small flashlight from his jacket pocket and moved in.

"Really," Carlotta continued, ignoring him this time around, "you'd be amazed at the cruelty of responses from the folks in Iowa. These are people with a real sense of humor. One was 'Iowa, gateway to Wisconsin.'" She sold the joke with a broad sweep of her arm, but didn't get much for the effort.

"Go the fuck back where you came from," yelled the heckler. Bob was standing directly behind him and briefly turned on the flashlight over the troublemaker's head. Carlotta was looking in his direction and nodded.

"My favorite slogan by far, though, was 'Iowa, it makes you want Dubuque.'" This got a pretty good response from the audience but the heckler started to laugh uproariously. He knocked his drink over, spilling ice and alcohol onto the floor, and grabbed onto the edge of his table, laughing convulsively. He looked up at Bob, with something close to panic in his widening eyes. Bob grabbed the man under his sweaty armpits and hauled him into a standing position, then guided him toward the exit. The heckler got his legs under himself quickly and Bob was afraid he might try to resist being ushered out the door. Luckily the man seemed relieved as Bob pushed him outside into the heat.

"I wouldn't come back," Bob said, as a parting shot, and gave the man a practiced stare for good measure. The heckler said nothing, but walked slowly away down the pavement.

Carlotta was leaving the stage to scattered applause when Bob made it back to the interior of the club. Mutt and Jeff had disappeared, which was okay with Bob. "Thank you ladies and gentlemen," he said to the audience. "She's here Friday, Saturday, and Sunday. Tell your friends."

Bob met her backstage with a half-smile. "Not your best, but not awful, given the circumstances." He'd guessed Carlotta's wild card ability and had bluffed the truth out of her a few weeks earlier. She couldn't do any real harm with it; make a crowd giggle, a few people laugh out loud, or—if she focused it on one person—completely incapacitate them.

"Right." Carlotta wiped her forehead and combed back her damp hair.

"Thanks for the help, but I had him spotted. Jerks seem to grow on trees in this burg."

"That's a fact, my dear. After six months here, I'd think you'd come to expect it. New York's reputation didn't manifest itself out of thin air."

Carlotta headed for her tiny dressing room. Bob followed. "God help me if I ever get used to rude assholes," she said without looking back at him. "The dirt, yes. The noise, yes. Even the lack of anything green outside of Central Park or the A&P. But jerk-off morons are always going to piss this girl off." She turned around at the doorway of her tiny dressing room. "I haven't got time to talk. I'm meeting someone."

"You're certainly not a very traditional girl." Bob fingered his watch and waited for a reply, but received only a roll of the eyes. "Most people suck up to their boss a bit, unless they're very, very good at their job. You certainly don't have more than one 'very' and possibly none at all."

"You're not going to get rid of me just yet, Mr. Cortland," she said, and closed the door with finality.

Too true, Bob thought to himself. He wandered back over to the bar and poured himself a half-shot of scotch, wondering what it would be like to win a round with her. She certainly wasn't smarter than he was. *Well probably not.* But he couldn't match her obstinacy. "To good humor," he said quietly. "Mine. And patience."

He saw her flash out the rear exit in a short blue dress and almost-matching heels, blonde hair bouncing, and decided, with the help of the scotch, to try another approach on her. He had until he caught up with her to figure out just what that might be.

Once outside, the July heat swallowed him like a chip of ice in a cup of steaming coffee. Even in the early morning hours, the still, furnace-like air sucked the life out of everyone and everything. Carlotta was disappearing down the alleyway, but stopped short on the far side of a dumpster. Two men emerged from the darkness and stepped into her path. Bob couldn't see them well and slipped into the shadows on the dark side of the alley, carefully removed a small revolver from his right jacket pocket. It felt bigger in his hand that it really was. He was hoping the same psychological phenomenon applied to the men he was going to try to stop.

"You're coming with us. Any trouble, I hurt you." The taller of the two men grabbed Carlotta by the arm. She tried to wrench away, but was pinned by his grip.

Bob moved out from behind the dumpster and trained his weapon on the man holding Carlotta, recognizing the pair as Mutt and Jeff. "Let her go," he said, in as even a tone as he could manage. "I'll shoot you both if I have to."

Mutt stared at him, unblinking. "Now why don't I believe that?"

Taking a deep breath, Bob pointed the end of the revolver slightly to one side of the man and pulled the trigger. The gun kicked uncomfortably in his sweaty hand and the bullet ricocheted off the brick alley wall and into a pile of crates, spraying chips of wood. "Because you're stupid," he suggested.

The pair turned and bolted toward the street. Bob aimed the gun toward the Mutt's receding back, realized he wasn't up to that, put the safety back on, and slipped the weapon back into his pocket.

Carlotta still stood unmoving, fists clenched. Bob quickly put his arm around her and got her moving back toward the club door. "You never have any shortage of admirers. Ever seen them before?"

She let out a deep breath. "No. Not until tonight. Show business isn't all it's cracked up to be." Carlotta looked into his eyes for a second, then turned her head. "Thanks."

"You want to tell me anything?" Bob tried to make eye contact with her, but she looked away and walked slowly back into the club. "Somehow, I didn't think so."

He was in his favorite seat at the club, lazily rubbing his thumb over a cigarette burn on the table's hard wood finish. Bob was tired and it was only late afternoon. The excitement of the previous night had kept him from sleeping. Not that insomnia was unusual for him. It even helped if you ran a late-night business. Even though he'd put on fresh clothes, he felt rumpled.

Carlotta had seemed more scared than he would have expected if Mutt and Jeff were just muggers, and she didn't spook easily as far as he could see. Not to mention the fact that comedy clubs like his didn't really pay very well and any thief with half a brain would know that. Something was up, he was sure of that, but he didn't have a clue what it might be. Maybe Carlotta just made him stupid. He took a sip of lukewarm coffee. It was his fourth cup of the day. If he had to be tired, at least he would be alert.

Wes the bartender walked over with a half-empty pot of coffee and gave Bob a warmup, then headed back to his work cleaning glasses behind the bar. A native New Yorker, Wes was physically large, but not particularly good-looking, loved to laugh, and only poured heavy for regulars and attractive women. He was the first person Bob had hired when he opened the Village Idiot and the only original employee the place still had.

"Wes, am I an idiot?" Bob asked, without looking for inspiration in the steam swirling in his cup.

"No, boss. No one who has the good sense to hire me could possibly be an idiot."

Bob knew Wes could have made a comment about Carlotta. The bartender had a good pair of eyes and a quick mind. "Thanks, Wes."

"How about a raise?"

"Don't hurt me, Wes. You know how things are."

Bob heard a key turn in the front door and Carlotta stepped in. Even in the dim light, he could see she was paler than usual. She was wearing a royal blue halter-top that was sweat-soaked to the skin and her hair was plastered to the sides of her face.

"What the hell are you doing here?" Bob asked. "You look like, well, like last night."

"Funny about that." Carlotta clutched a chair back and took a deep breath. "Because that's how I feel."

"Okay. Sit down and tell me about it." He motioned to Wes. "You want anything to drink?"

"A shot of brandy would be nice."

"Coming up." Wes grabbed a glass and a bottle. "Anything for you, Mr. Cortland?"

"Not just yet, Wes." He put a finger under Carlotta's chin and raised her head. "Let's hear it."

Carlotta took the glass of brandy Wes had hurried over and had a sip. "Okay. I'm shopping on Eighth Street. Checking out some clothes and whatnot, and I wind up in a bookstore. This guy comes up to me and starts talking. Gorgeous guy. Tall. Blonde. You'd hate him."

"I do," Bob said. "I'll take that brandy after all, Wes."

"Right. Well we really hit it off and he asks if I want to get a cup of coffee. I figure he's looking to get laid, which isn't exactly objectionable in my mind, so I'll just entertain the possibility and see how it goes."

"Playing hard to get again."

"Forget that, okay." Carlotta shot him an agitated glance. "I don't need you to ride me right now. In any case, we're having coffee and it turns out he likes the same things as me. Russian composers, and Monet, and Woody Allen, and iced coffee." She ticked off the coincidences on her fingers as she named them. "And I realized that this was beyond Kismet and into something really creepy. This guy came after me, same as those goons last night. Only he was using sugar instead of trying to strong-arm me." She paused and took a deep breath, then another swallow of brandy.

"So where is he now?"

"Damned if I know," Carlotta said. "I crawled out the window of the ladies room at the coffee shop to get away from him and came straight here."

"All right," Bob said, nodding. "Do you think there's any chance you're being paranoid or overreacting because of last night?"

"No way."

Bob picked up his brandy and drained the small glass. "Then let's go. We've got somebody to see."

Carlotta hadn't been excited about a trip to Jokertown, but the fact that she hadn't protested either indicated to Bob that she was genuinely scared. Not that Jokertown was that bad these days. In fact, it was one of the few areas of the city that didn't live in fear of the '44 Caliber Killer known as the Son of Sam. There were a few nutballs suggesting a joker was the murderer, but most people weren't buying it, particularly in Jokertown.

"Pull over next to the newsstand," Bob told the cab driver. The cabbie whipped the car over, his tires squealing slightly as the rubber met the concrete curb. Bob handed him a twenty, too much really for such a short ride, and helped Carlotta out onto the sidewalk.

No place on earth, at least that Bob had seen, was like Jokertown. The streets and building looked and smelled a little different, and the residents ranged from almost passably normal to grotesque, but that wasn't what struck him every time he came here. It was that the rules were somehow not quite the same inside Jokertown, and outsiders never knew where the lines of acceptable behavior lay.

One of the few people he did know and trust down here ran this newsstand. Bob walked over with Carlotta in tow. The proprietor was wearing one of his trademark Hawaiian print shirts. Even in the gathering shadows of dusk, the colors looked electric.

"Jube," Bob said, extending his hand. "Got a minute?"

Jube, who resembled nothing more than an upright, badly dressed, walrus, extended a blubbery gray hand. "Well, if it isn't the owner of the Jokertown Idiot."

The walrus always gave Bob grief over the fact that the Village Idiot was technically closer to Jokertown than Greenwich Village, even after Bob explained that a club named the Jokertown Idiot not only wasn't clever sounding but would fold in less than a month.

"Thanks. I need your help. Actually," he indicated Carlotta, "she does."

Jube's lips tightened appreciatively across his tusks and into a smile. "Whatcha need?"

Carlotta looked Jube up and down and lightly shook her head. "You didn't tell me he was a redhead." She pointed to the crimson tufts on Jube's head. "Could be more trouble."

Jube gave a deep, rumbling chuckle. "She's a live wire, Bob. One of yours?"

Bob nodded. He was relieved Carlotta hadn't shed her sense of humor. "Yes, but only as an employee."

There was a rapid skittering noise behind them. A coin flew lip over the lip of the newsstands wooden front and landed in Jube's open palm. Something thin and semi-transparent whisked away a copy of the *Jokertown Cry*. A short, indistinguishable form folded the paper and shot across the street into the shadows.

"Thanks, Speedy," Jube said, tossing the quarter into the register. He turned back to Carlotta. "Now, where were we?"

"We," Bob said, emphasizing the word, "need someone for a protection job. Someone very good."

"Mmmm." Jube leaned forward. "And cost?"

"Is a consideration, but not a deterrent to hiring the best." Bob had an Uncle Scrooge vision in his mind of dollar bills flying away on angel wings.

"I'll pay you back, don't worry." Carlotta smoothed her hair back with both hands. "Just tell us who to see."

Jube pulled out a beat-up notepad and wrote a name and address on it. "He's the best I know of. Doesn't ask too many questions and gets results."

"I sense a qualifying 'but' coming here," Bob said.

"No, not really. He's a . . . changeable guy, but reliable. Just pay him what he asks and tell him what he needs to know to do the job and you'll be fine." Jube tore the paper from the pad and handed it over.

Bob turned the paper around and peered at it, unable to make out the letters. "What's his name? Start with a 'C'? Can't quite read it."

"Croyd, just Croyd. I'll call ahead and let him know you're coming," Jube said. "Hey, you know how many jokers it takes to screw in a light bulb?"

"I don't have time to find out. Thanks, Jube."

Whoever Croyd was, he didn't have a standard address. Bob walked carefully down the alleyway with Carlotta a couple of steps behind. Dumpsters, baked by the incessant heat, clogged the alley with the actively unpleasant smell of accelerated decay. Bob checked Jube's instructions with his flashlight and kept moving forward, looking for a door.

"Are we there yet?" Carlotta was trying to maintain her sense of humor, but Bob wasn't laughing, or even smiling.

"Just about, I think," he replied.

"I'd turn back if I were you," the voice came from behind a stack of half-empty boxes. There was an old, bearded man sitting there, nursing a bottle of something. His threadbare clothes were soiled with what looked like a decade's worth of stains. He looked them up and down and then turned back to his bottle.

"I do believe in spooks, I do believe in spooks, I do, I do, I do believe in spooks." Carlotta's voice had a bit of the spunky tone Bob associated with her, which was okay because his courage and confidence were beginning to head south. He came to a door and rapped hesitantly on it.

"*Entre vous*," came a deep, raspy, voice from the other side.

Bob opened the door and stepped into a small, high-ceiling room. There was a low-light lamp in one corner next to a large mattress and the opposite corner was screened off. Something was sitting in against the wall opposite the door, covered in a massive gray-brown tarpaulin. There was an odd smell, but no Croyd was visible.

"We did hear somebody, right?" Carlotta was right on his heels.

"Yes, you did," came the same deep voice. What Bob had thought was a tarpaulin began to slowly unfold into two massive, leathery wings, spreading until they almost touched either wall. Between them was a humanoid-type creature with a horned head, slitted, yellow eyes, and a fanged mouth. One of the yellow eyes winked and the mouth curled into something of a smile.

Except for a small, belted garment at the waist, the creature was naked, not that it mattered. "You must be Jube's friends."

"Yes," Carlotta said, "Well, he is anyway." She pointed to Bob, who was trying to get his mouth to shut.

Croyd stood up on feet that, although sporting four clawed toes each, were more or less human. "He said you need protection. Afraid the Son-of-Sam is after you?"

"No," Bob said, finally able to speak. "He doesn't work Manhattan anyway. I thought Jube would have explained, Mr . . . Croyd." Bob then covered the story of the heckler in the alley for the second time that night.

"Do you have any enemies that you know of?" Croyd turned his horned head lazily toward Carlotta.

"No. I'm from Iowa."

"Well, you seem to now. Nothing I can't handle, though." He gently placed a taloned finger under her chin. "I aims to please." He emphasized the word "aims," obviously aware that it was a town in Iowa.

Everybody's a comedian, thought Bob. "And your fee for protecting Miss DeSoto will be?" He was trying to get Croyd's attention. The last thing he needed was someone else trying to horn in on Carlotta, literally or figuratively. That line was already long enough.

"She's not a DeSoto." Croyd gave Carlotta the slow once over, which she didn't seem to mind at all. "With curves like that, she's more like a Mustang." Croyd cleared his throat. It was an unpleasant noise. "You can have me for five hundred a day, one day's pay in advance and the rest when the job is over." He walked in an ungainly fashion to the partitioned area of the room. Bob heard the sound of a bottle-cap coming off and being replaced, a drawer opening. Then Croyd emerged with a small amber bottle held between a massive thumb and forefinger. He carefully opened and dabbed some of the liquid contents on one his fingers, then scooped Carlotta's blonde hair back and applied it gingerly behind her ears. *"Et, voila."*

"What's that for?" she asked, sniffing. "It's definitely not Chanel."

Croyd handed her the bottle. "No, but if someone does get their mitts on you, the scent will help me track you, so take good care of the stuff."

Bob was equal parts tired, suspicious, and annoyed. If Jube hadn't vouched for Croyd, there was no way he'd deal with him at all. Not because he was a hideous joker, but because in spite of that fact, he was still charming.

"I don't have that amount of cash with me," Bob said. "But once Miss DeSoto is safely home, you can follow me to my business. I'll pay you there."

"And just what is your business?" Croyd leaned his head toward Bob's face.

Bob held his ground, in spite of Croyd's unusually hot breath on his face. "I own a comedy club in the Village, the Village Idiot. I'll meet you in back of my place, show you what happened and where, and give you your retainer."

"You know," Croyd said, "I find the fact that the name of your club is the Village Idiot to be completely believable."

"I work there," Carlotta said, stifling a yawn. "So show some respect. By the way, you do fly don't you? Those wings aren't just for show?"

Croyd laughed. It was a deep, booming sound, and in spite of the source, Bob liked it. "I fly like a bat-out-of-hell, just wait and see. And if you spot something on a building that looks like a misplaced gargoyle, don't worry. It means I'm on the job."

"You can't cover her 24 hours a day," Bob said, hoping the comment didn't reveal his paranoia. "When you're asleep, I'll take over."

"I won't be sleeping on this job," Croyd said. "Later. I'll sleep later." There was a hint of something in Croyd's demon voice that to Bob almost sounded sad. With that thought in his head, he smiled.

They hadn't seen Croyd since hiring him, although Carlotta said she thought maybe she'd spied him a time or two, a dark, still shadow on the rooftop of the building opposite her apartment. Bob was fine with the situation. *Out of sight, out of mind,* as far as he was concerned. A grand every other day was a steep price, but sooner or later the Mutt and Jeff, or maybe the pickup artist who spooked Carlotta, would try again. If Croyd did his job as advertised, that would be their mistake.

He'd offered to buy her dinner at a steak house off Central Park West, knowing she'd have a hard time saying no. Bob knew what she took home in pay, and it didn't allow room for passing up a free meal. She also had to overcome the fact that it was the 13th of the month and she was deathly superstitious.

They got to the restaurant early enough to beat the crowd, and darkness was settling in over Manhattan when their food arrived. Bob had ordered a t-bone smothered in onions, while Carlotta had gone for the filet mignon. It was 10 ounces and he hoped she'd let him poach off her plate if she wasn't up to finishing it.

"This is one thing my people could never get right, cooking meat," he said after downing a particularly tasty bite.

"Your people?"

"The English." He dabbed a spot of juice from his chin. "I'm a Brit, you know that."

"You're a New Yorker in denial, you mean." She shook her head. "You spent what, two years in England after you were born and have been here the rest of your life. You're just a New Yorker with a slightly different pedigree. Live with it." Carlotta pointed to her filet with the fork. "This is great, by the way. Thanks."

"You're welcome, and I'm English, thank you very much. My parents lived there for ten years before we moved to NYC, and raised me to be a repressed, cultured snob."

"Bet your mom would smack you if she heard you say that. You'd deserve it, too." She gave him a lascivious smile that promised only torment. "At least you're right about the repressed part."

"Oh, that's great, coming from the Ado Annie of Iowa. You wouldn't know repressed if it bit you on the ass, and it's probably the only thing that hasn't."

"No," she said, smiling. "That would be you."

Bob wagged a finger in her direction. "No dessert for you." The lights inside the restaurant flickered and went out, tried to come back on for a second, and then went completely dark.

"Looks like they've blown a fuse," Carlotta said.

Bob turned and looked out the windows toward the street. There was light, but it was fainter than it should be. "I think the whole area has a power outage. The street lights are gone, too."

The waiters were moving from table to table, lighting candles. One particularly lanky fellow made it over to where Bob and Carlotta were seated to furnish the couple with their meager source of light.

"Any idea what's going on?" Bob asked.

"No," the waiter replied, shaking his head, "and wouldn't you know the manager would be off today. Like he didn't know it was the 13th. Someone's on the phone though, checking into it. We'll pass on any word we get." He hurried off to another table.

"A man after your own heart," Bob said, smiling. Carlotta's face, lit by the flickering candle, had an almost sinister cast. Her round features, lit from beneath, reminded him of the face in the mirror from Disney's *Snow White*.

"If you want to make jokes, you should get up on stage and try it sometime." She took another bite of steak. Bob's hope of leftovers was quickly disappearing. "You don't have any superstitions?"

"No. Only fact-based fears." One of them, that Carlotta would completely finish her steak, had already been realized. He raised his arm and waved it in an exaggerated fashion, trying to flag the waiter, who noticed after a few moments and wove his way expertly through the mostly empty tables toward them.

"No word yet, sir, but I believe it's city-wide."

"Thanks. Could we have the check?"

"Certainly, sir," he said, and quickly disappeared in the direction of the register.

Bob fingered his shirt's topmost button uncomfortably. "It's getting pretty warm in here without the a/c. Want to stop by the park and see if we can get some ice-cream?"

"Sure. My relatives in Wisconsin would tar-and-feather me if they found out I passed up a dairy product. I wonder what it's going to be like on the streets?" Carlotta pulled a compact out of her purse and checked her face briefly. "Like anyone will be able to see me."

Their waiter returned and set the tray with their bill in front of Bob. "Our credit card machine is down, sir. I hope cash won't be inconvenient."

"Not a problem," Bob said, pulling out his wallet. "Thank you." He carefully stacked several twenties onto the tab and helped Carlotta out of her seat. "Let's have a look outside."

The street was unreal in the dim moonlight. People stood in small groups talking quietly, and a family, probably out-of-towners, waved in vain for an available cab. The traffic was crawling at best, but drivers were still jockeying from lane to lane, trying to find an opening. Bob looked up and saw the stars. Normally, the city lights washed them out completely, but now they were clear and distinct. In contrast, Central Park loomed darkly across the crowded, hot asphalt.

"It's going to be murderous getting you home," Bob said. "Even the subways are going to be useless. Maybe we should reconsider our plan."

"We're not going anywhere until the power comes back on." She headed across Central Park West, moving around the cars that were momentarily at a standstill. "Might as well kill the time as best we can."

"Alright," Bob said, "wait for me."

After half an hour wandering along the edge of Central Park looking for an ice-cream vendor, Bob was ready to give up. He'd also noticed a group of kids following them at a distance. Even if they were just wandering in the same direction, it made him uneasy. He was glad to still be carrying the revolver.

A sharp snapping noise, followed quickly by another, stopped them in their tracks. Screams began to drift through the still, hot air from nearby.

"What the hell is going on?" Carlotta asked, looking quickly from side to side. "It's just a blackout."

A dark shape appeared at the tree line and grew in size. More snapping. Bob realized it was the sound of branches being split. Several people were sprinting directly at them. One of them screamed "*The ape! It's loose.*"

Bob knew in an instant how much trouble they were in. The giant ape had been a mainstay at the Central Park Zoo for over a decade. Every now and then it broke loose and started looking for a young, blonde woman to clutch to its massive chest. After abducting its Fay Wray stand-in, the beast invariably headed in scripted fashion for the top of the Empire State Building. His mind registered that the monster ape had first appeared during the blackout in 1965, but there was no time to dwell on coincidence. He grabbed Carlotta by the wrist and bolted for the street. She had no trouble keeping up, matching him stride for stride in the race to reach the hoped-for safety of a building interior.

A kid running full-tilt crashed into a garbage container and sent it rolling in a tight semi-circle right into their path. Bob felt a pain in his knee and sprawled headlong, Carlotta's hand wrenched from his grasp. There was an animal roar that rattled his fillings and he scrambled to his feet.

The ape knuckle-walked toward them, its eyes fixed on Carlotta and her blonde hair. She struggled to stand and backed slowly away from the monster. Then stopped. "Knock-knock," she yelled. The ape bared its teeth and snorted. "Who's there?" Carlotta answered to her own question, at the top of her voice.

Bob pulled the revolver and pointed it between the ape's luminous, yellow eyes. She'd panicked and was trying to use her power on it. "You can't make a gorilla laugh," he yelled. "Run."

The giant ape regarded him for a second, then returned his attention to Carlotta, taking another giant step in her direction. "Banana, banana, banana, banana," she continued, ignoring Bob's advice.

He tightened his finger on the trigger, and the ape lunged for Carlotta, scooping her up with a giant, hairy paw. She screamed and then went limp. The ape gingerly propped up her head with a single finger and made what might have been soothing vocalizations in ape language. The monster turned suddenly and saw Bob. It snarled and bared its teeth.

Bob suddenly felt very alone, the useless gun heavy in his hand. He'd be a dead man in a few seconds and the punch line to a bad joke for years to come if he didn't do something. So he got flat.

He didn't lie flat; that would have been no help at all. As a particularly shy teen-ager, Bob had been forced by a zealous drama teacher to take a role in a Moliere comedy. During a dress rehearsal, he felt sick with stage fright and, right before his entrance, literally flowed puddle-like to the floor. The sensation of giving up his physical form was even more frightening than performing on stage. His vision and hearing became almost non-existent. Worse, he couldn't move any more than a beached jellyfish. After a few long moments, he'd reconstituted, naked, as he'd puddled right out of his clothes. A few of his fellow students saw what happened, or thought they did, but the school kept it quiet. He was dismissed from the play and told his parents it was because he called Moliere an over-praised, humorless Frog. Over the years he'd worked with his ability in secret, and had even mastered a sort of pseudopodal movement. Bob assumed part of his attraction to Carlotta was the fact that they'd both been touched by the wild card, albeit a glancing blow.

Bob had a feeling that, flat or not, if the giant ape stepped on him, he'd be crushed to death. He felt the thunderous footsteps move toward, and then past, him. He waited until the vibrations seemed a safe distance away and pulled himself back together. The few people who hadn't left the area were looking at the ape, which was about a hundred yards distant. Bob hurriedly donned his clothing and put the gun back into his pocket. The ape was making good time. Bob knew he'd never catch it on foot, and with traffic snarled because of the blackout, a car was out of the question, too.

He heard a horse neigh and turned to see an empty carriage not far away. Abandoned by its driver, the horse, coal black with a white patch on its forehead, regarded Bob warily as he approached. He moved slowly toward the spot on the ground where the reins lay. The horse snorted as he gathered the slim, leather leads into his hands.

"Good boy," Bob said, clambering up into the carriage. Once seated, he tried to plot a course in the direction the ape and Carlotta had taken and then shook the reins.

The horse didn't so much as twitch. Apparently, he didn't have the voice of authority. "Yaah!" he yelled, and tossed the reins violently. Nothing.

"I'm not in the mood for this," Bob said, pulling the pistol from his pocket. He fired off a round into the air and the horse immediately bounded away at full tilt, hooves pounding the earth. Bob's back was slammed into the driver's seat by the carriage's abrupt start and he fought to pull himself back into a position to drive, not that he had any idea what he was doing. The hot summer air whistled in Bob's ears and he noticed they were veering a bit to the left of his best guess at the ape's path, so he pulled on the right hand rein but got no response from his charging steed.

"Damn," he said, and pulled harder, but the horse galloped hell-bent onward. Bob saw what looked like a curbed pathway directly ahead and reached for the side of the carriage to brace himself for the impact, but his reaction was a second too slow. The carriage's front wheels slammed into the curb and the front of the vehicle vaulted into the air, tossing Bob out of the carriage and down onto the grass on the far side of the sidewalk. He rolled to a stop and sat up. The now riderless carriage was disappearing into the darkness. Bob let out a deep breath and there was a rush of air around him that raised a cloud of heavy dust.

Croyd landed next to him, chuckling. "Can't even keep a girl safe at dinner, eh?"

Bob bit back on his anger at Croyd's nonchalance. He needed help to save Carlotta and Croyd was it. "If you were watching, why didn't you do something?"

"I'm tough, but no match for a giant gorilla. Keep your shirt on, though. As many times as this has happened, not once has the ape's captive blonde been hurt, unless you count soiled clothing." Croyd helped Bob to his feet, a glint in his yellow eyes. "There's a bit more to you than I thought."

Bob felt sick. He'd guarded his secret for years and Croyd was one of the last people he would have picked to share it. "That's not important now. Let's get going."

"You da boss." Croyd slipped his taloned hands under Bob's armpits and began beating his wings. The pair rose slowly from Central Park.

Bob felt more than saw the world falling away. The noise level faded as they headed into the sky. Car headlights lit the streets and avenues at ground level but everything else was inky black, except for the occasional dim window he assumed meant someone inside had lit a candle or two. To his relief the air cooled a bit as Croyd carried him upward. Combined with the rush of Croyd's wings, the sensation was almost refreshing.

"You're not going to throw up are you?" Croyd's breath was warm on the top of Bob's head.

"No. I'm okay." Which was true as long as he didn't think or look down. "Where are we going?"

"Empire State, Mr. Village Idiot. The ape always climbs it, if he gets that far. And we can pick up some reinforcements there. Like I said, I can't handle him alone."

"Aces High?" Like everyone else, Bob had heard of the famous restaurant atop the Empire State building and knew that as often as not there was an ace or two having dinner there.

"Give the boy a cigar." Croyd's breath was becoming a bit raspy. "You're not exactly a lightweight. This whole thing is going to cost you extra, by the way. Not exactly what I signed on for. Might cut you a deal for a couple of rounds with your girlfriend, though."

"Have you even got genitalia?" Bob snapped.

Croyd let go of Bob with one hand and lowered him level with the demon's crotch. "Care to check?"

Bob grabbed hold of Croyd's sinewy arm with both his hands and clutched it tightly. "Okay, okay. You made your point."

Croyd made a sibilant noise that sounded like a giggle. "An attitude and altitude adjustment. Good thing. You'd feel like one stupid shithead during the time it took you to fall. Here we are."

The observation deck of the Empire State Building stood out in faint shades of gray and silver. They landed softly on the concrete and Croyd took a deep breath. Bob was both happy and sorry to have his feet on something solid again. Nothing else he'd experienced was quite like the flight he'd just had.

"Here's how it's going to work. I'm going to shadow the ape and grab Carlotta on the off chance he makes a mistake. How fucking likely that is I don't know, but we can't count on it. You go inside and tell Hiram that I sent you. See what help you can round up and have it waiting when our hairy friend shows up." Croyd grabbed Bob by the shoulders and spun him around, then gave him a shove toward the door. "Do it." Then he was gone again.

Bob opened the door and groped his way down the stairs as quickly as he could, and when he reached the first landing felt around for a doorknob. He couldn't turn it and started pounding on it as hard as he could. "Open up. I need help." He was silent a moment to try to hear any sound from inside but there was only silence. He was groping for the handrail when he heard a door open not far below him.

"Who's there?" The voice was deep, male, and irritated.

"A friend of Croyd's," Bob said, his hand finding the metal of the railing. He was halfway down the flight of stairs when a flashlight came on, blinding him momentarily.

"A friend of Croyd's who isn't a woman? That's a novelty." The voice took on a somewhat more amiable tenor. "Come inside."

The man holding the door open for him had to be Hiram Worcester. Bob had seen pictures of him in the papers and magazines. Hiram was tall and broadly built with a distinctive spadeshaped beard. Even in the candlelight spilling from the restaurant Bob could tell every aspect of Hiram was perfectly groomed, right down to the crisp lines of his white tuxedo.

"Thanks." Bob stepped into Aces High and was taken aback by its elegance. The tables, punctuated here and there by exotic-looking plants or objects d'art, were ideally situated to provide patrons with a view of the entire establishment while still maintaining a degree of privacy for conversation. Aces High was illuminated with the flickering light of least a hundred candles, reflecting polished crystal and silverware, giving the restaurant a romantic, ethereal glow.

"Have a seat," Hiram said, gesturing to an empty table. "And tell me what's going on."

Bob sat down and took a deep breath. "You heard the ape is loose?"

Hiram shook his head. "No. I told Emil to listen to the radio and let me know what's going on, but he clearly hasn't done it. Would you like a brandy, by the way?"

"That would be great."

Hiram caught a waiter's eye and raised two thick fingers. The man nodded and disappeared. "So what do you have to do with Croyd and the giant ape?"

"The ape has my girlfriend." Bob was surprised to hear himself refer to Carlotta that way, particularly since it was far from true. "And Croyd is, well, in my employ. He flew me here and then took off to see if he could get Carlotta away from the ape. Most likely it's climbing the building by now. Are there any other aces, beside yourself, who might be able to help? Croyd said there might be." Each of Bob's phrases came out quicker than the one before. He hoped he didn't sound hysterical.

The brandies arrived and Hiram took a sip of his. Bob drained half of the liquid in his snifter and the bracing quality of the liquor made him feel instantly calmer. "You can see we're a bit less crowded tonight than usual, but there's someone here who might be helpful." Hiram gestured toward a young woman sitting alone at a table.

Except for her magnificent, curled wings, or maybe because of them, she was the most beautiful girl Bob had ever seen. He'd seen her on the *Tonight Show* and in *Playboy*, repeatedly. His mind groped for her name. "Ptarmigan," he said, realizing the name was wrong the instant it passed his lips.

Hiram smiled and took another sip of brandy. "Peregrine, actually. I'll introduce you, but let me do the talking."

They walked over to Peregrine, who Bob was shocked to see alone, given her looks and notoriety. "Peri, we've got a bit of a situation," Hiram said. "A giant ape is headed here with a captive blonde, this gentleman's girlfriend." He indicated Bob. "We're going up to the observation deck to rescue her. Would you mind helping?"

"Sounds like fun." Peregrine stood and kicked off her heels, then studied her gown, which was a shimmering aqua and tighter than a Scotsman with his last nickel. She fingered a slit in the dress that rose to mid-calf one side and tore it open by another fifteen inches. "That should help." She carefully removed a pair of metal talons from her purse and slipped them over her wrist. "Let's go."

Hiram led the way up the stairs with his flashlight and helped open the door to the observation deck for Peregrine and Bob to step outside.

"Peri, why don't you see what you can see," Hiram suggested, but at that moment a giant paw appeared over the railing in front of them. Peregrine shot into the air and Hiram hustled Bob around the corner. Bob heard the metal railing buckle behind them, and breathing so heavy only a fifty-foot ape that had just climbed a hundred story building could have made it.

The ape scaled the building's domed apex and roared. Bob picked out a pair of flying shapes darting around above them, but Croyd and Peregrine, either together or singly, didn't seem to Bob like much of a threat to the monster.

Hiram agreed out loud. "They'll never be able to get her away from it. I wish the Turtle were here. This would be no trouble for him."

Bob and Hiram craned their necks to follow the flying figures darting by the ape. It kept the beast looking up instead down at the deck where they were. Although it was too dark to really be able to tell, Bob thought Croyd was paying as much attention to Peregrine as he was to the ape, who stood unmoving except for the swiveling of his head to keep its enemies in sight.

The ape looked like it was going to set Carlotta down. She was conscious again, but not struggling very much. Croyd swept in and the ape thrust out a giant arm out to fend off the perceived attack, catching Croyd with the back of his hand and sending him spinning down toward the street. Peregrine instantly disappeared after him.

Hiram sighed. "I suppose that leaves me." He turned to Bob. "Unless you do something."

"I stay out of the way pretty well," Bob replied, "but I'm willing to try anything you've got in mind."

Hiram looked up and slowly made a fist. The gorilla's broad shoulders slumped and its arms dropped to its sides. "A bit heavier," Hiram said, more to himself than Bob. The top of the building began to creak under the strain of the extra weight Hiram was adding. "Now," he said and the ape leapt upwards, almost appearing to hover in the air momentarily. It dropped Carlotta and grabbed at the top of the building with both paws, its momentum carrying it to the other side of the dome. "And heavy again," Hiram mused. The ape slammed into the top of the dome, sending fragments of stone and metal onto Bob and Hiram.

"Up the ladder and get her," Hiram said. "I'll keep our guest where he is."

Bob did as he was told. He gathered Carlotta into his arms and tried not to look down and he guided her to the ladder. They were joined on the observation deck by Peregrine. Bob pulled the winged beauty to one side. "How is Croyd?" he whispered, afraid to hear the answer.

"Not too bad," Peregrine said. "He landed on one of the setbacks about ten floors down but must have got his wings going right before he hit. He can't fly, though, so I'm going to take him home."

"Thanks." Bob reached to pat her shoulder, then stopped, realizing her wings prevented it. "I really do appreciate it."

"My pleasure. See you soon, Hiram." Peregrine fluttered into the air and then down into the darkness at the building's edge.

Bob returned to Carlotta's side. "We need to get you home."

"The sooner the better." Carlotta said, sniffing her hands. "God, I smell like that thing." She extended her hand to Hiram. "Whoever you are, thank you."

"Hiram Worchester." He gave Carlotta's hand a shake and looked back up at the ape, who's breathing was again labored. "Will you stay for dinner, once this is fully taken care of?"

"Some other time," Carlotta said, turning to the doorway. "I don't think I could really appreciate it right now."

"I'll look forward to it," Hiram said, smiling.

Bob turned off the transistor radio and set it down on the coffee table. "Anything new?" Carlotta poked her head out of the kitchen area. In spite of the heat, she'd insisted on cooking as much food as possible to keep it from spoiling.

"Not really. The ape is back at Central Park Zoo. They're keeping him sedated until the cage is repaired."

"I hope Croyd is okay. It's good for a girl's health, not to mention her ego, to have a protector like that." There was a momentary pause. Bob figured she was expecting a jealous comment and kept his mouth shut. "Anything else?"

"Major fires in Jokertown and the Bronx. Looting. Rioting. Just your average day in New York." Bob walked over to the open, third-story window and looked out onto the street. It was late afternoon and the power had been out over 20 hours, but residents and visitors in the Village were treating it like a holiday. People were milling about, sharing stories over warm beer, or clustering around a radio for news. "Doesn't seem bad at all around here."

"Good," she said, stepping into the living room. "We've got plenty to eat for dinner this evening, but I never got my ice cream last night and I'm feeling sugar-deprived."

"I'm not sure there's any unmelted ice cream left in this town, but I could use the exercise." Bob looked at her. Even in sweat stained clothes she was an attractive woman.

"First things first. I'm taking a shower." She started unbuttoning her blouse. "Want to join me?"

Bob delighted in what he was looking at, but his back still hurt from the hours he'd spent trying to sleep on her couch the previous night. "You're just taunting me."

Carlotta took her top off and fingered the snap on her bra. Her lovely curved flesh lowered Bob's I.Q. 20 points or so. "You're right, I am. Would it kill you to play along?" She disappeared into the bedroom and there was the delicious sound of running water.

"You never can tell," he said, suddenly aware of just how nice it would feel to get clean, even without Carlotta's company. He walked into her bedroom, which had several candles burning, as much to take a look at it as for proximity to the bathroom. It was tidy, with a couple of tasteful but inexpensive art prints on the wall, probably from the MoMA. Other than the garments she'd just stripped off to shower, all her other clothes were put away. There were several framed pictures of the folks back home on her dresser and bedside table. Nothing that looked like a boyfriend, although she'd had plenty of those since coming to New York. "I'm next," he said loudly.

"Okay by me," she yelled back.

Bob sighed.

The heat was as bad as it had been all week, with temperatures in the low hundreds. The concrete and asphalt gave it nowhere to go but into the air and the living things on the island of Manhattan. Carlotta had made a point of putting on the scent Croyd gave her. Bob still wasn't sure whether or not to tell her Croyd was out of action indefinitely.

"Have you wondered why I had sex with so many other men, but not you?" Carlotta flashed him a challenging smile.

"Why no, that hadn't even occurred to me. Of course, I'm not sure why you're fixated on ice-cream, either." Bob raised a single eyebrow, a trick he'd learned watching Vincent Price movies as a kid.

"For that I should keep you in the dark, but I figure you deserve to know." She crossed the street to avoid a cascade of water from an opened fire hydrant. Bob followed. "Number one, you're a smartass. Number two, you're the boss." She paused, maybe to give him a chance to object to number one. He didn't. "And number three, you've got possibilities."

Bob's eyebrow shot up again, this time of its own accord. "What do you mean, possibilities?"

"Long term possibilities."

Her comment hung in the air like a float at Macy's Thanksgiving Day Parade.

"Wait a minute," Bob said, and was on the verge on launching into a tirade when he felt a strong hand on his shoulder.

"No, you wait a minute, tough guy." The hand had an accompanying voice, and, unfortunately, he recognized it as Jeff the bad guy.

Bob turned his head slightly and saw that Carlotta had company, too. Mutt had her by the elbow. She was casting her eyes upward, looking for help Bob knew wouldn't be coming. He felt something press firmly into his back. A brand new limo pulled up beside them and its rearmost door on their side opened up.

"Get inside."

He and Carlotta slid onto the leather seat between their captors. The tinted windows were less than comforting and the truly humorless men surrounding them were even less so.

Jeff slid Bob's revolver from his pocket, holding it firmly by the barrel-end. "Know what happens next?"

"You all commit suicide," Carlotta said, and there were several giggles.

"Not now," Bob thought, and then consciousness fled his body through a portal of blinding pain as the gun smacked into the side of his head.

He was lying down when he came to. Bob opened his eyes with deliberate slowness. He was lying on a couch and Carlotta was sitting opposite him in a straight-backed wooden chair, a concerned look on her face. "Where are we?" he said quietly, his head throbbing.

"In a house." She reached over and pushed Bob's hair out of his eyes.

"A little more information would be appreciated, if you've got it." He eased himself into a sitting position.

"Okay, a big house. An estate. Big walls, wrought-iron gate, you know the type. I think we're on Long Island."

"That's not good." Bob realized that if they hadn't bothered to keep Carlotta from describing where they'd been taken, they weren't expecting her, or either of them, to be able to talk to the police later. He looked around the room for exits. There were two windows, both barred, and one door. "Who are these people, and what do they want with you?"

"Like they'd tell me that," Carlotta said. "But that one guy, the tall one, he really doesn't like you."

"I have no trouble believing that." The pain in Bob's skull was spreading into his jaw and neck. "We have to come up with a plan to get out of here. Clearly, making them laugh in the limo didn't work."

"No. They gagged me with a stupid little plastic ball thing. My power doesn't work at all if I can't talk. I don't know how they knew that." Carlotta stood and walked over to the window, staring into the darkness.

The door opened and three men stepped in. Bob recognized Mutt and Jeff. The third man was a head shorter than Bob, and was casually dressed in a pricey, dapper manner. He was balding on either temple, and there was a quickness about his movements that was almost birdlike.

"Hello, Jane." He sat down in the chair Carlotta had been occupying.

"Jane?" Bob said, mystified. "Look friend. I don't know what your game is, but her name is Carlotta Desoto. So your goons obviously bundled the wrong people out here. Let us go and maybe we won't press charges."

"I should have known it was you." Carlotta's eyes were livid with anger. "My name was legally changed, and I'd appreciate it if you'd call me Carlotta."

Bob felt like whatever play he was in had just dropped a scene. "What in blazes is going on here?"

"My name is Breton Earle. Carlotta," he said the name as derisively as possible, "is my wife."

"Ex-wife," Carlotta corrected, folding her arms. "That part was legal, too. Your money doesn't change the fact that you're a loser and a jerk."

Bob couldn't believe that all they'd been through the past few days was because of a jealous ex-husband. "Sounds like her mind is made up, Mr. Earle, so why don't you just let us go. Like I said, we'll leave the police out of it."

Earle turned to Jeff. "Mr. Mueller, who is this?"

"Robert Cortland. He owns the club she worked at."

Earle nodded. "You and Mr. Layden will have to take care of him on your own dime."

"No problem."

"What do you mean, no problem?" Carlotta walked behind her captors. The suited men kept a careful eye on her. "You kidnapped me. That's a federal crime."

Earle laughed, but it wasn't Carlotta's doing. "You're welcome to address your grievances to the police if you're ever in a position to do so, but I don't think you will be."

"Why did you bring Bob?" Carlotta shook her head. "He doesn't mean anything to you."

"He does to me," said Mueller. "I don't like anyone taking a shot at me."

"Why do you want her back?" Bob was stalling for time, trying to come up with some plan of action. If there was one thing smug egomaniacs like Earle shared with entertainers, it was the need for an audience.

"I'm glad you asked me that question. I could say she makes me laugh, or that the sex was incredible." Earle feigned a yawn. "But that's not it. The truth is, she made me look ridiculous. A man with my position in life can't have one of his acquisitions leave him of its own accord. That's all she was to me, an attractive acquisition. So, in return for her disloyalty I want to make her miserable and I want the pleasure of seeing her miserable every day of her wretched life. May it be a long one."

"You're a fool," Carlotta said. "It's a damned shame money can't buy sense. Maybe then you'd understand."

Breton Earle folded. "With my money, I'm hardly restrained by your idea of what's sensible, Miss Desoto."

"Don't have to go begging to daddy anymore?" Carlotta gave Earle a nasty smile.

Earle's eyes took on a hard quality. "My father died 19 months ago. After the estate was fully executed I gave some of my best men the job of finding you, which they did. I bought this house to work from. It's a more expensive prison than you deserve, but who knows where I'll ultimately keep you."

"Asshole," Carlotta said.

"It's a shame you didn't fall for our blond Adonis. He was very disappointed when you disappeared from the coffee shop." Earle shook his head. "You're such a slut. You'd have enjoyed that."

Carlotta raised her chin. "The last person in the world to know what I'd enjoy is you, Breton."

"What exactly are you going to do to her?" Bob planned on keeping the questions coming as long as Earle was in an answering mood.

"Whatever it suits me to do at any given time. I'm sure whatever it is, it will be better than what happens to you." He headed for the door. "Shall we, gentlemen?"

Mueller bent down and whispered in Bob's ear. "I'm betting we've got an oil drum in your size. If not, I'll just have to break some of your bones to get you in." He grinned and followed Earle and Layden out of the room. The door clicked shut and Bob heard a lock being set.

"Okay," he said, removing his shirt and shoes. "Put these away. They'll be back in a minute."

"What?"

He tossed her his pants. "Hide them."

She picked up his clothing and gave him a long look. "So, you're going to die and I'm facing a fate worse than death and you want to score with me as a dying request?"

Bob dropped his underwear at her feet. "No."

Carlotta stared at his crotch and Bob realized that the adrenaline had gotten to him in an unexpected way. "Those who are about to die salute you," she said. "No wonder you're the boss."

It was good she was still cracking jokes, however lame, but now was not the time. "I'm going to show you something, and I don't want you to freak out. Okay, my dear?"

"You've already showed me something, but okay."

Bob puddled, waited a few seconds, and reconstituted.

"Holy shit. You're one too." Her mouth closed and eyes narrowed. "You never told me, even after you knew about me, you never told me." She slapped him.

Bob raised a cautionary finger. "My head really hurts, so don't do that again. I was going to tell you, after we had sex the first time."

"Oh, that's cute. I can't believe you didn't tell me something that important." Carlotta sat down. "So where does this get us?"

"Out, with any luck." Bob padded over to the door and pressed his ear to it. He heard footfalls approaching at a brisk pace and ran to the far corner where there was a large, heavy rug with a Middle Eastern design. "Don't tell them a thing, and try to keep them from stepping on me." The door began to open. He centered the rug on the top of his head and got flat.

The vibrations were heavy, frantic and all around him. He prayed not to get trod on, fearing one of his vital organs might be turned to paste. Bob would have held his breath, but he was doing the equivalent anyway. His flat body was incapable of respiration and the oxygen to his tissues was quickly depleting.

After what seemed to him like the eternity of a bad comedy routine, Bob resumed his normal form. He was alone in the darkened room. He heard voices outside the door, but they were growing fainter. He had two options for escape, the door and the window. After groping his way to the door, he tested the knob, but it was still locked. Judging by the crack of light under the frame, he might be able to slide under, but it would be quite a squeeze and he might wind up in the lap of Earle's goons. He fumbled under the couch where Carlotta had tucked his clothes and pulled them out, then moved to the window and slowly opened the blinds. It would be no problem for him to get under the bars, but that would still leave him on the outside looking in. Doubtless, they were searching the grounds for him right now, possibly with dogs, although he was relieved not to hear the sound of any barking.

He unlatched the window, lifted it silently up a foot or so, and pushed his clothes out under the bars. Decision made. Bob thrust his arms under the bars and began to slide out. By the time he was completely flat, enough of his body extended past the windowsill that he was dragged down the wall and onto the ground. The impact didn't bother him and Bob pulled himself together and hurriedly put on his clothes. The tiny flashlight was still in his pocket, but along with his car keys, those were his only tools.

He circled the perimeter of the house, amazed and disgusted at the size of the place. Although only one story, Earle's mansion had to be five or six thousand square feet of house, minimum. Most of the rooms were dark and he quickly passed them by. He came to a well-lit corridor that was, for the moment anyway, deserted. The window was unlocked and unbarred. Taking a deep breath, he opened the window and went in. There was a door on either side of the hallway, but Bob decided to move further into the interior of the house, maybe catch the sound of voices and overhear something about Carlotta. More likely, he'd get caught or shot, but he wasn't going to run for it. He wouldn't ever be able to live with that. About 20 feet in was a large living area, lit by a single lamp. The ceiling arched upward from all sides to an oval skylight.

He heard a noise behind him, then to his left was a sound better than anything he could have expected, laughter, rising into hysteria and nearly convulsive choking. Bob ran to where he heard the noise and opened the door, ready to get flat if he had to.

Carlotta was kneeling on the floor, chewing at the duct tape on her wrists. She looked up at him, clearly surprised. "Close the door, and get me out of this."

Layden was curled up drooling on the floor, his eyes red, his barrel chest heaving. Bob rolled him over and put a knee into the man's back. He reached behind and fumbled to get Layden's shoelaces off, contorting himself uncomfortably to do so, then used them to bind his captive's hands behind him.

"Me now." Carlotta held out her hands. Bob used the edge of one of his keys to saw through the tape. It was tough work and took the better part of a minute.

He got up and closed the door. "Why didn't they gag you?"

"Well, they did." She indicated a rubber ball and a handkerchief on the floor.

Bob wrinkled his brow. "How did you get him to take it off?"

"You don't want to know." She pulled the remains of the tape off her wrists and snatched up the red ball, then pushed it firmly in the bound man's mouth.

Bob picked the silk handkerchief up off the floor and tossed it to Carlotta. "Of that, I'm sure. Tie this around his mouth, just to make sure he doesn't start yelling." He moved to her side and checked the man's pockets, retrieving a revolver from his inside coat pocket. "Come to daddy," he said, recognizing it as his own weapon. He took a deep breath and stood, and helped Carlotta to her feet.

"Time to get out of here," she said. "Let me go first, just in case someone's waiting."

"What's the point of that?" Bob asked, but she was already out the door.

"Don't move, bitch." Mueller's voice was clear, steady, and close. "If you so much as open your mouth, I'll put a bullet in it."

Bob pulled out his gun and readied it, then stepped into the hall. His large nemesis had drawn down on Carlotta, but shifted his weapon's aim to Bob when he saw him. Mueller was standing on the far side of a couch in the living area. Bob's finger tightened on the trigger. He wondered if he could squeeze off a round and get flat before the return shot nailed him. "Drop it," Bob said, knowing it was overly optimistic.

"No chance. I'm better at this than you." Mueller lowered his head a bit so that he could sight down the gun's barrel.

"Don't bet the farm," Carlotta said.

Mueller snarled. "One more word and you're dead, lady. End of story."

Darkness swallowed them as the lights went out. Bob dragged Carlotta to the floor. "I don't fucking believe it," he said. "Not again."

"What now?" Carlotta whispered.

Bob pondered for a moment and thought he caught a glint of something in the darkness. He kept his voice low. "Start telling a joke and follow my lead. Stay behind something or keep moving so you don't get shot."

"If I can't see him, I can't make him laugh," Carlotta said.

"Just do it."

"What do you call a hundred lawyers at the bottom of the ocean?" Carlotta's voice didn't sound strong, but that might be because she was behind something. Bob started laughing.

"A good start."

Bob increased the pitch and tenor of his laughter, moving in the general direction of the glint he had seen.

"Layden, is that you?"

Bob could hear the confusion in Mueller's voice, which was exactly what he was hoping for. He intentionally gave his laughter a raspy, desperate quality.

"Why did the chicken cross the road?"

There was a shot in Carlotta's general direction. Bob popped off two rounds of his own, but the muzzle flash from Mueller's gun put stars in his eyes and spoiled his aim. One of the slugs hit something breakable, a lamp maybe, and Mueller started screaming. "My eye. Get over here, Layden. I'm hit in the eye."

Bob reached out and caught Mueller's wrist, steadied it, and before the man knew who he was dealing with, Bob swung and nailed him on the temple with his revolver. "Lights out. Are you okay?" he asked loudly of Carlotta.

Before she could answer the skylight shattered and something fell through. It looked to Bob like it might be a person, but in the semidarkness he couldn't be sure. Someone groaned and Bob heard glass crunching. He pulled out the flashlight, but didn't turn it on. It would make him an easy target.

"A monster," came a nearly hysterical voice. Bob recognized it as Earle's. "Someone save me."

"Monster?" Bob didn't need another problem at this point.

"That would be me," came a voice from above. A winged shape dropped down through the shattered skylight into a crouching position. "Fie-fi-fo-fum. I smell a good looking woman, yummm."

"Croyd,", Carlotta said, like his name was the answer to a prayer.

"A couple of minutes ago would have been timelier." Bob was happy to hear the sound of Croyd's voice just the same.

"Complaining about my timing will cost you extra," Croyd said, folding his wings against his scaly back.

Earle was whimpering on the floor, but pulled himself together sufficiently to start crawling away. Unfortunately it was in the direction of Bob, who trained the beam of his flashlight on Earle's tear-stained face.

"Stop right there, Mr. Earle," Bob said. "Or we'll feed you to our demon."

"Your demon?" Croyd snorted and fluttered across the room to where Bob, Carlotta, and Earle were faced off. "I am mighty hungry, though."

"No." Earle covered his eyes with his fists. "It's not fair."

Croyd picked up Carlotta in his massive arms and sniffed delicately behind her ears. "If there's one thing that gets me hot, it's a woman who actually does what she's told." He turned to Bob. "Can you handle him for a minute?" He jerked his head at Earle.

"No problem, but where are you . . ." Croyd shot up through the hole in the roof with Carlotta. ". . . going?" Bob trailed off.

There was a moan from across the room. Mueller was coming to, which Bob did not want to allow. "Time for your second helping." He brought the pistol butt on forcefully down onto Mueller's head with a stinging whack. Bob looked down at Earle. Rich boy's eyes were still shot through with fear.

Croyd swooped back into the room and clapped his hand over Breton Earle's mouth. "Don't bite, or I'll bite you back." Croyd bared his sizable yellow fangs. The message got through. Earle didn't even whimper as he was carried out into the open air.

Bob waited an uncomfortably long time. Mueller was beginning to make a lot of noise and there must be other people searching through the darkness of the home. Croyd dropped back into the room just as Bob's paranoia was beginning to bloom.

"You cut the power." Bob said.

Croyd grabbed him under the armpits. "Leave it to Mr. Village Idiot to state the obvious." Bob felt a rush of air as they rocketed into the warm night. The sense of being airborne was magical and slightly scary, given Croyd's unusual nature.

They landed far from the house, by Carlotta and Earle, whose hands were bound behind his back with Carlotta's bra. Bob gave her an accusatory look.

"We had to use something," she explained. "Or he might have run off."

"When I took it off, I couldn't really see that much, but we may have to rectify that later, as part of my payment." Croyd kissed his fingertips.

"Please leave me alone. I'll give you money." Earle was enough of himself to try to strike a bargain.

Croyd laughed. "I've got business with Mr. Earle. So we'll have to figure out a way to get you two back to the city. I'll bet neither one of you can hotwire a car.

"Figures." He flew over to a nearby sedan and opened its driver's side door. A few moments later the engine turned over and the headlights came on. Bob grabbed Earle by the collar and led him over to the car. Carlotta was ahead of him. She was from Iowa, so she actually knew how to drive.

"What are you going to do with him?" Bob handed Earle over to Croyd.

"Please. You can't just kill me." Earle looked from face to face. "I didn't hurt anybody."

"Rich boy and I have a date with the Atlantic Ocean." Croyd slapped Earle hard on the back. "He's going to do some motivational swimming."

"No, I don't swim well at all," Earle protested.

"I'll meet you at your club later, and you can pay me then. What I did tonight falls under the bonus clause, just in case you didn't know." Croyd flew up with Earle and was quickly lost in the darkness. The screams of protest from Earle faded quickly. Bob got into the passenger side of the vehicle and shut the door.

"You know how to get us home?"

"Watch me," Carlotta said. Bob turned on the radio when they hit the main highway. The version of "Night on Bald Mountain" from *Saturday Night Fever* was playing. He drifted off to thoughts of a white-suited Croyd dancing with Carlotta.

The comfort of seeing the New York skyline lighting the horizon vanished when they finally made it back to the club. They'd ditched the car just north of Jokertown, taken the subway up, and been greeted with a burned-out building surrounded by yellow police tape. Bob walked to the center of what once had been his club, still-warm ashes crunching under his feet. Carlotta walked quietly behind him for a few moments, then gave him a hug.

"What to you think Mickey and Judy would do?"

"You'd have to hit me with your deuce to make me laugh now." Bob crouched and picked up a handful of burned rubble.

They stood there silently for a few minutes, ignoring the people on the street, the cars, and the other sounds of the city. With a rush of leathery wings, Croyd dropped down next to them.

"No riots around here. Maybe a parting shot from Earle's goons." Croyd shook his horned head sympathetically.

"I won't be able to pay you until tomorrow," Bob said. "I can go to the bank and get the money."

"Good. If not, I'll have to kill you." Croyd tangled his fingers in Carlotta's hair. "Or take it out in trade."

Carlotta laughed.

"I know that laugh," Bob said. "You're out of luck where she's concerned."

"Tomorrow," Croyd said, and he was gone.

Bob had paid Croyd off handsomely, and Croyd had suggested that he and Carlotta get out of New York and adopt new identities. Croyd had plenty of useful tips on creating another persona that would be undetectable by the authorities or people like Earle. Croyd didn't much care for Earle and remarked that the millionaire peed better than he swam.

After settling with the insurance company, Bob and Carlotta hit the road, with her at the wheel, of course. Driving was one thing he'd promised he was going to learn how to do. He didn't know where they were going to end up, but he wanted to get away from New York for good. They stopped off to visit his parents on the way out and were now headed to Iowa to see hers. He wondered if he could tolerate that much homespun Americana. After Carlotta had demonstrated to him the benefits of "long-term possibilities" he was ready to try.

The sun was coming up across the plains when they entered her home state.

"How many New Yorkers does it take to screw in a light bulb," she asked.

"Only one, if the right person asks."

Carlotta smiled at that. "Want to hear some new 'knock-knock' jokes?"

To Bob's surprise, he actually did.

Age of Wonders

THREE

January 2004

"THIS IS REALLY GOOD," Gavin said, looking at Raleigh over the February issue of *Aces!* hot off the presses, as the saying went. They were having lunch together at a deli on Sixth Avenue, and as soon as they sat she offered him the magazine with a mix of pride and trepidation. Her first feature article, the piece on Alice Smith/Carlotta DeSoto. It felt strange being proud of her work. She had to suppress this urge to apologize while Gavin read through it. *Oh no, it's nothing, I got lucky . . .*

The article had started as a quirky sidebar, a human-interest story from the wild card virus's weird past. Here was a woman, an ace, but her power wasn't flashy, *she* wasn't flashy. For thirty years she'd been balancing a desire to be out in the world, to show off who she was and what she could do—and a fear that made her want to hide away from it all. She loved comedy, and when the spotlight was no longer a possibility—well, she kept it lit for others. These days she preferred to be called Alice; it was the name she'd had the longest.

One of the wild card virus's small stories. There were thousands of them. Not earth-shattering like the Swarm, not filled with power and mayhem like the Astronomer, not anything like the strongest man in the world, the world's most powerful telekinetic. Not glamorous like any number of celebrities *Aces!* had put on its cover over the years. People might laugh at their harmless middling powers, might overlook them entirely.

But maybe they shouldn't. The whole idea felt overblown and kind of cheesy, except the more Raleigh thought about it, the more it drew her.

She'd sent the photographer back to the club and he'd gotten a great portrait of Alice, sitting on the stage, wearing a sober-looking suit and blouse, one foot on the floor, one heel hooked over the rung of her stool, hands folded on her knee. Her smile was winning, and the lights caught a glint in her that suggested she spent a lot of time laughing. The story itself wasn't sensationalist, didn't go into the details of the mess that had burned down the Village Idiot and sent her and Bob Cortland—a.k.a. Ralph Smith—into hiding. But it did talk about a woman who'd survived and gone on to make a difference. The story asked the question—was this because of her ace power or in spite of it? It left the answer to the reader.

"Once I got her talking she did all the work," Raleigh said.

"No . . . you were the one who saw there was a story there. This is *good*."

She and Gavin had officially been dating for two months. The first time he called the number she gave him it was to tell her he'd found some old clippings she might like to look at. The second time, he asked her out for coffee. Over the holidays, they'd made a day of it, afternoon at the Met and a nice dinner after. Then they'd spent the night together for the first time. He'd asked about her bracelet then, worried—was it something he should know about? Just allergies, she insisted, moving his hand from her wrist to her backside. They went to Times Square for New Year's, and spent *a lot* of time kissing after the countdown. So far, so good.

He was thoughtful, well read—of course he was. He had opinions and loved talking about them almost as much as she did.

"So is she an ace or a deuce?" Gavin asked, and Raleigh smirked because he'd asked her the same question about himself and she'd dodged.

"Depends on context," she said. "Like you—erasing bookmarks for scratch paper? Definitely a deuce. But if you erased some politician's speech right before they went on stage?"

"Everybody uses teleprompters now," he said grouchily.

"Or the evidence in a big case just before the trial? You could change the world."

He got a sour look and shook his head. "I'd rather not change the world like that. But what do you think—is it cheating, trying to be a comedian when you have the power to force people to laugh?"

"That didn't work out so well for her in the end, did it? She insists she rarely uses her power anymore at all."

"You believe her?"

The stakes were so low in this case, the answer hardly seemed to matter. Comedy specials weren't being filmed in her club because she was forcing people to laugh. "I do."

He sat back, brushing crumbs off the magazine before putting it carefully in his courier bag, which gave her a warm fuzzy feeling. "You think about this stuff a lot, for being someone who isn't in the middle of it all."

She was keeping secrets from him. She didn't like it, but she rationalized that keeping secrets gave her insight into someone like Carlotta. A lot of those folders in Digger's archives represented a lot of people keeping secrets. Raleigh liked to think she understood.

This one wasn't really a secret. He was going to find out sooner or later. "I'm a lot closer than you might think," she said. "I haven't told you about my mother, have I?"

"Just that we can't go back to your place because you're living with her and she's nosy."

"She has a nice place," Raleigh said. "But yeah."

"So what about your mom?"

"She's an ace. Well, maybe a deuce. She's Aurora."

The blank look in people her own age that followed this declaration was familiar. Their parents would know who she was, and might even be impressed. Then they'd ask, *Wait, is she still alive?*

But Gavin gave her the blank look and she had to explain. "She's an actress, was in a lot of movies in the seventies and eighties. Got her own paragraph in that Tom Wolfe book about wild card chic. Anyway."

Then came the donning of polite recognition. No doubt he'd run to the library to look her up later. "So your mom's a movie star," he said thoughtfully. "That's where you got your looks, hm?"

She grinned at the obvious flattery. She'd take it. "You're very sweet."

"I guess it's a little early to talk about taking me home to meet her or anything." That flirty smile of his made her toes curl.

Was she ready to introduce a guy to her mother? She was sure Gavin would behave himself. Would Aurora?

"And your dad?" he asked.

"Not in the picture," she said, and left it at that. That part—that he'd also had the virus, that she was latent—she didn't want to see his expression after that declaration. Back at the office, she'd set up a file of her own, a list of possible candidates to research.

"So what was it like, growing up with an actress mom?"

"I didn't see a whole lot of that side of her. She'd had her last big film role by the time I came along. A few of the tabloids said she had me just to get some publicity, but I think she really did want a kid. I maybe had a lot of babysitters during stretches when she was out on gigs, but mostly it was normal, I think. As normal as you can get growing up around theater people in Manhattan. We went trick-or-treating at Halloween, she helped me with algebra homework, cried at my graduation." She shrugged. This was a longer answer than she usually gave the question. "Still, Mom will always happily point out that she did the surprise baby thing way before Peregrine ever thought of it. Not that the tabloids were ever as interested in us the way they are in Peregrine and the mysterious John Fortune."

"I guess you didn't have a famous ace dad to boot."

Maybe. Maybe. Aurora had known a lot of famous men, and the secret list of possibilities had a few names that would make things, well, *interesting* if they turned out to be The One.

"I'd love to get an interview with him. John Fortune, I mean. I bet he's got some things to say." Biracial latent with a celebrity mom? The two of them had a ridiculous amount in common. Like she was a low-rent version of him or something. Then again, maybe they had *a lot* in common. Fortune's father was the famous, ultrapowerful ace Fortunato. *What if . . .*

Gavin glanced at his watch. "I need to get back, I think."

"I'll walk with you."

He beamed, his eyes lighting up. They held hands en route, and pausing on the steps of the library, she gave him a lingering kiss.

Yeah, maybe it was time to bring a guy home to meet Mom.

Technically, Raleigh had her own office at *Aces!*, but it was back in the asthma-inducing storage room with the decades of dust and bare-bulb lighting. As an alternative, she'd claimed a spot in the main bullpen with the rest of the reporters and a scrap of sunlight. A small desk shoved up against the wall, but still, it brought her closer to the rest of the staff, and the arguments about whether Buddy Holley's latest album held up to his work of a decade ago (the musician was beyond judgment at this point, as far as Raleigh was concerned) or whether the Turtle was ever going to come out of retirement (she hoped not, give the man a rest).

She'd hung a corkboard on the wall and pinned clippings to it: the old publicity headshot of Carlotta DeSoto, a picture of Fidel Castro laughing with Richard Nixon at some postgame photo op. A list of actors, singers, and vigilantes who'd been big in the eighties and were maybe due for "where are they now" pieces. She'd put her mom on the list but was waiting for the right time to pitch. She might have to put some spin on it, writing about her own mother. But that spin might be just the hook that would make it a good story. She'd been through stacks of back issues looking for gossip about Aurora. Lots and lots of pictures of her on the arms of handsome men, actors and politicians and everyone in between. More than a few possible candidates. Raleigh was impressed in spite of herself.

In the year, give or take a few months, before Raleigh's birth, Aurora had been romantically associated, in public, with two men. Three others, she'd been photographed with attending parties and galas and the like, but publicly stated that there was no relationship. Then there were the men she'd worked with, actors and directors on two movies and one stage play. Then the outliers, the men who moved in the same social circles. In late-seventies Manhattan, those were big circles.

Raleigh didn't pin that list to the bulletin board.

Next to her desk were the boxes, the ever-present archives, hauled into the light from the back room to air out, to give up their secrets.

When she got back to the office after lunch, she had her mind on work, had intended on making a beeline straight for her desk, when the receptionist brought her up short. "Herself wants to see you." Ally handed over a scrap of paper with exactly that message, scrawled in the editor in chief's florid handwriting.

"Is she angry?" Raleigh asked.

"I don't know, that's all I got." She gave a pained smile in sympathy. This could have meant anything.

Raleigh had only had a few interactions with Margot Dempsey outside of general all-hands meetings and layout reviews. Since Raleigh wasn't high-ranking enough to have an opinion on layouts, she stood in the back and tried to learn. The only time she'd spoken with Dempsey was right after she got here, a brief welcome-aboard, friendly enough but the editor obviously had little time to spare. Raleigh had gotten the impression that as long as she did her job and didn't screw up, Dempsey would be happy with her.

A summons like this? She walked to the editor in chief's office, down a posh carpeted hall that smelled of gardenias, as if she marched to an execution.

The office door stood open. Raleigh arranged herself, standing tall and trying to keep her breathing steady, knocking on the frame with confidence. "Ms. Dempsey, you asked to see me?"

"Yes, Raleigh. Come in, please."

Dempsey's office was half the size of the bullpen all by itself. She had a seating area with an armchair, a loveseat, and magazines spread over what was probably an exceedingly expensive mid-century coffee table that looked aerodynamic. In case anyone wanted to throw it out the window or something. Another area was for layout: a waist-high table, big enough to hold meetings around, where the staff could review photos, rearrange spreads, decide what was good enough for the cover and what was going into the trash. The May issue was all over the table now, pages and advertisements slowly coming together.

Margot Dempsey herself sat behind a wide desk that was as neat as the rest of the office was cluttered. A phone, a blotter, a legal pad and pen, and a neat stack of rival magazines and file folders. Taking notes on the competition. She had an amazing view of the Chrysler Building. She was in her fifties, white, had frosted hair swept back in a sculpted hairstyle. She wore a simple blouse and loose trousers, a couple of bracelets and diamond stud earrings. Nothing that stood out. She was the sister of the previous editor, Bob Lowboy, and granddaughter of the magazine's founder. Dozens of framed photographs of the two men hung on the wall behind the seating area, shoulder-to-shoulder with all manner of celebrities: the elder Lowboy with his arm draped around a rather dazed-looking Jetboy, wearing his classic leather bomber jacket. Bob with Dr. Tachyon, who seemed to be distracted by the women in cocktail dresses surrounding them at what must have been a hell of a party. *Aces!* was one of the last family-run publications of its size left anywhere. Margot had worked her way up in fashion magazines before taking over here—the real deal, not just coasting on the legacy. Raleigh imagined this office had looked a whole lot different when her male relatives ran things.

"Hi," Raleigh said earnestly, standing before her like a kid called to the principal's office. Her backpack still hung on her shoulder. Maybe she should have left it outside. She waited for the ax to fall.

Dempsey regarded her a moment. Then, she smiled. "Nice work on the Carlotta DeSoto piece."

"Really?"

She reached to a set of files on the shelf behind her, found a manila folder, and presented it to Raleigh. "We've been getting a lot of calls on it. The good kind. Go on, look through them."

Raleigh did. Many of them seemed to be phone messages, but there were a few postcards and printed emails as well. A call from someone who remembered seeing her at the Village Idiot back in the day and wondered what had happened to her. An email thanking her for reminding them of a piece of old New York. And many from people who were intrigued by a story that wasn't the same old celebrity exposé.

This . . . Raleigh hadn't expected this. She knew, intellectually, that her words were going out into the world, that people were reading them. But to get a reaction? A *good* one?

"This . . . this is great," she said, not really sure how else to respond. "Thanks."

"Two things I want to ask you. Can you do more like this? Slice of life, profiles of people who aren't celebrities. People relate to Carlotta, and I think you tapped into that. Peregrine's up on her nest and she'll never come down, but Carlotta? You might run into her at the corner store. There's something to that."

"Yes, of course, this is exactly the kind of thing I want to do more of."

"Second, you ever hear of something called a blog?"

"A bunch of my friends have them." For journalists and freelancers, blogging was a way to keep in the writing game between gigs. Bare your soul to everyone, with no barrier to readership but who was on the internet. Raleigh anticipated the next question.

"Think you can write one for the magazine? *Aces! Online?* I've been wanting to do more with the website, and I think this may be the thing. It's not the place for big profiles, but maybe tidbits, girl-on-the-street insights? Make it personal."

How personal, she wanted to ask. But the trick was not getting personal— it was pretending to, making people think you were baring your soul. She didn't know what such a thing would look like, but she answered, with enthusiasm, "I'd love to."

"Good. Send me your first five posts so I can see if I like the direction. Can you have them in two weeks?"

She didn't know if she could, but that hardly seemed important at the moment. "Absolutely."

Dempsey offered a thin smile and turned back to her work. Raleigh resisted an urge to bow as she backed away from the desk, then turned and escaped the office.

Back at the bullpen, the entire staff seemed to be gathered, collected around Digger Downs' desk, to witness the aftermath of her summons by the matriarch. Raleigh wondered if they had a pool going. "Well?" Digger asked. "You get an 'attagirl' or you get fired?"

She crossed her arms. "What do you think? I'm serious, what do you think about the job I'm doing around here?"

"She's smiling," Suzy said. "She got an attagirl."

Raleigh straightened, tipped up her chin. "I'm going to be writing a blog for the magazine."

"*Aces!* enters the twenty-first century!" Eddie called. "Right on!"

Downs said, "Did you ask for a raise? You should have asked for a raise."

"Damn," Raleigh said. She didn't realize she could do that. Next time.

Eddie and Suzy both looked over her shoulder at her bulletin board. Her vortex of ideas. It was getting full. Overwhelmingly full. Sixty years of the wild card virus in the world—that was a lot of material.

She was talking. Rambling. Thinking out loud. "The thing is there's hundreds of wild carders out there trying to make it with whatever powers they have, and no one ever notices. In show business alone there's hundreds. You ever see that guy in Times Square with sparklers for fingers, skating around in his underwear? Like I guess he makes a living doing that?"

"Just in music there's hundreds," Suzy said. "Like, you could do a piece on all-wild-cards bands. Like the Jokertown Boys, you ever seen them?"

"They're old news," Eddie said. "Joker Plague's the hot band now."

Raleigh sat up and dug through a stack of folders. "The guy with six arms and his own drum set? We got the press kit here somewhere."

Downs called from his desk on the other side of the room. Raleigh didn't even know he'd been listening. "You know, kids, we're called *Aces!*, we should be covering aces, not novelty joker music acts."

"That's discriminatory, Mr. Downs," Suzy called over her shoulder. "We cover topics related to any aspect of the wild card in pop culture."

"Oh Jesus I forgot we had a mission statement now, please spare me," he muttered, and walked out of the room.

"That guy is going to have an *amazing* midlife crisis," Eddie observed.

Raleigh said, "You guys have been over the whole thing where Peregrine is technically a joker, right?"

"All those pinups . . ." Suzy groaned.

"Circulation's down, and if we want a younger audience we need to cover younger celebrities. And that means Joker Plague." She'd found the press kit and held up the astonishing picture of Michael Vogali, all six arms flung out from his bare torso, each one holding a drumstick.

Suzy said, "But I like the Jokertown Boys. You can actually dance to their music."

"Tell you what," Raleigh said. "I'll put a call out to both and see who gives me an interview first. It'll be like a race." Then she would need a good angle. Anything can be a story if you find a good angle.

"I'm totally starting a pool on that," Eddie said, and reached for a piece of scratch paper. "Who's in?"

♦

The one that called her back? The Jokertown Boys, which wasn't a surprise. Their last album hadn't been a flop, necessarily, but hadn't produced a hit, either. The kids today? Wanted the noise and rebellion of Joker Plague. The Jokertown Boys were hungry for publicity.

And the angle? Well, turned out they'd done this show a few years ago that went kind of pear shaped. . . .

With a Flourish
and a Flair

by Kevin Andrew Murphy

"PLEASANT EVENING, ARTIST. A present. And a responsibility."

Sam looked up from his sketchbook just in time to see miniature squid attempting to escape from pirouline cookies, the pastry flutes impaled in a goblet filled with guacamole mixed with pomegranate seeds, winking like demonic eyes behind the round facets. While on one level he knew it was meant to be an exotic appetizer, fusion cuisine of the East-meets-West-goes-South-then-hits-the-other-side-of-the-galaxy school, the end result looked like nothing half so much as a sundae for the Elder Gods.

Hastet benasari Julali Ackroyd, earth's first and currently only Takisian chef, set the eldritch offering on the table in Martha Stewart's "It's a *good* thing" presentation position.

Sam knew enough to smile, trying to avoid the wide-eyed *"Help me!"* stares and frantic tentacles of the squidlets which were, he noted out of the corner of one eye, frozen into position with strands of carmelized sugar.

"And the responsibility?"

"Inclusion in tomorrow's brunch menu?" She preened, smoothing down her apron. "Since you're already redoing it, I thought this might be Starfields' new feature item."

It looked more like a feature from the Bowery Wild Card Dime Museum. A diorama of the Swarm Invasion perhaps, or one of the more disturbing examples of the Monstrous Joker Babies. But Sam knew it would not be politic to say so. Not if he wanted to keep his job. "Um . . . could we do it as table placards?"

"As you like," said Hastet. "I just showed my husband, and he said it would be perfect for Halloween." She beamed at the mass of tentacles, then frowned. "But that's not till Wednesday, isn't it?"

Sam gestured to the patrons in costume about the restaurant. "People celebrate early."

"Oh good." She pursed her lips then. "I haven't given it a name yet. I was thinking 'Takisian Surprise,' but given the last one, I don't think that would sell." Absently, she tucked a stray brown curl under her chef's pepperbox.

"Jay also said something about 'Lovecraft' when he saw it. But that would be for Valentine's Day, wouldn't it?"

Sam pictured Cthulhu got up as Cupid and was immediately sorry he had. "No, not exactly."

Hastet rolled her eyes. "You earthlings have too many holidays." She gave a grandiloquent wave of dismissal to the tentacle parfait, which Sam guessed to be the Takisian equivalent of 'Whatever.' "I trust your judgment. Just let it speak to you." With that, she slipped back through the arch to the kitchen, leaving Sam alone with the otherworldly *hors d'oeuvre*.

He leaned closer and gave it a wary glance, half expecting it to go scuttling across the table.

It was looking back—A nameless thing from the far depths of space. Bloodstone eyes watched below, flat lavender ovals stared above. Lidless. Unblinking. Alien. Sam wondered how it could possibly speak to him, afraid that it would.

Then it did: "Nice hat you have there."

A lifetime of living in Jokertown had taught Sam that the most unlikely things could speak. Plants. Animals. Even the urinal in Squisher's Basement. Things that had once been people, and horribly, on some level, still were, the wild card twisting their bodies into forms no longer even remotely human. But only rarely did they become entities as bizarre as Hastet's new appetizer. "What?"

"I said 'Nice hat,'" the dish of tentacles and avocado ichor repeated, its voice incongruously dulcet and feminine, albeit slightly annoyed. "Had it long?" Sam then realized that none of the squid were moving their lips, and unless the eldritch sundae were telepathic—always an option when dealing with victims of an alien virus—it was more likely that the speaker was someone behind it.

He sat up straight and looked past the sugar-frosted cephalopods.

The voice belonged to a woman. A nat woman to all appearances, mid-thirties but damn fine for all that, as petite or even more so than Hastet, with one of those figures you usually need corsetry to get, displaying it to best advantage in a tux shirt, black tie, swallowtail coat, black satin short-shorts, and cobweb-patterned black fishnets over stiletto heels. This ensemble was topped off with a top hat, worn over masses of Titian curls somewhere between Dr. Tachyon and the naturally vain girl from Peanuts. Accented with devil red lipstick and nails, the whole look said either stage magician or hooker, or something with the same effect thrown together for a semi-elegant semi-trashy evening of clubbing the Saturday before Halloween.

Sam heartily approved of the outfit, and the woman in it, and not just because his was almost the same, except he had the cobweb lace as cravat and cuffs, jeans instead of short-shorts, Docs in place of stilettos, and slightly more gothic taste in nail polish. And black velvet gloves, at least on his left hand. He tapped it to the brim of his own top hat. "No, just picked it up." Sam felt a grin steal across his face as he took in the sights, since up close she looked even better than when he'd first noticed her an hour ago. "Nice threads yourself. Columbia, or Sally from *Cabaret?*"

She paused for a moment. "No, Topper."

"She was one of the SCARE aces, right?" Now that she mentioned the name, Sam could see the likeness. " 'Cause if you're supposed to be the guy from the old ghost movies, I never would have gotten it. But speaking of spirits, can I buy you a drink?"

She raised an eyebrow. "Are you old enough to drink?"

Sam grinned. "ID's are *not* a problem." He chuckled then. "Of course, if you're Topper, you'd just pull whatever you want out of your hat, right? Get me a Long Island?"

She gave a strained smile. "I'd be happy to, assuming I had the right hat . . ."

Sam shook his head. "Nice try, but wrong answer. You got the costume perfect, but the real Topper can use any hat—top hats, bowlers, sombreros. And she never does requests." Sam grinned further. "Besides, she retired that outfit when she quit the Justice Department."

"Aces High is having a costume party. So sue me." She put her hands on her hips. "So, how do you know so much about the 'real' Topper? Ace groupie?"

"Nah," Sam shook his head, "someone donated a bunch of back issues of *Aces!* to the J-town orphanage. Topper was on the cover in the eighties. Had a pinup and everything." Sam shrugged. "Haven't made the cover yet myself, but we aces like to keep tabs on each other."

She arched the same eyebrow. "New ace, huh?" Her eyes flicked over him. "So who are you then, the Artful Dodger?"

"That's sort of the look I was going for," Sam said, still smiling, "but actually, you can call me Swash."

"Swash?"

"Well, it's either that or 'His Nibs,' but even a goth can only be so pretentious." He held up his ungloved right hand, which had been hidden behind his sketchbook. "Pardon me if I don't shake, but I'm a little inky right now."

He watched her eyes start, a pretty cerulean blue, as she took note of his hand, which was stained with that shade and several others beneath his hooked black-enameled Fu Manchu manicure. It wasn't a joker, but it still had shock value, like an unexpected tongue-stud.

Sam laid his sketchbook flat, displaying the Art Nouveau letters and dancing pumpkins of the menu he'd been re-illuminating. He flexed his fingers, letting a drop of ink come to the tip of each split sharpened crow-quill pointed nail, glanced to Hastet's nameless appetizer, then flipped to a fresh page and clawed down it. A twitch here, a slash there, a drop of the chartreuse of revulsion and the pale lavender of disquiet, and he'd pretty accurately captured his impression of the tentacular delight. He tossed in a few word balloons with the squidlets saying, *"Eat me!"* instead of *"Help me!"*

then added a banner borne aloft by Cupidthulhu putti with a caption in dramatically dripping Salamanca script: *"Dare you partake* of LOVECRAFT'S MADNESS?"

With one more jig of his thumb, he signed it Swash. "See?" He used his gloved left hand to turn the book around. "Not just my ace name, but my artist's signature too." He blotted the nails of his right on one of Hastet's no-longer-immaculately-white napkins. "Like I said, ID's are not a problem."

The woman applauded lightly. "Nice trick."

"Thanks." Sam grinned.

"Can I have my hat back now?"

He picked up his spare glove and slipped it on, sliding his fingertips into the special pencap sheaths. "Uh, you're wearing it." He shook his cuff so the lace fell properly, black cobwebs on black, stealing a glance up from beneath the brim of his own top hat.

"No, I think you're wearing it." She gestured to the bar. "About a half hour ago, when the waiter dropped his tray? Someone bumped into me and knocked my hat off."

Sam remembered the loud and spectacular crash, which had not only made him jump and squirt ink all over a page, ruining one of his sketches, but had also had caused him to dig in his nails, injecting pigment into several pages previous, destroying hours of work. Which in fact was why he was still here, recopying pages and hitting up Hastet for snacks to refill his ink reservoirs. "And . . . ?"

"And my grandfather was a stage magician. I know all about misdirection." She looked pointedly at a spot a few inches above his eyes. "Likewise the bump-and-switch." She reached up and tapped her hat. "And while this is the same size and vintage as the one I came in with—even the same haberdasher's mark—it's *not* the same hat."

Sam grimaced. He should have known it was something more than just mutual admiration of gothic finery. "If you wanted to look at my hat . . ." He doffed it, stray bits of blond mane falling into his face, ". . . all you had to do was ask." He extended it to her. "Was yours a rental prop?"

"No," she said coldly, grasping the brim, "but it had a lot of sentimental value." She then thrust her arm inside his hat, up to the elbow. Her hand came out the other end, where the crown was partially detached, becoming even more detached as she did so, and Sam watched as her expression changed, from a look of smug satisfaction, to puzzlement, then to worry as her painted nails fumbled at the air, to red-faced embarrassment as she caught sight of them over the brim of the hat. "Wha—?"

Something in her expression made him flash back to the teenage girl on the cover of *Aces!* and he realized that, with the exception of Golden Boy, most aces didn't stay unchanged since the early eighties. "Wait a second," Sam said, "you really *are* Topper, aren't you?" She looked at him and that look cinched it. "That article, it was wrong, right? SCARE disinformation. Your ace crutch isn't just any hat, or a top hat, it's one top hat in particular, the one you got from your grandfather. You hid it inside that sombrero and—"

"*Not so loud!*" she hissed, withdrawing her arm from his hat and abruptly sitting next to him. "I don't want everyone to—What's the matter?"

Sam gritted his teeth to keep from screaming. "*You're sitting on my tail!*" She looked. "Uh, it's a nice tail coat but . . ."

Sam twitched his real tail, hidden down the sheath in the lefthand train of his own swallowtail coat where it had been stretched out in the booth, and Topper's eyes started. She abruptly raised back up so he could yank it under himself, having a moment of trouble as it got tangled with the tails of her coat and the velvet of the upholstery, but at last he got it situated. "My Jokertown membership card, a little joker to go with my deuce." He blinked back the pain, even though his tail was still smarting. "Okay, now you know my secret too."

She sighed. "I'm sorry. I won't tell if you won't tell." She grimaced and covered her eyes with one hand, shaking her head softly. "Good god, if Jay ever finds out that I've lost my hat, I'll never hear the end of it. . . ."

"Hastet's Jay?"

She dropped her hand and nodded. "I work for his agency."

Sam glanced down at her fishnets through the hole in his hat. "What sort of agency . . . ?"

She followed his gaze, then muttered, "There was a reason I retired this costume. . . ." Then she glared at him. "*Detective* agency. Gads, I work for Popinjay, not Fortunato." She looked then at Sam's top hat, with its crown falling out, and gave a sheepish grin that made her look years younger. "Sorry about that. . . ." She glanced around the restaurant. "Do you see any other top hats?"

Sam looked himself. Starfields was packed, and given the night, he saw every sort of hat imaginable, from the odd dozen ostrich-plumed cavalier hats worn by the Dr. Tachyon lookalike waiters to representational foam rubber creations liberated from the Theatre District, looking to be cast-offs from last month's *Wild Card Follies*, everything from the Great Ape climbing the Empire State Building to Dr. Tod's flaming blimp. But no top hats.

"Right now?" He smoothed his hair back with one velvet glove and replaced his battered hat with the other, pushing the crown inside. "Excepting mine and the one you're wearing, no."

She bit her lower lip. "Earlier?"

Sam thought back. "Several. Let me look". . . . He picked up his sketchbook, blowing once across it so that the snot-trails from the Salamanca script would be dry, then flipped back past the buffer of blank pages he'd left to protect from bleed-through until he got to the ruined section. He pried open the last two sheets, still damp from the accident, revealing a giant multicolored Rorschach blot of sprayed ink, one hue bleeding into the next, predominantly the shocking pink of surprise. But underneath that, still visible on the lefthand page, were a series of sketches, including an image of the

Starfields bar just minutes before the crash. Counting top hats, there were seven individuals of note, the first six wearing tail coats, the last without.

First was Topper, holding a martini, perched at the edge of the bar in her fishnets. Next, a short ways down, was a crippled boy with polio crutches. Then came a young man with a blond mane and velvet gloves, the very image of Sam himself, turned and talking to a darkly handsome man with black hair and a permanent five-o'-clock shadow, fiddling with a small hand-held black box. Then there was a set of improbably wide shoulders, facing the bar and taking up at least three seats, the top hat worn atop a perfectly average, even narrow, head. Next a pale horse-faced giant with a long white goatee and a spiked and spiraled Mohawk, his top hat artfully and absurdly impaled on the twisted spikes. Then, finally, there was a fetish girl, a long, lithe, willowy woman, thin as a supermodel and almost as tall, dressed head to toe in latex. Her catsuit and platform-soled dominatrix boots were all of a piece, broken only by buckles and straps, and her face was hidden by a pantomime mask, a single tear on one cheek. This was backed by long honey blond tresses and topped with a vintage silk top hat.

"Here." Sam handed the book to Topper.

She scrutinized the page like a rogues gallery. "Do you know any of these people?"

"Everyone except the women on the ends." Sam paused. "Though I'm getting to know the one of them."

Topper looked at him, and their proximity, and smirked. "Don't push it. I'm old enough to be your babysitter."

Sam shrugged. "I grew up in an orphanage. I never had a babysitter." He paused. "Though I did have fantasies."

Topper didn't touch this, focusing instead on the mystery woman. "So, the Vinyl Vixen here—any idea who she is? Is that an ace uniform? A joker disguise? A Halloween costume? A really kinky fashion statement?"

Sam shrugged. "All of the above? Go to bondage night at the Dead Nicholas and that's a pretty common look." Then he added, "I do their club flyers."

"Is it just me, or does it look like she has an Adam's apple under the latex?" Topper looked closer at the illustration. "Or is that an inkblot?"

"Hard to tell. When I sketch fast, I just—" He caught a flicker of movement out of the corner of one eye, a flash of silver buckles and golden hair. "Though maybe you could just ask Latex Lass yourself." He pointed across the restaurant to where the same woman was coming out of the ladies room.

Topper looked, then shoved his sketchbook into his hands, standing up and rushing from the booth. Or really, attempting to. Sam felt a tug on his tail, and realized that when he'd tucked it under himself for safe keeping, he'd taken Topper's along with it, the cloth ones on her coat. The antique wool snapped back like a pair of suspenders in a vaudeville act, and Topper screeched, overbalancing on her stiletto heels, clawing to save herself, grabbing the tablecloth. Silverware, glassware, and the prodigious greenness of Hastet's tentacled appetizer clattered down atop her as Sam forewent chivalry to protect his sketchbook, springing back out of the way and halfway atop the booth.

There was, as with all such accidents, a swift silence, followed by even swifter sarcastic applause. Then Takisian Three Musketeers extras were helping Topper to her feet and offering words of solicitous concern while Fetish Girl crossed Starfields' star-spangled foyer, pushed open the nebula-frosted glass panels of the entrance, and made her exit. Topper gave a strangled shriek of protest, attempting to evade the well meaning interference of the wait staff, and sprinted for the crack in the stars as fast as petite legs in stiletto heels could carry her.

Sam struggled across the wreckage of tablecloth and *hors d'oeuvres* and was faced with a snap decision: He could stay, finish his work, and try to explain the mess to Hastet, or he could follow Topper. It was an easy choice. Besides which, Hastet was Takisian, and as such, she knew that chivalry had its demands, as did attractive women in fishnet stockings. And while Sam wasn't tall, he was taller than Topper, and he caught up with her just as she passed through the doors. He leapt through the gap in the nebula after her, his tail pinging the edge of the glass, then it was down the stairs, no waiting for the elevator, and out to the sidewalk.

Topper took three steps outside and looked up and down the street, then back at him. "Where is she?"

Sam looked too, taking in the bustle of Park Rowand trying to spot a latex-clad supermodel in a vintage top hat, then shook his head. "Gone. I'm sorry, I—"

"Do you have any idea where she went?"

Sam shook his head again. "No." Then he paused. "Or actually, yes. I'm pretty certain I do. Follow me." Topper looked ready to grasp at the slimmest hope, and Sam gave it to her. *"Taxi!"* he shouted, jumping out into the street and flagging one down.

Sam went into chivalry overdrive, opening the door for Topper, who piled in, with him following.

The driver had a beard and a turban and a wide smile. "What is your destination on this fine night, oh most—" The man stopped, goggling in horror at Topper, as if she'd just sprouted an extra head.

Sam looked. She had. Well, actually no, but the effect was remarkably similar, one of the cephalopod confections caught in her curls, staring at the driver with the same wide-eyed expression, like Father Squid being subjected to an unexpected proctology exam.

It was against Sam's better judgment, but if he'd learned one thing growing up in Jokertown, it was this: Sometimes you had to freak the nats. Plus Hastet expected him to taste her creations, not just draw them, so the time had come to bite the bullet, or at least the squid.

Sam removed it from Topper's curls and popped the pirouline into his mouth, biting down. It was crunchy and spicy-sweet, a little like Japanese spider roll, mixed with the dry caraway flavor of kimmel cracker. Then his

eyes began to water. *Takisian Surprise* was right! Hastet had spiked the guacamole with wasabi or some otherworldly equivalent.

Topper looked at him. "Edible?"

Sam swallowed and thumped his chest. "Like Candy Mandy's fingers."
He wiped the tears with the back of his glove. "Girl I knew back at Jokertown
High. Edible fingers. Really."

There was really no response to this, and Topper didn't try to make one.
Half the Jokertown stories were "No, really" bullshit, and the others were un-
believable, but still true.

The driver was still staring his own rectal-examination stare, and Sam
had a bad feeling in his own tail, but pressed ahead anyway, smiling as if
nothing could be more natural. "Jokertown, please. Club Chaos."

At last the cabby's expression changed, going from a mask of shocked
horror to righteous indignation. "This cab, by the Light of Allah, does not go
to the abode of the unclean!"

"What if we gave you some unclean money?"

The mask faltered for a moment. "How much?"

"Five hundred bucks," said Topper.

"Let me see it."

"Fine." Topper took her hat off and started to reach inside, then stopped.
"Oh shit—I left my wallet in my other hat." She looked to Sam.

He shrugged. "Don't look at me. I don't carry that sort of money."

"Can't you . . ." She wiggled her nails and gestured towards Sam's sketchbook.

Forge five hundred dollars on the fly? And without the right paper? "I don't
think so."

"Get out of my cab. Allah spits on jokers and liars."

Sam thought, remembering the rantings of the Nur, who'd glowed as
green as if he'd swallowed a *Lite Brite* set, which seemed pretty close to a
joker by most people's definitions. "If I remember correctly, Allah thinks
aces are just spiffy." Sam stripped off his right glove and brought five beads
of Nur-green ink to the tip of his nibs, luminous poison green, the color he'd
always associated with malice. "See these, dickweed? Allah gave me poison
claws, and if you don't take this fucking cab to Club Chaos before I can say
'Allah Akbar,' Allah tells me I get to poison your ass dead."

"*Allah Akbar!*" the cabbie agreed fervently and Sam nearly got whiplash
as fast as they took off down the street.

Topper stared at him, and Sam didn't know whether he'd just crossed
the line to become her knight in shining armor or a dangerous psychopath—
likely something of both—and he wondered how long he could bluff a religious fanatic with what amounted to a handful of fountain pens.

Topper turned to the cabbie. "I'll also have you know that I'm a federal
agent, or at least I used to be. You move so much as a finger towards that gun
under your seat, I'll drop you before poison boy here even gets in a scratch."

She had one of her stiletto heels off in her hand, pressed into the vinyl in back of the cabbie's seat. "That okay?"

"*Allah Akbar!*" the cabbie swore, turning left on Chatham Square and into Chinatown, and left again with a squeal of tires onto Confucius Place.

Conventional wisdom said it took only three minutes to get from the Village to J-Town, but Confucius said that men fearing for their lives could get there in less than two, even when all they were threatened with was stiletto heels and fountain pens. "With the grace of Allah, we are here!" They screeched to a stop in front of Club Chaos. "Do not harm me, oh most beloved of Allah!"

"Stay where you are," Topper told the cabbie, opening her own door, and Sam did the same with his, wiping his nails clean on the headliner as he exited, leaving the cabbie with the message, in elegant *sihaja* script, *Allah says you're a dickweed.* Actually, it was probably something more like, *Allah, the compassionate and most merciful, says you're a putrescent camel penis steeped in mint-fennel sauce,* but most of Sam's Arabic came from falafel house menus.

The cab sped off the moment the doors were shut and Topper grimaced. "Idiot," she said, balancing flamingo-style as she replaced her shoe.

Sam didn't know if she were referring to him or the cabbie, and didn't ask. "Did we just commit a felony?"

"Do you actually have poisonous claws?"

"No."

"Then no." She shrugged. "I came closer to it, but I never actually said I had a gun, and I have friends in the Justice Department." She walked over to him and looked up at the Club Chaos sign, the latest work of the Jokertown Redevelopment Agency. In place of the broken and blighted marquee of the long defunct Chaos Club, there now stood a fifty-foot tall neon version of the new club's owner, veteran joker comedian, Chaos, back after many lucrative years in Vegas (and a split with his old partner, Cosmos), bringing some of the glitter and tinsel with him to mix with the city's matching funds. He juggled spaceships and planets with his six arms, while below his feet, sporting considerably less neon, was a television van plastered with a twirling *MTV* logo. A huge mass of teenage girls, most of them nats, were standing behind police barricades while a single, albeit large and brown-scaled, police officer attempted to keep them in line. The joke of it was, they were all dressed like Topper—top hats, tail coats, and more than half of them had figured out that fishnets were the way to complete the ensemble, even those who should have considered something else.

Topper stopped and did a double take. Then turned to Sam. "When did my outfit suddenly come into fashion?"

Sam felt a bit uneasy. "Um, it didn't. I think my outfit came into fashion."

"Come again?"

"Ever hear of *The Jokertown Boys?*"

She paused. "They're a gang, right? Like the Werewolves or the Egrets?"

"Um, no." Sam reached to the back of his portfolio and pulled out a flier done in the Bauhaus style, with blocky Bremen lettering that had required cutting his thumbnails square. He passed it to Topper and let her read it:

♠ ♥ ♦ ♣

♠ **8 PM, Saturday, October 27th** ♠
♣ **CLUB CHAOS!** ♣
♥ **The Jokertown Boys** ♥
CD Release Party
♦ **'Top Hat, White Tie, and Tails'** ♦
Wear Yours and Get in Free!

♠ ♥ ♦ ♣

Below that was a pen-and-ink portrait of the five guys in formalwear from the bar, facing right and sporting canes and white gloves, the pose something Sam had modeled after one of the old posters for Grand Hotel.

Topper looked to Sam and blinked. "You're in the band?"

"No, I just live with them. I sang backup on a couple tracks, that's all." Sam pointed to illustration. "People mistake us all the time, but that's my brother, Roger."

"So that wasn't you by the bar?" Topper scrutinized the flyer, then bit her lip. "You know, except for the guy with the shoulders, they look awfully nat for Jokertown."

"Looks can be deceiving." Sam brushed his tail in its swallowtail sheath against Topper's leg. "Trust me. They're all jokers and they're all from J-town." He paused. "Well, Dirk there's from the Village, and we've been renting the upstairs of his mom's shop since we left the orphanage. But *Village People*? Don't think so." He looked at the van, watching a guy in a wizard hat atop it working the crowd, and realized it was Carson Daly. "Since when did they hook up with *MTV*?"

There came a squeal from the line of girls and a louder one as he made the mistake of looking, and Sam came to a sudden grim realization: Once again, his fraternal resemblance had carried too far.

"It's Roger!" screamed a girl in a domino mask, and her screams were picked up by the next teenybopper in line, and the next, like a chorus of howler monkeys at the zoo: "Roger!" "Roger!" "Roger, we love you!" The crowd pressed forward and the barricade overturned, the girls trampling the scaled police officer in their mad rush.

It wasn't the Jokertown Riots, or the Wild Hunt from the Rox War, but it was the closest thing Sam had ever experienced to either. Screaming girls. Clawing girls. A huge slavering hound's muzzle thrust in his face. "I'm not Roger, I'm his brother!" Sam protested, but the clawing and screaming and tearing at his clothes continued until Topper and the scared police officer, who'd somehow crawled *under* the crowd, linked arms before him and held them back, bellowing things about the NYPD and federal agents.

Then autograph books were waved in his face past them. This, at least, was something he could deal with. *Roger,* he signed, and *Roger!!!,* and *To my dearest fan,* and then he was confronted by part of the hunger and madness of the Rox War made flesh, the drooling, panting muzzle of one of the Gabriel hounds, white fangs glistening, fierce and sharp. Except the hound had bows in its hair and was holding an autograph book, and Sam realized he was looking at a joker fangirl with the head of an afghan. He signed all five band members' names in her book simultaneously, one with each digit: *Roger, Jim, Alec, Dirk and Paul,* each signature in the respective hand, then did a second line with their wild card manes: *Ravenstone, Grimeraek, Alieorn, Atlas* and *Pretty Paulie,* with extra hearts and smiley faces.

Then Topper was shoved aside by sheer bulk. "Sign my breasts!" screamed an obese nat girl who'd exceeded the recommended weight allowance of her halter top.

Sam did not want to scratch her—not that her fellow autograph-seekers had any such reservations when it came to him—but it was not as if these girls were jokerphobic anyway, so he flexed the toes of his left foot, letting his nails piss ink into his Doc Marten, then slipped his tail out of its sheath, dunked it into the impromptu inkwell, and whipped it up and around and through the flourishes of Japanese brushwork. *Roger* he wrote on the right breast and *Ravenstone* on the left.

"I'm going to have it tattooed in!" the girl squealed.

Her fellow fanatics howled for more, surging through the gap, then one grabbed his tail and two others grabbed his arms, wrestling him for his sketchbook, and a fourth clawed for his face, snatching off his hat. Then she gasped in shock. "His eyes are blue!" she screamed. "Both of them! And where are his cute little horns?"

"Where's the raven?" demanded another.

"Wait a second," said the girl behind him, "since when does Ravenstone have a tail? And wouldn't it be a devil tail? This is a lion's tail? What sort of rip is this?"

"I read about him in *TeenBeat!*" screamed a slightly more knowledgeable fangirl. "That's Roger's brother, Swish!"

"That's *Swash!*" Sam roared, snatching his hat back and jamming it on, wresting away his sketchbook, and jerking his tail free. The crowd fell back, the scaled police officer shouting for the girls to get their butts behind the barricade. Sam lashed his tail, splashing drops of ink, and stomped forward, his coat torn, his left boot squishy, his hat jammed down around his ears. He hoped Roger had brought spare socks.

Topper scanned the crowd as they walked past. "Any sign of Bondage Babe?" Even with the stiletto heels, she wasn't tall enough to see more than the teenyboppers just behind the barricades.

"You mean Fetish Girl?" Sam wasn't much taller than Topper himself. "Not that I can see. Not that that means much." He shepherded Topper around the side of the building, past a few more autograph seekers, drying off his tail by painting the Chinese characters for *Luck, Joy* and *Get-a-Life* on the proffered books.

"You think she's inside with the band?"

Sam just shrugged, going up the steps to the stage door. There was a bouncer who blocked it, via the simple expedient of being the same size and shape. "Passes?" he asked in a dull monotone.

Topper took off her hat and started to reach inside, then stopped and looked to Sam.

"Check the door list. Sam Washburn and . . ." He glanced to Topper. He didn't even know her real name.

"Melissa Blackwood," Topper supplied.

The doorman looked. "You're on it, she's not."

"Let me see." The doorman did, and Sam ran a finger down it, not very impressed. Childish roundhand, two steps from Palmer method. "Right here, in the middle." He tapped the list, dotting the i in *Melissa.*

The doorman checked again and it was a testimony to his dullness or his professionalism that he just shrugged and stepped aside, crossing them off and handing them passes once Sam flashed him his driver's license and Topper flashed some leg.

The back of Club Chaos was an old hemp house, an off-Broadway theatre unchanged since the thirties except for facelifts out front, with nothing else special about it, except for the welcome. "Hey, look everyone, it's His Nibs!" Alec Hamer, alias Alicorn, the lead guitarist, waved, easy to spot by virtue of him being something over seven feet tall, not counting the three-foot ice blond spiked Mohawk, which easily put him over ten.

Paul O'Nealy, alias Pretty Paulie, the main vocalist, swung forward on his polio crutches, the lines of his tux somewhat spoiled by the elaborate armature of head, shoulder, back, arm and leg braces necessitated by his rubberized skeleton. With a top hat covering his perpetually unruly brown hair, this and his sweet smile made him look more than a bit like Tiny Tim, posterchild for cute sick boys everywhere—despite the fact that he stood around six feet, depending on how he adjusted his braces that morning. "Sam! I thought you were stuck at Starfields till you redid those menus."

"Change of plans. Hastet's not going to find anyone else who can do Takisian calligraphy on short notice, and so long as I get everything there before brunch tomorrow, she won't kill me."

"You need to find a different job." Jim Krakowiez, alias Gimcrack, the band's keyboardist and tech wizard, looked concerned and not at all a joker, with black hair, intense green eyes, and a permanent five-o'-clock shadow that also made him look far older than his nineteen years. However, looks could be deceiving. Despite the male model face and the tall, toned and perfectly muscled nat body that went with it, the wild card had touched him deep inside his head, making him possibly the most gullible man in the universe, and certainly the most literal-minded. "I know Takisians take their honor seriously, but she shouldn't kill you just because you messed up a menu. That's not right and it wasn't your fault anyway." He blanched then. "Did she kill the waiter? The one who tripped?"

"No, Jim, he's fine." Sam patted his friend on the arm. "Hastet's not really going to kill me."

"Are you sure?"

"Yes."

"Looks like someone tried to." Roger stood in the shadows of the proscenium, looking like a young Odin, with a patch over his left eye, and his pet raven, Lenore, on his right glove. "Sweet Joker-Jesus, Sam, what happened to you?"

Sam sighed, pulling up on his sleeve where the seam had been ripped out at the shoulder. "Some of your fans just tried to play Stretch Armstrong with me."

"Hey, that's my shtick!" Paul protested.

Sam ignored him, turning to his brother. "What the fuck's going on out there?"

"It's a long and complicated tale," Roger began, coming forward from the shadows. "I'm not certain where to start. . . ."

"Britney Spears got food poisoning!" Alec exclaimed, then started to laugh, nearly braying. "Puked Pepsi all over Bob Dole!"

Paul giggled, then made a strangled ralphing noise, followed by a perfectly inflected, girlish, "Oops! I did it again!" The wild card had elasticized his vocal cords along with his bones, giving even more justification for his nickname, a talent for mimicry rivaled only by his vocal range. "Yeah, and she was supposed to be over at Radio City tonight doing the Halloween show for *MTV*!"

Alec nodded wildly, his Mohawk bobbing like a sail. "But, puking Britney—they had to cancel."

"And our video just trashed everyone on *Total Request Live!*" Paul exclaimed, bouncing up and down on his crutches.

Alec continued to nod, the motion revealing that the bowsprit of his coiffure was actually a spiraled ivory horn, hidden like the Purloined Letter just below his forelock. "And Britney said she thought Paul was cute!"

Paul grinned from ear to ear—literally. "And we were having a concert tonight anyway, so they moved the show here!"

"In a nutshell . . . yes." Roger stroked Lenore, smoothing down her ruffled feathers and keeping a tight hold on her jesses. "Chaos told us the deal when we got back from dinner."

It was all a little bit much to take at once, surreal in fact, and Sam just took it in stride when a parade of thirty women, all dressed like Topper, filed by in back of the band.

"*The Rockettes,*" Jim explained. "*MTV* said if they paid for them, they were going to use them, and they already know all the Irving Berlin numbers anyway." Jim smiled. "We didn't see the nutshell Roger said they came in, but I'm guessing it was a big one, kind of like the giant flying seashell Dr. Tachyon uses."

"Oh," said Sam. Topper just stood there in stunned silence, watching the seemingly endless display of top hats.

Alec angled his Mohawk towards her and stroked his equally long, silky and silly goatee. "You're not a Rockette, are you?" He loomed over Sam. "Going to introduce us to your friend, Swash?"

"Uh, yeah." Sam shook his head, realizing he'd been forgetting his manners. "Guys, this is Topper. The ace."

"Alec," said Alec, bending down to shake hands, "the joker." Their size differential made them look like Teniel's illustration of Alice and the Unicorn, except Alec was only horse-faced in the nat sense and Alice didn't wear a top hat and fishnets. "Or 'Alicorn,' if you want my joker name."

"Nice to meet you," she said, his hand enveloping hers as they shook. "I remember seeing you at Starfields." Sam saw her glance to Alec's immense Mohawk-impaled top hat and immediately discount the possibility.

"People tend to do that," Alec remarked as he straightened back up and uncricked his back. "It's the height."

Topper nodded. "People overlook me. Same reason."

"That's not true," said Jim. "Paul kept looking at your legs. He said they looked totally hot, which kinda confuses me, 'cause in fishnets you'd expect they'd be cool."

"*Jim!*" Paul exclaimed, his voice jumping three octaves. Then he looked to Topper, blushing furiously. "Pardon me while I curl up into a ball and die of embarrassment. . . ." He glanced to Jim. "No, Jim. I'm not really going to. It's just a metaphor. People don't really die of embarrassment."

"Yes they do!" Jim protested. "Don't you remember Margie? From the orphanage? Five years ago she got her period and stained her choir robe, and she said, 'Oh God, I'm so embarrassed, I'm going to die!' Then she *did* die, right there next to us in the middle of church. She drew the black queen, and Father Squid said it was embarrassment that made her card turn, just like she said. And he had a whole sermon next Sunday about the evils of shame and how it kills jokers." Jim's lip began to quiver. "And I've seen you curl up into a ball. You can even bounce."

Paul gave Jim a look halfway between sympathy and exasperation. "It's okay, Jim. I'm not going to die. And shame doesn't really kill jokers. Usually." He paused then, taking a deep breath. "And none of us are latents anymore anyway. Even Roger's drawn his card."

"I haven't," said Jim, blinking at tears. "I'm still a completely normal. . . ."

"Jim, you're an ace. A crazy powerful one."

"Am not."

"Are too."

"*Am not,*" Jim insisted.

Paul let it drop, and there was an uncomfortable silence, which Roger broke with the rolling tones of a born showman: "I believe we were in the middle of introductions. If I may, allow me to introduce Jim and Paul, alias Gimcrack and Pretty Paulie. And this is my assistant, Lenore," he said, gesturing to his raven. "While as for myself . . ." Roger held up his left hand, showed the glove's palm then the back, then with a flourish, produced a business card from thin air.

Lenore snatched it from him, holding the card in her beak.

"Give it to the nice lady, Lenore," Roger coaxed, holding the raven towards Topper. "Give it."

Lenore looked at Topper, then at Roger, then defiantly took the card in one claw and began to shred it into confetti. Roger caught it in his left hand, squeezed tight, then opened it with a flourish, presenting the card to Topper, miraculously restored, if missing a corner. "For you, my good lady. The Amazing Ravenstone, at your service."

She accepted it with a smile. "A fellow conjurer, I see."

"But nowhere near your level of skill, I'm afraid." He retrieved the last corner from Lenore's beak. "I'm afraid my ace at present only extends to parlor magic. But I'm working to expand my repertoire." He handed the torn corner to Topper. "Would that I had your skill. Or that of your grandfather."

"Likewise," Topper said, putting the missing corner to the card and seeing that they matched. "I only pull rabbits out of my hat, not tigers."

"The legendary Blackwood Conjure. . . ." Roger gave a wry smile. "A most impressive feat, especially since Lafayette Blackwood accomplished it without apparent access to curtain, trap door, or gimmicked stand—and this years before the advent of the wild card." Roger gave her a sidelong glance from his unpatched eye. "I know that almost all his props and effects were destroyed in a fire, but did he ever by any chance pass on the secret personally?"

"Grandpa took it to his grave, I'm afraid." Topper gave a sad shake of her head. "He always said that a magician's secrets were meant to be lost, stolen, or traded for one equal, never given outright or sold for cheap."

Roger nodded, then quoted, "'For to do so would cheapen the magic and destroy the wonder, and the world needs mysteries, now more than ever.'"

Jim applauded wildly, then smiled at Topper. "That was the end of the 'History of Magic' spiel he gave when we worked at Dutton's Magic and Novelty Shop." Jim smiled wider. "Roger always said it just before trying to sell people 'Topper's Big Box of Ace Magic Tricks.' He got a commission."

"Oh God," said Topper, "they're still selling those? I thought the license expired years ago."

"Mr. Dutton bought up the warehouse. He told us to jack the price and call them collectibles, and if we could unload them, we got an extra twenty percent." Jim smiled. "I worked there too. I sold more X-ray specs than any other employee."

Roger glared. "That's because you used your ace to make them actually work, Jim."

"I did *not*," Jim protested. "They work just fine for anybody, so long as you adjust them right, and it's not my fault if people keep breaking them after they leave the store."

"Jim, regular people can't see through walls."

"Sure they can. All they need are X-ray glasses. Or windows." Jim glared at Roger. "You said the same thing when we were kids and you were upset because your sea monkeys didn't look like the ones on the package and mine did. Just because I know how to follow directions and can get products to work the way they're supposed to doesn't make me an ace."

Roger left the statement unchallenged, as did Sam. There was no point in arguing with Jim, especially when he got in a mood, since the flipside of absolute gullibility and literal-mindedness was absolute faith, and when the universe catered to your belief in it, this was not necessarily misplaced. Even if that belief was mostly in the outrageous promises of advertising, particularly the products in the backs of comic books and supermarket tabloids.

Jim still looked hurt. "You should remember what it's like, Roger. You were a latent too, before the wild card gave you a black eye."

Topper looked at Roger, incredulous. "A black eye?"

Roger nodded. "Jim is being accurate here. I got a black eye." Roger raised his hand and flipped up his eyepatch. His left eye was black, totally black, without trace of white or iris. "As you can see," Roger said with a wink before hiding the eye again, "Ravenstone is not just my stage name or my *nom de ace*," He tapped the brim of his hat, "but also my *nom de joker*."

Topper looked at his hat. "Nice hat," she remarked. "Finchley's Fifth Avenue?"

"Of course," said Roger. "The classic magician's hat. And a good old New York firm too."

"May I see it? I collect hats."

"You and Cameo should talk," Paul remarked.

"Our costume designer," Roger explained, doffing his hat to reveal a pair of small black horns. "She also collects. Though not just hats." He handed his to Topper. "She found our costumes for the show."

"Or made them," Alec added. "Hard to find my size, even in Jokertown."

"And she wouldn't punch holes in a vintage number anyway," Roger pointed out. "She'd consider it murder." His eye flicked to Sam's mangled hat. "I suggest you ask for a loaner, Sam. We may want to drag you on stage later and I can't have my brother dressed like that."

"On stage? Oh please."

"You're our cover artist. Take your bows." He smirked. "Besides, we may need a backup singer, in case Alec suddenly gets hoarse. . . ."

"Please God no . . ." said Alec.

Sam was in agreement. "I don't sing that well, Roger."

"Better than Alec would," Roger said. "Besides, you know all the songs."

"Thank you," said Topper, returning Roger's hat and saving Sam from further argument. "May I?" Jim and Paul showed her their hats as well, but

Sam knew from her expression that theirs weren't hers either. "Of course," she added, "the hat thing is just a hobby. I was hoping you boys could help me with something else. I'm a private investigator, and I was looking for a woman you may have seen at Starfields—who incidentally also wears a top hat. Swash, could you show them your illustration?"

Sam took his cue and opened the sketchbook. The ink had smeared even more and the pages were almost glued together, bits of paper tearing off in little shreds, but at last he showed them the sketch of the Vinyl Vixen.

"I remember her," said Jim. "Paul said she was totally hot too. But that made sense, 'cause she's wearing all that latex."

Paul blushed slightly. "So I've got a thing for rubber. Go figure."

Roger shrugged. "If I recall, she stumbled into the waiter. Likely couldn't see much with that mask. I helped her up and returned her hat, and last I saw, she ran off for the ladies room, presumably to wash off the Takisian margarita he'd spilled down her back."

"Presumably," Topper said.

"I bet she was a fan," Alec said. "She kept looking at you, Roger, like she was thinking about asking for your autograph."

"Roger was looking at you the same way," Jim told Topper.

Roger gave Jim a withering look, then glanced to Topper. "Well, I'll admit, I am a fan. Though mostly of your grandfather. The man was amazing."

"So are a number of things," Topper said, glancing to Roger, then Sam. "Joker-deuce brothers. The odds are what? One in a thousand? Ten thousand?"

"Somewhere in there." Roger flashed his devilish smile. "Scarce as hen's teeth and twice as weird."

"Not that we're complaining," Sam added. "The Croyd outbreak killed our parents and left us infected and unadoptable. Same with lots of kids, actually. After I drew my card, I was afraid I was going to lose Roger. After all, look at the odds."

"We survived. That's what counts." Roger stroked Lenore's feathers. "And the same with some of our friends from the orphanage." He nodded to Jim, Alec and Paul.

"We didn't just survive—we're freakin' *huge!*" This last was said, without apparent irony, by Dirk Swenson, alias Atlas, drummer for the Jokertown Boys, who despite a face with delicate, almost Takisian, features, had shoulders about as wide as he was tall, with muscles to match. "I just carried Jim's piano out on stage and snuck a peek through the curtains and you won't believe how many girls are out there!"

"And let us not forget our loud friend from the New York School for the Arts . . ." Roger said in an aside to Topper.

Dirk was loud in more than one sense of the word. He'd swapped out of his custom tail coat and tux shirt and into a sunburst tie-dye, presumably for the set up, and Sam wondered if the rumors were true, that he was Starshine's lovechild. Certainly they had the same fashion sense, though

that just might be due to the fact that the muscleboy had been raised following the Grateful Dead until Jerry Garcia died and Dirk's mom had moved
back to the Village to take over The Cosmic Pumpkin.

"I can't freakin' believe it!" Dirk boomed. "This is absolutely wild!"

Sam was in agreement, but from a slightly different angle, since "wild"
was a pretty accurate description of the nat girls they'd encountered out
front.

"Dirk?" Roger said, getting his attention. "Allow me to introduce you to
Topper, the famous ace conjurer—Topper, Dirk, our piano-lifting drummer.
Dirk, I need you to get back into costume before we do a sound check, but
before you do, Topper was wondering if you'd seen the woman in vinyl from
the bar." He pointed to Sam's illustration.

"Oh, yeah, Bondage Girl," said Dirk, looking at the illustration. "She was
hot."

"We've established that," Topper said. "Do you know her? Did she by any
chance say anything?"

"Nah," said Dirk, "I think she was doing the mime trip. But I gave her
one of the flyers Sam did for the show. I hope she gets in," he added, "Chaos
said it's, like, going to be standing room only, and the shows around us'll
have to deal with our overflow."

"The toilets are going to back up?" asked Jim.

"Nah," said Dirk, "that's theatre talk. Means girls who can't get in will
go to other clubs."

Topper looked more than slightly alarmed at this, but only said, "Is that
your coat and hat over there? Let me get them for you."

"Cool. Thanks." Dirk pulled off his tie-dye, revealing musculature like a
classical statue of Atlas reinterpreted by an eighties comic book artist, while
Topper went to where his ordinary hat and incredibly huge shirt and jacket
had been laid over an amp. She came back with them, but Sam could tell
from her look that Dirk's hat had been eliminated from the running as well.

"Here you go," she said, handing him his clothes. "Mind if we go sneak
a peek at the audience? I don't think I've ever seen this many . . . girls . . .
in one place ever before, and I'd like to see them all before the fire marshal
turns anyone away."

"Yeah, go greet my fans," Sam said, pulling at the lining hanging out of
the torn pocket of his coat.

"Sure," Roger said, "we need to go over some stuff anyway. Glad you
could make it after all—and nice to meet you." Roger tipped his hat to Topper
and he and the boys went over to the stage area and started a sound check.
Meanwhile, Sam and Topper slipped around the edge of the proscenium,
coming out past the red velvet curtain. There were cheers and screams almost
immediately: "Roger! Roger!" and "Show us your horns!"

Sam didn't oblige, just looked out at the main floor of the club. He had
never seen so many girls in his life. Girls in black formalwear and fishnets,
leather and lace, shiny patches of vinyl and acres of bare midriffs, with

mime masks and dominos and occasional headbands with animal ears or maybe just joker ears sticking out beneath their hats. Top hats. Everywhere. And there were more girls and more than a few boys pouring in all the time, forming a sea of high silk hats on either side of the runway that led forward from the main stage, taking seats at the tables in the upper mezzanine, or swarming through the shadows of the upper balcony.

"Oh my God . . ." said Topper, stricken. "I haven't seen this many possible suspects since the Democratic National Convention. . . ."

Sam watched the bouncing, waving, shimmying sea of fans. "Well at least my brother and my friends have been lined out." He glanced to her. "They have been lined out, right?"

"Sorry," Topper admitted. "First rule of detective work—everyone's a suspect until you solve the crime. Or the innocent mix-up. But if we don't figure it out soon, it may become an unsolved mystery. . . ." She looked out at the sea of top hats. "Can you spot our mystery woman?"

Sam looked. "No. I'd need opera glasses." He glanced back to Topper. "Got any?"

"If I had my hat, that would not be a problem." She smiled to the crowd and managed a feeble wave. "But if I had it, the point would be moot." Topper's smile looked like it had been affixed with a staplegun.

"We could ask Cameo," Sam suggested. "If anyone has some, she would."

"Cameo?" She looked glad for any excuse to look away from the audience. "The costumer for the band?"

"And the Jokertown Players. And Broadway. And the Jokertown High theatre department." Sam held up his right glove and waggled his fingers, girls in the audience screaming in response. "Made me these. Even recommended Roger and the rest of the guys for the School for the Arts." He waved again, eliciting more screams from frenzied girls, which was sort of fun now that he wasn't in the middle of them, but only slightly. "She always has this bag of props. Seen her pull out everything from a feather boa to a frying pan."

"Worth a shot," Topper said. "But you ask. I don't want anyone else to have even a chance of knowing what's going on."

"Sure thing."

She pulled Sam back past the edge of the curtain and sighed, then looked at him. "You know what, Swash? The girls out there are right—you are cute. *Way* too young for me, but cute." She gave a nervous grin. "Now let's go see about those binoculars, Mr. Teen Idol."

Sam felt a blush stealing into his face. "Sure thing."

It took a bit of asking around backstage, but they finally located Cameo in the wardrobe room. "Got a sec?"

"No, but tell me what you need anyway." She emerged from behind a rack of costumes, dressed as a twenties flapper in a fringed tea dress and cloche hat, her only departures from cutting the perfect *IT girl* figure being a tape measure in place of a string of pearls around her neck and the sudden expression of shock on her face as she stopped, gaping. Then the moment passed. "Sam! What have I told you?" She went over to him, clucking her tongue, clearly more distressed by the rips in his jacket than the scratches on his face. "Old clothes are like old people. You have to treat them gently."

"Tell that to Roger's fans."

Cameo just shook her head. "You take that off before you do any more damage to it." The cloche hat framed her face, beautiful as a nymph from a Mucha poster, a few spit-curls of golden hair pulled loose to make it a mirror of the face on the cameo she wore on a choker around her neck, her one constant amid her constantly shifting display of vintage outfits and re-creations. "I'll find you a loaner till I can fix it. Something black you can't stain."

Topper looked around at the racks of clothes and the stacks of hats, including a huge number of top hats, lingering for a moment on a collection of wigs, one long blond one in particular. "Nice collection," she said, turning at last. "All this yours?"

"Heaven forfend," Cameo said, "I do *not* have the space. Most of this is on loan from Dutton's Theatrical Supply. We're in rehearsals for *The Boy-friend*." She turned to face a rack of tuxes and rifled through them. "Alec misplaced his cummerbund. I was hoping there might be one he could borrow."

Topper stared at Cameo's throat until she turned. "That's a lovely brooch you have there. Antique?"

"Why yes," Cameo said, her hand going to it. "Family heirloom." She dimpled. "And source of my nickname. My real name's Ellen."

"Melissa," Topper said, her eyes flicking to Cameo's golden spit-curls. "Were you at Starfields earlier?"

"Me?" said Cameo with a slightly alarmed expression. "You must be joking. I can't stand eating in restaurants. The tables are never clean enough for me, and the silverware . . . Ugh! Just the idea of how many people have had it in their mouths . . ." She shuddered delicately. "Give me a nice new styrofoam box and disposable chopsticks any day."

Sam nodded. "You're talking to the Queen of Takeout here."

"Too true," Cameo sighed, going back to her search. "Call it an eccentricity, but until they invent a fashionable hazmat suit, the most I'll be able to stand is the occasional stand-up buffet with plastic champagne glasses and cocktail pies."

Topper gave her a long look. "Aren't you an ace?"

Cameo chuckled. "If I say 'yes,' Marilyn Monroe's lawyers will sue me. Word to the wise, but never accuse an international idol of card sharkery on national television. Especially if the only proof you can give is 'revelations from the spirits.'"

"So you're not an ace?"

"I'm a trance channeler and psychic—for entertainment purposes only—and do seances for the tourists over at the Dead Nicholas. I'm also a famous fraud." Cameo chuckled. "Peregrine kicked me off her Perch and Hiram

Worchester had me barred from Aces High once it came out that my only ace powers were my skills as an actress and the same medium scam that goes back to Houdini. And a positive blood test for the wild card."

"Positive?" Topper asked.

Cameo nodded, then struck a melodramatic pose, her head cast back, her wrist to her forehead. "Alas, I'm cursed. I'm doomed. I live under a cloud of knowing that any day I might suddenly drop dead or suffer some unimaginable fate—which, if you think about it, sounds pretty much like a joker, not that you can convince many jokers of that," she said, dropping the pose. "But since being a latent means always having to say you're sorry, I decided to quit waiting for the damn card to turn and just picked something out of the deck myself." She chuckled again. "After all, you don't have to be a real psychic to go to a murder scene and scream about bad vibes. Besides," she said, waving to her dress, "aces have an excuse to wear the coolest outfits. And people treat you like a celebrity. What's not to like?"

Topper chuckled as well. "Do you want a list?"

Cameo paused. "You're Topper, aren't you? The conjurer ace?"

"Yes, I—" Topper broke off, spotting something hanging from the corner of one of the costume racks. "Excuse me, what's that?" Sam looked—a white pantomime mask, a single tear on the cheek. The same as the fetish girl had been wearing back at Starfields.

Cameo glanced over to it. "Oh," she said, then waved in dismissal, "that's the mask for Pierrette." She took Sam's jacket and put it up on a hanger.

"Pierrette?"

"'Poor Pierrette,' actually," Cameo said, looking through the tux rack as Topper went over to examine the mask. "Pierrot's lover, from the *comedia dell'arte*. It's one of the numbers in the show." She pulled out a swallowtail coat. "Here, try this."

Sam put his arms in the sleeves and shrugged it on. It was good fit, and black, but there wasn't a sheath for his tail. "Um . . ." he said.

Cameo gave him a sharp look. "It's Halloween in Jokertown, Sam. If you've got it, flaunt it. Except for that hat," she said, removing it from his head. "This the handiwork of those crazed fangirls?"

Sam looked to Topper. "One of them."

Topper glared while Cameo grimaced and said, "That kind of woman you do not need," tsking over the ripped seam at the crown. "Now to find you a replacement. . . ."

"Mind if I help?" Topper gestured to the tux rack and the top hats on top.

"Please do," Cameo said. "We're looking for something in a small."

Topper got a step stool and began to inspect the hats, and Sam could tell she was not just checking their size.

Cameo set his battered hat aside on a work table, then picked up an overstuffed ragbag from the floor and set it next to it. "Let's see what I've got in my bag of tricks. I'd rather not borrow from Dutton if I can help it. . . ." She opened the bag and rifled through her assortment of costume pieces, pulling out another top hat, collapsed flat. She held it in her hands for a long while, contemplating it, then shook her head, and with an expert flick of her wrist, popped the top out into shape.

She turned, stopping, and looked up at Topper where she was perched on the stool. "That's a lovely hat you have there, Melissa," she said at last. "Had it long?"

Topper looked at the one in her hands, then set it down and reached up and tapped the one on her head. "Why yes, actually. My grandfather gave it to me shortly before he died. . . ."

"I'm . . . so sorry for your loss. Were you fond of him?"

It was kind of a forward question, even for Cameo, and Topper stopped searching through the top shelf for a moment. Then continued. "Very. But it's a mixed bag. My grandpa was a stage magician—really great in his day, before the wild card. But it destroyed him." She grabbed for another stack of top hats, popping them out and checking inside. "He used to work places like this, have bookings all over the country. Then . . . nothing." She grimaced. "He was very bitter about it—I mean, who wants to see someone pull a rabbit out of a hat when in the next tent there's a woman who can turn into a flying elephant?"

Cameo turned the hat over in her hands. "And then you drew an ace from that infernal deck. . . ."

"I didn't tell him," Topper said, trying another hat. "Or anyone else for that matter. Not until after grandpa died."

"He knew," Cameo assured her. "Trust me, he knew. He just didn't say anything."

Topper cocked her head. "You really think so?"

"I know so. Grandfathers know these things." Cameo gave a dark chuckle. "Besides, it's hard to keep a secret from a professional magician." Her mouth twisted in a wry grin as she contemplated the hat, turning it over again. "So what did you do after . . ." She paused, as if trying to come up with a delicate way to phrase it, then failing, ". . . your grandfather's death? If you don't mind me asking. . . ."

"I'm a private eye. I'm used to questions." Topper sighed and shrugged. "I went into government work. I didn't want to be one of the aces who took the spotlight away from him. That, and the fact that I hate being on stage." She grimaced. "I must be the only person who ever had the wild card turn from stage fright. Right in the middle of my high school talent show no less."

"And your grandfather never told you that he knew. . . ."

"If he did know." Topper shook her head. "Trust him to die leaving me a mystery."

"Or two." Cameo chuckled. "The world needs mysteries now more than ever. . . ." She laughed long and loud, as if she'd just heard the best joke in the world, then abruptly shook her head and stopped. "You know, Sam," she said, turning the hat over in her hands, "I don't think this hat will fit you after all." She collapsed it, far less deftly than she'd popped it out, then turned and began to replace it in her ragbag.

"Are you sure?" Topper asked, coming down off the steps. "Could I see that one?"

Cameo paused, then shrugged and pulled the flattened top hat back out, flipping it to Topper like a Frisbee. Topper caught it and popped it out, turning it over in her hands and reaching inside to check the lining.

"You see," Cameo said, coming over next to her and retrieving the hat, "this is a seven and a quarter, and we need more of a six and seven-eighths or a seven." She put the hat on Sam, demonstrating where it went down too low on his forehead, then collapsed it and put it back in her ragbag. Topper gave Sam a look he couldn't read.

"Here," Cameo said as she came back, "until I can fix the silk—*if* I can fix the silk—why don't you just make do with ordinary felt?" She went to the rack where Topper had been searching and took down a modern top hat with rounded corners, checked the label, then put it on Sam's head where it fit perfectly, if inelegantly.

"Socks?" Sam bent down and began unlacing his left boot. "And do you by any chance have any opera glasses or binoculars?"

"Are you on a scavenger hunt?" Cameo located a single clean sock, pointing him to a trash bin when he offered her the ink-soaked one. "No binoculars right now. Maybe a lorgnette?"

Topper shook her head lightly. "No, sorry," Sam said.

"Ask Jim," Cameo suggested, collecting her ragbag. "I need to go check the greenroom for cummerbunds. Alec isn't someone you can just fit off the rack."

She left and Topper came over as Sam finished tying his bootlaces. Sam laughed. "So, your talent show? Mine turned in detention."

"What?"

Sam waggled his fingers. "My deuce. I was busted for graffiti. The VP tossed my artwork in the furnace." He paused. "You know, mental cruelty to a latent is a firing offense. . . ." He stood up and retrieved his sketchbook from the floor. "But hey, I survived, and so did you. Nothing wrong with that."

"Yeah," said Topper. "Is it me, or did she pull a Bobo Switch?"

"A what?" Sam asked.

"A Bobo Switch. It's a magician's pass that lets you swap one coin with another. You could do it with collapsed hats."

"Why?"

"I don't know," Topper said. "I would have sworn that the top hat she just had there was mine. And she's asking all these questions about my grandfather. Then next thing, she starts to put it away, then hands it back, and that's the exact way a magician would swap one coin for another." She gave him a sharp look. "Trust me, I may not be great at it anymore, but that was one of my tricks for the talent competition."

Sam looked at her. "Again . . . why?"

Topper waved at the air. "I don't know. I'm just making suppositions here. She's the right height and build, and that mask there is awfully suspicious. And while her hair's too short, it's the right color, and it's hard to tell length anyway with that hat, so maybe she has it pinned up. Or maybe she wore a wig—there's plenty of them here." Topper gestured to the room. "Plus that brooch of hers—that could have made a lump under the latex that would look like an Adam's apple. And that weird crack about fashionable hazmat suits—what was Rubber Maid wearing if not that?"

"Or Bondage Babe could have been Mr. Dutton in drag," Sam pointed out. "He's thin too. He owns all these wigs and costumes, and he can certainly afford a pair of fake breasts."

"Or that," Topper conceded. "That's the maddening thing about detective work. But was it just me, or was Cameo acting seriously weird?"

"Seriously weird? Remember, this is Jokertown, and you're talking to a man who's housemates with Jim. The guy's almost twenty and still sends letters to Santa—which would just be pathetic, except Christmas morning, there's extra presents under the tree and the milk and cookies are gone." Sam let that sink in for effect. "Weird is relative. Cameo's a theatre person. Weird, yes. Seriously, no. Or at least she always acts like that. We think she's had one too many method acting classes." Sam chuckled. "Roger got her drunk at a cast party and she did this hilarious crazed hunchback impression. You should have seen it."

"Crazed hunchback?" Topper inquired, then shook her head and took a deep breath. "You're right. I'm being paranoid. Let's just go see if Jim has any binoculars then check the audience again. The show should start soon."

They went downstairs and over to the stage where the guys were talking over the sound of an impatient audience coming through the curtain. "What do you think, Sam?" Alec asked. "Ditch the formals? 'Cause I've got this Green Knight outfit I was planning to wear for second set—I mean, it's Halloween and all—and I can't find the stupid cummerbund and we're going to be on national TV. Plus the whole tux business makes me look like Lurch anyway."

"Better than Tiny Tim," Paul said, glaring. "If I hear 'God bless us, everyone!' one more time, I swear, I'm gonna whack someone."

"'Top Hat' is our big number, that's all I'm saying," Roger pointed out, "and it'll look pretty stupid to have four guys in formalwear plus the Rockettes dancing around a Ren Faire refugee. We close on 'Top Hat' at the break, then we change costumes, and then you can be the Jolly Green Giant all you want."

"It's not the Jolly Green Giant! It's the Green Knight! From the tale of Sir Gawain!"

"Right, Alec. We all know about your Arthurian fixation. Even the wild card virus knows about your Arthurian fixation. Now lay off and tell us where you hid the cummerbund."

"I didn't hide the—Wait a sec," he said, breaking off and looking down his very long nose at Topper. "Couldn't you just pull my cummerbund out of your hat?"

Topper stared at him with a deer-in-headlights expression, then slowly shook her head. "Sorry. No requests. Firm rule of mine."

"Can't you break it?"

"Only if it's life or death. Is a cummerbund that serious?"

"You ever been on stage?" Alec's nostrils flared, making him look even more horse-faced. "With people calling you 'Lurch?'"

Dirk looked up at Alec. "Hey dude, we could shave your head the rest of the way. Then you'd look like Uncle Fester instead."

Alec glared down at him. "And if we dressed you in stripes, you'd look like Pugsley."

"If Pugsley bleached his hair and did a whole ton of steroids," Paul remarked.

"Shut up, Timmy," Dirk told him. "It's not my freakin' fault I've got muscles like this."

"Well," said Jim, "if you use the Charles Atlas system for more than five days, what do you expect? You keep saying I'm crazy, but at least I followed the directions." Jim stood there, cutting a perfect figure in his tux, then added, "But if the problem is Alec being too tall for the lineup, and we need a quick fix, what if we just made Paul taller instead? After all, it's a lot easier to stretch someone who's already stretchy, and his braces are fully adjustable."

Paul waved a crutch. "You know how long it takes me to put these things on, let alone change the settings. We don't have time."

"Sure we do," Jim said. "Look what I just got."

You could have heard a pin drop at that moment. Jim's *Look what I just gots* were usually followed by something spectacular and sometimes frightening, occasionally destructive. He held up his latest gimcrack, what looked like a remote control, with a few extra wires and sparkling diodes held on with strips of duct tape. "It's a universal remote." He displayed it with all the pride of a child showing off the new toy Santa had brought him. "The box said it would control all my appliances, electronics, entertainment and audiovisual equipment. I had to fiddle with it a bit before it worked right, but now it does, and doctor always calls Paul's braces appliances. And look, here's the *vertical*." He pointed the remote at Paul and a jolt of electrical energy shot forth, connecting with the rubber boy's braces and arcing along them like a Tesla coil.

Paul began to get taller and taller, rapidly nearing Alec's height then going somewhat beyond, his body becoming correspondingly thinner, like a life-size Stretch Armstrong doll. "Gimcrack! Cut it out!" Paul's leg braces were clearly visible beyond his highwater tux pants, getting higher still as electricity crackled and adjustment pins on the braces clicked and ratcheted spasmodically, inching higher and higher.

"Cut what out?" asked Jim.

"He means stop," Roger said. "There's a *stop* button, isn't there, Jim?"

"Sure," said the ace, "it's right here." Jim pressed the remote and the electrical charge zapped into nothingness, Paul's braces locking just short of eight feet. His elongated midriff stuck out below his shirtwaist and above his tux pants, held up by his massively strained suspenders.

Topper leaned over to Sam and whispered in his ear, "On second thought, let's not ask about the binoculars." Sam nodded.

The rubber boy looked down at himself. "Hey, actually this is pretty cool." He stilt-walked a couple steps towards Alec. "Hey look, Alec, I'm even taller than you!" He smiled then, the corners of his mouth curling up like a caricature. "I can even touch your horn. . . ."

Paul reached his elongated arm for the forward point of Alec's Mohawk and the tall joker jerked away. "Don't you touch it, you fucking rubber chicken!" Alec reared back, his goatee flying. "I *know* you're not a virgin!"

Paul grinned even more wickedly. "Hey, when you can beat all the other guys at Freakers annual 'Whip it out' contest, the girls can never get enough of you!"

"Really?" Jim looked perplexed again. "That hasn't been my experience. I keep getting emails about how to 'Add extra inches,' and those work, of course, but there's never any 'Lose unwanted inches' programs, at least for your penis."

There was another of those pin-drop silences. "Jim," Roger said, shaking his head, "please, whatever you do, don't mention that once the curtain goes up. And Alec, Paul—that goes double for you two. You should know better. This is our first live broadcast and we don't want to piss off the network."

"The Network?" Jim repeated. "The celestial intelligences I hear with my pyramid hat?"

"Well 'celestial intelligences' may be going a bit far, but they're the ones who cut the checks," said a woman's voice from behind Sam. "Remember, we're talking *MTV* here."

Sam turned, seeing a tall brunette in a gold dress with more sequins than the Sultan of Brunei, her hair elaborately coiffed up with pins tipped with gold coins with a matching necklace and drop pendant earrings, and a pair of beautiful brown-and-white-feathered wings behind her. And equally spectacular cleavage in front. Peregrine, the flying ace model and talk show hostess.

She swept forward, regal as the Queen of Angels, which was probably the general idea. "I hope you boys excuse the liberty. I was wanting to talk with you about a possible appearance on my Perch, and Chaos invited us backstage." She waved behind herself, then partially unfurled her left wing, to both shelter and backdrop two other individuals. "I also wanted to introduce my son, John Fortune. He's a great fan of yours. And this is his date . . ." She glanced back.

"Velvet," supplied the girl, "Velvet Brown."

If it was possible to eclipse Peregrine, this girl did. Posed against the feathered curtain, which made her even more radiant, was a startlingly beautiful young woman, no more than sixteen, gorgeous as a Hollywood starlet of another era, with long dark curls, flawless ivory skin, and intense violet eyes. She was dressed in a velvet riding habit, circa 1940s, and a pert little top hat, and had one slim hand laid on the arm of a young man about the same age. This lucky boy was as gorgeous as his mother and almost as tall, with the extra perk of being genuinely exotic, at least on the nat end of the scheme, with *cafe-au-lait* skin, kinky hair the color of burnished gold, and huge almond-shaped brown eyes. This didn't exactly fit with the round black glasses or the purple scar makeup in the shape of a lightning bolt at the edge of his hairline, but having a mother who could actually help you fly was probably consolation for a less-than-convincing Harry Potter costume.

"Wow!" said John. "This is so cool, I can hardly believe it! You guys are really all jokers?"

"Well I'm not," Jim admitted. "I'm only a latent." He said this, as always, with a straight face, though this time while holding a universal remote wrapped with duct tape and diodes and arcing with weird electrical energy.

John Fortune looked askance at it, as did Velvet Brown and Peregrine. "There's so much shoddy workmanship these days," Jim apologized further, "but then I guess you get what you pay for." He waved it, making it spark and causing Paul to grow an inch. "I picked this up off the bargain table at the five and dime, so I really shouldn't complain."

Alec put his finger next to his ear and twirled it in the universal crazy signal, then looked away and pretended he was primping his Mohawk the moment Jim glanced back.

"I'm a latent too," said John, smiling the trying-to-make-conversation-with-the-nice-crazy-person smile.

Jim smiled back. "My sympathies."

"Perhaps you might make your friend a bit shorter, dear?" Peregrine interrupted gently. "Say, six-three, six-four? A little more in the shoulders, a little less in the hips, the Fabio proportions?"

"Okay. . . ." Jim pressed a couple buttons, causing the static to arc, and Paul began to get shorter and slightly wider, at least across the shoulders, while Jim looked back to John. "Roger was a latent until a little while ago, but he was lucky enough to draw a joker-deuce, and he's working on making it into an ace."

"As should we all," said Peregrine. "Being an ace is an attitude. Though a good fashion designer helps." Sam realized then that she wasn't got up as the Queen of Angels but the Queen of Pentacles, wearing what had to be a Bob Mackie original.

Jim began to look distraught, then showed the remote to Peregrine. "I checked all the buttons, but there isn't a hip-narrowing function. . . ."

Peregrine smiled. "Oh yes there is. I was in more than enough beauty pageants when I was younger." She furled her wings and moved closer, checking out Paul's butt, now that he'd reached a more reasonable height. "Do you have any athletic tape?"

"No," said Jim, then produced a silver roll from the pocket of his tux, "but I have duct tape."

Paul's eyes almost popped out of his head, literally. "You're not going to duct tape my ass!"

Peregrine's wings rustled softly as she laid a perfectly manicured hand on his shoulder, her nails as gold as her lipstick. "Trust me, dear—there are no jokers, only aces with bad publicists and fashion designers."

"Yeah, all Bloat needed was a muumuu. . . ."

Peregrine only smiled. "And a press kit. This is showbiz. We're selling a fantasy." She cast a glance around, then locked eyes with Topper standing next to Sam. "Melissa! My goodness, I didn't even notice you! What are you doing here?" She smiled her most dazzling smile, an advertisement for the virtues of toothbonding and cosmetic dentistry. "I know you have athletic tape in that hat of yours. Could we trouble you for some?"

"Uh . . ." said Topper, and Sam realized that the world's chattiest ace talk show hostess was the *last* person that Topper wanted to know that she'd lost her magic conjuring hat.

"Good luck," said Alec. "She won't even give me my cummerbund."

"Which I just found," said Cameo, appearing from behind Dirk. "It was behind the couch in the greenroom."

"Cameo!" Peregrine exclaimed. "So lovely to see you."

"Say it on camera and I'll believe it, Peri," she replied, taking a moment to adjust her hat. As she brushed by Peregrine, there was a sudden loud *ZOT* and a flash of electricity and ozone, and the only thing Sam could figure was that the beads on Cameo's flapper dress had somehow acted as a conductor and allowed the static electricity from Jim's remote control and Paulie's braces to arc to Peregrine's copious amounts of metal jewelry. Her hair went up like the Bride of Frankenstein and her wings spread-eagled on reflex, the feathers whacking the front edge on Alec's Mohawk, and the spiraled ivory horn.

Alec screamed and the scream turned into a whinny as his face elongated, becoming more horselike, and his body became more staglike, and his legs became more goatlike, and his tuxedo split apart, revealing a lion's tail, very much like the one Sam possessed, except in white, with an elaborate tassel at the tip, like the one possessed by a heraldic lion—or a unicorn, which was what Alec had become. Only his spiraled horn, Mohawked mane, long white goatee and mass remained constant between forms. He waved his cloven hooves, pawing the air as the remnants of the tuxedo fell to the stage, then he came down hard on them, looking at Peregrine with fire in his eye, an accusatory snort, and his horn pointed straight at her heart.

Lenore was squawking and screaming and trying to become airborne while the static in Peregrine's hairdo collapsed, and she stood there, a wisp of smoke coming from the underwires of her support bra. "What happened?"

"You're not a virgin!" Jim exclaimed.

"What?" said Peregrine, dazed. "Of course I'm not a virgin—I'm a mother! How many mothers are virgins?" She blinked, starting to focus on the unicorn in the top hat in front of her.

"Alec shifts if anyone who's not a virgin touches the tip of his horn," Jim explained. "He can only change back if he has a virgin ride him."

"What sort of 'ride?'" asked Topper.

"A short one. Five, ten minutes, tops." Jim paused and bit his lip. "As for virgin mothers, there's Sister Mary Immaculate over at Our Lady of Perpetual Misery. She's given birth the last seven Christmases in a row, and she's the one we get to ride Alec if there aren't any other virgins handy."

Velvet Brown put up her hand. "So any girl who's never had sex with a man counts?"

"I think so," said Jim. "Lesbians can still be virgins, if that's what you're wondering."

Velvet smiled her starlet smile, then threw her arms around Alec's neck and announced, in the worst British accent Sam had ever heard, "Pie's the best horse! I'm going to ride him in the Grand Nationals!" With this, she planted a kiss right at the base of Alec's horn and swung herself up on his back, posing as if she were ready for her closeup.

Alicorn the unicorn's eyes went wide and then he screamed, rearing up, champing the air, Velvet Brown clinging frantically to his mane as he shook his head till the ridiculous top hat flew free.

"I don't think she's a virgin," Jim said. "Alec gets very upset if someone who's not a virgin gets—" Jim broke off abruptly as Alicorn's hoof lashed out and knocked the universal remote from his hand, sending it spinning and skittering across the stage, weird energy arcing in all directions, grounding itself into every bit of metal in sight, then some beyond it as the curtain began to rise, the ropes of the gaffing system beginning to pull it up via electronic pulley.

"What's happening?" Peregrine demanded.

"My remote!" Jim screamed. "He smashed it! And I think he hit *play!*"

On cue, the bands' instruments behind them, everything from Dirk's drumsticks to Roger's electric fiddle, rose up into position, borne aloft by strands of phantom energy, and started into the opening strains of Irving Berlin's 'Top Hat.' Then a gap opened in the curtain as the drapery swags parted and the unicorn made for it, still screaming, running out onto the runway spit accompanied by the screams of Velvet Brown mixed with those of countless other girls.

A camera operator ran in, wearing headphones and a mike. "Peri! The cameras are acting like they're possessed, but that doesn't matter—we've somehow got a live network feed! We're live! *We're live!*"

"It's all audiovisual and entertainment. . . ." Jim said plaintively. "Did you say The Network?"

Peregrine and Roger exchanged looks, then, with the instincts of veteran showpeople, they turned to the wings and called, "Cue the Rockettes!"

Peregrine then took the cameraman's headset and stepped forward, into the breach, announcing, "Ladies and gentlemen, live from the new, and aptly named, Club Chaos, *MTV* is proud to present a special Halloween show—New York's new hometown favorite, *The Jokertown Boys!*"

Sam balked—Alec had become hoarse all right. Or horse. Or unicorn, as was the case, and he had the choice of joining the band as replacement singer or chasing after his friend. It was an easy choice, and not just because of the rattle of tap shoes behind him or the screams and wild applause as the unicorn ran the length of the runway, Topper running after him and Velvet Brown screaming, "Jerry, you idiot!" as they vaulted into the aisle. Sam followed, National Velvet Jerry or whoever she was still astride Alicorn's back as the unicorn ran into the lobby, out the main doors, and up the street, vaulting cabs.

Somewhere in the lobby, Sam realized that John Fortune was with them, in fact outpacing Topper, Quidditch robes far better suited to running than stiletto heels, and they all caught up with Velvet Brown just as she was dumped on her ass in the middle of the roadway, Alicorn continuing up the street without her.

"That was wicked cool!" John exclaimed, while Topper and Sam couldn't do much more than pant.

A moment later, Peregrine landed next to them. "John Fortune!" she exclaimed, using all her stage presence and the fury of mothers everywhere. "What on earth do you think you're doing running off like that?"

John pointed to his date, who Sam suddenly realized was a dead ringer for long dead movie starlet, Elizabeth Taylor. "You said I was supposed to stick with my bodyguard, Mom."

"That is not your bodyguard," Peregrine intoned with barely controlled rage. "*That* is someone who is so fired she'd think J.J. Flash had done it."

The girl went pale. "And our Agency?"

Peregrine paused. "Has proven itself on other occasions," she conceded, looking to Topper. "Melissa, are you free?"

"Fraid not. I'm on another case."

Peregrine looked sour at this, but didn't bother to plead or argue, merely took her son by the shoulders and said, "Young man—I will, of course, be furious if the answer is no, but I need an honest answer to a simple question: Are you a virgin?"

John Fortune's eyes went wide behind the Harry Potter glasses and he nodded. "Yes ma'am."

"Good," said Peregrine, "then you get to ride a unicorn. Assuming . . ." She looked askance to Sam and Topper.

Sam nodded. "Male virgins count." He pointed up the street. "He went that way."

"Good," said Peregrine, gathering John Fortune into her arms and winging off down the block.

Jerry-Velvet-Elizabeth got up and dusted herself off, looking after the rapidly disappearing Peregrine, then simply shrugged and walked over to them. "Back to the club?"

"For us. You got fired, remember?" Topper took a couple steps in that direction then stopped, the girl still following. "Yes, Jerry?"

"What sort of case are you on?"

"Um . . ." Topper looked stricken, and Sam realized that, the same as Peregrine, Jerry was also someone who under no circumstances could know that Topper had lost her hat.

"Actually, she's not on a case," Sam said, taking Topper's hand. "We're on a date."

"Yes, a date." Topper hugged close to him, putting her head on his shoulder for a moment.

The fallen starlet looked at Topper, then Sam, then back. "I thought you said you didn't go for younger men."

"No," said Topper, "that's just something I told Pete. I don't date guys who habitually insult people and smoke huge cigars as overcompensation. But I was trying to be polite." She looked to the faux Elizabeth Taylor, then Sam, then pulled him into a kiss, full on French, no holds barred.

By the time it was over, Sam felt almost as dazed as Peregrine had been after the jolt. "See?" Topper said. "Date." She led Sam a few step back towards the club. "And if you tell Pete about any of this, I'll tell him about you and the dalmatians."

"*What* dalmatians?"

"You know Pete," Topper said. "I don't need to tell him any more than that." She paused. "Maybe a number. A hundred. A hundred and one. He already knows you have a thing for Glenn Close."

"You wouldn't."

"Try me, Cruella."

They continued back towards Club Chaos, Jerry-Velvet-Elizabeth tagging along like a kid sister. "Oh well," the girl said, "even if you're not on a case, there's still one mystery left." Topper looked askance at her until finally the girl let it out: "Do you think Cameo zapped Perry?"

"That's your mystery?" Topper looked exasperated. "Cameo? We both saw the sparks from Gimcrack's gizmo."

"Yeah, but that would give her the perfect cover."

Topper snorted. "But why? And with what?"

"Her ace," said the starlet.

"Ace? Jerry, she's a famous fraud." Topper bit her lip. "Even if she isn't, she's what, a spirit medium? I didn't see any seance tables. What could she do, zap Perry with ectoplasm?"

"No," said Jerry, "with a dead ace's ace."

Topper balked, bringing her and Sam to a dead stop. "Come again?"

"I went on a mission with her once," Jerry explained. "Secret government stuff. Very hush-hush. Billy Ray was there. You used to work with him. He tell you?"

"We're talking Billy," Topper said. "No."

Jerry looked smug. "Cameo's ace lets her channel the dead by touching something they had in life—Something important to them. Like your hat, Melissa. If you were dead, I mean. And if the dead person was an ace, she can channel their powers too." Jerry looked at Topper's topper. "Actually, that hat would be a real score for her. Cameo's payment for the mission was going to be Black Eagle's jacket, but if she had your hat, she could pull out that, Brain Trust's pearls, Cyclone's flight helmet—hell, whatever she wants."

"If I were dead," Topper amended.

"Yeah."

"And this shocking ace?"

"Dunno," Jerry said, "Cameo had all this junk in her backpack. Said she could summon a shocker with some hat. Never saw it, I . . . left the mission early."

Topper squeezed Sam's hand, and he squeezed back, and they walked a long while in silence before Topper said, "So you planning to out her? For putting her ace back up her sleeve, I mean, after Peri and everyone laughed at it?"

"Well, maybe Peri . . ."

"Would laugh at you too," Topper finished. "Face it, Jerry—Cameo may have the perfect motive, but she's also got a perfect alibi. And even if she confessed, Peri wouldn't believe her." She paused. "And in the scheme of ace pranks, zapping someone's butt is pretty trivial. You'd out someone for that? You, of all people?"

"It was probably Jim's remote anyway," Sam said.

Jerry paused. "This sort of thing happens?"

"Since we were lads. You should have seen it when he took drivers ed. The car was an automatic."

"You know, Jerry," Topper said, "you could still catch a movie. . . ."

"Hmm . . . the Metreon is showing all the Hammer *Draculas*. Including *Brides*." The starlet looked pensive. "Those girls in the nightgowns are really hot. . . ."

"And they're waiting for you," Topper said. "Look, there's a cab."

Jerry looked, then ran for it, waving.

"She's bisexual, right?" Sam asked. "'Cause regular lesbians don't set Alec—"

"Jerry's a special case," Topper said, shutting him off, "and yes, our agency is a detective agency."

"Isn't she a bit young?"

"You're not one to talk, young man." Topper squeezed his hand. "But you should see Pete. Not that that matters right now since we know—"

There was a flutter of feathers and gold sequins as Peregrine alighted. "You're needed on stage, Sam."

"But—"

"But nothing. You're the best thing to happen to jokers rights in ten years." She scooped him up in both arms and Sam and his sketchbook were pressed against the famous cleavage as the flying ace took off, speaking into her headset, "Got him. Cue the Boys for our entrance." They swept up into the air, then down, and Sam felt his stomach lurch as Peregrine folded her wings in a power dive, fanning them out as they entered the lobby, then folding them again as they plunged through the doors into the main theatre, swooping over the heads of the audience. The crowd went wild, with cheers and screams, and Roger's voice boomed, "LADIES AND GENTLEMEN, MY BROTHER, SAM—OUR ACE COVER ARTIST, SWASH!"

Peregrine landed with him and Roger pressed a microphone into his hands. "*Jokertown Blues*, Sam. C. C.'s version—your lead."

Sam felt his mouth go dry, but Dirk pressed a bottle of water into his hand and Sam took a swig, realizing that the drummer's presence meant that Jim's mad ace was somehow still playing the instruments. He hoped it could take a cue: "And a One-Two-Three!

If you go down to Jokertown
Anyone you might see
Might be a little old lady
Name of Juju Marie
She might look like you
She might look like me
But there's mighty mean momma
Name of Juju Marie

The radios had played that fourteen years ago, C. C. Ryder's version of the old Mr. Rainbow song, when Sam and Roger's parents had taken them to Jokertown for the day. And while they hadn't met the old blues witch, they'd run into her counterpart, Typhoid Croyd, their parents dying, Sam and Roger going to the J-town orphanage.

If you go down to Jokertown
Better watch what you say
Or that little old lady's
Gonna blow you away
"Toads and Diamonds,"
That's what she sings,
"Jokers, and Aces,
And Black Queens and Kings"

Sam put his heart into that verse. "Kings" was J-town slang for latents, shorthand for "suicide kings," the sword of Damocles of the wild card suspended over every latent's head until it finally dropped, usually ending in death, sometimes maiming even worse than death.

He'd been a latent for eleven years and a deuce for only three. He knew what it felt like.

If you go down to Jokertown
You better pray hard
That a little old lady
Don't deal you a card
You might start to weep
You might start to wail
You might feel an urge
To start a-shaking your tail!

Sam did so, flaunting the thing that set him apart from human, the joker that he could have but would never have removed. The audience went wild, girls screaming, snatching and grabbing for it as he danced out of the way.

Then his lion's tail wasn't the only one on stage. Alicorn leapt onto the end of the runway, John Fortune dismounting, and the unicorn began slowly walking along the ramp to the adulation of the virgins and somewhat less virginal teenyboppers on both sides as the rest of the Boys joined in on the next verse:

If you go down to Jokertown
Well, you might just stay there
'Cause that mean ol' woman
Who deal cards, she ain't fair
If you lose, you win
If you win, you lose
What I'm talking about
Is called the Wild Card Bluuuuuuues. . . .

On the long sustained note, the unicorn reached the end of the runway and reared up on his hind legs, morphing from Alicorn into Alec—Alec, totally naked—and Sam realized that when he'd catalogued his friend's changes earlier, he'd been inaccurate. Aside from his horn, mane, and mass, Alec's unmentionables remained relatively unaffected by the transformation: He was hung like a horse in either form. Girls screamed in appreciation while the Boys got in front of him, strategically placing Dirk's shoulders between the cameras and Alec, handing him a microphone for the encore:

You'll get no release!
You'll get no reprieve!
And if you go down to Jokertown
You might never leave!

The crowd went wild while various individuals attempted to enforce decency standards: cameramen battling to restrain possessed and prurient audiovisual equipment, Jim puzzling over his smashed remote, and Cameo running from offstage carrying a giant green tunic which she threw to Alec. Just as he put it on over his horn and got it low enough for at least regimental standards of decency, the weird electrical energy evaporated into nothingness and the instruments clattered to the stage. As the curtain began to come down, Jim triumphantly held up the universal remote in one hand and the batteries in the other.

"That was fun," the crazy ace said, turning to the rest of them. "Do you think we'll be able to top that with the next set?"

"God I hope not . . ." Alec prayed. "I must have looked like Herne out there."

Jim nodded. "A lot like he did in 'The King of Spring'."

"Jim," Paul said, "that's not a good thing. That's a joker porn video."

"It is not," Jim insisted. "I read the box. It's a French art film."

"Where Herne fucks twenty nuns."

"It's symbolic. He's the King of Spring."

Dirk snorted. "King of Sproing is more like it."

"You're not being helpful," Cameo said, then to Alec, "Honestly, Alec, you do not look like Herne."

"Herne has antlers," Jim said helpfully, "you have a unicorn horn. No one could mistake you. Above the waist, at least."

Alec groaned while Cameo said, "Let's just get you your tights."

They went offstage to the changing area where the most noticeable thing was Cameo's ragbag spilled across the floor. The next most noticeable thing was when Topper snatched the cloche hat off Cameo's head. "Alright," she said, stuffing it inside the inverted top hat she held in her other hand, "and for my next trick, I'd like to hear some serious answers. That is, if you ever want to see your own precious hat again."

Cameo turned and began to glow blue with St. Elmo's fire, electricity sparking off the bobby pins of her bizarre hairdo, which consisted of her long honey blond tresses pinned up and over a battered fedora, squashed from where it had been hidden beneath the cloche. "I don't know who you are, lady," she growled, "but you stay away from Ellen or you'll have to answer to me."

"And who are you?" Topper asked, stepping back, her hand still down her hat.

"That, I expect, would be Nick Williams," said Peregrine, stepping in front of John Fortune, "a dead private investigator. And a dead ace. Will-o'-the-Wisp, the Hollywood phantom."

"Who—" said Cameo, turning, then, "Oh, the winged bimbo who called me a liar. Ellen too." A small ball of energy had formed in the air, levitating above her right hand like an *ignis fatuus*. "Going to call us liars again?"

Peregrine stood there, her face a mask of regal calm. "No. Though you were less than forthcoming with all the particulars of your story."

"I told you everything," Cameo said. "I was an ace up the sleeve, and I was murdered for it. Only thing I didn't tell you was that when Ellen calls me back, she calls my ace too."

"Is that why you stole my hat?" Topper asked.

"What?" said Cameo, then looked distracted, as if she were listening to someone. "Ellen says she didn't steal your hat, she stole your grandfather's hat. She needed to talk with him." Cameo looked distracted again. "Says he's a stubborn old bastard, and he's pissed as hell that you kept your ace up your sleeve. But tit for tat, you never told him your secret, he never told you his."

Topper's eyes went wide. "That's what this is about? Grandpa's tricks?"

The electrical charge faded back into Cameo and she shook her head. "Yes," she said, "I'm sorry for borrowing your hat, but you can use any hat for your tricks, while I needed this one in particular."

Topper looked to Sam, then back to Cameo. "You read that same damned *Aces!* article, didn't you?"

"Actually, I did," said Roger. "I won't let Cameo take the rap for it alone. I put her up to it. The article said that after the fire, the only personal effects Blackwood the Magnificent had left were his hat—"

"And the International Brotherhood of Magicians pocket watch he was buried with," Topper finished for him. "And you didn't want to desecrate his grave. I guess I should thank you for that." She paused then and grimaced. "Grandpa forgive me . . . hopefully soon. . . ." She reached deep into her hat and came back with a corroded silver pocket watch, covered with dust and grave mold. She tossed it to Cameo.

The medium caught it in one hand, then gazed at it for a long moment. Then she popped the catch and looked at the watch face, remarking, "This is going to need to be cleaned if you expect me to be wearing it." She looked up then, smiling. "Melissa. How are you, my dear?"

"Grandpa?" Topper asked.

"The same," she said, "or different. Don't be so amazed. Swapping places with an assistant is old hat." She chuckled. "Besides which, if Houdini managed an escape from the grave, why should you be surprised when I play the same trick?"

"This afternoon . . . you didn't tell me it was you."

"You didn't ask. Besides which, it wasn't my trick to reveal." Cameo raised her eyebrows. "Anything you'd like to tell me now, my dear?"

Topper bit her lip, then let it out all in one breath: "I'm an ace, Grandpa."

The medium nodded. "There, that wasn't so hard. I'm glad to hear it. But as I can see from the faces here, that secret has been spread rather thin. Indeed, I heard you tell it this afternoon to one who you believed was a complete stranger. Not quite worth the price of the Blackwood legacy." She looked about the group. "Are there any other takers?" She looked to Roger.

"You, sir, the gentleman with the handsome raven—I'm informed you quest after magic. Is this so?"

"Of course," said Roger. "You're one of my idols."

"A flattering thing to hear in a weary world," Cameo responded, "but flattery is cheap, and you know my price: A secret for a secret. But a bit of professional advice: A good magician has more than one trusted assistant. If you can take those present here into your confidence, I suggest you do so."

Roger looked around, lingering a long moment on Peregrine and her son, but she nodded as did he. "Alright," Roger said, "I'm not an ace. Not even a deuce. All my tricks are parlor magic."

"Anything else?"

Roger paused, then took a deep breath. "I'm not a joker either." He reached up and lifted his eye patch, then opened his eye and pinched out a large black lens. "Theatrical contacts."

"But you have horns!" Jim protested. "I've seen them!"

"Those are real," Roger said, "just not mine. I got them from Hodge-Podge."

"Hodge-Podge?" Peregrine asked.

"Back alley psychic surgeon," Roger explained. "She takes bits off animals and put them on people." Roger replaced his contact and eyepatch, then lifted his hat." Somewhere there's a small African antelope missing its horns."

Everyone looked at Sam's tail until he tucked it between his legs. "Uh . . . guys, this is original equipment."

"Same here," said Alec.

"Not here." Roger dropped his hat. "I'm a latent. That's all."

"No," said Cameo, "you are also a skilled illusionist. I can see from the faces here." She gazed about the circle. "I also find this very droll—an ace pretending to be a latent aiding a latent pretending to an ace." She glanced over to Topper. "And teaching my granddaughter a valuable lesson in the bargain: A good magician never relies too heavily on one trick. Enjoy your hat, Melissa. And adieu, for the moment."

Cameo clicked the watch shut and shook her head. "He's gone."

"May I have his watch back?"

Cameo paused, then pressed the stud again, raising a cloud of dust, and fixed Topper with haughty look. "Really, Melissa. It's my watch, and last I checked, the dearly departed were allowed to take their grave goods into the afterlife however they please. This is how I please. Once Ellen assists with costume changes, we intend to watch the performance—and my new apprentice."

"I thought I was your apprentice."

"You were, my dear," Cameo said softly, "but there's a difference between something you do to please your grandfather, and something you do out of love for the art. And despite my current state, I still have standards. This young man meets them. Masquerading one magic as another, well, that has a certain flair, don't you think? You are all assistants in a grand illusion, one final Blackwood trick." She paused, listening. "And Ellen tells me that it is time for a certain young man to get into his tights. It appears the theatre has not changed much in the years since my death, and I take some comfort in that, so again, adieu for now." Cameo clicked the watch shut again and said to Topper, "My hat?"

Topper pulled the cloche out of her topper and tossed it to Cameo, and as she and the Boys set about costume changes, Topper came over next to Sam and sighed. "Trust grandpa to upstage me, even after all these years."

"Trust my brother to join him," Sam said.

"They're two of a kind, aren't they?"

"Seems like. Anything for the show. Your grandpa ever drag you onstage?"

"When I was five. . . ." Topper bit her lip. "You know, I was planning to go to a costume party at Aces High. Care to blow this popstand and join me?" She paused. "What's wrong?"

"That phrase." Sam nodded to where Cameo was helping Jim with a Dr. Frankenstein costume. "Do you know how many sodas have names like 'Burst' and 'Blast'? Jim blew up the 7-11 once." Sam switched his tail then. "Do I meet the dress code?"

"You've just had thousands of girls screaming for you. Hiram's a snob, not an idiot. And it's a charity masquerade anyway." She paused. "The only problem is that I only bought one ticket and it's sold out. And while Hiram keeps extras in his desk," With a flourish, she produced a sheaf from her hat, "they require his signature to be valid. . . ."

"What's the charity?"

"J-town Clinic, same as always," Topper said, handing him the passes. "I can slip a few thousand in the till when he's not looking."

Sam grinned, laying them out on the cover of his sketchbook. "Got an example?" he asked, pulling off his glove.

Topper produced one, and with a flair, Sam forged both Hiram Worchester's flamboyant up-and-down signature and his peacock blue fountain pen ink. "Cast party is on me," said Topper, taking the extras and handing them to Peregrine, "but tell the Boys that I've absconded with their backup singer." She replaced her hat, tapped the top, and extended her arm to Sam. "Care to join your fellow aces?"

Sam accepted her arm. "Sure thing."

Age of Wonders

FOUR

July 2004

"MS. BLACKWOOD, I'VE GOTTEN the story from five audience members, an MTV cameraman, three of the band members, including Sam Washburn—"

"Sam actually talked?" Melissa Blackwood, ace name Topper, asked.

She hesitated. "Not . . . exactly. The thing is, none of the versions match up. I'm still not sure what really happened."

"And you never will be," Topper replied.

Raleigh had interviewed the band members together. Sam, his brother Roger (a.k.a. Ravenstone), and Jim "Gimcrack" Krakowicz were happy to talk to her. And over each other, interrupting, changing their story in mid-stream. They'd been nice and endearing, even when she couldn't quite tell them what the story was about because she still hadn't hit a good angle. Something here wasn't fitting together—which of them were aces again? Whose power did what? Cameo wouldn't talk to her at all. Someone—maybe everyone—was hiding something.

"Off the record then," Raleigh said.

Topper laughed outright. "I don't trust you clowns over there!"

Topper had been a staple at *Aces!* back in the eighties and early nineties, had her own share of striking covers and had enough notoriety to appear in the gossip column, so her not trusting the magazine was perfectly understandable. Raleigh hadn't learned yet how to get past that obstacle—trying to interview people who associated *Aces!* with Digger Downs' aggressive and unapologetic snooping.

Raleigh said, "Ms. Blackwood, maybe you can tell me a little more about your hat?"

Topper hung up.

Instead of uncovering a secret ace, Raleigh had to be content with a feel-good write-up of a boy band that was all grown up. Wasn't often you could pinpoint the moment a band or musician broke out to widespread acclaim.

Buddy Holley's comeback at the 1987 Funhouse Wild Card/AIDS Benefit. Tom Marion Douglas, "the Lizard King," and his participation in the riot at People's Park in '70. That last-minute MTV live broadcast at Club Chaos had been that moment for the Jokertown Boys. Now, a couple of years later, what did the band members think? What did they remember, and how did that line up with how they felt about it now?

She got her story. But the secrets still nagged. She was trying to land an interview with Peregrine herself, who had also been there.

But Peregrine had staff. She had layers of personnel between herself and anyone who wanted to talk to her, especially anyone with the press. Raleigh couldn't get through, and briefly considered lying in wait outside the doors of her building. Except that was something Digger Downs would do and maybe that wasn't the best idea if she wanted to get a better reputation in the business.

Raleigh submitted the story on the Jokertown Boys without that last interview and tried not to feel like she'd missed something. And then, a week or so after the story ran, she got a call at work. A male, secretarial voice announced, "Is this Raleigh Jackson? I have Peregrine on the line for you."

Raleigh didn't have any of her notes ready, didn't have any of her prep work at hand—and that might have been why Peregrine called on her own time, out of the blue. Lesson learned.

Raleigh took a calming breath and said smoothly, as if she were in control, "Yes, I'll take that call, thank you."

The line clicked, a new voice spoke. "Hi, Raleigh Jackson? I understand you wanted to speak with me."

It really was Peregrine, that bright voice that seemed to have a hint of a laugh behind it, that made her sound like your best friend. Raleigh had been listening to that voice, to *Peregrine's Perch,* her whole life. And now she was talking to her. She almost started crying but managed to pull it together. "Hi, yes, thank you so much for replying to my messages, I really appreciate it."

"The only reason I'm talking to you at all is because of that piece you did on Carlotta DeSoto. I like that you tried to get insight into her as a person, and not just go for the sensationalist punch. Not really what I'm used to seeing from *Aces!,* to be honest."

"I just want to tell good stories." It sounded corny, but it was true.

"So do I. How can I help you?"

"A couple of years ago you were at the live broadcast of a Jokertown Boys concert. I wondered if you could talk to me about what you remember from that night—"

Peregrine had spent almost her whole life in the spotlight, dealing with the press, and she had her story down pat. A couple of amusing asides, some genuine laughter, enough of a personal take to appeal to the audience's emotions but nothing too revealing. She was a real pro at this. A little prompting encouraged her to share a couple of anecdotes about her own early days in show business.

The material would be great for a couple of blog posts. Draw readers in, make 'em comfortable. Peregrine was nothing but charm.

"Of course I dreamed of being an actress. Anyone who loves movies thinks about it, however briefly. But I realized pretty quickly the roles for someone with wings were never going to be about the acting." She laughed, maybe a little wistfully.

"Do you think that's a problem, that a lot of people who have the wild card virus are limited by their abilities and appearances, and maybe don't get a real chance to develop their talents?"

"I think we're all just getting by as best as we can. Some doors close, others open. My wings opened a lot of doors. But you want to talk about limited roles, talk to Dr. Bradley Finn over at the Jokertown Clinic about that. He did a stint in Hollywood when he was in college. He's got opinions."

Raleigh made a note to do just that. "Bands like the Jokertown Boys or Joker Plague certainly seem to make the most of their appearances."

"Like I said, we're all just getting by. You use what you got."

There was a pull quote. Raleigh put an asterisk by the line. She had one more question, the one that was pushing her luck. But the interview had gone so well . . . "I wondered if by any chance it would be possible for me to talk to your son about what he remembers from that show? Get the perspective of the band's target audience, maybe?" She held her breath.

Peregrine made the kind of sigh game show hosts let out when the contestant had bet everything and lost on a stupid guess. "Oh, I'm sorry, that won't be possible. We're very protective of John's privacy."

"Oh yes, I understand." And Raleigh did. She should just say it. *I'm latent, too.* . . . Get the woman's sympathy. And . . . she couldn't do it. Even now she had to keep that secret. "Maybe another time," she finished, because this was a contact she very much wanted to cultivate. "Thank you so much for taking the time to speak with me. Can I ask what's next for you?"

"A trip to L.A., I think. My production company is developing a couple of projects. I can't say any more than that—you'll just have to tune in."

"I'll do that."

Raleigh pulled a collection of photos from the archives at *Aces!*, dated from the late seventies and early eighties, when Aurora and whoever her father was would have been together. Many of them were publicity shots from her various movies and stage plays, often showing her arm-in-arm with her handsome co-stars. Others were candid shots at red-carpet events or after-hours parties. Aurora had done a lot of those, it seemed. Wild Card Day dinners at Aces High from years gone by, seventies disco fashion on full display. For a brief period, Manhattan's most public aces had flaunted skin-tight jumpsuits with flared bell bottoms. There was a blog topic: ace fashion disasters.

The criteria for men who might be her father still stood: they had to be wild card positive, and to have contributed to Raleigh's brown complexion. She tried to find as much information as she could. When she went to her mother, she wanted to have ammunition.

Aurora had been photographed on Raul Julia's arm at the Tony Awards the year he'd been nominated for *The Threepenny Opera*. Raleigh daydreamed for a moment about a discovering a long-lost Puerto Rican family. Unfortunately, he'd passed away in 1994, so she couldn't just go ask him.

Aurora had seemed to know just about everyone with any connection to show business in New York in the seventies. Raleigh found pictures of her with Sidney Poitier, Richard Roundtree, Morgan Freeman, Stevie Wonder, Sly Stone, and a dozen or so others who Raleigh would have been thrilled to discover were her father. But if any of them had the virus, they'd kept it secret.

It was easy to spin out fantasies. Fairy tales with no basis in fact, no evidence to support them. Tabloid fodder, not serious journalism.

But then, she'd had a lot of practice spinning fairy tales about the wild card.

If her card turned, when her card turned, if . . . maybe it wasn't the death sentence everyone treated it as. Maybe she'd be an ace. She'd been just a kid, six or so, when she really understood what being latent meant, when she was able to read the engraving on her MedicAlert bracelet and ask pointed questions. Her mother hadn't sugarcoated it. "You need to know what might happen, so if something happens . . . you'll know what it is." Effervescent, dramatic Aurora had been very serious for these discussions.

But Raleigh had been sure she'd be an ace someday. Cyclone's daughter was an ace, wasn't she? They even had the same powers. Maybe Raleigh would have beautiful shimmering lights like her mother, maybe she'd be able to fly like Peregrine . . . except maybe she would have whatever power her father had. And she didn't know who he was, what his powers were, if he even had powers.

And maybe she wouldn't get powers at all, when her card turned. For about six months during her teen years, she'd refused to speak to her mother at all except to yell about how irresponsible she was, how could she possibly think of having a child and basically condemning that child to a horrible, awful death or disfigurement. In hindsight, Raleigh understood a little better. Aurora had played the odds. Took a chance.

Child Raleigh had been sure she'd turn an ace. Adult Raleigh wanted to discover a secret Hollywood romance between her parents. No harm in dreaming, right?

A few other candidates were probably more likely. A photo showed a really buff black guy in an ACLU press-release photo: Mordecai Jones, the Harlem Hammer, one of the world's strongest aces. He didn't move in show business circles; Raleigh had no evidence that he and her mother knew each other. But she kept him on the list of possibilities. Another photo featured a striking black man in an impeccable suit, with two impossibly gorgeous women wearing skintight cheongsams standing on either side of him. Neither was Aurora. This was Fortunato, who ran a notorious prostitution ring and battled the archvillain the Astronomer for the fate of the planet, once upon a time. He'd retired. Raleigh wasn't sure Aurora had ever met him, but then again there were those crazy Aces High Wild Card dinners. He was John Fortune's father. He went in the "maybe" file.

The men in the next two pictures weren't celebrities. These pictures hadn't appeared in the *Aces!* gossip and events columns. Outtakes, they'd been filed in the archives. But Aurora was in them both, with men whom Raleigh had never seen before.

One was labeled as entertainment lawyer Graham Carter, a well-built black man with no obvious wild card powers or features, but who seemed at home at the Wild Card Day party at Aces High where the photo had been taken. He and Aurora were laughing at a joke. Her hand was on his shoulder, his arm presumably on her back. Was this flirting or something more?

The second photo must have been at some nightclub. There was booze everywhere, everyone in the crowd had a glass in hand, a disco ball and flashing lights seemed to distort the image with lighting effects, but Aurora was at the center of a crowd of men and women, her arm around one man, kissing another. Again, Raleigh had no way of knowing what was actually going on here. But one of the men had what looked like a lizard's tail sprouting out from the back of his jeans.

At some point, Raleigh was going to have to start talking to people.

The next time Raleigh had dinner with her mother, Aurora was very impressed that she had interviewed the mighty Peregrine, even if it was just over the phone.

"You guys must have known each other back in the day," Raleigh said. "Hung out together at all?"

Aurora shook her head, chewing salad and scooping up the next forkful. "Not so much. She was on the way up when I was on the way down. Pretty young thing like her wouldn't have much to do with me. My God, the first time we met I was in my *thirties*." She smiled, and Raleigh was glad her mother could laugh at these things now, at least a little. "Though I did get a spot on the *Perch* once, when I was in that play with Dustin Hoffman." Aurora paused a moment, remembering. "She was very nice. I've never heard anything otherwise about her."

"She seemed nice, yeah."

"And I just want to point out that along with having a cute baby in the prime of my career, I did the 'legally change my name to a one-name name' thing before she did. Nobody ever gives me credit for that one, either."

Raleigh smirked at her. "Sure thing, Mom."

Aurora paused for a sip of wine. Then, "I like this. It seems like you don't get home for dinner much anymore."

"I've been busy," Raleigh said neutrally.

"Busy, hmm."

Raleigh set her fork down. "Mom."

"It's just I would like to meet this boy you've been spending so much time with. Maybe we could all go out to dinner sometime."

Raleigh resisted the urge to reflexively argue. Asked herself why she was so resistant to introducing Gavin to her mother. Because . . . because . . . no, she wasn't embarrassed by Aurora. She'd brought plenty of friends home to meet her, everything had been fine then. So what was different? Besides the fact that she was sleeping with him . . .

Maybe that was it. They'd meet, it would come out that he had powers, and Aurora would say something. Raleigh still hadn't told Gavin she was latent, and the longer she waited the harder it would be. Because after this much time, it definitely looked like she was keeping it secret. And when Aurora and Gavin finally met, if they met . . .

Raleigh wasn't ready for it. She just wasn't.

"We'll see," she said offhandedly, hoping not to sound too stressed out about it. "I'm sure we can work something out. If you're sure you're ready to meet him." If Raleigh was ready . . .

"Sounds serious," Aurora said.

"So . . . speaking of relationships," she started carefully. "I have a couple of questions for you."

"Is this about your father?" Aurora leaned back in her chair and narrowed her gaze.

"I mean how can you *not* know? Didn't you even try to figure it out?"

Her gaze went distant. "Maybe I didn't want to. Maybe . . . I didn't want to share you. Are you sure you really need to know this?"

In fact, she wasn't. And she didn't. She'd made it this far without knowing, hadn't she? Would knowing change anything? It was like daydreaming about becoming an ace. It was just daydreaming.

"Don't you want to find out if I have some gigantic inheritance waiting for me?"

Aurora glared at her over the rim of her wineglass. "If there was a gigantic inheritance involved I'd have tracked the man down myself."

Raleigh leaned in. "I have a list. You don't even have to say anything. I'll say a name and you just, like, nod or something if it's even a possibility." In other words, which of the men on this rather long list had she, in fact, slept with during the appropriate window. Once again, Raleigh wondered if she really wanted to know, and plowed ahead.

Aurora poured a new glass of wine, almost to the rim. "All this hard-hitting journalism has gone to your head."

"You bet it has."

"All right. Go."

The first few she threw out were pretty firm "no"s. They were something like controls. Get her mother's reaction on an absolute negative, so she could better judge the positives.

"Okay. Hiram Worchester?"

"No, honey," Aurora said, rolling her eyes a little as if to say she would flirt with the man, but never more. Especially given what had happened to him over the last decade. The once brilliant, ebullient restaurateur and gravity-controlling ace had been convicted of manslaughter in 1989.

"Okay. Jack Braun?"

"Oh give me some credit, won't you?"

Yeah, Raleigh had been pretty sure that was a negative. "The Harlem Hammer?"

Aurora shook her head. "I never met him. I don't think he was really into parties."

"Charles Dutton?"

Her brow furrowed. "How'd you come up with him?"

It wasn't a no. . . . "I found a picture of you two together. At a fund-raising gala at the Bowery Dime Museum in 1979?" In the photo, Aurora stood close to Dutton, one of Jokertown's more prominent businessmen, a tall man enveloped in a black cloak and hood, his face obscured by a simple white mask, à la Phantom of the Opera. Her mother had been smiling; it was impossible to judge the man's expression. The Bowery Wild Card Dime Museum cost a lot more than a dime these days, but the museum still ran on its cheesy displays and waxworks depicting wild card history. A waxwork of Aurora had been part of the Hall of Beauty for a few years.

"Oh, I do remember that—that was a fun night. But me showing up in a picture with someone doesn't make him your father."

Raleigh shrugged. "All I really know about my father is he probably isn't white and he has the virus. And I don't know, something about the picture made me think you liked each other."

"He was polite. I was a flirt. He'd think it was hilarious that he made your list."

"But that's a no."

"No."

Raleigh was almost disappointed. Now, there would have been a story. . . . "Next name. Raul Julia?"

Aurora seemed startled. "Wait—did he have the virus? I never heard that."

"Mom. Are you telling me you slept with Raul Julia?"

"I don't think he can be your father. Timing's off."

"Mom—"

"Next name."

"Fortunato?"

Aurora sighed wistfully. "I would have, if he'd even looked twice at me, which he didn't."

"Mom!"

She sat back and imperiously waved a hand. "Who's next?"

For the next ones, Raleigh brought the pictures and set them out on the counter. The entertainment lawyer, and the anonymous partiers she hadn't been able to find names for. All the pictures had been taken at various show business and Broadway parties in the year before Raleigh's birth.

Her mother touched both photos. Picked them up and studied them. Smiled with what seemed to be sadness. "I don't think I realized that anyone was even taking pictures those nights. I guess I should have known. When those photographers start following you around, they really follow you. You know I miss it sometimes? At least you know you're a marketable thing, when the paparazzi show up."

"You really were a total flirt, weren't you?"

"Oh yes I was," she said, unapologetically.

"So which of these guys did you sleep with?"

"All three of them." She shrugged. "Not at once. Different times."

"But close together."

"Yeah . . ." That sigh was definitely wistful. "I was on a bit of streak that year, wasn't I? Anyway, by the time I knew you were on the way, I guess I was embarrassed. I didn't get in touch with any of them, and I decided it didn't really matter—I was going to march into the next part of my life without a backward glance. Just you and me, kid." She reached out, and Raleigh took her hand and squeezed.

"If you tell me to leave it, to not look for these guys, I'll forget all about it."

She studied the pictures again, then looked at Raleigh. "You really need to know, don't you?"

She didn't *need* to. She'd gotten this far without knowing. But those secrets would always nag. . . . "I kind of do, yeah."

"All right, then. Go be an intrepid reporter and tell me what you come up with."

Raleigh was never going to get through all of the archived files. She was reconciled to that. It was fine, perfectly all right to leave some stories for the next person. That left her to sort through and try to find the gems, or at least the ones she thought were gems. She took Peregrine's suggestion about the Jokertown Clinic's Dr. Finn, and was surprised to find a connection to him in one of the files she'd already picked out. A tale straight from Hollywood with all the drama she could wish for—and like so many of the others, she didn't quite believe it, which made it worth tracking down. With Dr. Finn, there was an eyewitness to those events right here in New York.

Dr. Bradley Finn, the joker chief of staff at the Blythe van Renssaeler Memorial Clinic in Jokertown, was startling if you didn't know what to expect. He really was a centaur, with the torso of a white man, around fifty years of age, with graying hair and a collection of laugh and worry lines in about equal number, and the body and legs of a palomino pony. His tail was neatly braided; his hooves were covered in protective rubberized booties. He wore a garish blue and yellow Hawaiian shirt under his lab coat, and specially designed trouser scrubs.

"Thanks for meeting with me, Doctor," Raleigh greeted him. He'd taken her to a small conference room, clean and spare. In the corner was a giant beanbag-type cushion, which he backed himself onto and used as a chair.

"I've got some arthritis and this is easier. Turns out a hip replacement might be a little problematic in my case." He smiled, full of good humor.

That was a whole other idea for a set of stories—when standard medical care wasn't. She had the best source of information right here. But that was an interview for another time.

She launched right in. "I've been working on a series of stories about the wild card virus and show business. I know this must seem like it's coming out of left field, but I wanted to talk to you about Grace Kelly and Stan Whitehorn-Humphries. I understand you actually knew them?" The pair at the center of the story had passed away in the mid-nineties, and Raleigh was sure this wasn't the first time she was going to regret that no one had gotten to Downs' files sooner.

At her question, Finn would either shut down and refuse to talk about that long-ago part of his life, or open up with the fond memories of it. He chuckled, shook his head, and she wasn't sure if that was good or bad. "That's a pretty good story, I have to admit," he said. "Wild cards and show business. That's a rabbit hole, for sure. How'd you dig up my name?"

She kept Peregrine out of it. "Your father, and some files in the archives at *Aces!*"

"Digger Downs put you up to this?"

"No sir, I'm getting into trouble all on my own."

He laughed, and she decided she liked the guy. "Can I ask you a couple of questions first? Your mother's Aurora, right? Yeah, I did a little homework on my own. Have you written any stories about her?"

"Not yet, but I want to. When I can get her in the right mood."

He leaned forward, laced his hands together, and she suddenly felt like a lab specimen. "This is a nosy question I have no right to ask, and my interest is purely medical and anything you say won't leave this room, I swear it. But given the circles Aurora moved in, is by any chance your father positive for the wild card, too?"

Her heart stumbled over a beat. *She* was supposed to be asking the questions here, her secrets weren't the interesting ones. But maybe . . . He was a doctor, right? He wouldn't tell anyone. And *why* didn't she want anyone to know again?

She waited too long to answer, and Finn nodded. "I'm going to take that as a yes."

Just like that, the secret was out. Her cheeks flushed with the revelation. "And . . ."

Joker, ace, something in between—or something not at all. "Latent," she said softly. First time she'd ever said it out loud to anyone but her mother and doctor. And the ceiling didn't fall down on her. It was almost a relief. Finn's expression remained kind, nonjudgmental. Professional.

"How has that been?" he asked cautiously.

"I mostly don't think about it."

Which wasn't entirely true. Downs had told her she wrote about Joker-town like a local. At one point, when she was in college, she'd scouted out apartments in the area, which was gentrifying around the edges and had a fascinating arts scene. She told herself she wanted to be in the middle of an up-and-coming neighborhood. She also told herself she might as well move there now, just in case. On the off chance she turned a joker.

She discovered herself playing with the chain of her bracelet. Finn glanced down at it, and she stopped, closing her hand in a fist. "You know about the plaid kidney theory?" he said. "Your card might have already turned and given you a plaid kidney. We'd never know unless you needed surgery. Some latents may not actually be latents, so maybe . . ." He shrugged. "Maybe you're right to not worry so much."

"How many latents are there? Do you have any statistics?"

"We can make guesses, based on infection rates and the number of sur-vivors. But we don't know for sure. We don't have good ways to track the difference between a latent turning their card versus a new infection."

She was furiously making notes. This was good stuff. "Can I quote you on this? Can I come back when I have more questions? Do you have any ar-ticles or something I can read?"

"You want to do a story?"

"Yeah, I kind of do," she said. "But after this one. I'm supposed to be ask-ing you about how you met Grace Kelly and Stan Whitehorn-Humphries."

"Then let's start with that."

A Face for the Cutting Room Floor

by Melinda M. Snodgrass

DUST FILTERED DOWN FROM the rafters, shaken loose by the grips who scurried like a tribe of apes along the ancient wood catwalks. It glittered and spun gold in the bright work lights. Bradley Finn stared mesmerized at the spinning motes and wished he'd spent less of the night drinking Tequila Sunrises down in Santa Monica.

Finn and the rest of the Myth Patrol were perched on a fabricated cliff. Below them sat the deck of the Argo. The nat actors, including the stars of *Jason and the Argonauts,* David Soul and Arnold Schwarzenegger, were back in their trailers sipping Evian and keeping cool. The excuse for keeping the jokers was that they were hard to light, and the D.P. wanted another crack at it.

Finn sighed and tried to find a more comfortable position on his platform, which wasn't easy since he was a pony-sized centaur. The action called for him to rear. He wasn't relishing the prospect. The wood didn't offer much traction for his hooves, and he'd left his rubber booties at home. Not that Roger Corman was going to let him wear booties in the shot.

So Bradley figured he was going to pitch backwards off the platform, fall twelve feet to the floor, break his back, and end up with a little wheeled cart so he could drag his back legs. There were five jokers in the cast, but the E.M.T. wasn't certified in joker medicine. Finn knew. He'd checked. Which meant he'd probably be dealing with any injuries to the Myth Patrol—unless he was the myth who was down.

It was a sweltering August day in southern California, and he could feel damp on the palomino hide along his flanks. The stink of rancid make-up, stale coffee and donuts just added to his joy. The big air conditioning unit on the roof of Sound Stage 17 came to life with a grind and a rumble that shook more dust out of the rafters.

Clops looked up from his copy of *Variety*. His single eye was magnified to the size of a goose egg behind the fold-down lens which was mounted on an old fashioned surgeon's headband. It was tough to be an actor when you were that nearsighted.

Of course Clops had other disadvantages—like being seven feet tall, and having only one eye in the center of his forehead. Finn thought.

"You realize that dust may have been around when Mary Pickford was a star," the cyclops said.

"I don't think Pickford was ever at Warner's," Goathead responded.

"Hmbruza #** muffel wanda," said Cleo. She was lying on her stomach while one of the snakes which sprouted from her head gave her a neck massage. Cleo, whose full name was Cleopatra Reza, was Turkish, didn't speak a word of English, but never let that stop her. She commented on everything. The other jokers just agreed with her, and so far none of the men had gotten slapped.

When Finn had first been introduced all he could think was that her parents must have hated her. *It would have been like naming me Seabiscuit,* Finn had thought, *and why Cleopatra and not Medusa?* Clops thought it was because Cleopatra had died from the bite of an asp, and because Cleo was breathtakingly beautiful while Medusa was so hideous that she turned men to stone. Finn had to admit that Cleo was very beautiful—if you could ignore the tangle of snakes growing out of her head.

"You know what I mean. This is historic. This sound stage was built in 1927," Clops said.

"Yeah, well, I wish we were on a new sound stage with real air conditioning that we didn't have to turn off for every shot," Goathead groused. Goathead was your basic asshole who never missed an opportunity to trash anything and everybody. Finn just wished he wouldn't cut at Clops, who was a gentle soul and completely star-struck. Clops had left his Kansas home at seventeen and headed west determined to be a star. *Except he was seven feet tall, and had one eye.*

Finn quashed the thought and glared at Goathead, hoping the other joker would correctly interpret the look as a *stop pissing on Clops's birthday cake.* Apparently he did, for Goathead muttered that he was hung-over, which for Goathead amounted to an apology. Cleo rattled off another of her incomprehensible comments.

The D.P. threw the lights, and there was a magnificent geyser of sparks from one transformer. Firemen rushed forward with extinguishers, but the sparks were all she wrote.

"Shit!"

"Fuck!"

"Hell."

"Damn!"

The curses rose from all over the stage, erupting from the D.P., the First A.D., the director's assistant, and Goathead. Finn got the assistant's attention. "Mary, can we please take a break?" Finn pleaded.

"Sure, go ahead. Nick, when do you want the Myths back?" she shouted at the D.P.

"Give me an hour."

Clops just climbed down the front of the plaster cliff. It wasn't that far for him. He then reached back up and, handling her as if she were made of spun glass, he lifted Cleo to the floor. She gave him her thousand-watt smile. *If only it weren't snakes,* Finn thought, and sighed.

Finn and Goathead had a ramp off the back of the cliff. Their hooves rang hollowly on the wood, and Finn felt the ramp sag under his weight. His stomach was suddenly too light, and heading for the back of his throat. Finn froze, waiting or the ramp to break. After a moment where nothing happened, Bradley resumed his cautious descent.

Once Finn was safely on the floor he trotted over to the craft services table. His stomach had been too off for breakfast and now he was starving. He surveyed the array. M&M's, stale donuts, Oreoes, peanut butter, jelly and bread. A jar of pretzels. Corman was known for being a tightwad. Finn decided to head over to sound stage 23 where his dad was shooting *The French Lieutenant's Woman.* Finn Senior kept an elaborate spread, but of course he was making a twelve-million-dollar extravaganza staring Grace Kelly and Warren Beatty, not a cheesy B action movie.

Finn slipped out the stage door, into the hazy but intense California sunshine. The white walls of the stages loomed like breakers on either side of the street. He kicked it into a lope, and went clattering past Teamsters tossing around footballs, (he got the usual calls of Hi Ho Silver, which was annoying because he was a palomino) past stars in their golf carts and lines of Star Waggons parked against the sides of the street. Spinning red lights indicated they were shooting on the various stages. There were a lot of lights. The movie business was booming.

He waited in front of his dad's stage until the light went out so he could enter the set. Pulling open the door, he stepped into a Victorian drawing room complete with dark wood, red velvet and innumerable knick knacks on every available surface. Grace Kelly, looking like a swaying calla lily in her white gown, was gliding off the set. Stan Whitehorn-Humphries, dapper in his bow tie and tweed jacket, was blotting her make-up as she walked.

She passed close by Finn, and he caught a scent of sweat under the perfume. It was somehow comforting to know that someone that beautiful was still human enough to perspire. Kelly stopped. Finn gaped at her. Stan, a smile lurking beneath the brush of his white mustache, gave a nod, and Finn realized his pony's ass was blocking the door. Muttering an apology, he swung his hindquarters out of the way. Kelly glided out, and Stan gave him a wink.

"You've just seen an example of what they mean by 'stunningly beautiful,'" Finn said to the elderly make-up artist.

"She is quite remarkable, isn't she?" Stan gazed for an instant at the closed door as if conjuring a picture of the star. "So who did your make-up? You look dead." Fifty years in Hollywood hadn't blunted his upper-class British accent. Of course it was an affectation after all this time, but no one cared. It was part of the legend of Stan Whitehorn-Humphries.

"I'm supposed to look scary," Finn said.

"Sorry, dead. Come over to the trailer after you get a bite and sup, and I'll touch you up." Whitehorn-Humphries walked away before Finn could thank him.

Finn cut through the set, admiring the design. Next week the production was scheduled to move to England for the exteriors. Finn would love to go along, but he badly needed to replenish his bank account before the fall semester. He glanced over to where his father was discussing the set-up for the next shot, and briefly wished his dad had been the typical Hollywood parent—just throw money at your kids and hope they don't embarrass you. But G. Benton Finn had clung to his mid-western roots, and believed his kid appreciated what he had to work for and disdained what he hadn't. He would pay for Bradley's medical school tuition, but if his son wanted to live away from home he had to swing it himself.

Finn stepped delicately over the snaking wires and cords, and got a glimpse of the craft service table. He broke into a smile. From here he could see salmon, cream cheese, bagels, fresh fruit, and an assortment of pastries and cookies. There was a gaggle of nat starlets gathered around the table—two blondes, a redhead and a brunette. The taffeta dresses hissed and crackled as they moved, and they were showing a lot of bosom for Victorians. *Still, with bosoms like that you didn't want to hide them.* These girls were stunners.

Finn briefly wondered if his father had ever availed himself of the casting couch. A moment's consideration, and Finn decided that Finn Senior probably had, but mom had sense enough to look the other way. There were a lot of temptations and vices in Tinsel Town. You picked the ones you could tolerate and lived with them.

"I looked it up, she was born in '28," one girl was saying, as Finn stepped over the final power cord.

"That means she's . . ." The brunette's brow furrowed.

"Fifty-two," said one of the blondes. She was tinier then her companions, and she reminded Finn of the figure in a music box, perfect in every detail. Then he got a look at her eyes.

A figurine constructed out of hard glass, he thought, as he waited for them to react to him. Jokers, even rich ones, learned to gauge a nat's reaction before approaching too close.

"She's got to be an ace," mumbled the brunette around a mouthful of cookie.

"It's illegal for them to be in professional sports," said the redhead. "They should have done that in Hollywood."

"Then Golden Boy couldn't have had a career," objected the zaftig blonde.

"Another good argument for banning wild cards," murmured the petite blonde dryly. Finn swallowed a chuckle. This girl was quick.

"Kelly's never said she's an ace," offered the brunette.

"Never said she isn't," countered the redhead.

"There's a blood test that will tell if you've got the wild card," mused the gimlet-eyed blonde, almost to herself.

The redhead picked a shrimp out of the melting ice and savagely chewed her way to the tail. "You'd think she'd want to move on." The girl bit off the words with the same force she had shown to the shrimp.

Again the tiny blonde answered. "Why? Why would she? She's been a star for thirty years. Every major role has been hers. Why quit?"

"So some of *us* could have a chance," said the brunette.

"I wouldn't do it," said the gimlet eyed blonde.

"Yeah, but we all know you'd kill your mother for a part," shot back the brunette.

The blonde gave her a look that clearly said, *And what's your point?*

This time Finn couldn't hold back the laugh. That did get their attention. The brunette and the zaftig blonde looked disgusted and walked hurriedly away. The redhead gave him a nervous smile, then made a show of checking the brooch watch which was part of her costume and hurried away. The tiny blonde held her ground.

He grabbed a plate and started loading up. "I'm sure you believed that watch really worked," remarked the blonde.

Finn lifted his shoulders and dropped them. "Hey, at least she pretended to have an excuse."

"You're Mr. Finn's son, aren't you?"

"The one and only."

"I'm Tanya."

Finn shook the proffered hand. "I'm Bradley Finn. Pleased to meet you."

"Well, I better go and walk off some of this," she indicated the table ". . . spread."

"It's really hot out there. It's not so bad when you're down by the beach. I was at Santa Monica last night, and it wasn't bad. It's always worse in the valley. I'm a native Angelino and we know to avoid the valley." Finn realized he was babbling. He tried to bite back the inane flow, only to have the worst of the inanities escape. "So, where do you live?"

"Oh, don't worry, Bradley, I've got the right area code and an acceptable Beverly Hills address. The casting directors call."

"I'm sure they do," and he knew there was no way that line was going to come across as anything but a leer. Bradley cringed. He'd grown up talking to actresses. He wasn't usually this gauche.

That's because your gonads are talking, you dope. And she thinks you're a freak so shut up!

She surprised him by saying, "I've never had a decent meal or good time in Santa Monica. Maybe I need native guide. Nice meeting you." She gave a little wave with the tips of her perfectly manicured fingernails and walked away.

A freak whose daddy is a director, Finn's cynical side amended.

Still, Finn figured he'd get her number. He was male and twenty-three, and she might be adventurous.

Finn came trotting down the sidewalk toward his Spanish bungalow apartment, and checked at the sight of the man standing in the shade of the trailing bougainvillea. It wasn't that he looked threatening. No one that short could be threatening. It was more the fact that he looked like a garden gnome.

The man's face was a full moon with the wide, surprised eyes of a child. A fringe of graying brown hair ringed a bald pate. An open-necked shirt revealed a mat of graying chest hairs mashed flat by a tangle of gold chains. The barrel chest was supported on an even broader belly. Finn noted the Rolex watch and the expensive slacks, then boggled at the sight of the high-topped red tennis shoes.

The man surged out from beneath the brilliant red flowers with the rolling gait of a sailor. "Harry Gold," he announced, and Finn found a card thrust into his hand.

Shiny slick red paper with the name embossed in gold and the title PRODUCER beneath the name.

"I don't have any input with my father on his projects," Finn said automatically.

"I don't want your dad . . . not that he isn't a great director, but I don't want him. I want you."

"I have an agent." Finn began sidestepping toward the safety of his front door.

"Of course you do. You're a savvy kid, but I knew he wasn't going to let me get near you," Gold replied. "So I decided to talk to you myself."

Far from being alarmed by this admission, Bradley found himself amused. He now had a pretty good idea of the kind of movies that Harry Gold produced. There was a bubble of laughter filling his chest. He forced it down, and propped his hindquarters on a nearby planter.

"That's right, take a load off, though it's gotta be easier with four than two," Gold said. "Where was I?"

"Wanting to talk to me."

"I don't want to just talk to you. I want you to star in my next film. What do you think of that?" The little man's chest puffed out like a satisfied pigeon's.

The devil was in Finn prompting him to ask, "A speaking role?"

"Absolutely. That's what makes you so perfect. You can talk."

"Harry, do you make porno movies?" Finn asked.

The little man drew himself up. "I make male art films."

Finn heaved himself back onto all four feet. "Thanks, but I'm not interested."

"I'll pay you *ten thousand dollars.*"

It was a ton of money for a porno flick. *And you'd get some,* said the bad Elmer Fudd who suddenly appeared on Finn's left shoulder. He pictured his father and mother's reaction. *How would they ever know?*

Because some teamster or grip would talk.

Finn hunched his shoulders, trying to dislodge his baser self. "Sorry, Harry, can't do it." He unlocked the door of his apartment.

"You've got to. You know how hard it is to train a real pony?" came the disconsolate cry as Finn closed the door.

"The frightening thing is that a woman would probably rather fuck a pony than a joker," Goathead said the next morning when Finn finished telling them about his meeting with Gold. They were in the extras' make-up area. Clops flushed to his eyebrow at the use of the profanity, and cocked his head significantly toward the joker woman seated nearby.

"What?" Goathead demanded. Clops cocked his head further this time and waggled his eyebrow. "Them? Hell, they don't want to fuck a joker either," Goathead said, upping the volume even further.

Finn sighed and looked up at the rafters. Goathead's attitude was definitely starting to wear thin. On the other hand, Goathead had grown up poor in Detroit while Finn had grown up in Bel Aire, a child of privilege blessed with parents who had never treated him as different. He had had playmates and girlfriends. . . .

And how many of them were with you because your daddy is a famous director? came the hateful little voice. They did always end up wanting to be "friends" and only one had ever put out, and Finn later heard she'd been busted in one of L.A.'s more notorious sex clubs.

Clops looked pained. "I don't think that's true. There are whole magazines about us." He held up a copy of *Aces* to prove his point. Goathead stuck a nicotine-stained finger under the title. "A. C. E. S.," he spelled. "Aces. You see a magazine called *Joker?!,* you dumb shit? No."

"Would you sit still?" the make-up man grumbled, trying to glue on Goathead's horns. Despite the legs and hooves of a goat, the joker lacked horns, and Corman wanted big horns on his satyr.

Clops shook his head. "I think women pick men because of what's on the inside, not on the outside."

"Oh, God you are such a goober," Goathead said. "And like how often are you getting any?" Clops flushed again and ducked his head. "Never? Right?"

The make-up man made a moue of distaste. "You're done. Go away." He made shooing motions with both hands, and Goathead went clattering away on his cloven hooves. Finn reflected that they were going to have to refinish the ancient wood floors after eight weeks of his and Goathead's hooves.

The terribly sweet boy who was doing Finn's make-up smoothed the foundation over his nose, and reached for the powder. "Did you hear about the commotion over on the *Lieutenant* set?" He punctuated every word with a little gusting breath.

Finn knew it was stupid. It was just a movie. But it was his dad's movie, so he felt his stomach clench down into a small tight ball. "What?"

"Somebody broke into the production offices last night."

Finn blinked. He had been prepared for a dead star, a fire on the set, lost film. "Was anything taken?"

"They don't think so. The file drawers were all open, and they found the petty cash box by the open window, but all the money was there."

It was an odd enough occurrence that Bradley decided to talk to his dad when the *Argonauts* broke for lunch.

There was a cafeteria on the Warner's lot where extras, day players and the below-the-line people went to eat. The food was plentiful and cheap. You would often see writers in there, which said something about the self-image of Hollywood writers.

Then there was The Warner's Restaurant—table clothes, linen napkins, wines and gourmet food. This was where the powerful "did lunch." Finn swung on down the street to the entrance to that restaurant. Steps led up to the etched glass doors. The doors opened out, and he had to lower his hindquarters down a step to make room for the swing of the door. Eventually he was inside. They had just repainted the place in azure blue and cream with pale blue upholstery on the furniture. Beneath the scent of fresh cut gardenias in a vase on the maitre d's desk there was the tang of newly dried paint.

Tony, the Maitre d', grinned. "Hear you been slumming over at the cafeteria."

Finn slapped his gut beneath the Hawaiian shirt. "I couldn't take too many more gourmet meals and keep my boyish figure. Dad here?"

Tony indicated the direction with a cock of his head. "Corner right."

"Thanks."

Finn minced his way between the tables, exchanging hellos with various actors, directors, producers and studio heads. He had practically grown up on this lot, and in fact been the focus of a law suit between Disney and Warner's in the late fifties. Warner's had used Finn in some of their promotional material, and Disney had screamed infringement of trademark, citing *Fantasia*. Since Finn had been two at the time, he wasn't sure how it had all been resolved. He just knew it was a favorite dinner tale of his father's.

His dad was eating with Ester Flannigan, the most perfect of personal assistants. There was a slight frown on his long, lantern-jawed face, and he seemed to be talking more than he was eating. Which meant Ester was taking shorthand instead of eating. Finn came up behind her, placed his hands on her shoulders, and gave her a kiss on one wrinkled cheek. "Doesn't the union have something to say about working through lunch?"

Benton Finn looked down at their virtually untouched plates and gave Ester an apologetic smile. "Sorry, we'll finish this after lunch."

"What's got your shorts in a twist?" Finn asked as he swiped a cherry tomato off his dad's salad plate. He bit down and savored the tart/sweet explosion. He swallowed and added, "The break in?"

"So it's all over the lot, is it?" Finn asked.

"I don't know. It's at Corman's."

"It's all over the lot," Ester broke in. "Jenny called to ask about it, and she's over in the bungalows."

"Why is this a deal?" Finn asked. "Nothing was stolen."

"Because everything on *Lieutenant* has to go smoothly and if you look close enough at any production you'll find problems, and Coppola will use it," Ester said in singsong voice while Benton glared at her.

Finn gave his dad a look. "Wow, you are being paranoid."

"Coppola wanted this movie, and Bernie told me Coppola told the Chairman I didn't know how to pull something new and fresh out of Kelly. Kelly doesn't need to be new and fresh. She just needs to be Kelly."

"You've directed her in three other films. These other guys don't know how to work with someone from that generation," Finn soothed.

Ester closed her eyes briefly, then mouthed to Finn *wrong thing to say*.

"Meaning what?" Benton asked low and cold. "That I'm also from that generation so I know how?"

"No, that you're a gentleman and Kelly is a real lady," Finn babbled, and hoped his dad would accept this statement of the public's view of Kelly even though everyone in the industry knew she slept with every hot young star who came along. "These young . . . er, new guys don't know how to work with someone like that."

Benton looked mollified. "You're sure right about that. These new guys are punks. They have no respect for the institutions. . . ."

Finn cocked a back foot for greater comfort and settled in to listen. He also helped himself to the sole almondine on his dad's plate.

Finn heard the sharp clatter of high heels on concrete, and suddenly an arm was slipped beneath his. The redhead from the *Lieutenant* set had attached herself limpet-like to his side.

"Hi." The word emerged on a puff of coffee-scented breath. "Sorry I had to run off back there. By the way, I'm Julie."

"Pleased to meet you," Bradley said.

He waited to see if Red would ask for his name, but apparently she had discovered that the joker with the pony's body was the director's son, and she wasn't bright enough to realize that she needed to pretend that she hadn't. Finn had long ago stopped being angry over these sudden shifts in attitude from eager young starlets. What he hadn't totally resolved was whether to laugh or cry about them.

"So, are you in the business?" she asked as she tried to adjust her steps to match Finn's length of stride.

"No, not really." He watched the glow of interest in her eyes die. "I'm in medical school." A touch of interest returned. *So we've established what motivates you, Julie. Looks like . . . money. Which is probably good because you sure can't act.*

"So, how do you like it out here as compared to the Bronx?" Bradley asked.

Julie pouted. "Oh, pooh! I've been working so hard to lose the accent."

In your dreams, baby. "And you have," Finn said diplomatically. "It's more intuition. Native Angelinos are few and far between."

"So you were born like . . . here," the girl suddenly amended.

"Yeah, born at the Hollywood Presbyterian hospital. Went to Hollywood High. And I expressed my wild card moments after birth. Which was good, because if it had happened in the birth canal I would have killed my mother, and that would have really sucked." He smiled at her brightly. She blanched at the image his words had elicited. Which showed she had some imagination.

"So it sounds like you really know the ropes here, and that's good because I could sure use some advice." It was the dogged delivery of a rehearsed line, whether it fit into the conversational flow or not. It also made it very clear relationship she envisioned—friend, mentor, confidant.

"Sure," Finn answered. "My cards are in my briefcase on the *Jason* set. I just keep a wallet in my pocket." He tapped the breast pocket on his Hawaiian shirt. Julie's eyes flicked toward his gleaming palomino haunches.

Years ago the sisters at his elementary school had forced him to wear pants. His father had declared that Finn looked like a bad clown act, and they'd found another school. Finn was careful to keep his penis sheathed, but nothing could hide his balls, and even pony sized they were still the envy of every male and a terror to most women.

"Why don't you come back after shooting, and I'll get you a card." His bad angel prodded him to add. "We could have dinner."

"Uh, I'm busy tonight. Sorry. I'll get the card . . . later." She glanced hastily at her wristwatch. "Well, gotta go." She gave him a perky smile, waved, and hurried off between the stages.

Finn allowed himself a laugh. It felt a little hollow.

The next day Corman was shooting coverage on Jason and his merry band of Argonauts. Finn decided to use the free time to head down to U.C.L.A, and buy his books for the fall semester. He enjoyed medical school, but it seemed like the summer had just started, and he wasn't quite ready for the grind yet.

He stood between tall bookcases, his arms stretched around a giant stack of books, squinting at the class list perched on top, and realized he only had half the required texts. He wondered if he could make it to the front of the store for a cart, or if he should just leave the books here and come back. But there had only been one copy of the epidemiology text, and some bastard would probably swipe it if he left them.

"Man, these suckers are *heavy*," a voice suddenly said. Startled, Finn let out a yell and dropped the precariously balanced stack of books.

Harry Gold was peering around a bookcase like a malevolent leprechaun. He stepped around the case, and began to gather up the strewn books. "You shouldn't try to carry these things. You'll herniate yourself. You should get a cart."

"Thanks," Finn gritted.

Gold had stopped stacking, arrested by the picture of Dr. Tachyon on the back flap of his introductory text on Joker Medicine. "I hear this guy is a real stud, but he sure looks like a poufftah," Gold said. "I tried to make a movie about the Four Aces back in the fifties, but Universal shut me down because of their movie. Actually it worked out great because after their movie came out I could do a parody and they couldn't touch me. The *Four Deuces*, Golden Hotdog, the Enema, Cock Tease and Black Stallion." Gold smiled fondly at the memory. He picked up another book and did an elaborate double take at the price. "Seventy-five bucks? These suckers are expensive."

"Yes, and heavy," Finn said.

"Look, I've been thinking about it, and now that I see the kind of expenses you got I realize I wasn't being fair. I'll give you *twelve thousand dollars* to be in my movie."

"Mr. Gold. I don't want to be in your movie. I'm not an actor. . . ."

"I can teach you."

"Look, Mr. Gold, I was trying to be polite. I'm not interested in being in a porno movie. I couldn't face my family, my friends, and. . . ."

"You could wear a mask." Gold was charmed with the idea. "Yeah, like Zorro. . . ."

It was hard to get out the words past the laughter. "Like nobody would recognize my big palomino ass bouncing up and down on the screen. How many joker centaurs do you think there are?"

"One. Which is why I need you. Look, I specialize in wild card porn. I got guys with double dicks, and gals with three boobs, but you're unique."

"Goodbye, Mr. Gold."

Finn took the joker medicine text out of the producer's hands and set it on the top of the stack. He slowly bent his forelegs until he was resting on his knees and picked up the pile of books.

"You're being very unreasonable about this," Gold grumbled. "I'm telling you ponies are a pain in the ass."

I'm sure your star would think so too, Finn thought, but successfully resisted the impulse to say it. Instead he replied, "So get two guys and a horse suit."

"That would look cheesy," Harry complained.

Like your movie won't? Finn thought, but he didn't say that either.

Benton Finn was footing the bill for a bon voyage party at City, one of L.A.'s more trendy restaurants down on Melrose Boulevard. Personally Bradley hated the place. It bowed to the new trend in interior design, which decreed there should be no color, no fabric, no softness and no warmth. There were concrete walls and floors, exposed pipes in the ceiling, gleaming metal track lighting, and black metal tables. The wealth of hard surfaces amplified every sound, so forks connecting with china became a hailstorm, the drone of conversation a roar, and the background music an irritating beat with no discernible melody. Worse, from Finn's point of view, was the footing. The floor offered no traction so he was forced to wear his booties, and while they were practical he thought they looked dorky, especially with a French cuffed shirt, tuxedo jacket and black bow tie.

He spotted Julie sitting with the same group of females from the set. Since two of the four had indicated they would tolerate him he decided to head over. The plump blonde spotted him first, grabbed up her plate and bolted for the buffet. Finn found himself watching her behind in the satin sheath dress and thought nastily a *few more runs to the chow line and she'll be vying for the Shelly Winters roles.*

Julie gave him a too bright, too large smile, Tanya coolly surveyed him, and the brunette eyed him nervously but this time held her ground.

"EVENING LADIES," Finn bellowed.

"HI," Julie shouted back. The brunette's mouth opened and closed, but he couldn't hear what she said. Tanya just inclined her head with the air of a queen. Again Finn felt respect for the girl. She knew how to avoid looking ridiculous.

Finn bent at the waist and put his lips close to Julie's ear. "Who's your friend?" He indicated the brunette with a jerk of his chin.

Julie turned to place her mouth near his ear. Wisps of hair tickled his nose and cheek. He could smell the hair spray. "Anne," Julie replied.

"Hi, Anne." Finn waved at the brunette. She gave him a tense smile.

"Nice party."

It wasn't that he heard her, but years at these events had taught him a form of ESP crossed with lip reading. It was the safest and most inane thing the brunette could say so Bradley suspected that was what she had said. He gave her a broad smile and nodded enthusiastically.

Tanya was watching him. The intensity of her gaze was such that he found himself looking at her rather than at Julie, who was trying to talk with him. Since he was only catching one word in four, it wasn't working. Tanya lifted her champagne glass, quirked an eyebrow at him, and jerked her head toward the bar. Finn nodded. He makes his excuses to Julie. From her expression when he walked away he gathered she hadn't gotten the drift.

Tanya led him around the bar where it dovetailed into a corner. Amazingly it was almost quiet in the cubbyhole. Finn looked around at the rows of glittering bottles, and the racked glasses hanging like bulbous stalactites. A short hallway ran past them leading to the bathrooms. It made for an odd mixed smell of spilled beer and toilet bowl freshener.

"How did you know about this?"

"Used to tend bar here," Tanya answered.

"A woman of many talents." Finn cringed again.

Tanya gave him a smile. Her lips quirked up higher on one side than the other which gave her a gamin look. "You really keep walking into them, don't you?"

"Sorry, I'm not usually this gauche."

"Should I take that as a compliment?" Tanya asked.

"Yes. You're quite beautiful and you fluster me."

"Good. Can you fluster your dad for me?"

Finn was disappointed. He'd thought this girl might avoid the worst of the actress clichés. He realized she was watching him very closely with a measuring expression.

"Is this a test?" Finn asked.

"Yeah. I figured I'd do it for Julie and save both of you the embarrassment."

"I never use the relationship on anyone's behalf."

Tanya pulled down a bottle of scotch and poured a couple of fingers into her champagne glass. "I'll pass the word."

"Guess this means I won't be hearing from her," Finn said.

"Oh cut the crap. If you really want to connect with women that way you'd be making promises whether you could keep them or not."

Grace Kelly came gliding down the hall from the bathrooms. Stan followed a few steps behind. He was shoving a small make-up case back into his shoulder bag. The elderly make-up artist made himself unobtrusive and slipped away along the back wall. Kelly gave Finn and Tanya a smile, then swept on and rejoined Harrison Ford at their table. She had arrived with the actor, so Finn figured the fling with Beatty was over. Finn looked back down at Tanya and found her staring across the room at Stan Whitehorn-Humphries where he sat alone at a small table.

"So, you want to dance?" Finn asked.

Tanya kept looking at Stan. "I don't think either of us want to look that absurd." It stung, but Finn had to admit it was an accurate assessment. "Actually I think I'm just about funned out. See you around, Bradley."

She waved her fingertips and slipped away. Finn looked back at Stan. The Englishman was watching Kelly. His expression was both fond and regretful. Stan had never married. Finn now thought he knew why. Bradley looked from Kelly glowing and radiant as she leaned against Ford's shoulder, to the withered old man who watched her with such longing. They were separated by a vast gulf of age and status and it wasn't going to be bridged. Finn glanced back along the length of his horse body. He looked at all the pretty girls. Suddenly he was all funned out too.

Three days later Finn had a late call, four p.m. He parked his van, and backed the length of the stripped interior and out the rear doors. There was a tendril of smoke hanging over the hills of Griffith Park, and the hot Santa Ana winds carried the acrid scent of burning.

The high walls of the sound stages blocked out the wind, and Finn's shirt was soon sticking to his back. He trotted toward stage 23, and stopped dead when he saw the knots of people hanging around in the street. The small groups would split apart and coalesce in new configurations. Cigarettes were being nervously puffed, flipped onto the pavement and crushed. New ones were lit. Finn knew what this looked like. It looked like trouble.

Edgar Burksen, Finn Senior's favorite director of photography, was pacing in small circles outside the stage door. Finn joined him.

"Hi, what's up?" Finn asked the Dutchman. "Warren shut down the production?" The rising star was known for his insistence on perfection.

"No, Kelly."

Finn goggled. In all the long years of her career the actress had never shut down a production. "What happened?"

"We don't know. She won't come to the stage. She won't let your father in the trailer." The D.P. gave a very European shrug.

A big black limo came nosing down the street and stopped almost at the door of Kelly's trailer. The driver climbed out and knocked. The door of the enormous Star Waggon abruptly swung open and with such force that it slammed against the metal side of the trailer. Everyone jumped, then stared as Grace Kelly emerged.

Her head and neck were swathed in scarves and enormous sunglasses hid her eyes. She almost jumped the two feet separating the trailer from the limo, and dove into the back seat. The back door was closed, the driver took his place and the car rolled away. Nothing could be seen through the darkly tinted windows.

Everyone released a pent up breath and began talking at once. Finn stared at Edgar. "She looks like Marilyn dodging the press," Finn said.

"At least with Marilyn you knew why she was shutting you down—pills and booze," Edgar said. "This is just a glamour fit."

"About what?" Finn asked.

"Stan didn't show up to work today, and she won't let anyone else do her make-up," Edgar explained.

"Did somebody check on him?"

"Your dad sent a P.A. over to his house. He wasn't there."

There was a tingle of concern down the length of Finn's human back and into his horse back. It manifested in his white tail beginning to swish madly. "Or he couldn't answer. Stan's seventy if he's a day."

"We can't exactly break in," Edgar answered.

"Does he have family?"

Edgar gave the shrug again.

Finn felt really bad. Because Benton had directed so many Grace Kelly movies, and because Stan was her preferred make-up artist, Finn had gotten to know the English émigré pretty well. He had always treated Finn with courtesy and respect, and not just because of who his dad was or how much money they had. Finn hoped the old man hadn't had a stroke or a heart attack. Finn glanced at his watch, and realized he was late for his call.

"Keep me posted," he said to Edgar and kicked it into a gallop.

"Coppola has already been over to Diller's office telling him that he knows how to handle a real star. That he's an 'actors director.'" Finn senior provided the quotes with his fingers, then twisted his lips in disgust.

"Be sure to seed the cucumbers," Alice Finn said, as she bustled past Finn where he stood chopping salad fixings at the marble cutting board. "They give your father gas."

"I'm discussing the eminent end of my career, and you're discussing cucumbers?" Benton Finn demanded.

Alice paused to kiss her husband on the top of the head, "Actually your reaction to them," she said, and headed across expanse of marble floor to the oven.

The family was gathered in the giant kitchen of the Bel Aire house. Black granite counters stretched out in all directions like an alien monolith. There were two ovens, a convection oven, a microwave oven, and an open hearth rotisserie. The refrigerator was hidden behind cherry wood panels, and glass-fronted cabinets threw back the light from the track lighting. It looked like a movie set, but for the incongruity of a battered Formica breakfast table with cheap chrome chairs which sat in the bay window of the breakfast nook. Benton Finn was seated at the old table morosely drinking wine.

"So what is the deal with Stan?" Finn asked as he sprinkled on dressing. The pungent scent of vinegar and pepper made him sneeze.

"God bless you," said his mother placidly.

"Who knows?" Benton replied. "The cops say they can't enter the house until he's been missing twenty-four hours. By then my career will have ended."

"By then Stan might be dead if he's fallen or had a stroke," Finn said.

Benton flushed. "Look, I'm worried about Stan too, but I've got two hundred people working for me. . . ."

"Would you get the butter, dear?" Alice sang out to her husband as she pulled the pot roast out of the oven.

Benton started for the refrigerator. The phone rang. Benton answered it. "Grace, my God, we've been so worried. . . ." His voice broke off abruptly, and he began listening intently. Finn stood holding the salad. Alice held the roast. The aroma of roasted potatoes and gravy filled the room. It was so quiet in the room that Finn could hear the tick of the grandfather clock in the hallway.

"I don't think Dr. Tachyon is the right choice," Benton finally said. "You're not a wild card." Benton listened again. "You think you caught it this morning?" His father rolled a desperate eye at Finn.

Finn shook his head. What the actress was describing was virtually impossible. If she had somehow caught a spoor she'd be dead . . . or a joker. Which might explain her demand for Tachyon.

"Look, I'll try to get him here, but it'll take a day. . . ." There was obviously some kind of explosion from the other end of the line, because Benton broke off abruptly. His father was nodding, muttering *uh huh, uh huh;* finally Benton blurted out, "My son is in medical school. Specializing in wild card medicine. Let me have him take a look at you."

I'm going to lose my license before I ever get it. Finn thought.

"Okay, just hang tight," Benton was saying. "We'll be right over." The director hung up the phone, and headed past his wife and son. "Let's go," he snapped to Finn.

"Dad, I'm starting my *second year* of medical school. I barely know how to find the pancreas."

"And dinner's ready," Alice protested.

Benton didn't pause. He slammed out the pantry door into the garage. Finn heard the whine of the garage door going up. He looked at his mother and shrugged. The horn of the van started blaring in sharp staccato honks. Finn put the salad on the table, and headed out.

"Oh . . . Holy . . . Shit . . . !!"

It probably wasn't the most diplomatic thing his father could have said, and it had the effect Finn expected. Grace Kelly started to cry.

The tears went washing down her cheeks, catching in the net of wrinkles around her eyes and racing down the crevasses on either side of her mouth. It wasn't that the wrinkles were so deep; what was shocking was that they were there at all. From her debut role in *Fourteen Hours* in 1951 she had never changed. At least not physically. Her acting had become more elegant and nuanced, but the perfect face had retained the smoothness of porcelain. With other actresses of her generation it was apparent the wrinkles were being tucked away beneath their hairline. Not with Grace. She was perpetually twenty-two.

Now she was fifty-one. A beautiful fifty-one, but not the stunning ingénue currently staring in *The French Lieutenant's Woman.*

Benton Finn was staring blindly at the far wall of the living room of the Los Feliz mansion. He was unconsciously combing his hair with his fingers. Grace, huddled on the curved sofa, pulled out a handkerchief and blew her nose. Finn shifted his weight from foot to foot to foot to foot, his hooves sinking in the plush beige carpet. He wondered how long the silence was going to last.

"Is this the wild card?" Benton finally rasped out.

Finn and Kelly's eyes met. Her expression was desperate pleading. She drew in a shaky breath and said, "No."

"Then why the hell did you want Tachyon?" the director asked.

"I was hoping he might know an ace or a shot or something that could . . . fix me. Give me back my youth."

Now it was Benton's turn to give his son the desperate look. "Do you think there is such a thing?" he asked.

"No." Finn looked at Kelly. "I'd say Ms. Kelly had the market on the Fountain of Youth cornered."

"So what the hell happened?" Benton demanded. He swiped his hand through his hair again. It looked like a gray/blond haystack.

Finn thought furiously. It couldn't be a substance or others would have discovered it. Kelly's demand for Tachyon indicated it was wild card related. Which meant it had to be . . .

"*Stan!*" Finn blurted. "It's Stan, isn't it?"

Kelly stared at him with the air of deer caught in the headlights, bit her lip, and finally nodded.

His father stared at him, his brow furrowed in confusion. Benton pointed at Kelly's face. "No make-up man is this good." Kelly gave a gusty sob and held the sodden handkerchief to her eyes.

"He is if he's a wild card," Finn replied. He looked back at Kelly. "I'm right, aren't I?"

The actress nodded. "We met on the set of *High Noon*. I had been out too late the night before. I asked him to cover the shadows. He gave me this smile." The woman also smiled at the memory. "He leaned in close to me, and whispered he'd make them vanish. And he did." She twisted the handkerchief between her fingers. "He's been with me ever since. On every film."

"So where is he?" Benton asked.

"I don't know," Kelly wailed.

"Have you checked his house?" Finn asked. Kelly's eyes slid away.

"How could she?" Benton asked. His voice had lost the stridency of a few minutes before and he was taking on the director's smooze tone.

"Because the effect obviously doesn't last very long, which means he's got to be doing her make-up before every date, every preview, every meeting. She probably has a key to his house." Finn wasn't a director and didn't need to coddle stars. He simply laid it out baldly.

Kelly didn't relish the tone. She gave him a dirty look. "He's not there. His car's there but he's gone."

"Was the door locked or unlocked?" Finn had often been an extra on *Jokertown Blues*. He suddenly realized he was sounding a lot like Captain Furillo.

"Locked."

"So you have got a key." Kelly bit her lip, then pulled the key out of a pant pocket, and held it out. Finn automatically took it.

"Any sign of a struggle?" Finn asked.

The actress looked startled as if that hadn't occurred to her. *Probably hadn't.* She was far more concerned with the ravages to her face than Stan's fate. "No. Well . . . maybe. His dinner was on the table. He'd eaten a little."

Finn faced his father. "We need to call the police."

"No," wailed Kelly.

"Impossible," snapped Benton.

"This can't get out," they both concluded in concert.

"The man is missing," Finn argued.

"This is directed at me," came the duet again. The director and the star paused and looked at each other.

"Somehow I think Stan would think it was directed at him," Finn said with some asperity.

"Stan's just a pawn," said Benton. "Coppola's been after me for a couple of years."

True, Finn thought.

"And a lot of actresses resent me," Kelly said.

Also true, thought Finn.

"So, what are we going to do?" Finn asked.

Neither his father nor Kelly had an answer for that. Instead there was a lot of toing and froing about how she really hadn't changed all that much. She was still beautiful. Then they moved on to whether Benton was going to recast the movie, since it was unclear how long Kelly was going to be off the set. Finn's stomach, which had been expecting dinner two hours ago, let out a loud rumble. Kelly gave him a startled look, and his dad frowned at him.

"I took you away from dinner, didn't I? Let me order in a meal for you," Kelly said. It was nice of her to offer. Most actresses were far too self-absorbed to notice the people around them. And Grace Kelly had every reason right now to be totally self-absorbed.

Benton shook his head. "We really need to get home. I need to reassure Alice that *you're* all right."

Kelly looked pleased. Proving yet again that an actor always assumed everything was about them.

They let themselves out of the large double doors, and Finn skittered down the steep flagstone path to where the van was parked in the driveway. Behind them the Griffith Park observatory loomed like a white ghost castle on the hilltop.

Finn took over driving. His dad wasn't terribly adept with the hand controls. "So are you going to recast?" he asked his father as they turned onto Los Feliz Boulevard.

"I've got twenty days in the can. The studio would never agree to that much reshooting. If we don't find Stan this movie is dead."

Neither of them said anything else for a number of blocks. "How do you think she kept him working solely for her?" Finn asked, desperate to break the morose silence.

"Probably threatened to have him killed," came the equally morose answer.

"Doesn't seem like her style."

"The guy could have made a fucking fortune," Benton said. "Gone from studio to studio, set to set, keeping actresses young." Benton reflected for a moment. "Probably a good thing he didn't. It would have killed the industry. The public wants a new flavor at least every few weeks."

Finn was pondering something else his father had said. "But does he really keep her young . . . physiologically young? Her face may look twenty-three, but what kind of shape is her heart in? Her lungs?" They were rolling down Sunset Boulevard at the best speed the van could manage. Mercedes, Porsches, and Rolls went flying past their tail lights like malevolent red eyes. "The *break-in*," Finn suddenly blurted.

"What?"

"The break-in a few days ago. Nothing was taken, but the files had been rifled. The insurance policies are in there, and a medical exam is attached. It would prove that Kelly wasn't a wild card."

"So, what's your point?"

"They'd know it was somebody near her, and Stan is the only constant."

"Hey, I've directed most of her movies," Benton argued.

"*Most,* not all. You heard her. Stan's done her make-up ever since *High Noon.* She's never married, and she never stays with any leading man much past a few months. It wouldn't take a genius to figure out who held the wild card."

"So who took him?" Benton. "And did they kill him?"

Worms seemed to suddenly go crawling through the pit of Finn's stomach at his father's blunt statement. "I don't know. It depends on who took him. It's a power worth preserving. I think. I hope."

Finn turned up the hill toward Bel Aire and they rolled past the guard gate. The guard gave them a wave. A few minutes later they were home.

His mom was full of questions, and Finn began giving her the rundown while he wolfed down a slice of pot roast. Through the kitchen door they could hear Benton making a call in the living room.

". . . Grace is down with the flu. I'll be rearranging the schedule, but it's no problem."

Since Finn's last remark to his mom had been that Kelly looked like the *portrait* of Dorian Grey, he and his mother exchanged incredulous looks at the lie. Benton hung up the phone and reentered the kitchen. Finn waved his fork at his father. "How can you say that? You said yourself, without Stan there is no movie."

"So we find him," Benton said. "You find him."

"*What!?*" Finn's voice rose to a squeak. "I'm a med student."

"You're a joker." Finn watched his mother flinch, and he felt the beef turn to bile in his gut. His parents had always been careful to call him a "wild card" not the pejorative "joker." Now his father had said the word, and he felt an aching grief as if the love and acceptance which had been the foundation of his life had suddenly proved to be a fraud. "You know the world. I can't involve studio security or the police, and you've already had some great ideas. I'm depending on you, Bradley." His father's eyes were pleading. "I'm close to retirement. I just wanted to go out on top, not fired off my last film."

We all have our griefs, Finn thought.

After dinner Finn went to Stan's house. He had the key that Kelly had thrust at him, and it was where all the detectives started in the TV shows. It was a tiny white bungalow on the south side of Los Feliz Boulevard. On the north side were the Hollywood Hills and the homes of the rich and very famous climbing the scrub-covered folds and canyons. On the south were modest houses and ethnic restaurants, groceries, laundromats, shoe repair shops—the kind of place where normal people lived.

The front door opened directly into a long living room with hardwood floors underfoot and several throw rugs. Finn avoided them assiduously. He had learned the hard way that hooves and throws didn't mix. There was a shabby green recliner in front of a television set, and a couch that hardly looked used. There were built-in bookcases on most of the walls, and they were crammed with books.

There was a double glass door that divided the living room from the dining room. It was a charming room with built-in buffets on either side of the west window, and an array of china displayed behind the glass mullions in the doors. There was a plate on the table with the remains of fried chicken and mashed potatoes, a salad on a salad plate, a glass of red wine. It was sad and very uninformative.

Feeling like a voyeur, Finn proceeded to the bedroom. There was a large four-poster bed, meticulously made with a canopy and dust ruffles and throw pillows. There was a large window looking northwest toward the hills. Finn gave a glance out the window, then snapped his neck around for a longer look. From the window he could see the upper story of Kelly's house. Finn trotted back to the main rooms of the house. All the drapes were tightly closed. He returned to the bedroom and those wide-open drapes.

After another look at the lights in the movie star's house Finn began riffling through the bookcases in the bedroom. Not surprisingly there were a lot of books about the movie business. There were also a lot of books about Grace Kelly. Finn flipped through a few of them skimming a sentence here, a paragraph there.

On the dresser was a framed picture of Stan standing next to a marlin hanging by its tail from a wooden scaffold. This was a familiar picture to Finn. Every male in southern California had a picture of himself next to a big fish he'd caught in Mexico. In the photo Stan was a good deal younger, and he was smiling off to the side as if to someone out of camera range. That was odd. Most of the mighty hunters beamed directly into the camera. The frame was also anomalous. It was an elaborate silver affair.

"Must have been really proud of that fish," Finn muttered as he turned over the photo and looked at the back. There was a handwritten notation. La Paz, June 1954.

The date hit some memory or association. Finn stood struggling with that sense of reaching for something just beyond reach. Then it hit. He lunged back across the bedroom, and pulled down one of the biographies of Kelly. He flipped quickly through the pages.

The start of principal photography was delayed on To Catch a Thief *due to Kelly's exhaustion. She recuperated for several weeks in Mexico before returning to begin work. . . .*

There was more, but Finn had what he needed. Kelly and Stan had both been in Mexico in June of '54. Question was, were they together? Finn flipped forward a few more pages to the section about Prince Rainier of Monaco.

Odds makers in Vegas were offering two to one that Kelly would wed the dashing prince, but it was the cynics who didn't believe in fairy tales who made the best choice—in 1955 Hollywood's princess declined the offer to join European royalty.

Finn closed the book. He looked back at the framed photo. He looked out the window at the distant lights in Kelly's home. The lights went out. Grace Kelly had gone to bed. "She didn't marry Rainier because she couldn't," Finn said aloud. "She was already married to you. Wasn't she, Stan?"

It was an idiotic thing to say, but it was the only thing that made any sense. The only explanation for why the make-up man had stayed so loyal for all those years.

"All those years while she was fucking every new leading man. You were a schmuck, Stan." Finn shoved the book back into its place on the shelf. "And you need to go home and go to sleep. You're talking to yourself, Bradley, my man."

The next morning he put in a call to the Myth Patrol. He knew he needed help, and he didn't know whom else to ask. They met at Dupar's, and Finn outlined the situation.

"So tell me again how all us wild cards are brothers under the skin, and how I ought to spend my free time rescuing an ace," Goathead mumbled around his double bacon cheeseburger.

Finn hadn't counted on ace envy entering into the equation. "He's not an ace. He's a deuce. This is not a major league power."

"He's a seventy-year-old man who can make women look young," Goathead argued. "If that's not a sure means to unlimited sex I don't know what is."

"I wish you wouldn't always put your head in the gutter," Clops said. He rolled his eye at Cleo.

"She can't understand a fucking thing I say." Goathead leered at her. "Hey baby, want to fuck like frenzied ferrets?"

"##$%&&*****" Cleo dumped her chocolate malt in Goathead's lap.

Clops grinned as Goathead cursed and mopped at the sticky mess. "Looks like she understands just fine."

"Guys, could we focus here," Finn said, waving his hands in the air. "Where do we start?"

"Hollywood and Cahuenga," Clops said confidently.

The Myths were standing beneath an old brownstone building on the corner. The dark upper windows threw back the sunlight in sharp jagged glints. Cleo was glaring at a drunk who stood swaying and leering at her from across the street. Goathead was leering at a couple of female hookers just down the block. Finn stared at Clops.

"Okay. We're here. Why are we here?" Finn asked.

Clops pointed to a corner window. "That was Philip Marlowe's office."

Finn fought down the urge to rip off the cyclops's head. Forcing a mild tone, he said, "I hate to break this to you, but Marlowe was a character in books. Then he was a character in the movies. He's not real."

Okay, Finn thought, as Clops looked like a kicked puppy, *it wasn't your most diplomatic moment.*

Surprisingly it was Goathead who came to the big joker's defense. "No, he's right. We've got to get in the space. Think like a detective. Find the character."

Wonderful, beneath Goathead's hairy chest beats the heart of a method actor, Finn thought.

"I think a tough, no nonsense Bogart approach," Clops began, only to be interrupted by Goathead.

"Well, that leaves you right out," replied Goatboy. "Whoever plays our detective, you're destined to be the loyal sidekick. You're not leading man material."

Cleo glared at Goathead, and all the snakes *hissed* at him. The joker jumped back. Cleo laid a hand on Clops's arm, and gave him a blazing smile. Finn was dazzled. She really was beautiful, if you just ignored the snakes. There was a barrage of Turkish being directed at Clops, then one halting English word.

"Gorgeous," Cleo said, and smiled up at the Cyclops again.

A tide of red swept from the base of Clop's throat to the top of his ears. "You really think so?" he asked the joker girl. She nodded vigorously. "Would you like to have dinner tonight?" he asked. Cleo nodded again.

"Gee, isn't that just . . . swell," muttered Goathead. "I'm going home."

"Wait," Finn cried. "We haven't. . . ."

But Clops and Cleo were strolling off with her arm tucked through his, while tourists on a bus gawked out the window and shot photos. Goathead went clattering off around the corner. Finn took a last look up at Marlowe's window. Inspiration did not descend. Finn headed off down Hollywood.

In the old days the Boulevard had been a magical, glamorous place. Now it had fallen on hard times. The street was lined with cheap tourist shops selling tee shirts, tacky memorabilia and maps to stars' houses. Hookers, male, female and joker, worked the corners, fading down side streets when an L.A.P.D. cruiser would roll past. Down those side streets the robbers waited. They generally left the hookers alone. Tourists were easier targets.

Finn, depressed and in a brown study, wasn't paying much attention to where he was going or who he passed. He had to tell his father he couldn't do this, and they had to call the police. Then a familiar voice called out to him. "Hi, Bradley."

"Tanya." He looked around, but he didn't see any evidence of a boyfriend or even one or two of the Bimbo Battalion. "Are you alone?"

"Yeah."

"This is not a good part of town for you to be in." She laughed. "No, I'm serious."

"So escort me," she demanded.

Finn felt like a sun had started burning down in the pit of his belly. The warm good feeling spread upward and broke out in a broad grin. "Sure. Where do you want to go?"

"I was going to Musso and Franks. Have you eaten?"

Banishing the thought of the short stack of pancakes, egg and sausage he had consumed only two hours before, Finn shook his head no. "But Musso's is tough for me. Pretty much nothing but booths and narrow isles. Do you like Chinese?"

Tanya nodded. "But only in Chinatown."

"Do you know Hop Li's?" She shook her head. "Come on, you're in for a treat. I'm parked over by Grauman's." She slid her arm through Finn's and the bright glow seemed to explode out the top of his skull. He forgot about Grace Kelly, the movie, even Stan. He was prancing down the Walk of Fame with the prettiest girl in Hollywood.

Tanya did have a pretty good location—off Melrose on the fringes of Beverly Hills. Lunch had been terrific, and he didn't mean the food. They had talked for two hours, and by the second hour Tanya kept laying her fingers gently on his wrist. Once she had even brushed a hand through the hair at the nape of his neck. Finn offered to drive her home. She agreed with a secretive little smile and then briefly touched the tip of her tongue to her bottom lip. Finn sensed she was going to invite him in. Then during the drive to North Hollywood Finn had started to worry. *What if she lives in one of those nineteen-fifties apartment buildings with the concrete and metal exterior stairs. There is no way I can negotiate those.*

Tanya directed him up a quiet street off Melrose, and Finn felt his spirits soar. The street was lined with nineteen-twenties duplexes. Most were not aging well. There was missing stucco, missing tiles on the Spanish roofs. Tanya's was differentiated by the fact it had beautiful landscaping.

She followed his look. "I take care of the landscaping in exchange for half the rent."

"Wow, you're an incredible gardener. You could do this professionally," Finn said enthusiastically then realized from the way the skin around her mouth tightened that he'd said the wrong thing. "Look, I wasn't suggesting it as the fall back position when you don't make it as an actress."

She gave him a smile, and it was the first one Finn had seen that didn't seem calculated. "You're a nice guy, Bradley Finn." He felt the same rictus tightening of his cheek muscles as his smile went thin. "And no, I don't mean that as a kiss off. I mean it as a come on." And she leaned over and kissed him on the lips. Her tongue flicked out to explore his lips. Finn suddenly couldn't breathe. "Now come on in."

The duplex was sparsely furnished, something which he suspected had more to do with poverty than design. But it was clean and almost obsessively neat and the spicy scent of incense gave it an exotic feeling.

Tanya walked backwards down the short hallway, unbuttoning his shirt as they went. Finn was willing to follow. At that moment he would have followed her anywhere. She yanked off her tank top, took Finn's hands, and cupped them around her breasts. The skin was warm, slightly sweaty, and very soft. He ran his thumb across her nipples, feeling the roughness as they puckered. She pushed his shirt off his shoulders. He felt it slid across his back and down his side and his horse hide quivered at the tickle.

Gasping, he pulled her close and kissed her. The flesh on their chests seemed to lock together, glued by sweat. Tanya tugged him forward. Finn opened one eye to see where they were going.

It was then that, if not sanity, practicality returned. Finn looked at the bed. "I can't use that."

That seemed to rattle her. "What?"

"I can't get down like that. And even if I could I'd squash you. I weigh about four hundred pounds." She retreated several steps. *Too much information,* Finn thought with a cringe. *Didn't need to mention the weight thing.* He could feel his erection dying.

She glanced at the walls of the room. "So what do we do?"

"Put the mattress on a table." A new worry intruded. "Do you have a dining room table?"

She looked around the room again. "Yeah, but I don't want to make love in there."

"We could carry it in," Finn suggested and cringed because he thought he was sounding desperate. Probably because he was desperate.

"There's not enough room," she said.

"Yes there is if we set it horizontal to the foot of the bed."

She was looking desperately around the room again. "It won't work. Look, what do you say we hold this thought, and you come back later. I can get some help moving the table. . . ."

"What, you need movers? How big is this table? I can move the table."

She was staring past his shoulder. Nausea replaced the earlier hot tingle of arousal. For the first time Finn took a hard look at the bedroom. He noted the way the track lighting spotlighted the bed. He spotted the tiny shotgun mike nestled next to one of the light cans. Careful mincing sidesteps with his hind feet brought him around to face the side wall. It wasn't a large hole. He wasn't sure if he saw or only imagined the glint of light off the camera lens. It didn't matter. He gulped down tears of rage and shame and went galloping out the door of the bedroom.

Harry Gold popped out the bathroom door, and waved his arms over his head. "Whoa, *whoa!*"

Finn reared, forelegs pawing the air. It was a trick that usually made people step back. Harry Gold froze and stood staring admiringly up at Finn. Suddenly Finn realized what was holding the producer's unwavering attention. Finn felt his balls trying to retreat, and his penis pulled as far back in his sheath as was possible. He dropped back to all fours and rushed past the porn producer. He felt his horse shoulder connect with Gold. There was a loud thump and a shout of pain from the little man.

Finn didn't look back. He sprinted for the front door. As he charged through the living room, his hind brain noticed the dents in the carpet where furniture had stood. Far from being sparsely furnished, the room had been packed with furniture. They had moved it for him so he would have a straight shot to bedroom, led by his dick. Shame and humiliation were a foul and oily taste on the back of his tongue. Bradley yanked open the front door.

He shot through the colorful flower beds. Flower petals and leaves flew up around him chopped loose by his churning hooves. He cleared the low chain link fence like the front runner in the Grand National. Reaching his van, Finn realized his keys and his wallet were in his shirt pocket back in the apartment. He grabbed the spare set of keys from the magnetized box from beneath the chassis, got the doors unlocked, and staggered the length of the van. He could feel the muscles in his left stifle and hamstring starting to tighten. The physical pain was nothing to the shame he felt.

"Hey, no harm, no foul" said Harry Gold.

Finn had tracked down the producer at his offices in a rundown strip mall in Van Nuys. The walls of his office were lined with movie posters commemorating some of Harry's classics, and huge blow-up photos of his stars. Finn tried to keep his gaze away from the equipment being flaunted by Jetballs and Dr. Tachydong.

Harry sat behind an acre wide cherry wood desk. It was loaded down with photo stills of actresses and piles of scripts. Finn didn't know porn movies had scripts.

"And you can't blame me for trying," the little man added.

Finn rested his fists on the desk and leaned in on Harry until they were almost nose to nose. "I do blame you, Harry. I liked that girl. I thought she liked me. But you spoiled it all."

"Hey, it's not too late. We can set up only this time do it right with a table . . . a table. I didn't even think of that. . . ."

Finn cut across the flow of words. "Did you roll film?"

Harry held up his hands, palms out. "No. You were only warming up. Nothing to get."

Finn spun around and let fly with his hind legs. His hooves connected with the front of the desk and wood splintered. The desk collapsed, falling forward to shed scripts and photos like a paper avalanche. Harry gave a yell of alarm, jumped out of his oversized leather chair, and retreated against the back wall. "What? Are you nuts?"

"No. I'm pissed. And tired of being lied to. Give me the film."

The producer's hands were trembling as he opened a filing cabinet and pulled out a cassette of film. "You are, like, way overreacting. Sure she owed me, but she could have said no, so she had to like you a little."

Finn clutched the film and started for the door. Then it penetrated. He looked back. "What do you mean she owed you?"

"N . . . nothing. I gave her a start. That's all. She's one of my kids and I look after my kids even when they move on. . . ."

"Christ, Harry, I hope you don't play poker because you are the worst liar I've ever met." Finn leaned over and grabbed the phone off the floor.

"What are you doing?" Gold asked.

"Calling the police."

"What! Why? Because of this?" Gold pointed at the film under Finn's arm.

"No. For aiding and abetting in a kidnapping and possibly a murder."

"Kidnapping? Murder?" Harry squeaked. "You are nuts. I just put her in touch with a grip I know at Warner's. B and E guy. Nothing violent. Gentlest guy you'll ever meet."

Finn glared at Gold. "Is that God's own truth, Harry?"

"Yeah, yeah, I swear it!" the producer panted. He pulled out a big blue handkerchief and mopped sweat. This time Finn believed him.

Benton was taking the opportunity during Kelly's "indisposition" to shoot crowd scenes. Finn called over to the set and learned that Tanya was there. He thought she might have had the decency to quit. Then he realized that she knew damn good and well that Finn wasn't going to tell his father what had occurred, and nothing was going to keep Tanya from getting in front of a camera.

A call to the first A.D. established when the extras were going to be released. There was only one parking area on the Warners lot for extras, day players, and visitors. Finn parked his van down a side street which led to the back lot and waited. Eventually Tanya came walking into the lot. She wove her way through the parked cars to a dilapidated Nova, climbed in, and headed out onto Pass Avenue. Finn was right behind her.

He figured since he knew squat about tailing a car he'd just hug her bumper. Hopefully she knew squat about being tailed and wouldn't notice. She led them over the hill and at Sunset Boulevard she turned west. They rolled past the entrance to the Bel Aire Heights where Finn's family lived. He was surprised. This was high dollar country. Not the usual place to hide a kidnapping victim.

Then she turned north up the road to the Beverly Hills Hotel. Finn's brain was starting to feel like it was spinning inside his skull. She went to the hotel, and parked in the free lot. Finn swept around to the entrance and availed himself of the valet service. He knew the dining room gave a pretty good view of most of the paths so he waited there. A few minutes later Tanya arrived. She headed through the lobby and out the back doors. Finn noted the path, and rushed out to find a busboy and a room service cart.

It required some significant greenbacks, but he was soon outfitted in a white jacket, pushing a cart in front of him. If he hunkered down a bit the long tablecloth hid his centaur body. Finn was worried he would lose her in the maze of paths and bungalows, but he caught a lucky break. He heard her voice over a high wall. "Julie, what the hell are you doing out here?"

"I was bored. I wanted a swim. Like, take a pill," he heard Julie answer. "Besides, Susan said she'd watch him."

Susan, Susan, Finn thought trying to place the name. Then he realized that was the plump blonde.

"She's not on shift now," came Tanya's voice, sharp with suspicion.

"God, you are so anal. What difference does it make who guards him?" Julia replied. "And Anne stuck me with two shifts so I was due for a break."

Is every starlet in Hollywood in on this? Finn thought, and he bit back a chuckle. Given the surroundings he was no longer worried about Stan's physical well being.

"You are so stupid," said Tanya. Finn heard the click of her heels retreating across the concrete.

"Well, fuck you too," Julie shouted.

A moment later Tanya swung around a corner. Finn quickly looked away. She went up to the door of a bungalow and let herself in. Finn rumbled closer with his cart.

As the door was closing he heard Tanya say, "*Out!* Get your shirt on and *get out!*" The door shut. Finn started to grin.

A few moments later the fat blonde came flying out the door. One cheek was bright red, and her eyes were watering. Finn waited until she was out of sight, and then rolled up to the door. He knocked.

"Who is it?"

"Room service," Finn sung out as loudly as he could.

"We didn't order anything," came Tanya's voice.

"Actually I ordered some champagne," Finn heard Stan say.

"Great, this is already costing us a fortune." Her voice was getting louder as she approached the door. She threw it open. "We changed our minds. We don't want. . . ."

Finn knocked her down with the room service cart.

Stan was seated in an armchair with a large basket of fruit close at hand. "Hi, Stan," Finn said. "I'm here to rescue you."

"Why thank you, Bradley, but you might want to look out for Miss Tanya," the elderly make-up artist said mildly.

Finn turned and found himself looking down the barrel of a small pistol. Tanya held it in a very confident and very businesslike manner.

"I see you've noticed Miss Tanya's assets," Stan said. Finn's errant brain suddenly flashed the memory of the warmth and weight of a pair of breasts cupped in his hands. He shook it off. "I found it a very compelling argument for accompanying her," Stan continued. "Now that I've gotten to know her I realize that she wouldn't shoot me." The rigidity in Finn's back started to slump toward his withers. "But she might shoot you." The steel rod shot back up the centaur's back. "I don't think there's anything that Miss Tanya won't do in pursuit of a goal."

"Yeah, no kidding," Finn said dryly. Tanya glared at him. Finn then did an elaborate scan of the opulent bungalow. "Hell of a hide-out."

Tanya's lips compressed. "Oh, don't blame Miss Tanya," Stan said. "She very sensibly had me stashed in a dingy little apartment over in Irvine. But I convinced Anne that I might be more willing to become her personal make-up artist if I were more comfortably situated. Since then Susan keeps taking her clothes off for me. . . ."

"Stan, you're a dirty old man," Finn said.

"No, I simply saw no reason to argue. Susan is an unaffected child of nature."

It sounded like a quote, but Finn couldn't place it.

"Susan is a moron," Tanya said. "What did Julie offer you?"

"Just money. Very unimaginative."

Finn jerked a thumb at Tanya. "And Annie Oakley here just offers to shoot you?"

"No, she's offered me nothing which inclines me to help her over all the others," Stan said.

"I don't want your help. I just want a chance," Tanya spat out the words.

"And taking out Grace Kelly is going to help you how?" Finn asked.

"When the sun's up you can't see the stars. Why look for anything new when she's there?"

"Tanya, it's over. You've got to let him go," Finn said.

"No, sooner or later the press will get a look at her, and then it'll be over."

"What are you going to do with me?" Finn asked.

"Keep you too. And I think when I tell your dad what went on between us he'll want to keep me happy and quiet."

There was a massive throbbing behind Finn's eyes. A headache made up of equal parts rage and hurt. He fists clenched, but before he could react Stan *tsked*. "No, no, my dear. Crude threats are not the way to go. Now it's time for you to ask for something. Let Bradley call his father, and negotiate a speaking role for you."

Finn watched the calculation in her pale eyes. She then tucked the pistol back into her purse and gave a nod. Finn released the pent-up breath he hadn't realized he'd been holding.

There was a reason Stan had survived in Hollywood for fifty years, Finn thought.

Finn didn't bother to take Stan home. He just drove the make-up man straight to Kelly's house.

"Is there a reason you've brought me here?"

"It's your home, isn't it?" Finn countered.

"Home is where the heart is," Stan said lightly, but there was a shadow in the back of his eyes.

"Then that would be here. I figured out about Mexico. You married her, didn't you?"

The net of wrinkles around Stan's blue eyes deepened as he smiled. "You're a danger, young Bradley. Well, let's go in to her." Stan climbed out of the van.

They went around to the back where Stan unlocked the kitchen door. "Grace, my dear," he called.

They heard her steps overhead. Stan led them into the foyer. Kelly came running down the grand curved staircase and into Stan's arms. Finn side-stepped his way through an archway and into the living room. A few minutes passed and then they joined him. They were holding hands. It was really sweet.

"Would you like something to drink, Bradley?" Stan asked. "Would you get him something, dear, while I get my kit?"

Stan took a step only to be caught by Kelly. "Stan, wait. I've been thinking a lot during the past two days."

Stan started shaking his head. "No, Grace. This is a beautiful movie, don't. . . ."

She put a hand over his mouth. "I'm tired, Stan. My back hurts. I'm hungry all the time, and I have to exercise twice as long now to stay the same size. I'm not twenty-three. You just let the mirror give me back that picture." Stan stood silent, just staring at his wife. A wave of insecurity passed across her face. "You can't love me like this?" She touched a wrinkled cheek.

Stan grabbed her into a tight embrace. His voice was thick as he murmured against her hair. "No, my love. I just want you to be sure before you give it all up."

Kelly wasn't trying to hide her tears. She kissed him hard. "But I'll finally have you. For whatever time remains to us."

The emotions—love, regret, joy—were like electric currents in the room. It was overwhelming, and Finn had to get out of that room. He placed each hoof with elaborate care. They still rang hollowly on the wood floor of the foyer, but neither Stan nor Grace noticed.

Amazingly, the movie continued. Kelly offered to split the cost of the reshoot with the studio. Benton recast, and the production moved to England. The tabloids made much of Kelly and Stan's love story. SHE GAVE UP BEAUTY FOR TRUE LOVE! Stan hired bodyguards. And Finn started back to school.

One evening the phone rang.

"Hello," Finn said around a mouthful of Chef Boyardee ravioli.

"Hi, Bradley." It was Tanya.

Finn swallowed, and felt the inadequately chewed food hit his stomach like a lead ball. "Hi."

"I was wondering if I could take up the offer of a native guide to Santa Monica?"

"Last time we met you aimed a gun at me, and the time before that you tried to trick me into a porno movie."

"So? It's not like it was personal."

"And that's why I think Santa Monica is a bad idea."

"Coward." He could hear the laughter in her voice.

"Tanya, would you fuck a pony?"

"No. But a centaur might tempt me."

Age of Wonders

FIVE

August 2004

WHILE WORKING ON THE story about Grace and Stan, Raleigh watched a lot of old movies. She saw Roger Corman's *Jason and the Argonauts* with Dr. Finn as an extra, in all its high-concept low-budget glory. He'd mostly been in the background, but she was still able to get a pretty good look at him. He'd been so young, baby-faced, several decades removed from the careworn middle-aged doctor she'd met with. Except, of course, that he was still a pony-sized centaur. His palomino coat had a whole lot of gray in it these days.

Just like there were aces and deuces, there were jokers and then there were *jokers*. The Peregrines and Bradley Finns on one side, with faces for the movies and a lot of goodwill built in. Then there were the Father Squids and Snotmans. The jars of "Hideous Joker Babies" in the Bowery Wild Card Dime Museum.

It wasn't just three cards Raleigh might draw. It was a whole deck, and every one of them different. If she just *knew* . . .

There was another story to be had in here, about how well some jokers did depending a lot on how their families reacted, and whether their families had the resources to move the world for them. These circumstances seemed to make a huge difference, and that meant something, said something about economic disparity and privilege. *Aces!* might not have been the best place for that article, though. She could hear Margot now, mildly questioning what any of this had to do with Oscar season. But Raleigh made notes anyway.

Gavin joined her for lunch one day at the library while she was reviewing a few more odds and ends on video from the library's collection. He'd reserved one of the private study rooms for her, that had its own TV and VCR—she had a stack of VHS tapes, old school—and brought in a bag of deli sand-wiches.

"What are we watching?" He leaned in for a kiss, which she gave. He settled into the chair beside her and put his arm over her shoulder while she snuggled into his embrace; she was needing a hug. The TV screen showed black-and-white footage of a tall middle-aged man in a purposefully badly fitting suit, playing a ukulele and singing in a comic falsetto.

"It's a documentary on the postwar Catskills entertainment circuit. That's Timothy Wiggins. He's the guy who coined the term 'deuce.' 'If I'm an ace, I'd hate to see a deuce,' he said."

"What's his power?"

"He could change his skin's color. Like, he'd sing songs about colors, 'Yellow Rose of Texas,' or whatever, and change his skin's colors with them. This is the only film I've found of him, but it's black-and-white. It doesn't really show how his power works." Wiggins' shading would change, but it looked more like an effect of bad lighting than a wild card power.

"That's . . . really sad, somehow," Gavin said.

"It gets worse. He was called to testify before Congress during the Ace Scare and blacklisted. When he couldn't find work, he committed suicide."

"Oh no," Gavin murmured.

"This is all that's left. No one really knows about him anymore."

In the clip, the audience laughed, applauded. They seemed to be enjoying themselves. The act didn't seem like much but he must have had a rapport with the crowd. It all seemed a bit silly now. Silly, and sad.

"You're going to write about him?"

"Yeah. Probably on the blog. Another 'Hey, look what we've all forgotten' story. His daughter is still alive but I haven't been able to get her to talk. His grandkids never knew him. Whatever I write is going to end up being really depressing, I'm afraid. All this work I've been doing, digging up these stories and writing these profiles—I'm happy that people like them. But it just feels so . . . frivolous. I'm not really making a difference. Am I?" She frowned, and the film clip of Timothy Wiggins cut away to a bespectacled scholar going on with some analysis or other about the historical implications of blacklisted Catskills musical comics.

"I think you're making a difference," he said, kissing her cheek, holding her. "You're making people care."

"But is this really what people should care most about? Timothy's story— it's sad, and it's important. But is it going to change the world?"

"So you want to change the world? Is that why you're doing all this?"

"I don't know. Did you ever think about keeping your power secret? Like, did you ever think it would get you in trouble if people knew?" He so rarely used it, most of the time she forgot about it. Not like with herself. His card had turned; he *knew*. She was waiting, waiting . . . "Or did you ever think about publicizing it?"

"Not really, one way or the other. It's such a stupid power. I suppose I could hide it so as not to embarrass myself."

"I think you sell yourself short."

"That's because you think the best of everybody. But I don't know . . . I'd like to have kids someday, you know? But I don't know if I should, with genes like that. The odds are never good. And you—you're a carrier, right? Because of your mom? That's some dice we'd be rolling, if we had kids."

A chill touched her spine. No, they could absolutely not have kids. If she were just a carrier, if it were just her mom with the virus, maybe. But she was *latent*. She had the wild card gene, too. Their kids would have it. Her thoughts stumbled over themselves in a tangle.

Gavin's smile fell. The expression on her face must have been stricken, obviously horrified. "You don't want kids, do you? Did I just screw up by bringing up kids?"

Now, she should tell him now that she was latent. Right now was the perfect time. They couldn't have kids together, and if that was a deal breaker they needed to know that *right now*. To think, at one time she had assumed that once she got past the danger of puberty this would all get easier. She smiled and touched his face, hoping to bring that smile back. "To tell you the truth, I'm not crazy about the thought of kids. Not right now."

"Well of course not right *now*." *But someday?* his hopeful gaze seemed to ask.

"I'm sorry, I'm not really in a fit state to have a serious conversation. Not with 'Yellow Rose of Texas' stuck in my head."

He chuckled, and the tension broke, for now. But this only delayed the conversation. She frowned at her files spread over the desk, the sad story of Timothy Wiggins playing in the background. She might be done with the show business angle. People with the wild card virus used their powers in other lines of work; they didn't all subject themselves to the performance circus, though Raleigh could be forgiven for taking such a long time to figure that out, seeing how she grew up with Aurora for a mother.

New project, then. And she bet she wouldn't even have to go that far to find a good story.

Tasty

by Mary Anne Mohanraj

Jokertown, July 1990

JESÚS GASPED AS ALONDRA moved her hips one last time above his, pleasure whiting out every last thought in his brain, so that he barely heard the rattle of the ceiling fan above their heads.

"*Amor!*" Her voice, alarmed, yanked him back to himself. He managed to fight the satisfied lassitude spreading through his body, pulling himself up in one smooth motion. Arms reached above his head, to where they could just touch the base of the fan. Enough. He sent his power out, a tingling, tiny wave, fixing the cracking housing where it was coming apart from around the bolt. Again. The metal smoothed, seamless.

"You said you'd fix it properly." She frowned up at him—not a look he enjoyed seeing on the woman he loved.

"I will, I will." Jesús slid down into the bed, pulled Alondra against him, a warm, brown bundle of soft flesh and long bones. "It's on the list, I swear." It was just easier, using his power to make a quick fix, even though those fixes never lasted more than a few weeks. And now he was even more tired.

"*Sabes que te quiero, mi amor, pero . . .*" She frowned, pulling back and sitting up in the bed. "But you're always doing things for other people. Will I always come last? Must I be murdered by a ceiling fan before you take me seriously?"

"*Aieee, exagerada!*" He laughed, and brushed a fond finger down her cheek. Alondra glared at him a moment longer, before she gave in, laughing too.

"Fine. But one day, *te lo juro*, you'll regret neglecting me so!" She bent above him, her hair swinging down like a dark curtain, and her breasts . . . ah.

Jesús whispered, "I give you permission to castigate me for all my flaws when that day comes. For now, I want to taste that sweet mouth of yours. Come here . . ." He pulled her down, losing himself in her again. Outside their apartment window, a summer thunderstorm began, rain crashing down in heavy sheets. A bird shrieked in protest. But inside the protective walls, everything was just fine.

The next morning's sunrise found Jesús at his grandmother's house. The old woman didn't sleep much these days; she was always awake in the early hours. "I'm sorry, *abuelita*. I can't help you." He sat back on his heels and shook the loose dirt off his hands, careful not to shake too hard. Wouldn't want to lose a finger. They didn't usually drop off that easily, but still, best to be careful. "*Lo siento.*"

"*No te preocupes, querido.* You said it wouldn't work, but I had to have you try. Seeing how patchy the grass is around that old black walnut—*itan gacho!* After you and your men have done so much to make *mi casa muy bonita* . . ." Xiomara gestured towards the neat little house, freshly painted in spotless white, boasting a cheery yellow window box at every window, crimson petunias cascading down.

"It's nothing, after all you've done for me." The old woman had practically raised him and his sisters, with his mother working double shifts at the pickle factory and with no patience for the kids when she came home. Jesús still winced at the memory of her slipper whistling down; only *abuelita* had been able to soften Carmen in one of her black rages. As for his drunk of a father—better that they rarely saw him. "But I can't do anything with living things."

He'd tried to encourage the grass to grow, to spread, but there was nothing there for him, no whisper of power working. Jesús couldn't heal the scrapes he and his crew got on the job, either—the best he could do was thicken their bandages a bit and strengthen the adhesive, so that they'd hold better. The fix wouldn't last more than a few weeks—it never did.

But a few-week fix wasn't nothing. When Tony gashed himself on that busted metal pipe, the bandage held his leg together until they got him to *la clinica*. There was a reason jokers (with powers or without) fought to be on Jesús's crew. Mexican, Italian, Polish—it didn't matter. He ran the only mostly-joker handyman crew in the city, and his guys stood by each other. None of them cared that Jesús's card turning had left him with bits that fell off from time to time—he'd periodically lose fingers, toes, chunks of skin, even an ear. That's why people called him Retazos. *Scraps.* The bits always grew back, so it didn't really matter that they fell off sometimes, and his short-term fix-it ability could be helpful on the job.

But grass—he couldn't do anything with grass. Jesús pushed himself to his feet, rubbing the last of the dirt off on his jeans, pondering the problem. "Why don't we make you a mosaic? I can swing by Norton's junkyard, find bright tile and glass. We'll make a garden of flowers out of them, like your paintings." His *abuelita* painted murals for the neighborhood, walls blossoming with brilliant color. You knew when you'd crossed over into Jokertown's barrio because of her paintings—flowers and fantastical beasts. The mayor had even sent her a certificate, honoring her contribution to the community, and they'd run a piece about it in the paper. She kept stacks of those papers in her spare room. He went on: "Crackle's good with tilework—you lay it out, and he'll make you a beautiful patio. I can fix up a table and some chairs for you, and you can take your chocolate in the shade."

"*Que buena idea, mi amor*," she said, beaming, the mass of wrinkles of her face smoothing out with the smile. "*Podría ver un quetzal magnifico, azul y amarillo. Y rosas rojas, para tu pobrecita hermana.*" And the smile slipped away, leaving sad wrinkles behind. It had almost broken her, when Rosita's card had turned, and the black queen stole her youngest grandchild away. Every time Jesús used his small power, he thought of little Rosita; he would give the power up in a moment, to have her back with them again.

Now his grandmother frowned. "*Tienes tiempo, verdad?* With another Staten Island job—*porque necesitas ir* all the way out there . . ."

"When Mr. Dutton calls, you answer," Jesús said. "It's good money, *abuelita*. Enough that I can loan Juanita the last couple hundred for her community college fees this semester."

"College!" His grandmother harrumphed. "That girl—her nose always in a book. She should concentrate on finding herself a good husband." She smiled, remembering. "*Que linda fue* at her quince! Almost as pretty as your Alondra!"

Jesús smiled. That was a fond grandmother's eyes talking—Juanita had a beak of a nose and ears that stuck out. It was a good thing she liked studying so much, because those features combined with her sharp tongue meant that she had had little interest from the neighborhood boys, which seemed to suit her just fine. Juanita spent all her time at the library, studying with her best friend, Bibiana—and Jesús had his suspicions about that *friendship*. But that wasn't something he'd ever say to his *abuelita*.

The important thing was that Juanita was going to be the first in their family with a college degree, even if Jesús had to drive her to every class himself. Whereas Alondra—just the thought of her soft lips and dark eyes made him dizzy with desire. If he hurried, maybe after the junkyard, he could stop at home, steal twenty minutes with her. Wake her up before her alarm went off, and she started getting ready for her hospital shift. It wasn't even five a.m. yet, and Mr. Dutton wasn't expecting the crew until nine today, when the new chandelier was due to arrive. He had time.

"*Necesito irme, abuelita.*"

"*Si, si, nieto—momentico, por favor.*" She ducked back into the house for a moment, the screen door swinging shut behind her. Then came back out, arms laden with heavy plastic bags. "I packed you some tamales—make sure you share them *con tu novia. Y con el Señor Norton.*"

Jesús wasn't going to turn them down—just the scent of them made his stomach rumble. Abuelita's tamales were always so tender; she'd have steamed them just before he arrived, so they were perfectly fresh. He'd forgotten to eat breakfast again, too busy helping his neighbor with the broken window that some *cabrón* had smashed the night before. Weaving together all those little pieces of glass had used up more of his reserves than he'd realized.

It really hadn't made sense to do the fix—Jesús could've gotten her a new piece of glass installed by the weekend. But Señora Hernandez had been so upset—her daughter had started running around with the same boys who had probably smashed the windows, and now Señora Hernandez couldn't sleep at night. When Jesús patched the window, she smiled and patted his head, saying that he must make his mother proud. It was worth the trouble to give her a little ease. But now Jesús wanted nothing more than to go home and eat these tamales with Alondra. He'd lick the tangy green tomatillo sauce from her lips. . . .

He needed to adjust himself—but not in front of his grandmother! Jesús turned away, fighting a blush. He might be almost thirty, but he still felt like a child around her.

Jesús pulled up to the junkyard. He couldn't help himself; he ate one more tamale before he stepped out of the truck. It wasn't as good without the tomatillo sauce, of course, but his will was weak, and the masa still melted in his mouth. He licked his lips, and a little chunk of skin fell off, onto the floor of the truck. Oops. He'd get it later.

His *abuelita* did something special to the chicken, so it was moist and just a little salty. It made him want a beer to go with it—but Jesús hadn't had one of those in three years, and he wasn't about to start again now.

"Hey, Ralph! I brought you something!"

Ralph strode out of his trailer, a broad smile stretching his wrinkled orange face. "*Retazos, compadre!* It's good to see you. And are those your *abuelita's* tamales I smell?"

Jesús didn't love his nickname, but given when he could do with his minor power, and what his body did on its own these days, it felt appropriate enough. What were people, after all, but a collection of mismatched parts? At least from a man who lived in a scrapyard, *Scraps* was a compliment. "I only have two left, but I saved them for you." He was saving a few in the truck for Alondra, but Ralph didn't need to know that . . .

"It's a kind thought, young man. Just because I *can* eat anything—" Ralph reached out and casually picked up a printed piece of cardboard from a nearby stack and stuffed it in his mouth—"doesn't mean it tastes good. This particular piece does have a nice spicy bite—I think it's the acids in the ink. But it can't hold a candle to those tamales."

Jesús smiled as he handed them over; it was a pang to part with them, but he knew where to get more. They had a good arrangement, he and Ralph. He'd found more than a few treasures for the job at this junkyard, and it was a pleasure, watching Ralph stuff his wide mouth. That big body, built of rolls like the Michelin Man, had plenty of room for massive meals of junk *and* a whole host of tamales. Next time, he'd bring more.

When Ralph had finished the last crumb of masa, licking it off his thick fingers, he asked, "So what can I do for you, Retazos? I heard you were back working at Dutton's—you need something for his job?"

"No, no." Jesús stifled a laugh, not wanting to offend. Ralph was easygoing, but still, no reason to insult him. A man had his pride. "You know Mr. Dutton—everything there has to be just so."

Jesús *could* unearth some neglected treasure here—all kinds of stuff ended up at the junkyard, including pieces from fancy old houses gone to wrack and ruin. If the original construction was sturdy enough, he might be able to repair and restore it, given enough time, and Dutton was one of the few clients who'd indulge him in that. It was a rare pleasure, making something beautiful, something that would last. Usually, he just fixed things that fell apart again.

"Are you saying my stuff isn't good enough for Dutton?" Ralph swelled in outrage—but then laughed, letting the air out again. "Well, it *is* a junkyard!" He frowned, and the frown added a decade to his years. "Though even I don't know everything in here anymore. I used to be able to tell you exactly where every single piece of junk was, but now? I'm getting old, Retazos; I'm not sure how much longer I can keep this up. It's a young man's game, sorting the junk."

Jesús frowned. He'd never heard the jovial man talk this way, with such a somber edge to his voice. "Everything okay, Ralph?"

Ralph shrugged. "Oh, it's nothing. Some of the Demon Princes have been coming around, hunting for something—they won't tell me what, though, so how am I supposed to help them?"

"They giving you a hard time?"

"No, no." But that orange skin had a tinge of grey to it. Were those plump hands a little shaky? The Demon Princes were nothing to mess with: big guys, comfortable with guns.

Jesús knew what Alondra would say—*don't get involved.* But he could help a little, surely?

"Listen, I have an idea. Why don't I bring the crew by, help you organize the place a bit." Ralph looked like he was about to protest, so Jesús just kept talking, counting off his crew on his fingers. "You know Crackle—all those extra fingers make him a whiz at sorting. Slick's grease spit is great at getting things unstuck, and Goggles can generate a little heat; useful for a quick weld. Squeegee will help keep everything cleaned up as we go. As for Smokescreen and Short Step—well, I'll find them something to do. With seven of us working, we could get this place straightened up in no time. That'll make it easier to find things. Then if the Princes *do* tell you what they're looking for, you can get it to them fast, and get rid of them."

"I don't want to drag you into my mess," Ralph said, frowning.

So it *was* a mess. More trouble than Ralph had wanted to say. Too much trouble? Jesús frowned, hesitating; maybe this was more than he should take on. Not as if he and Ralph were family. Alondra was always saying he should pay more attention to her, to their life together, that it was time for them to start thinking seriously about children. Maybe Jesús had gotten carried away. "Well, never mind then." Ralph bit his plump lip, looking like he was regretting his words. Jesús hurried on. "I really just came by for some colored glass, for my *abuelita*. She needs a mosaic for a dead part of her lawn; Piotr's gonna make her a masterpiece."

Ralph beamed. "Ah, for that gem of a woman, I'll share some of my own gems. Come, take a look at this!"

Ralph led Jesús over past the back of the trailer, down a path between two piles of glass and into a far a corner. A massive metal bin sat there on a concrete pad, filled to overflowing with colored glass, catching the sunlight and scattering it around the junkyard.

"What's all this?" Jesús asked.

"It's from Our Lady of Perpetual Misery. Well, that's what they used to call it, until Father Squid reconsecrated it."

Holy glass—*abuelita* would love that. "These are the original stained glass windows? From the bombing?"

"It's a mix, actually. The wavy pieces are the originals. I like those the best—old glass is much tastier than new."

"You eat that too? Doesn't it cut your tongue?"

Ralph harrumphed. "I can digest anything, young man—that starts with the lips and goes all the way through, tongue to throat to stomach. My power wouldn't be much good if I couldn't get things past my mouth, would it?"

Jesús nodded; he'd never really thought about how Norton's power worked, but that did make sense.

"So there's the old glass, and then there's a bunch of unneeded stained glass scrap from when they were cutting the windows of the new church. Cobalt is the tastiest, like fine wine."

"Really?" Jesús frowned.

"Not really," Ralph said, grinning. "But it's true that I've eaten all the cobalt. Gorged on it, the day it arrived. I actually haven't been back here in a while; I'm not sure what else is in there."

It was good to see a smile on the big guy's face again; that's how he was meant to look. "That's all right. My grandmother wants blue, but it doesn't have to be cobalt. Blue and yellow for a quetzal, and pink for roses."

"Ah, your poor sister." And the smile was gone again. Ralph had never met Rosita, but he knew how Jesús had suffered after her loss.

"Yes." She had always been sunny, his little sister; it was impossible to be sad around her smiling face. They'd lost too much when they'd lost her. Jesús's brothers had taken off long ago, gone west, so it'd just been the three of them, Jesús, Juanita, and Rosita. He'd protected his sisters all his life, but he'd been helpless against the virus. The drinking had gotten pretty bad that year.

Ralph sighed in sympathy. "Well, go ahead and dig out whatever you like. I think there's some pink towards the bottom, but you might have to hunt for it."

Ralph really did know this junkyard backwards and forwards. Jesús pulled on his thick work gloves, climbed up on a metal girder propped against the bin, and started digging through the glass. Blue and yellow were easy. He was halfway into the bin before he saw the pink—just one piece, but a big one, the base sitting on the shadowed floor. If he could get it out without shattering, it should be plenty to cut apart for a mosaic of twining roses.

Jesús carefully grasped the edges and pulled—it seemed to be stuck, though he couldn't see anything holding it down. He could try force—but even though years of construction work had given him plenty of muscles, that was almost never the right approach on a job. Persuasion worked better; he rocked the glass back and forth, gently, exerting his power on it, though it didn't respond. It's not as if Jesús could mend this, after all—the rest of the pieces were gone, and it would never be whole again.

But a little rocking seemed to do it, or maybe it was a sharp edge of the glass—it felt like it had cut through the obstruction, coming free so suddenly that he banged an elbow against the metal bin, sending a blinding flash of pain up his arm. He almost dropped the glass. But he was too stubborn to let go, and when the pain subsided, Jesús gently lowered himself, and the glass, safely to the ground. Triumph.

"*Gracias*, Ralph."

"My pleasure. Stop by again soon."

Six a.m. He'd handed the tiles off to Crackle, gotten him started at his *abuelita*'s. He didn't need to be at Dutton's for a few hours; there was time for a quick stop at home. He could drop off the tamales, and Alondra would be so happy to see them . . . She was still sleeping, no doubt, having hit the snooze button for the third time. That made him crazy, but he was crazy about her, so he didn't worry about it too much. Besides, she'd worked the evening shift last night, so who could blame her if she slept in a little? His gentle sweetheart of a nurse. She'd spent too much of her life washing body parts to be bothered by the way Jesús's sometimes fell off. He'd been lucky to find her.

"*Mi bomboncita* . . ." His little candy, because she was so sweet. Ah, the taste of Alondra, salt-sweat under his tongue. He and Alondra could save the tamales for afterwards. After three years, he still wasn't tired of sliding his rough hands along her impossibly soft skin, seeing those sweet *tetas* engulfed, and the way she moaned, arching into him, ah . . .

But his key was still in the door. His key was still in the door, and yet, Jesús could hear her, unmistakable, moaning. Ah. She had woken up *muy ardiente*, and her favorite toy was charged and waiting. Better than just fingers, claro, but once he opened the door, Alondra would cast it aside, her papaya dripping for him . . .

Ah, no. No, no, no.

He didn't know the man. He didn't know the man pounding into Alondra, didn't recognize the feathered wings that lifted her up, positioning her apparently *just right*, because the noises she was making now were noises he'd never heard before. She was screaming for this man, and his Alondra wasn't a screamer. Or hadn't been. Not for him.

When you throw a plastic container full of tamales at a mostly broken ceiling fan, the fan falls down.

It didn't hit them, though. The metal made just enough noise breaking apart to warn them, and Alondra shrieked, "Jesús!" as she rolled off the bed. The man—the man wasn't there anymore. He'd disappeared. The fan came crashing down on the bed, spraying plastic shards from the Tupperware and bits of tamale everywhere. A waste of his grandmother's food. And then Jesús's eyes parsed the chaos better. A large black bird, maybe a hawk?, circled the room and then shot out the open window. Another waited outside. They swept away together, weaving a dark twisted arc across the sky. Leaving Jesús standing there, staring at the wreckage of his bedroom, of his life.

"*Fucking puta traicionera.* Get out, get out, GET OUT!" The taste of the words lingered, bitter as burnt chilies on his tongue.

"I'm going!" She was stomping naked around the room, grabbing her clothes, stuffing them into suitcases. "I should've left a long time ago. Agares has been begging me to leave you . . ."

"Who the fuck is Agares?"

"He's a Demon Prince. *My* Demon Prince. He's moving up. Going to be a lieutenant soon. He has ambition; he wants something better for his life. Agares isn't happy to just wait around, doing the same old thing he's been doing for the last decade . . ."

Bitterness curdled in Jesús's stomach, acid rising. Alondra had wanted him to be more ambitious, or at least to make more money so she could go back to school, maybe become a doctor. Jesús had *wanted* to give that to her, but money wasn't so easy to come by as all that.

Maybe it was for some people, though—if you were willing to take it from someone else. "So that's what you want for your own life? To be some gangster's whore?"

Her face hardened. "Fuck you, Jesús. Like you offered me so much more."

Jesús tasted metal on his tongue. "I would have given you everything!"

He hadn't known her eyes could look like that, like chiseled glass. "Everything that was left out of your life, once you'd given it away to everyone else? I hope your fucking dick falls off, the next time you try to stick it in someone."

Then she was slamming the suitcase shut. Then she was gone, trailing lingerie behind her. Filmy crimson gauze and the scent of vanilla.

Jesús blacked out for a few moments then, or so it seemed—as bad as his worst binges, back in the day. When the room took shape around him again, he staggered to the open window, and there was Alondra in the street, stalking away. Even like this, she was beautiful.

He slammed the window down, hard, and the glass cracked, spidering brilliantly along a thousand fault lines. Jesús pressed his hand to the glass, heedless of the tiny cuts that opened up along the skin. *Heal*, he whispered.

Heal, heal, heal. And *así perfecto,* the glass sealed itself, was whole again, as if it had never been touched. Never fractured.

Of course, in a few weeks, it would just shatter again. Nothing lasted in his world. Nothing good.

His phone rang. Numbly, he answered. If it were Alondra . . .

"Ralph. No, no, it's okay. You're not interrupting anything." Everything was finished.

Norton sounded on edge. Another one of the Demon Princes was prowling around, had been giving him a hard time.

"Oh? I don't suppose you know his name? Kenneth. Got it." Jesús's voice was flat and cheerful, as if nothing had happened. Nothing at all. "Sure, I can swing by. I'll come by after work today, okay? Around 6? See you then." Not the same Prince. Jesús didn't care. He just wanted to hit someone.

It wasn't time to go to the island yet. He had thirty minutes to kill. That was dangerous; empty time led to the bottle. Jesús would check on his guy. It was one of the first lessons he'd learned as a general contractor—the guys were great, but needed supervision to do their best work. If you didn't keep an eye on them, they'd wander off and fuck random Demon Princes. Well, not exactly, but same idea.

Besides, he liked to check in. Taking care of people kept him busy. By now, the guys expected it. Back to abuelita's. He called Squeegee and told him to meet him there—the three of them could drive over to the island together.

Crackle worked fast. Not even two hours gone, but he'd already cut the glass into tiles and laid the base of the mosaic, inspired by one of *abuelita*'s sketches.

"Good work, man." Jesús nodded approval, then went inside to check in with his grandmother. What he really wanted to do was slump down into a little huddle at her feet, let her stroke his hair. The way she'd done when he was just a little boy, and the white boys had beaten him up at the bus stop.

But she wasn't alone. Juanita and Bibiana were chattering at *abeulita*'s sunny kitchen table when he arrived: "We're here to study! Big exam!" They worked here often; growing girls needed food, and his grandmother kept them well supplied. Though it wouldn't be long before *abuelita* made them put aside their books and drafted them into slicing tomatillos. School was important, but so was food. His grandmother already had the oil heating on the stove, and a massive pile of diced onions waiting. She smiled and nodded to the bowl full of green chilies; he dutifully started chopping them. If his eyes teared a little, no one would notice.

"*Abuelita* said you're all leaving at eight?" Bibiana asked. A little extra emphasis on the *all*, which wasn't for Jesús or Crackle, but for the third member of today's team, who'd be joining them soon for the drive over to the island. She seemed to have a crush on Squeegee, which Jesús did not understand.

With squeegees for hands, just what, exactly, did Bibiana think the man could do for her? He was great to have on the job, squirting water at need; he could clean up a work site faster than anyone. But off the job, he was pretty useless. And how would that work, if Juanita and Bibiana were also a couple? Maybe they were hoping to seduce Squeegee together.

Jesús would never be able to tolerate anything like that. One woman had always been enough for him. It had broken his heart when his wife left him for that nat after Jesús's card turned—not even a good-looking man, but "normal," which was apparently good enough for Consuela. She'd sworn she'd love Jesús forever, when they'd married in the little church at the end of the block, but she'd been too repulsed by all the bits that had started falling off Jesús. Even though they always grew back.

The drinking had gotten pretty bad that year, even worse than the year Rosita had died. Jesús had lost days, woken up in alleys, covered in vomit. Maybe a blessing in disguise. Losing Consuela had knocked him down far enough and hard enough that Jesús had finally realized he was in serious trouble. He'd gotten clean, and then found Alondra, who was hotter and sweeter than his wife had ever been. *La dulceza* . . . he could just lick her up . . . god. Jesús stuffed a green chili in his mouth and bit down, letting the sweet, sharp pain of it distract him for just a moment. Burn, baby, burn.

It was none of Jesús's fucking business what Juanita and Bibiana got up to, or whom they invited into their bed. The less he thought about that, the better. As long as Juanita kept her grades up, that was all he asked. For now, he was glad to have a job to do, his hands busy with the knife and the chilies. The rhythm of the cutting, a task at hand—hard work was good for fighting off demons. The kitchen's big picture window looked out onto *abuelita*'s garden, making it easy to keep an eye on Crackle's progress.

The man looked up, waving him over. Jesús soaped, rinsed, and dried his hands on a weathered orange dishtowel, then pushed the screen door open and stepped outside.

"Eh, Retazos. What do you think?" Crackle's pale, peeling hands carefully laid the last pieces of the mosaic, a shiny gold tile.

"It looks beautiful," Bibiana said, coming out of the kitchen with her camera in hand, snapping photos.

"Put the camera down, Bibi," Juanita said, joining them. The screen door clattered shut behind her. "Just enjoy the moment."

"You enjoy it your way, and I'll enjoy it mine," Bibiana said calmly, clicking away.

The tilework was stunning, whether you looked at it through a lens or not. A quetzal reared, proud and glorious, a cascade of bright colors against a field of jungly green. And pink roses flowered at its golden feet—but wait, no. Some of the roses were red; Jesús frowned, his chest twinging a little. He'd specifically told Crackle that Rosita had loved pink roses, that his *abuelita* had asked for them. He had to fix this before she came out and saw; it would upset the old woman.

"Crackle—" but before more than the name had come out of Jesús's mouth, the red roses bled redder. A contagion, the tip of one tile touching another, the color seeping in a slow wave. Within a few moments all of the roses had turned red, which was impossible. *"Madre de dios!"* he whispered.

Juanita let out a little screech and stepped back, banging up against the door, which had closed behind them. The red was spreading faster, eating into the green jungle tiles. The tiles were weeping blood, and now Crackle was swearing, a steady, bewildered stream of obscenities dropping from his mouth. He reached towards the tiles, as if to pick one up, or try to use his power on them—

"Don't touch it!" Jesús shouted, and dashed forward, knocking Crackle aside. He didn't know what was going on, but he knew he didn't want one of his guys touching whatever that cursed substance was. Something was horribly wrong here. And now the quetzal was going, every golden tile turning a dark, rusty red. The blue ones too, the entire circle of tilework submerged in a sea of red. What would happen when it consumed all the tiles? His heart was pounding in his chest, and his vision had gone blurry with panic.

"Out of the way, *nieto!*" Jesús turned, and his grandmother was running towards them, a huge pot in her small hands. It looked too big for her to lift, but she'd been cooking for decades, stirring massive pots of rice and beans. She had arm muscles tough and strong as iron, and Jesús ducked out of the way as she swung the pot in the air, sloshing liquid—corn oil, from the scent of it—over the sea of red.

The red was starting to climb the trunk of the black walnut, eating away at it, and it was Juanita who pulled a lighter out of her pocket—he'd *told* the girl he didn't want her smoking! But she lit a spark and threw the flaming lighter into the pool of oil. **Fwoosh!** It went up, a blast of heat beating at them, so that if they hadn't already been pulling away from the horror in the garden, it would have knocked them to their knees.

Flames raced the ground, climbing a tree that should've been too green to burn so easily. But it burned hard and fast. Jesús stood between the women and the fire, though what he would do against bleeding tiles if fire failed them, he had no idea. Crackle stood on the far side of the flames, hopefully safely away from it all. Juanita was sobbing now, but he didn't dare to turn to comfort her, eyes locked on the burning tree.

When it finally burned out, they were left with nothing but a dead walnut tree, scorched into a blackened caricature of itself, and a circle of equally dead ground.

"Concrete, *abuelita*," Jesús said, in a voice that he had to work to steady. "I'll be by tomorrow, and we're going to bury that spot in concrete. Tonight, you stay at Juanita's, okay?" Juanita had her arms wrapped around their *abuelita*, and Bibiana was close as a shadow by her side. Shock and horror on their young faces.

The little old woman nodded and said nothing. Arms crossed in front of her, staring at the remains of her tree.

The drive to the island passed in a blur, Jesús's fingers too tight on the steering wheel. Crackle filled Squeegee in, speaking softly. "What the hell was it?" Squeegee asked.

Crackle's voice was shaky. "*Hell* is right. Only God knows! There's some weird shit out there, you know?"

The guys must've read his mood. After that, they'd fallen silent. Jesús chanted the Apostles' Creed in his mind—according to the nuns of his elementary school, the holy words would keep the demons away, of whatever kind.

He ascended into heaven, and is seated at the right hand of God the Father Almighty; from there He will come to judge the living and the dead. Would his namesake protect him now? From demons, perhaps. Not from betrayals of the flesh.

I believe in the Holy Spirit, the Holy Catholic Church, the communion of Saints, the forgiveness of sins . . . What sins had Jesús committed, to have such misery wreaked on him? He tried to be a good man. He tried so hard.

. . . the resurrection of the body, and life everlasting. Life everlasting. Was that supposed to be a good thing?

When Jesús finished the prayer, he started again at the beginning. Over and over. It calmed him enough that when they pulled up at the door, Jesús was able to shift into work mode.

Mr. Dutton was important, and far kinder that one might guess from first impression. Someday, Jesús would like to introduce his *abuelita* to Mr. Dutton, if only to see just how fast she'd curse him to the Hell she'd be positive he'd come from. Yellowish skin shrunken down over the bones, red eyes; Dutton looked like a living skeleton, *como un calaca en el Día de los Muertos.* But like those icons, Dutton was more cheerful than terrifying. Maybe his *abuelita* would simply ask him to help her talk to her long-dead parents.

And if he could help her, Dutton would try, the way he lent a wealthy hand to all the jokers he encountered. There were plenty of handymen who lived closer and would get to his jobs faster, but Jesús knew that Dutton called *his* crew so he'd have an excuse to get a little more money into the hands of jokers in need. Jesús wasn't about to complain, even if it was a hike out here.

"What do you think, Jesús? Can you save her for me?" Dutton leaned on his silver-headed cane, and cast his red eyes over the crystal chandelier laid out on the entryway floor, the silver frame bent and mangled, crystals fallen and shattered across the split cobalt blue tiles.

Jesús frowned. "The tilework looks straightforward enough, since we have plenty more stored in the basement from when we first laid them." He turned to Crackle, the third member of their little group, kneeling on the floor and soberly contemplating the devastation of the chandelier. "What do you think?"

Crackle frowned, though given how the wild card had left his skin, cracked and peeled like a bad piece of laminate, it took most people a while before they could read his expressions. Great advertising for his tile work, though—one look at him, and homeowners started fretting about that bit of cracked tile in the shower, or the vinyl that had started wearing out in the kitchen. That wasn't why Jesús had hired him, but it didn't hurt.

"I can take care of it today; it'll be set and ready to walk on by Wednesday." He pulled himself to his feet and stretched out his arms, wriggling the extra fingers. Twenty fingers made for speedy tilework. Though it was his skill and artistry that had actually gotten him on this crew.

Jesús nodded. Crackle knew his stuff, and if he said a thing would happen, it would. It was a good thing he was a man with integrity; his turning card had also left him with a minor power, almost the inverse of Jesús's—he could lay hands on something and hurry along its destruction. Just a touch, but it was useful when he was trying to get a bit of adhesive to give up its stubborn hold on some old tile.

Jesús said to Dutton, "So the tiles should be fine. And Goggles can get this ceiling repaired in a jiff." Goggles loved working on the high ladder— it amused him how freaked out people got, when they realized a blind guy was up there. Sometimes his tuneless whistling did get on Jesús's nerves, but since Goggles used it to feel the dimensions of the space, he tried not to actually complain. They tolerated and compensated for each others' needs on this crew, even the annoying bits. Short Step didn't love it when one of Jesús's body scraps fell into one of his paint buckets, but he put up with it. It all went around.

Why couldn't Alondra understand something so simple? He couldn't just pull away from everyone, just for her. Everything would fall apart.

Jesús frowned, wrenching his thoughts back to the job. "The chandelier itself . . . I can pick up more crystals tonight, but it's going to be a long restoration job, getting the frame repaired properly." His fingers were itching to work on it—it was a chance to haul out his most delicate tools—but he had to be up front with the client. That was how you stayed in business for the long haul. "You might do better to just replace it . . ."

Dutton shook his skeletal head fiercely. "No, no. Do you know how long it took me to find this beauty? I searched the French countryside for *months* before this eighteenth-century treasure leapt into my hands." He reached down and caressed a gleaming curve of silvered metal. "She waited for me for over two hundred years. I need her restored, and properly. Can you do that?"

"It'd be a pleasure, Mr. Dutton." Jesús loved this kind of work; it was so rare in his daily rounds that he was allowed the time and resources to build something beautiful. "I'll take it home and get started right away—I should have something to show you within a few months."

Dutton frowned. "Oh, no. I need it by Friday!"

Jesús's heart failed; he shook his head slowly. "Impossible. I could do a quick patch that would hold it together 'til then, but it wouldn't be done right, and it wouldn't last." He'd been foolish to get excited about the job. So little really lasted in this world.

Dutton frowned. "Can you do the patch, and then pick her up Saturday, take her away and restore her properly?"

"Seems like a waste of your money," Jesús said dubiously. *And my time.* Make the patch, hang the crystals, then take them all off again so he could repair it properly . . . why would Dutton want that?

Dutton sighed dramatically, sounding very tired and very French. "I have an important investor dinner this Friday, and the investors are from Paris. I really need this hanging in the dining room for them to admire; it'll be high enough that they won't be able to see the details. If it'll hold together?"

"Oh, it'll hold." For a few weeks, reliably, so 'til Saturday should be no problem. Dutton wouldn't have a chandelier crashing down again—not unless he repeated his mistake of bringing a troubled joker into his house, one whose very footsteps made the earth shake. That's what had brought this down in the first place. Sometimes, his kind nature did Dutton no favors.

"Good, then that's the plan." Dutton grinned, a disconcerting expression on that face. "A pleasure doing business with you, Jesús."

"As always, Mr. Dutton. I'll get the crew to work right away—we'll be here first thing tomorrow, hopefully with the crystals in hand." Another reason to go to the junkyard tonight—that was his best chance at finding replacements.

"Wonderful. And oh, can I ask a favor? Bring me some of your *abuelita*'s tamales when you come in tomorrow? It's not easy to get good Mexican food out here, even for me."

Jesús managed a smile, though his heart wasn't in it. No need for Dutton to know that, though. He'd shared some of his lunch tamales with the crew and Dutton the second time they'd done a job here, and Dutton hadn't forgotten that taste. "I'm sure she'll be happy to make you some. It might be a day or two before I can bring them, though." He'd have the concrete poured in the yard tonight, have *abuelita* moved back into her house within a few days, if all seemed back to normal there. There'd be time to handle it all, take care of everyone. He could handle it.

"Perfect!" Dutton said, with a skeletal grin. He clapped a bony hand on Jesús's shoulder, then turned to sweep his way up the grand staircase, the tails of his Victorian frockcoat flaring behind him as he went.

The day went by, somehow. Hours dragged, but eventually, it was time to stop. Jesús sent a few of the crew over to take care of *abuelita*'s concrete. Crackle was still too shaken to go back. Jesús would go over and make sure everything was all right—it wasn't as if he had anything to rush home for. But first, Norton's, and the crystals.

Jesús paused outside Norton's chain-link fence—just out of view, voices came through clearly. The first was low, aggressive. "I told you, Ralphie. If you don't give us what we want, you're going to regret it."

"Hey, c'mon, Aggie . . ."

"It's *Agares!*" the voice barked.

Jesús balled his fists, hard, fingernails digging into his palms. His throat went dry. He took a small step forward, just enough to peer around the back of the massive fridge that sat at the edge of the parking lot. The man snapping the words didn't look particularly intimidating on his own, despite the long black cloak. But a massive bird rode hooded on his arm, and Jesús suspected that a wickedly sharp beak matched the claws digging into the leather. Not something anyone would want to mess with.

"Right, right. Agares." Ralph had his hands out, gesturing for calm. "Didn't mean no disrespect."

Jesús was trembling. What he *wanted* to do was storm in there, start swinging. It would feel so good to take him apart. Jesús was angriest with Alondra; she was the one who'd betrayed him. But that didn't mean he didn't also want to *murder* the man who'd been fucking her. Fucking her in his own damn bed.

But there was that bird, and whatever weaponry hid beneath the cloak. Demon Princes didn't just wander around unarmed. Ralph wouldn't be any good in a fight, that was for sure. The smart thing to do was to wait, let Ralph talk the guy down. Jesús pressed his forehead against the chain link, hard enough that he was sure he was leaving an imprint. The pain beat a counterpoint to the pounding in his brain. What he needed was a beer, or ten.

Ralph was babbling, a calming stream of words. It seemed to be working. Agares threw up his own hands in disgust and swirled away, cloak flaring. The bird on his arm hissed and bridled, but stayed put as they stalked away, into the depths of the junkyard.

Jesús waited until they were out of earshot, then stepped forward, slipping through the gate. "Ralph," he said softly. "You okay?" He was okay himself—the words were fine, clear. No sign of rage showing through.

"Retazos," Ralph said, his voice also lowered. "I shouldn't have called—it'll just make more trouble if you're here. Look, I pulled the crystals for you. Here. Take them, and come back Sunday with your crew, if you still want to." The man shoved a large cardboard box at him, stuffed with glittering glass.

"You sure, Ralph?"

"Yeah, yeah." He wiped a cushioned arm across his sweaty forehead. "Just go, okay? I'll be fine."

Jesús couldn't wait 'til Sunday to confront Agares. If he just had an excuse to come back, after he'd prepared himself—"Hey, look. I just got myself a mobile phone last month. Super-useful on the job. Here's the number. If anything worries you, you call me, okay? I'll be here. And I won't come alone."

Ralph smiled weakly. "I won't need it. But thanks."

"*No se preocupe.*" Jesús was walking away, all his concentration going to balancing the box carefully. He couldn't drop it—that'd shatter the crystals, and give everything away.

Maybe it was actually seeing the guy. Maybe that was what broke him. He stopped for a beer on the way, the sweetness of it almost bringing him to his knees. Then another. It had been so fucking long. Only knowing that Dutton and the crew were waiting kept Jesús from having a third. If he had a third, he'd start to forget. He wanted to forget everything.

Jesús knelt on the entryway floor, fingers spread across the twisted metal, straightening it carefully, bit by bit. He was trying to concentrate on his work, but it was so damn hard with Goggles whistling like that.

"Quiet down, Goggles."

"Sorry, boss."

Goggles *said* sorry, and would quiet down or even stop for a few minutes. But then, absent-mindedly, he'd start up again. Just a habit when he was on the job, or walking around, or even just awake. Whistling, whistling, all the time.

It wouldn't be so bad if the bastard could just whistle *on key*, but no. It was getting in his head, rattling around in there, and Jesús's head was way too heavy to take that too. He was trying to fucking concentrate here, didn't Goggles understand that? This was a tricky bit of work, persuading the metal out of its twisted form, back into an elegant, shapely curve. As lovely as the curve of Alondra's nalgas, rising up from the tops of her thighs as she lay sleeping in their bed, just waiting for him to wake her. . . .

"*weetwootweetweetwoohwoohwooh* . . ."

"Can you just fucking give it a rest! For five fucking minutes?"

"Hey—not cool, boss." Short Step was there, suddenly, beside him, in that annoying way he had. World's most useless teleportation power—three feet in a random direction. He mostly didn't even try to use it, but every once in a while, it took him exactly where he wanted to go. And right now, where he wanted to be was uncomfortably close to Jesús, a grim expression on his face.

"Yeah." Slick had stepped over too, putting her greasy hand on his arm. "Maybe you should go take a walk? Clear your head?"

Jesús shook her hand off, trying not to be too abrupt about it. He hadn't *meant* to snap at Goggles. "Sorry. Sorry, guys. Sorry, Goggles. It's been a day." He stepped back, a little more space between him and the crew, who were clearly worried about him. He never talked that way to them. "A walk's a good idea. I'll be back in ten."

He started walking down the first floor hallway, heading away from the too-crowded entryway. Jesús tried to breathe, slow and steady. In for four, hold for four, out for four, hold again. Parlor, ballroom, second parlor, dining room—how many rooms did one man need, anyway?

He'd told Crackle to take the rest of the day off. Tomorrow Crackle would be back, though, to repair the entryway tiling, and then they'd all be talking about what had happened at *abuelita*'s. Which was better than talking about him and Alondra, which would *also* no doubt get around soon enough. He'd met Alondra through Crackle, after all—they were cousins.

Jesús still had no idea what had happened at his grandmother's. He didn't want to think about that blood-red tide, creeping across the tile, swallowing up his dead sister's lovely pink roses. Dining room, kitchen. Butler's pantry.

He was standing in front of the liquor cabinet. Mr. Dutton never locked it, didn't lock anything in this house; he trusted Jesús and his men. They could pick up a five-thousand-dollar watch and walk right out the door. Or drink down a thousand-dollar bottle of whiskey. Whiskey had never been Jesús's drink of choice, but Dutton didn't keep cheap beer on hand. Whiskey would do.

Jesús reached out, grasped a bottle, the amber liquid sloshing beautifully. He'd be classy about this—use a glass, instead of drinking straight from the bottle. Cut crystal tumblers from the cabinet, and the liquor poured out in a glorious stream, only splashing a little on the zinc countertop.

It wasn't Jesús's fault; his hand was shaky. Stupid hand. Stupid body. Falling apart on him, all the time, and his brain falling apart too. Jesús was broken, and that's why Consuela had left him, that's why Alondra had cheated on him, and how could he blame them, stuck with such a . . . he didn't know the fucking *word*.

There had to be a word in Spanish that described exactly the kind of low-down nasty piece of shit that he had become, but he couldn't ask *abuelita*. It had almost killed her, seeing what drink had done to him. That thought slowed the path of glass to his lips. After the last time, after the nightmare of this morning, what would it do to the old woman, to hear that Jesús had fallen back into his old ways?

Nope. Not a good enough reason, not when he could *smell* the alcohol. And now the glass was at his lips, the whiskey mellow and smooth as it went down, oh God. He'd never tasted anything like this before. Maybe he was a whiskey man after all.

"Jesús! What the hell, man!" And Smokescreen was there, coalescing out of a cloud of smoke and dirt, grabbing the glass out of his hand. "You *promised* us. After the last time—no more!"

Bastards. "I don't owe you anything. Give me that."

"No way! Hey, guys! **GUYS!**" Smokescreen grabbed the bottle too, and disappeared into a cloud of smoke, so that Jesús would only look a fool if he tried to grab the glass or bottle out of it. But he couldn't help himself— he had to grab. He tried, and stumbled, staggering through the smoke and banging his head into the doorframe. *FUCK.*

"What's going on?" That was Goggles, crowding in, with Squeegee just behind. And they were all here, the whole damned crew, crowding into the tiny butler's pantry, and at least the glassware was safely behind leaded glass cabinet doors, because otherwise these clumsy fools would smash it all.

Or maybe that was him. The clumsy fool.

"He's drinking again!"

"Oh no!" "Boss, you *promised* us!" "Not fucking again!"

A chorus of voices, and Jesús's head was pounding now; between the beers and the whiskey and the doorframe, he couldn't think straight at all. "Shut up! Shut up shut up shut up!"

He was shouting, and maybe that was just too much for them, because the next thing he knew, Slick must've shot some grease onto the floor because his feet went out from under him. Jesús thumped down onto his ass, and then Goggles was saying, "Cool him down, Squeegee. You know what to do." And oh, no. Not again. Jets of ice cold water slamming into his face, drenching his head, his shirt.

"Okay, okay. Enough! Enough, guys." Jesús had buried his face in his arms, but the cold water had found its way through, water pouring down his cheeks, hiding the tears.

"You'll stop shouting?" Goggles asked sternly.

"Yes."

Smokescreen added, "You'll stop drinking?"

Jesús wanted to say yes. But how could he? Liquor was the only thing holding all the pieces of him together. The moment stretched, painfully long, and it was only the ringing of his new mobile phone that rescued him. He dragged it out of his jeans pocket, thankful that it hadn't gotten drenched too.

"Bibiana?"

"*Tío Jesús!* I figured it out! I went to the library and researched and it took me forever, but I just kept digging and digging, comparing photos—"

"Slow down, Bibi—"

"No, I can't! Where did you get that glass? You have to go there, burn it all down! That was a Swarm bud at *abuelita's!* There's no way there's just one!!!"

Fuck.

"This makes no sense, boss," Slick asked. "The Swarm are all gone, aren't they?"

"Apparently not." They hadn't let him drive; Slick had the wheel of his truck, and he'd been jammed in between her and Goggles. The rest were coming in Squeegee's van, and Crackle was going to meet them at the junkyard. He might've talked them all into going just to help out Ralph, but he didn't have to—once they heard what had happened with *abuelita*, they were all just as determined to deal with this as he was. That bastard Swarm had messed with *family*.

Slick pulled up, braking way too hard and grinding the gears, but it didn't matter. They were piling out of the jeep, the van, and when they heard the howl of despair from the junkyard, they raced through the chainmetal gates. Jesús was having visions of Ralph, swallowed up by a massive pile of Swarm goo. There couldn't just be a bud, after all—no, somewhere in the junkyard, there must be more buried, Swarm mass that had just been lurking, growing like yeast, for the past five years. And now, it had been exposed, and it was ready to attack . . .

He raced around a corner, and there was the trailer, and there was Ralph—but there was no mass of Swarm swallowing him up. Instead, three men in black leather circled him. Agares leaning in, hand on Ralph's throat, squeezing.

"C'mon, Mr. Garbage. You've been holding out on us. You gotta know where the Swarm's been hiding."

Did these idiots actually think they could *use* the Swarm? Like a weapon? They'd just get themselves eaten, and that would be fine with Jesús, except for the tiny detail that if the Swarm got loose, it would end up eating everyone else too. Everyone on the damn planet, and when it finished that, it'd eat the planet too. God, he NEEDED that drink.

"*Let go of him!*" Jesús bellowed it loudly enough that the guy holding Ralph was startled and released his grip. Ralph fell to his knees, gasping for air.

Fuck, now they were coming at his crew. Smokescreen disappeared into a cloud of smoke—good, hide, he was no good in a fight anyway. And Short Step teleported away—boop, boop, boop, dammit, wrong direction, boop, okay good, he had disappeared, probably behind a stack of junk somewhere.

That left five of them. Slick grinned and crouched in a fighter's stance, arms crossed in front of her, chanting a count: *one, two, three*—and on three, she shot, grease arcing out in a precise line, right to the feet of the charging Demon Princes. They might be kick-ass fighters, but they couldn't do much against grease. Their feet shot out from under them, just the way Jesús's had, back in the butler's pantry, and they landed on their asses, hard.

But then Agares's hawk was swooping down at them, and Squeegee's jets of water were just barely strong enough to beat the bird back. And the Princes were picking themselves up, and seemed to have learned their lesson about trying to charge. Instead, they were pulling out guns. *Fuck.*

"Boss, boss, what do we do?" Crackle was waving his arms around, wriggling his fingers wildly, but seriously, what good was a little degradation going to do in a junkyard? Everything here was falling apart already! Goggles had ducked down behind them—could he see *anything* here? He was whistling, but there was so much stuff here, it would take him forever just to suss out the shape of the place. And now the guns were lifting, in slow motion, or maybe it just felt that way. Everything was happening too slow and too fast, all at once, and Jesús's heart felt like it was going to pound its way right out of his body. *Shit!*

Jesús grabbed for the closest thing that might work as a shield against bullets—a car door, rusted solid. He couldn't budge it.

Crackle saw what he was doing, grabbed it, and it came loose with a screech. But that wasn't all that came loose. The whole car started to fall apart, and then dragged itself back together. Jesús felt the power go out of him, in a sickening surge that dropped him to his knees. He'd never used so much before, and he wasn't exactly *fixing* anything—he was fixing them wrong, so they fused together, the pieces of this car, and the next car, and the truck beyond that, and whatever the fuck that other thing was—a stove? All fusing together, rising up, to form a kind of garbage-monster.

He couldn't do this. He couldn't keep it up; Jesús could feel the power running out of him, like water, like blood. He wasn't strong enough; he'd never been strong enough. He was almost out of strength, his body falling to the ground, his hands digging into the dirt, clawing for one more ounce of strength. Because these were his guys, and he couldn't lose them.

He'd lost Consuela, he'd lost Alondra. Most of all, he'd lost his sweet Rosita, lost her too soon to the darkness that waited for them all. He wasn't going to lose any more of his people, not today. Not while there was breath in his body.

Somewhere, Jesús found one more ounce of strength, just enough to push forward the garbage-monster he'd created. It took a massive, creaking step, and slammed down between the Demon Princes and his crew, the metal groaning in protest. It was done, and so was he.

Maybe he'd done enough, though. He'd bought them some time. In those few seconds, Short Step finally managed to jump in the right direction for a change, long enough to grab a gun out of Agares's hand and jump away again. He stopped jumping then, and just fucking shot the guy. In the knee, which was maybe not the best option, but it was enough to get the Prince down on the ground, screaming. It sounded so sweet, Jesús almost didn't mind that Short Step had been the one to pull the trigger. For a moment, Agares started to blur, to shift into what must be the hawk form the wild card had gifted him, but maybe he couldn't do it with a gunshot in his knee, because a moment later, he was there again, solidly human and still screaming.

Then Smokescreen was there, sneaking up behind one of the other Princes in a cloud of dirt and grime, slamming a two-by-four down on the guy's head. *Boom.*

Jesús could see it all, from his prone position, through the cracks in the fused garbage-monster he'd created. One more to go—but then the third Demon Prince threw up his hands in surrender.

It was over, *gracias a Dios!* The garbage-monster fell to pieces in a shiver of relief, rusty metal tumbling to the ground. And Ralph was weeping, and honestly, Jesús couldn't blame the man, because that had been fucking terrifying. Jesús didn't even want a drink right now. Maybe it was the adrenaline; his head felt clearer than it had in months. Though his legs were so wobbly he could barely stand.

Jesús picked his way through the pile of junk he'd created—he still didn't actually know how he'd done that. The guys were gathered around Ralph.

"You okay, Ralphie?" "It's over now, whew." "Maybe we should get that guy Short Step shot to a hospital?" "What about the other one?" "Smokescreen, didn't know you had it in you!"

Jesús almost missed it, because Short Step was the one keeping his gun trained on the third Prince, but the guy shifted just a little, and something . . . wiggled? Inside his coat.

Jesús snapped, "What have you got there? Hey, hand it over!"

The guy shook his head, but Jesús darted forward and grabbed at whatever it was. *Gah*—a pulsing mass of tissue, taking some kind of shape. Small—barely as big as his fist. A Swarmling bud, not quite formed yet. "You can't keep this, you idiot! We have to burn it!"

The Prince snatched it back, frowning, not seeming to care about the gun Short Step was waving at him now. Jesús groaned and reached to grab it again, but before he could, Ralph had intervened, grabbing it himself.

In one smooth, beautiful move, Ralph shoved it into his mouth.

Jesús's own mouth fell open. "Ralph! What the hell, man! You can't eat—that, whatever that is!"

Ralph grinned, looking much too pleased with himself. "I think I can, actually."

"You, um, feelin' all right?" Crackle asked.

"Just fine, fellas." Ralph burped. "I can eat anything, you know."

"We have to fan out and search this place." It was the third Demon Prince speaking, in a serious tone, as if he expected them to listen.

"Who the hell do you think you are?" Jesús asked. He could still find the strength to punch someone. He was sure of it.

But the man said quietly, "SCARE. If I may . . ." he gestured towards his coat, and Jesús nodded reluctantly at Short Step, who lowered the gun a few inches. The man pulled out a badge and handed it over. **John Ramos. Special Committee on Aces Resources and Endeavors.**

Ramos frowned. "I've been undercover working on this operation for three months! You are going to be in serious trouble, Mr. Norton, if we can't find any more of the alien biotech here. I've been searching for years now, and all my leads pointed to this junkyard. I'm sure there's more here; we just have to look for it."

Ralph asked, "What are you going to do with it if you find it?"

Ramos smiled. "Oh, the government has a plan."

Jesús didn't particularly trust the government, *or* their plans regarding a piece of alien biotech as dangerous as the Swarm. But they did need to find the Swarm material, if it was actually here. "All right, guys. Let's make a search grid, start looking."

Ralph threw up a hand, stopping them. "I don't think that'll be necessary," he said. "Despite what I told you before, I do know this place pretty well. It's *mine*. While there may be some more bits here and there, that I'll be happy to hunt down, there's only one place I can think of where there might be a good amount of material. Come with me."

He walked over to the edge of the compound, and they trailed after. Finally, he stopped in front of the massive fridge by the gate, and pulled the rusty door open.

"*Madre de dios!*" Jesús whispered. Green and glowing. Every inch of it was jammed full of a pulsing monstrosity. He took an involuntary step backwards, and noted that the SCARE guy did the same. But Ralph just grinned and stretched, cracking his knuckles. "It's like Thanksgiving and Christmas rolled up into one. It's going to take me a little while to eat through all of that, but I'm ready, fellas. I've been training for this for *years*." Ralph reached in with two big, fleshy hands, and scooped up a huge handful of Swarm goop.

"But my sample!" the SCARE guy yelped.

Jesús frowned and shook his head, and Short Step kept the gun on Ramos. If Ralph could really handle this, better to finish it now. "Sorry, buddy. This is a neighborhood problem, and we've got our own solution. Better luck next time."

Ralph had the biggest smile on his face. They stood there, Jesús's whole crew, and watched the man eat until the job was done. It was always good to see someone really enjoying their meal. Jesús's *abuelita* would approve.

In the end, they'd brought Ramos back to *abuelita*'s; he had a piece of tech used to search for Swarm material, and even though Ramos admitted it wasn't as effective as he liked, he could certify the black walnut was completely free of Swarm. The man been disappointed about that, of course, but life was full of disappointments.

Maybe the disappointments weren't what mattered. Jesús still couldn't think about Alondra without flinching away in pain—like a nasty raw wound, that you couldn't help poking on occasion, and then suffering for it. But he was starting to think that there had never been much to the relationship. She'd been sexy, of course, and she'd tolerated what the wild card had left him. But they hadn't wanted the same things out of life. Maybe Jesús deserved better than someone who just tolerated him.

They were all crowded around the kitchen table now, hip jostled against hip, knee against knee. The concrete was almost done setting, and Crackle had plans to help *abuelita* paint it on the weekend. She was just finishing another batch of tamales, lifting them out of the steamer; Short Step was waiting with a platter, ready to serve. She hadn't blinked when Jesús introduced her to Mr. Dutton in the end, taking him entirely in stride. Jesús should have known she would. Now Dutton and Ralph flanked Ramos at the table, skeletal and blubberous, looking equally hungry and happy.

Somehow, along the way, they'd both become part of his community, his family.

As for Ramos, he managed to look both frustrated and anticipatory, his nostrils widening at the scent of the warm masa, savory chicken, simmering tomatilloes. Short Step lay a plate in front of him, and Ramos put fingers on a steaming tamale, ready to peel back the corn husk and dig in—but then paused, looking at Jesús.

"You're sure I can't convince you to reconsider? We could use you at SCARE. It'd be low-level work at first, but I think you have real management potential, and could move up quickly. The pay is decent for government work."

Jesús shook his head firmly. The money might be good. But what he had already was priceless. If things got bad again, if Jesús started to slip, he needed them, his family, to bring him back to himself. To put all the pieces together.

"*Lo siento, señor.* But no."

Ramon sighed, but then attacked his tamales with gusto. On to the next project, it seemed.

Now that all the guests had been served, his crew dug in, and the noise levels rose to happy family levels. *Abuelita* brought over his plate herself, along with a mug of atole. He still wanted a beer, but he didn't need one.

She patted Jesús on the shoulder and said quietly, "*A beber y a tragar, que el mundo se va a acabar.*" Or in other words, *eat, drink and be merry, for tomorrow we die!*

Yes, exactly. Jesús whispered a silent prayer to the heavens, giving thanks. Then he bent his head, and ate.

Age of Wonders

SIX

November 2004

NEW YORK WAS FILLED with people like Jesús Sanchez and Ralph Norton, with odd powers that turned out to be amazingly useful and earned not fame and riches but decent livings. A man with telescoping legs who washed windows. A bartender with low-level telepathy who could tell exactly when you'd had too much to drink—and pick up secrets on the side. Any number of cops with strength, speed, and agility that helped them in their work. The stories might not have been sensational, but one organization seemed particularly adept at tracking down people with unassuming but useful powers.

Raleigh tried to get a wedge into the Public Affairs office at SCARE to get statistics on wild carders in both crime and law enforcement. Failed.

"I'm just trying to get some basic statistics. Can you at least tell me how many people with wild card powers are employed at SCARE?"

"I'm afraid that won't be possible—"

"You know my next step is to submit a Freedom of Information Act request, since staffing of government agencies is of public interest."

The agent didn't miss a beat. "We look forward to receiving your request, Ms. Jackson." The line clicked off, and Raleigh dropped the phone back in the cradle.

Raleigh announced, to no one in particular, "Is SCARE or is it not the single largest employer of people with wild card powers in the United States?"

"I don't think anyone's ever asked that question," Suzy said.

"What if it is?" asked Liz, who ran the gossip column at *Aces!* "Does that mean the government really is going around scooping up everyone with wild card powers?"

"Not everyone, but a lot."

"Other countries do it," Eddie put in. "You know about MI7 in the UK, right?"

"The Silver Helix, yeah. They don't really go in for publicity, though, not like SCARE."

"Do they have anyone flashy we could do a profile on?"

"I'll check."

Raleigh interjected. "I mean, what does SCARE actually *do*? Besides give reporters the runaround?"

"Meddle," Downs answered. "They meddle."

"We are not doing an exposé on SCARE," Margot Dempsey said. She just happened to be passing through the bullpen, a mug of coffee in one hand and a folded newspaper in the other. She didn't even look up from the paper. In the next half hour the group had come up with a list of a half dozen public Silver Helix members they'd try to get profiles on, and started a pool on how likely it was that they would be able to get interviews. The odds ended up thirty to one.

Raleigh left those stories to the other reporters and kept on with her own project. The pile of folders from Downs' stash involving cops, special agents, criminals, crime, the mob, secret cons, and so on was big. Huge. She regarded it a moment.

"Or is organized crime the single largest employer of people with wild cards powers?" she asked in the next lull.

"If it turns out the Department of Labor has statistics on that, I'll give you twenty bucks," Eddie said.

"Cheapskate," she shot back.

Dempsey poked her head back in. "We're definitely not doing an exposé on the employment practices of organized crime. We're an entertainment magazine. Entertain me." She walked back down the hallway.

Raleigh and Eddie stared after her. "How does she *do* that?" Suzy asked.

So, tonight was the night. She, Gavin, and Aurora were going to have dinner together. They were nearing their first anniversary. It was well past time they met.

In the old days Aurora might have suggested whisking them off to Aces High, to show off her own social cachet. Raleigh had been to exactly one of Hiram Worcester's famous Wild Card Day dinners as a guest of her mother. She'd been six, just old enough to be trusted with adult utensils and real glassware. She'd worn a green party dress with a crinoline, black patent Mary Janes, the works. They'd gotten their picture in a big spread in *Aces!* And yes, that picture was hanging in the apartment along with other publicity shots Aurora was particularly proud of. Back at the office, Eddie had found that picture and had a laugh over it. Raleigh was more faded jeans and crazy patterned T-shirts these days. She didn't remember much about that night, except that she'd felt a little like Alice down the rabbit hole. Lots of people had oohed and aahed over her and she hadn't said a word. They'd left early—bedtime and all that.

She did remember wondering if *now* her card would turn, if being surrounded by aces would make her more likely to turn an ace, and she could come to the Wild Card Day dinner on her own merits and show off her power to a laughing Hiram, winning the admiration of all—

There should have been other chances to experience one of New York's premier social events, but then came Hiram's fall, and Aces High had shut down. Another restaurant had filled its space atop the Empire State, but it wasn't the same. Wild Card Chic was long gone, replaced by nineties cynicism and exhaustion.

No, a high-end intimidating dinner was not the way to go. They arranged to meet at Ramenrama, Raleigh's favorite Jokertown restaurant from her college reviewing days, an Asian fusion place with lots of character and excellent food, a block or so off Delancey Street. Bowls of steaming noodles and Japanese pop music on the PA. Comfortable and interesting, something to talk about if the conversation died. Her mother liked it well enough, but Gavin had never been, and Raleigh treated the outing as just the littlest bit of a test: how would he do, in a place where the jokers outnumbered the nats, or the seeming nats?

Bundled up in coats against autumn's first real chill, they waited on the sidewalk. Raleigh made sure to get there first, with Gavin in tow. Claim the high ground, as it were. The sky was dark, and street lights shone off the wet sheen of a recent rain. Late-afternoon traffic swarmed, people heading home from work or heading out for the evening. In just the few minutes they'd been here, a dozen had walked by wearing masks—a sure sign they were in Jokertown. The masks weren't as ubiquitous as they'd once been, when people here were more invested in hiding their identities or deformities. The younger generations tended to flaunt their faces with the extra noses and feathers for beards and the like. These days the masks were a retro fashion statement as much as anything.

Gavin stared at a giant of a man across the street, eight or nine feet tall at least, with bony-looking green skin, and hooded red eyes. He wore an ordinary parka and big fuzzy earmuffs against the cold. Meanwhile, a young woman in shorts and a sweatshirt with a weirdly shaped torso—barrel chest, wasp waist—ran by fast enough to blow out a wake of trash behind her. "You don't spend a whole lot of time in this part of town?" Raleigh asked.

"Not really," he said, breathing out a sigh. "Does it show?"

"Don't stare, you'll be fine," she said, and he smiled.

They had warning, when Aurora approached. She always gave a warning, a shimmer of red, a spark of orange fading to white. Muted, when she wasn't actively controlling it, but still visible. She hopped out of a cab a block away and hugged her stylish black felt coat tightly around her as she marched up the sidewalk.

Before Raleigh had a chance to make introductions, Aurora looked them both up and down. "Hey there, I'm freezing, let's get the hell inside, shall we?"

Gavin immediately relaxed a notch.

The interior was simple modern furniture, exposed ceiling from which hung a mix of Asian-style lanterns in every color imaginable. Sprawling

bamboo plants softened the corners. The place was full; about half the customers and waitstaff were jokers. One of the reasons Raleigh liked the place:
everyone got along and seemed happy to be here.

While they were arranging themselves around a black lacquer table, Raleigh made proper introductions. As expected, Aurora went in for the hug
and Gavin blushed and made some aw-shucks noises but was a good sport
about it. They ordered drinks, appetizers, and there was small talk around
bites of food—How is work at the library? You grew up in Brooklyn? An
amusing anecdote about Aurora's latest audition for a director who didn't
remember drunkenly spilling a bottle of champagne on her a decade ago.

"I didn't get the part. Maybe I shouldn't have reminded him about the
champagne," Aurora said, winking. "You don't realize what a small world
this is until you look around and see there's nobody left you haven't worked
with at least once."

"You ever think about acting?" Gavin asked Raleigh, who immediately
shook her head, Aurora along with her.

"I don't have the patience for it. I watched Mom on a movie set for exactly one day before I was bored out of my skull. You don't just have to be
good at the job, you have to be good at the job doing the same thing over and
over again for hours on end."

"My kiddo's too smart for acting. She was meant for bigger things."

"Oh, Mom."

"Raleigh still hasn't told me how you met," Aurora said to Gavin. "Maybe
you can tell me the story."

He shrugged. "Just a classic story of two kids at the reference desk. She
kept asking questions and I kept answering them. Then she gave me her
phone number."

"To call me with the information you found," Raleigh said.

"Yes, and ask you out for coffee. I think I impressed her with my amazing
ace superpower."

Aurora sat up. "You're an ace. Really?" She gave Raleigh a look, concerned
and motherly. Raleigh realized she hadn't told Aurora about Gavin's power.
It had seemed irrelevant. Gavin just threw off the statement like it didn't
mean anything. Party trick, he called it. Something to keep a conversation
going, like showing off your double-jointed elbow.

"More like a deuce. But yeah, wild card positive." He spread his arms like
he was embarrassed.

"Well, so am I. Technically a deuce, I mean. It's not like I can control
electricity or anything, but isn't it hilarious how everyone goes out of their
way to not call good-looking women anything but an ace?"

Raleigh said, hoping to change the subject, "To give Peregrine credit, she
points that out all the time."

Aurora said, "Since you're the one who brought it up, you have to tell:
what can you do?"

Gavin met Raleigh's gaze. She had her lips pressed tight in a fake smile that she was sure he'd see right through. He picked up the photocopied daily-specials menu, passed his hand over it—and the print disappeared. He offered Aurora a plain white sheet of paper. She stared at it.

"And you work in a library?" Aurora exclaimed.

"That's exactly what Raleigh said when I showed her."

"Hm, I wish we still had the Wild Card Day dinners at Aces High, Hiram would have adored this. But . . . you two have talked about this, right? You know what this means?"

"What does what mean?" Gavin said, chuckling.

Raleigh didn't want to talk about this. Not now. "We don't need to talk about this right now, Mom. It's okay."

"But you've told him, haven't you?"

Raleigh would love it if her card turned right then and there and gave her teleporting powers so she could instantly be somewhere else. Gavin was drilling a stare into her, and Raleigh was looking everywhere but at him.

"Oh," Aurora said softly, and reached for a pot sticker. "Anyone want wine? Where did our waiter go?"

Gavin said, choosing his words, "So . . . I take it that means you're also wild card positive. Ace? I mean, I've studied you pretty carefully and I don't think you're a joker—"

"Latent," Raleigh said. Gavin slumped back in his chair, and the pity in his gaze overcame his brief flash of anger. Looking at her like she was already dying in front of him. *That* was why she hadn't told him. "Most of the time I don't even think about it—"

"Which is stupid," Aurora said. "You can't not think about it, honey—"

"It's not important," Raleigh insisted. "It's not *relevant*."

But Aurora had already launched in on the tear. "I know this isn't any of my business and maybe you two aren't serious enough to start talking kids. But if you're both positive, you *can't*. Never mind what I think about being a grandmother or not, that's a conversation for another time, but you know what the odds are—"

"You were totally fine with those odds, once upon a time," Raleigh countered. Aurora clamped her mouth shut and glared.

Gavin had slid further down in his chair, his hands pressed together in front of his face. He just stared at Raleigh and seemed to be thinking hard. Raleigh pushed away from the table and stood. "Gavin, you want to take a walk? Maybe just around the block."

"Yeah, let's do that." Quickly, he also stood.

"Mom. Sorry. We'll be back in a second." Or at least, Raleigh would. She had no idea how this was going to go.

"Oh, don't mind me," Aurora said blithely.

Gavin grabbed his coat and was out the door without a backward glance. Raleigh followed.

The wind was bringing in a storm along with dead leaves, dust, and cold. They walked side by side, dodging pedestrians when they had to, hands shoved in coat pockets, before either of them spoke. "Why didn't you tell me?" Gavin finally asked.

After a moment she said, "I didn't want you to feel sorry for me, I guess. Everyone always feels sorry for me. And they shouldn't."

"You're sure you're latent and not something else?"

"Well, Dr. Finn says I might have a plaid kidney. But yeah, pretty sure it's latent."

"You could have said something. When I brought up kids. Maybe I shouldn't have brought up kids, maybe it was too soon for that. But you should have told me."

"Because we shouldn't have kids together."

"No, absolutely not, given the odds."

Any kids they had together would be positive for the virus. Would suffer the odds and probably die of the black queen. No, neither one of them was a gambler, not like that.

He put his back to a brick wall and looked out. "Being here doesn't bother you? Doesn't remind you about what might happen?" A figure passed by, not bipedal, with too many limbs and moving strangely under a wide coat.

"Maybe I want to be reminded," she said.

"You were born wild card positive, then. That means your dad—"

"Guess so," she said.

"Who—"

She put up her hand. "Don't ask. I don't know."

"How can you not know?"

"My mother was a popular actress in the swinging seventies. I've been doing some research, but . . ." She shrugged. She didn't want to talk about this.

"Lots of secrets, then."

"I'm sorry," she said softly. Preparing to say goodbye, to watch him walk down the street and return to the restaurant alone.

He said, "But also you should have told me because I care. Sure, I'll worry about you but I was already doing that."

"Yeah?"

"Yeah."

"I don't really tell anyone about it. You did feel sorry for me, for a minute. I could tell."

"You could tell, huh? You know me that well?" She didn't know him. She wasn't sure. She didn't want this to change anything. But it had. He went on, "You write about this every single day. You dig into other people's secrets like you're in a sandbox. But you can't talk about your own?"

"Nope," she said, her smile pained. "Look, Gavin, I know the kids thing means something to you, and if it's a deal breaker I understand—"

He touched her shoulder, pulled her hand out of her pocket to squeeze it. "Not a deal breaker."

"I really like you," she said.

And he kissed her. A weight came off, and she let herself rest against him, as he folded her safely in his arms. "We should go rescue your mom," he said finally.

"Not if she's flirting with that cute waiter with the blue skin."

"She was flirting with him?"

"Oh yeah." Hand in hand they walked back to the restaurant. "You want to know another secret? I've never told anyone this. Not even my mom."

"Oh?" He raised a brow; definitely interested.

"I gave myself an ace name. Just in case. I must have been about ten and I got it into my head that if I acted like an ace hard enough, I'd turn up an ace when I hit puberty."

"Oh my God I want to hear this. What was it?"

She took a deep breath and felt herself blushing. There was a reason she hadn't told anyone this. "Glitter Girl."

"Glitter Girl?" he said, started to laugh, then stifled the laugh. "That's kind of adorable. Aurora and Glitter Girl. That sounds like a team."

"I know. It was so goofy!"

"You could have worked up an act. A song and dance routine."

"Please, no, stop."

"And you never told your mom this?"

"No. And you can't tell her. She'll never let me live it down."

"Hmm," he said. "Leverage."

She laughed, grabbed his collar, and kissed him.

Raleigh had a list of names on the bulletin board. Each name from Digger Downs' files seemed to lead to five other names. As if the powers, the expressions of the virus, attracted each other. Sanchez's story led to a list of gangs that made up a tapestry of New York's underworld: Demon Princes, the Werewolves, Shadow Fists. Never mind the totally mundane and still dangerous Mafia. One name, a dangerous ace, came up over and over again: Demise. James Spector. He had his own file in Downs' archives, and it was filled with darkness.

She almost went back to show business, rather than tackle this nightmare.

Spector was dead. Most people connected with Spector were dead. That seemed to be the most common result of coming into contact with the man. Except . . .

She found another name, drew another line on her board of associations, and called Our Lady of Perpetual Misery to make an appointment.

Jokertown's religious center and long-standing cultural icon, Our Lady of Perpetual Misery, was at its third location—it had been the target of multiple hate crimes over the years, including a fire at the last location that had killed over a hundred parishioners. Still, the church was an institution that persisted under the leadership of Father Squid.

Raleigh found the rectory next door and knocked. A joker answered, a big man in a cassock who filled the doorway. His face was clammy and gray, and a cluster of small, twitching tentacles grew where his nose should be, covering his mouth like an unkempt mustache. His large, round eyes were gentle. He seemed like the kind of man who would stand between you and harm if the need arose.

"Hi, Father Squid?"

"You must be Ms. Jackson."

"Call me Raleigh, please." She held out her hand for shaking, which seemed to startle the priest for a moment. His own hand—gray, with circular impressions like vestigial suckers—emerged from the wide sleeve of his cassock. He folded her hand in his own, and his skin felt chilled. He invited her in, and had tea waiting on a coffee table in a sparsely decorated parlor. Raleigh felt like she'd gone back in time to a British period mystery.

"You want to know about Father Henry Obst?" Father Squid asked, settling his bulk on a wide sofa while she took the chair opposite.

"I'm working on some stories about how people affected by the wild card virus get caught up in crime. His name came up. I was just hoping to get his perspective but I can't seem to track him down. I hope . . . Is he all right?"

He made a thoughtful grumble, a little like surf rolling into a cave. "Father Henry was here to manage the parish while I was on the World Health Organization Tour. My goodness, that was a while ago now, wasn't it? Nineteen eighty-seven? I have to admit I haven't really spoken with him since. I'm afraid his time here wasn't idyllic." He chuckled wetly.

"Maybe enough time has passed he'd be willing to chat."

"Ms. Jackson—I hope you don't take this the wrong way. But I know some of what went on back then, some of the people involved. Very unpleasant business. You might not want to turn over some of these stones."

"Surely it was so long ago—"

"Yes, and some of these people have long memories. If they're quiet now—you might not want to shake them awake."

The warnings only made her want to delve more. This was history, it needed to be brought to light. But she placated the old priest. "I understand. I'm not trying to solve any crimes here or expose any dark secrets. It's just curiosity."

"I can tell you what I know about what happened, but I'm afraid I must respect Father Henry's privacy. I cannot tell you where he is."

She could still try to track him down. How hard could it be? How many priests had ever come through Jokertown? He had to have left a trail.

"I'd be grateful for anything you can tell me, Father. Is it okay if I record?"

Father Henry's
Little Miracle

by Daniel Abraham

This being my first time speaking to a genuine Jokertown congregation, I thought I should make something clear. I myself am not a joker. I looked like this before I drew the wild card, my daddy looked more or less like this himself, and his daddy before him. I stand before you now as a testament to the charitable nature of Southern women.
    [Pause for laughter]
                        —From the notebook of Father Henry Obst

Tuesday, February 3, 1987

JAMES SPECTOR—DEMISE—SURVEYED the carnage. The overhead light fixture had been shot during the attack, a bare bulb left shining from a neck of frosted glass with edges sharp as teeth. A low haze of gun smoke filled the apartment. Three jokers lay on the floor or the cheap kitchen table, red and green and florid purple blood spilling out of them. The Gambione men—both nats—lay among them. One joker moaned in pain, another tried to crawl for the kitchen at the back of the apartment—a dead end, but away from Spector's slow footsteps. He walked among them, turning the bodies over with the toe of his new leather shoes, staring into the eyes of the dying, adding his own constant pain to theirs, pulling death into them a little faster.

"Could you not do that?" Phan Lo snapped from the front room.

"What?"

"Whistle."

"I was whistling?"

"The song from *I Dream of Jeannie*. I hated that show."

"Sorry," he said and went back to killing people.

The apartment belonged to Zebra, a small time Jokertown drug dealer who'd thought the gang war was his chance to make it big by selling raw heroin to the Gambiones. But the Shadow Fist had found out about the deal, and Danny Mao had arranged a complication. Spector leaned over, peering into the eyes of a young Gambione. Nothing. The guy was already gone.

Zebra lay on the floor by the table, riddled with Phan Lo's bullets. Demise considered the corpse, the last blood blackening on its breast, and snorted. "Hey Phan. What's black and white and red all over?"

"Go back to whistling."

"How many you got up there?"

"Two," Phan Lo said. "Maybe three. One of them looks like he may be—you know—two. One of those conjoined things."

"I've got a five back here," Spector said.

"Yeah, but you got shot."

"A couple times," Spector allowed. The wounds were already closed, and he'd been careful to wear a suit he didn't care about much. "They all dead?"

The businesslike crack of a pistol split the air. "Yeah," Phan Lo said. "Yours?"

"Dead as fish on Friday."

"Great. Let's get the shit and get out of here."

"What's the rush? It's not like the cops are going to come to this part of Jokertown."

"The rush is I've got better things to do with my life," Phan said, stepping into the room. He was young, maybe nineteen, perfect skin and black hair pulled into one of those little ponytails in the back. Spector wondered how he'd look with his hair like that. Phan put his gun back into its shoulder holster. The Uzi was slung across his back, magazine empty. "Where's the shit?"

"Over by the table. Blue duffel has the money. The little suitcase thing has the horse."

"Where?"

"Right over . . . um. Fuck."

The patch of floor was empty, just a dead Gambione leg. Phan walked over to the spot, frowning. Spector stood beside him. Two oblong shapes were outlined in blood, but the bags were gone.

They glanced at each other, Phan remembering at the last minute to focus on Spector's nose. No eye contact if he wanted to live. Spector suppressed a little smile and shrugged. "It was right there."

"You take it?" Phan asked.

"No."

"Well I didn't take it. Check the bodies. See who's missing."

"How would I know who's missing?" Spector said. "I didn't take roll call. I just got in the door and started killing them, same as you."

Phan wasn't listening. He locked his hands behind him and began walking through the corpses, his lips pursed, his eyes shifting, searching like someone working a jigsaw puzzle. Spector scratched his moustache and sighed.

"The whore," Phan said.

Spector thought back. He'd come in the room, interrupting the meeting. The bags had been there, by Zebra's chair. Yeah, there had been a nat girl—black hair, pale skin—rubbing up against the joker. Then Phan had started spraying the room with Uzi fire and the whore had ducked under the table.

Spector hunkered down, peering over the dead bodies, hoping for a thin, pale-skinned corpse with a half-open blouse. He looked up at Phan and shook his head.

"I can't fucking believe this," Phan said.

"Hey, you were the one in the front room. You were supposed to be watching for people coming out."

"She didn't come *out* the front."

"Well, there isn't a back way," Spector said.

Phan moved back into the little kitchen without a word. Spector followed him. It was small—too small to hide in. But it did have a window; an open one with a thin ledge beyond. Spector poked his head out. It was eight stories down the street, but the ledge, thin as a sidewalk curb—led along the side of the building to a black metalwork fire escape.

"Oh," Spector said, pulling his head back in the apartment. "Well, that sucks."

Father Henry Obst watched Quasiman stir the sauce. The steak sizzled on the grill and the scent of the meat and the fried onions in the sauce filled the small kitchen in the church basement. Father Henry's spiral-bound notebook lay open before him on the table. He tapped the pages impatiently with his pencil.

"I was off my stride is all," Father Henry said. "I should have come in a day or two earlier, just to get my bearings. It's long drive from Alabama, and I ain't the young man I once was. Threw my timing off."

Quasiman looked thoughtfully over his shoulder as his leg flickered in and out of existence, but didn't speak. Father Henry took off his glasses and pinched the bridge of his nose between thumb and thick, pale finger.

"Dammit, though, I have never in my life had anyone *boo* a homily. It's rude, sir. It's just plain rude."

The hunchback blinked, considered him as if they were meeting for the first time, then smiled ruefully, nodding his head in sympathy. "Jokertown makes for a rough audience, even in church," Quasiman said.

"I'll do better next week."

"No, you won't."

"Oh, yes. Yes, I will. I've got better material. Y'all are always listening to Father Squid. Now he's a fine man, but somber, if you see what I mean. No sense of humor. I'm pulling out my Age of Empty Miracles sermon. Usually hold that one off for Easter, but I don't imagine many of these fella's will be coming down to Selma."

"He is a killer, risen from the dead," Quasiman said, his tone light and conversational. "Before that I think he sold insurance."

Father Henry put his glasses back on and the hunchback swam into focus. His expression was placid and helpful, like he'd just passed on some interesting piece of Jokertown history. Father Henry closed the notebook and considered for a moment what to say to his caretaker and guide.

"What in Christ's name are you talking about, boy?"

"I'm sorry," he said, shaking his head like he was trying to sober up. "I thought you said something."

With an apologetic shrug, the hunchback vanished. The spoon he had been stirring with slid into the sauce with a low plop. Father Henry looked at the sudden absence, shook his head, and went over to turn off the flame before the steak burned.

When Father Squid had called him with the news—the world tour with Senator Hartmann, the chance to see the fate of jokers in third-world hellholes around the globe—Father Henry had been half-afraid that the tentacled padre was going to ask him along. The request that he come up to New York and perform the Mass for a couple weeks had been such a relief that he'd agreed to it without really thinking. Now he found himself hundreds of miles from home preaching to a bunch of New York jokers and trying to keep a barely-present hunchback from scorching dinner.

He grabbed a fork and trawled the sauce until he pulled out the stirring spoon. It was too hot to hold. He found out by trying and dropped the spoon back under the surface.

The sauce wasn't quite right. Stirring with the fork with his left hand, he took a glass off the sideboard with his right, reached over for the faucet and started a thin stream of water flowing. He set his mind to the clear ribbon until his wild card surged down his arms, through his fingers, and the water blushed, bloodied, and became a cheap Merlot. He filled the glass and poured half of it into the sauce to let the alcohol cook off. The faucet was running clear again when he closed the faucet down.

He hesitated before emptying the glass, but he did. A thirteen-year-old Alabama boy, finding he can change water to wine, never took it as a sign he should become a priest. Like any right-thinking Southerner in the situation, he became an alcoholic. A thirty-six-year-old recovering drunkard and closet deuce, on the other hand, had been known to hear the call of the Lord. Even cooking with wine was actually against the rules, and tempting as it was to scootch a little farther off the wagon, Father Henry held to his resolve and had a pop with his dinner. The steak was good—juicy with just a little blood—and the sauce was tart and sweet, just enough to season the meat without drowning it. He'd give the hunchback that—the man could cook.

He cleaned his dishes when he was done and left the remains in a Tupperware box, in case Quasiman showed back up hungry. He looked over his notes one last time, sighed, and hefted himself up the stairs and out the rear sacristy door into the cool night air. Father Squid had lent him the use of the cottage for the length of his stay, and he strolled through the small herb garden and up to the locked metal door.

Back home in Selma, he would have taken a short constitutional, down to the coffee shop or possibly over to flirt for a few minutes with the Widow Lander, before going home to his own modest apartments, pictures of St. Peter's and a lovely Roman sunset over his own simple wooden desk. He might read or write letters for an hour or two before packing himself off to bed.

Father Squid's cottage was gray and close compared to his home, and it did smell like a fish market. His bags were still half-packed. He sat on the bed. It was barely eight at night, and still much earlier than he was used to going to sleep. He had hoped that the caretaker of the church might be put upon to show him around, but that had been before he'd actually set eyes on the man. Which left him with his present options.

Jokertown after dark, a lone yokel braving the meanest streets of New York or Takis or whatever you decided Jokertown was really part of. Sounded stupid. But ministering to the twisted bodies and souls around him without having the courage to meet them face straight on seemed like hypocrisy. With his luck, they'd find him floating in the bay, and Quasiman would have to find some poor Episcopalian to perform next Sunday's mass.

He snapped his fingers and snatched open his notebook. Flipping to a clean page, he wrote "In this age of empty wonders, a real miracle is something small and precious. Like me walking through Jokertown at night and not getting killed." He grinned, then frowned and crossed it out. Maybe when he got home. These New York jokers might not think that was funny.

He loaded up all the little presents his sister had sent him when she heard he was going to take the assignment—a hand-held stungun, a canister of pepper spray, and a large gaudy crucifix that mirrored the one above the pulpit with its two-headed joker Christ impaled on a DNA helix. It wasn't the sort of iconography that went over well with the Archbishop, but here it might mark him as belonging. And, of course, a camera so he could give a slide show when he got home.

"Oh, Mother," he muttered, "God bless you. You gave birth to a fool and a papist."

Despite the chill of the night, there was a good bit more foot traffic than he'd expected. Most folks ignored him, hurrying along their own business. Some jokers had their bare faces out, however disfigured. Others wore masks. Father Henry found himself falling into his old habit of smiling and nodding to people as he passed, like he was back home.

He stopped by the Crystal Palace because it was famous and, once he introduced himself as Father Squid's stand-in, had his picture taken with the eyeless bartender. The twist-spined, grey-skinned clerk at an all-night bookstore along the way home asked him with a genteel grace whether he was out whoring and still treated him respectfully when he said no. Even the thin figures standing around trash fires, rubbing their hands or tentacles seemed more benign than he'd expected. For all the fear and angry talk—joker orgies, gang war, streets it was death for a nat to walk down after dark—Father

Henry could name three or four roadhouses in Alabama that had felt more threatening to him than this.

There were some moments when he felt like he'd walked into a bad hallucination—once when a section of sidewalk yelped underfoot and shifted off to become part of a wall, another time when something like a giant tongue called to him from a storm-sewer grate and asked the time. Despite all that, by the time he stopped to buy a newspaper from a poor walrus-man, he felt almost at home.

"You're new around here?" the walrus said, smiling jovially.

"You could say that," he agreed. "Father Henry Obst. I'm filling in for Father Squid for a couple weeks."

"Well, welcome to the neighborhood," the walrus said.

"Thank you. That's very kind."

"And don't worry about it too much. I'm sure next Sunday will go better."

A true miracle would be a place without small-town gossip and slander, he thought, but kept his smile all the way back to the cottage.

The problem was, of course, how to get through the crust of anger and despair—and self-pity, worst of all self-pity—that came with drawing the joker. He'd spent enough years himself living with scorching self-hatred to know the smell when he was up to his asshole in it, as his sainted mother would have said. It was poison, but he'd seen strong souls overcome it.

The problem with despair, he thought, was that it wasn't really despair when you could see your way clear of it. If he could only . . .

"Father?"

He blinked. The woman was crouched down beside the cottage door. Woman, hell. Girl was closer. Maybe eighteen years old with black hair and eyes and a tiny little skirt. She didn't seem to be a joker of any stripe.

"Well now, miss," he said gently, "what can I do for you?"

She stood up. Poor little thing barely came to his chin, and Father Henry had never been called a tall man. Her face, now that it was more in the light, was sharp as a fox's and her shirt streaked with blood.

"You're taking over for Father Squid, right?" she demanded, crossing her arms.

"Yes, I've agreed to help take up the slack, as it were."

"So you're the priest?"

"Yes. But there's this other fella who's really taking care of the place. I've only been in the city since . . ."

"I've come to beg for the sanctuary of the church," she said, the phrase so formal it sounded rehearsed. "I'm in trouble. And I can't take it to the police because I'm a Jokertown whore, and they wouldn't help me."

She stood there, her chin jutting out like she was daring him to send her away—back to her pimp or her family or whoever put her out on these streets. Eighteen might have been guessing high. She could have been younger.

Well, Lord, he thought. *I don't know what you have in mind on this one, but here goes.*

"Well now. Let's see," Father Henry said. "There's a room in the church basement you can stay in tonight at least. We'll talk about this, see what seems like the best thing to do after that. You got a couple bags there? Let me help you with those."

Wednesday, February 4, 1987

JOEY PIRETTA KNEW KNOCKS. The cops, they knocked one way—bang bang bang like there was a pissed-off elephant coming through. Then there was the landlord, old man Fazetti; he knocked hard, but only once, showing his authority, 'cause he was the landlord and all, but still showing respect because if he didn't Joey might kill him. The one that woke him up, though, wasn't like either one of those. It was just a quiet double tap. That was Mazzucchelli.

Joey got up from the couch, adrenaline pumping, and didn't quite knock over the half-empty beer cans on the coffee table. He grabbed the orange prescription bottle off the floor and pushed it down between the rough beige cushions. It rattled like a fucking baby toy. He delivered a quick prayer up to heaven that Mazzucchelli hadn't heard it and crossed himself. The knock came again, a half a beat less time between the impacts. Joey pulled himself up, ran a hand through his hair, and tried to suck in his gut.

When he opened the door, Chris Mazzucchelli greeted him with a smile and a raised eyebrow.

"Hey," Joey said, faking pleasure and surprise. "Christ! How you doin'?"

"Fine, Joey. And you?" Mazzuccheli asked, walking into the apartment. "The wrists still bothering you?"

"They still hurt a little sometimes. The scar tissue's all messed up with the nerves. But you know how it is."

Mazzucchelli smiled and nodded to the door. Joey closed it, apologizing with a gesture. The apartment looked like hell and smelled like a cheap bar. He wished he'd gotten around to washing the dishes last night. It just didn't look professional the way they were all stacked up in the sink. Mazzucchelli walked into the living room but didn't sit. Joey stood respectfully back, crossing his arms and scratching absently at the recent pink flesh the size of a quarter on his right forearm.

"You're not still on the pain stuff," Mazzucchelli said.

"Nah. Not for weeks. Just some aspirin sometimes."

"Good. I have a job for you, Joey."

Joey tried to pull himself up a little taller and deepened his scowl, just so as Mazzucchelli knew he was taking it seriously.

"Someone interrupted a negotiation last night. They killed some of our men and the jokers we were doing business with. They also took the merchandise we were picking up and the money we'd taken to pay for it. Half a million dollars, untraceable, and a suitcase of heroin."

"Ah," Joey said, nodding.

"You understand?"

"Sure," he said shrugging. "Find 'em. Kill 'em. Get the stuff back."

"How about you start with just looking around. Once we find it, we can worry about killing people."

"Just look around. Check."

"You've been out of action for a while, Joey. You think you're up for this?"

"No trouble. None at all."

"Good. That's what I wanted to hear. I'll have Lapierre get in touch with you and . . ."

"Ah, c'mon boss. I don't need some smart-ass college fucker hanging off of me. I got sources. I can do this."

"You want to take this one by yourself?"

"Yeah. Look, if I find something, I'll let you know. Don't worry about before. The thing with Chrysalis and the arrow guy, that was a one-time thing. Never happen again."

Mazzucchelli paused, then walked over and clapped him on the shoulder. "It's good to have you back, Joey."

"Thanks, boss."

"Show some respect for yourself. Clean the place."

"I will, boss."

Mazzucchelli went out, closing the door behind him. Joey lumbered back to the couch and sat down heavily. He dug his hand into the cushions and came out with the rattling bottle of Darvon. He popped two of the great big hot pink capsules into his hand even though his arms weren't really aching much and swallowed them dry.

The pills seemed to lodge about halfway down his throat.

It just wasn't starting off to be a good day.

The Crystal Palace always looked worse in the daylight. Darkness and neon suited it better. Demise slouched across the empty lot beside it, Phan Lo two steps behind him and to his left. The day was overcast, but Phan wore dark Blues Brothers sunglasses all the same.

"Danny Mao was pretty pissed off, eh?"

"It's fine," Demise said. "I told him it was your fault."

Phan went silent for a moment, only the sound of their footsteps over the constant murmur of the city.

"You're fucking with me, right?" Phan said.

"Look," Demise said, sighing, "let's just get the shit back and then it won't matter what I said."

Demise reached the service entrance and pushed his way into the darkness. The storeroom was filled with kegs of beer and crates and boxes of harder liquor. A violet-skinned joker with a wattle like a rooster bent over a wooden crate of wine bottles, counting on his fingers. When he looked up, his eyes met Demise's briefly and a shock of pain appeared in the joker's face, the wattle shriveling and turning gray at the edges.

"We need to talk to Chrysalis," Demise said.

The joker turned and ran back into the building. Phan Lo strode forward and barked his shin on a crate.

"Take the shades off," Demise said. "You look like an idiot."

"Nah, man. I like 'em."

"Look, I *promise* not to kill you . . ."

"What do you want?" a man's voice demanded. Sascha, eyeless and frowning, walked toward them. Demise grimaced. Sascha always gave him the creeps.

"Where's Chrysalis?"

"India, I think," Sascha said.

"*Fuck,* that's right. She's on that thing with Tachyon and the senator, isn't she."

"What do you want, Spector?" Sascha asked again.

"What does anyone ever want from Chrysalis? We need some information. And we can pay for it."

Sascha's expression seemed to change. He nodded.

"There's about to be someone trying to unload about twenty-five pounds of uncut white heroin at fire-sale prices."

"And you're looking to buy?"

"No. We just need to talk with the seller."

"Since when are you working with the Fist?"

"Ran into the Sleeper a while back. He pointed out they might be hiring. The seller I'm looking for is an independent, though," he said. "Anything the Mafia's going to get pissed about has already happened. You'll be out of the crossfire."

"Leave a number," Sascha said. "I'll let you know if I hear anything."

Demise took a card out of his pocket and placed it silently on a wine rack, then nodded to Phan Lo and headed back out. A thin, cold rain misted down, and Demise turned his collar up against it.

"You must really hate that guy," Phan said. "He'd be a pain in the ass for you to kill. You'd actually have to shoot him."

"I'd manage."

"All right now," Father Henry said. "I just want you to listen here. Let me know what you think."

The church was empty except for the two of them. Quasiman sat in the first pew, his misshapen back making him look like he was praying. Father Henry, leaning against the altar, cleared his throat, pushed his glasses up to the bridge of his nose, and read from his notebook.

"Jesus could change water to wine, but it didn't put him in AA meetings the way it did me. These days, somebody walking on water would hardly get them looked at funny, and I know of two or three people who have raised folks from the dead. The virus has changed more than our bodies. It has changed what we mean by 'miracle' and . . . Now boy, you're laughing, and I haven't got to any of the funny parts yet."

Quasiman's attention had flickered away, his eyes fixed on a spot in the aisle. Something about the carpet seemed to have given him the giggles.

"Oh," Quasiman said, pointing to the space and grinning. "That's sad. I mean that's just . . . *sad*. I wish I was going to remember it."

Father Henry closed his notebook and smiled, trying to swallow his annoyance.

"I'm sorry, son. Am I interrupting something here?"

Quasiman flickered rapidly for a moment, reappeared without his left arm, and frowned vacantly at him.

"I don't know who you are right now," the hunchback commented. "There was something I was supposed to do."

Father Henry took a deep breath, letting it out slowly. Talking to the man was like preaching to an electrical problem.

"That's all right. We can try this another time."

"Try what?"

"You were showing me how to polka," Father Henry said and headed back for the sacristy.

He paused at the head of the basement stairs. He'd talked with the girl more in the night—her name was Gina, she was seventeen and running away from her pimp. That wouldn't have been difficult, except that the pimp was also an informant for the police, and so she wasn't likely to get help from that quarter. She needed to stay in town for a couple more days until her brother drove in from Seattle to get her.

He believed about half of it. Still, it was clear enough that she needed help. And if the Church wasn't there to help out whores in trouble, well then it wasn't the church Mary Magdalene had thought it was. Besides, he had a feeling about the girl . . .

Which didn't mean she'd be a good person to talk his sermon over with, but Lord knew she couldn't be much worse. He rapped his knuckles on the wall as he went down the stairs.

"Gina?"

"Hey, Father," she said. She sat on the cot, her legs tucked beneath her, watching a soap opera on the old, grainy television. He'd shown her where the clothing donations were, and she'd picked out a blue wrap-around skirt and an oversize white men's shirt. The outfit made her look like a normal girl, maybe just about to start college.

"You feeling better today?" he asked.

She nodded and turned down the volume on the set.

"Fine," she said. "Whatshisface got me a sandwich this morning."

"Good, good. I was wondering . . . well, I had a little trouble with the sermon last week. And I was working on some material, as it were, for Sunday.

And while Quasiman is a good hearted fella, he doesn't listen for spit, and I was thinking, if it wasn't too much of an imposition . . ."

"Cool," she said and thumbed off the TV. "The show's boring, anyway. Fire away."

He smiled, nodded, and opened his notebook, searching for a moment to find the right spot. Gina tilted her head, her expression serious.

"Jesus," he began, "could change water into wine . . ."

She listened patiently as he moved through the homily, cited the passages of the bible that supported him, cracked wise a couple times, then took the tone down to somber at the middle and ended with a bright, hopeful, but also realistic finish.

Gina leaned back, considering. He took off his glasses, polishing the lenses on his shirttail.

"No," she said. "Sorry, Father. You got it wrong. I mean it's a nice talk, but it's all about nats and aces. You're preaching to jokers. Jokers don't give a shit about miracles—except for miracles that make jokers not jokers anymore, I guess."

"But faith is a universal. The proof of Christ's holiness . . ."

"No one gives a shit," she said. "Sorry. I mean I know you're a priest and all, but really, jokers don't care. They want to hear about how even though they're fucking ugly, someone still loves them. Or that they have beautiful souls. Or that the righteous are made to suffer. Like with Job. That kind of shit."

"Watch your language, young lady," he admonished, but his mind was already elsewhere. "So you don't think it'd go over well?"

"You're not selling what they're buying," she said. "They don't want another challenge. They want comfort. It's what they come here for."

"I suppose . . ." he said, and sighed. "Yes, I suppose you're right. I hadn't looked at it like that. I'll go see what can be salvaged."

"Put in someplace how ugly men are better because the world makes them tough," she said.

"Oh, I don't know. That seems a little harsh."

"Always works for me," she said, shrugging. "We're kind of in the same business that way. Making jokers feel better."

She winked and lay back on the cot, turning the TV back on as she descended. Father Henry found himself speechless for a moment, then walked up the stairs laughing.

The revisions took the better part of an hour, but in the end, there was more that could be saved than he'd imagined. With a little work, he had his very first jokers-only sermon, and by God, he was proud of it.

So proud and so excited, in fact, that he forgot to knock on his way down the stairs.

". . . unload it now, Randy. Don't tell me you . . . buyer."

Father Henry stopped, slowly easing his foot back to the step above. Gina's voice was muffled, but he could still make out some words here and there.

"Hundred thousand . . . tomorrow . . . would never guess where I . . . shit, really? Is she okay? Shit . . . No, I'll call you."

The plastic clatter of the telephone handset slipping into its cradle ended the conversation, and Father Henry slowly backed up the stairs. That certainly didn't sound much like her brother calling in from Minnesota.

Well Lord, he thought, *if this lesson is not to get took in by a pretty face, I could have sworn we'd covered that already.*

He went back down, knocking this time. Gina was all smiles and pleasant company.

Oh yes. This little girl was going to take some watching.

Joey smiled. Not a hey-that-was-funny smile. More like hey-I'm-gonna-take-your-eyes-out-with-a-fucking-spoon. Jerzy didn't seem to know the difference.

"Human target, get it?" the skinny Jew said again, like repeating it would make it funny. "Like that guy with the arrows." He pantomimed plinking a bow at Joey.

"That guy with the arrows killed my boys and tried to cripple me," Joey pointed out coolly.

Jerzy shrugged, smile fading, and he sipped his coffee. It was the closest he ever came to apology. The foot traffic going past the cafe was pretty light for the garment district, but it was still early in the afternoon. Come five o'clock, the overflow from Times Square would fill things up a little more. Joey wanted to be out before then.

"You got the coroner's reports?"

"Nah," Jerzy said. "I don't make copies. What you want to know, I'll tell you. I got a photographic memory."

Joey looked around. The whole place was the size of a school bus—the short kind for the dumb kids. The guy behind the counter looked archly back at him. An old lady in a puffy blue ski jacket was sitting right up against the window and muttering to herself. Other than that they were alone.

Joey leaned forward.

"Okay," he said. "So I'm hearing there's something about the way they got offed? Something about aces?"

"Everybody's buying up aces. Mafia, Shadow Fist. Everyone," Jerzy said. He wasn't so stupid, thank God, that he didn't know to keep his voice down.

"Okay, but it's not like the ones the Mafia hired are gonna queer a Mafia deal, right?"

"Maybe yes, maybe no," Jerzy said, waggling a bushy eyebrow. "Thing is, a couple of the guys that died? They shouldn't have. It's like they were hurt, but not so bad they woulda died. You see what I'm getting at?"

Joey scowled and shook his head. Talking to Jerzy was about as much fun as talking to Lapierre.

"People hiring aces?" Jerzy said, his hand moving in a little circular come-along motion. "Guys dead for no reason?"

"Hey Jerzy. How about you fucking tell me?"

The woman in the ski jacket glanced at them, scowling.

"Shouldn't yell," Jerzy said. "We're in *public*."

"Sorry. Didn't mean to. It's the wrists thing. Pain makes me jumpy."

"Demise," Jerzy said and sighed. "Find whoever hired Demise, you'll find the shit."

"Demise," Jocy said, nodding. "Great. And, ah, what about the Percodan?"

"I can hook you up next week. You got enough Darvon to hold you 'til then?"

"Yeah, sure."

"What? What is this with the long face?"

"It's just the Darvon pills are all pink," Joey confided. "They make me look like a faggot, you know?"

Randy McHaley lived in a basement apartment with six other jokers. Two of them were there with him when Demise and Phan Lo got there. They were happy, though, to give the three of them a little privacy.

The place looked like the worst of the 1960s left to rot for a couple decades. Beaded strands substituted for doors, old psychedelic posters of the Lizard King yellowed and cracked on the grimy wall. Sandalwood incense mixed with something close to wet dog. And Randy slumped on the low couch with his hands between his knees.

The wild card hadn't been kind to Randy. His greasy brown fedora rested on a forest of spikes like a hedgehog. His pale, fishy skin wept a thin mucous, soaking his clothes. Tiny blind eyes opened and closed along his neck and down behind his shirt, some staring, some rolling wildly. Demise could see the distaste in corners of Phan Lo's mouth and it made him want to draw the conversation out.

"I don't know anything about it," the sad joker said again, wagging his head.

"Okay," Demise said. "Let me clear this up, fuckhead. A piece of shit like you can't—*cannot*—set up a hundred-thousand-dollar horse deal in this town without us finding out. Okay? Where's the meet?"

"I swear guys, you've got the wrong fuckup. I mean look at me," the joker smiled desperately. "Look at the place I live. I'm not dealing with that kind of money."

"You're a junkie," Demise said. "You and your buddies could blow that kind of money up your arms in a couple weeks."

"I swear to Christ, you guys got it wrong. I'm really sorry. I wish I could help, but . . ."

"Could we just do this?" Phan asked.

Demise sighed and nodded. It had been fun while it lasted, but business being business . . .

Phan Lo stepped forward, drawing a pistol. The little joker squealed and pulled back, but Phan leaned in, pressing the barrel under Randy's chin, forcing his head up. Demise stood, shot his cuffs, and leaned in close. When their eyes met, Randy was caught like a fish. Demise let the pain of his own death, the sick feeling of spiraling down into darkness, the visceral knowledge of dying flow into the joker for a second, two, three . . . and looked away.

Randy drew a long, grating breath like a diver who's been under too long, then bent over and retched. Phan Lo danced back, disgusted. Demise sat down.

"The meet," Demise said.

"Bryant Park. Noon tomorrow. She's supposed to bring a sample. Please don't kill me."

"Where is she now?"

"I don't know. She calls me."

"You believe him?" Demise asked.

Phan Lo shrugged.

"The buyer's a Brit. Looking to export. He's gonna be wearing an Aerosmith t-shirt and reading the *Wall Street Journal*."

"Probably won't be two of those," Phan said.

"Please," the joker whined. "That's all I know. I swear to God that's all I know."

"You know, Phan. I think that's all he knows."

Phan nodded and crossed his arms.

"You want to kill him, or you want me to?" Demise asked. Randy looked from one to the other, his jaw working silently, then curled up in a ball on the couch and started crying. Phan curled his lip and shook his head. Demise frowned and nodded toward the weeping joker. Phan shook his head again.

"If she's not there tomorrow, we'll be back," Phan said, holstering his pistol. "You understand?"

Randy wailed wordlessly, his shoulders shaking. Demise stood and followed Phan out through the kicked-in front door and up the steps to the midnight-dark street.

"What the fuck was that?" Demise asked.

"It's better for the mystique if some of them are alive and scared shitless," Phan said.

"That's the stupidest shit I've ever heard."

Phan shrugged and walked to the car.

"You felt sorry for him, didn't you?" Demise accused.

"Fuck you."

"You did, didn't you?"

"No. Get in the car."

Thursday, February 5, 1987

THE MORNING WAS WARM for February, and where the city didn't stink of car fumes and urine, it smelled like the threat of snow.

He'd called Mazzuccheli with his information about the killer ace, and Mazzuchelli had come up with an address that fit with it. It was teamwork. For the first time since it all got fucked up, he was really working with the team.

He hated it.

For weeks, he'd been down. Even after the wounds in his arms were pretty much healed up, he hadn't been able to focus or sleep through the night. He kept seeing his boys sprouting arrows, watching them die. And every day he couldn't pull himself together, he felt the respect of the family dropping. No one said anything—not to his face. But he knew. And now Mazzucchelli was helping him out when what he really needed was to show that he could handle it without. He didn't need a hand doing his work.

He stopped at the corner bakery for a pick-up breakfast before heading south toward Jokertown—the tastes of greasy, sweet pastry and bitter, hot coffee competing pleasantly, the chill of the morning pulling a little at the skin of his face. Joey pictured what it was going to be like.

He'd walk in to a restaurant, go over to Mazzuchelli's table. He'd sit down. They'd talk a little, then Joey would pass over the satchel with the drugs and the money. And then, in a separate little bag, he'd have the right hands of all the fuckers he'd killed getting the stuff back. Mazzuchelli would grin and welcome him back. And Lapierre, the little fucker, would be somewhere in the background boasting about how he could have done just as good, only no one's gonna believe him.

It was a pretty good daydream, and it got him to the flop. He dropped the nearly-empty coffee cup and the wax paper still dusted with powdered sugar into the trash and went down the steps to the basement apartment, flakes of rotten concrete scraping under his feet.

The door was open. Joey took the Beretta out of its holster and went in. The place had all the marks of being left in a hurry—empty dressers, a half-eaten sandwich in the bathroom. The big stuff—the television, the old stereo—was still there, but anything portable was stripped and gone. The lights were all burning even though there was more than enough leaking through the windows to see by.

So it looked like Demise knew he'd been spotted. He and his Fist buddies had gotten scared and skipped. Joey smiled. It was nice having someone scared of him again. He put away the gun and took the rattling orange bottle out of his pocket and popped a Darvon to celebrate.

The phone was one of those little lozenge-shaped ones. Joey guessed it had started out the usual colorless beige, but someone had painted it black. He scooped it up and dialed.

"What?" Mazzuchelli snapped after the second ring.

"Boss. It's Joey."

"What've you got?"

"I went to check out the place you told me about. Nothing there. I was thinking, though. You remember how you got those phone records on that guy in Soho?"

"How'd you hear about that?"

"I was there when you braced him, boss," Joey said, trying to keep his voice from sounding hurt. "I helped you break his knees."

"Oh. Right. Sorry."

"I was thinking maybe you could do the same for this joint. See who's been talking to them, see who they been talking to."

There was a long silence. Joey shifted his weight from one foot to the other.

"Okay," Mazzuchelli said. "Where can I get hold of you? You're not calling me from *there* are you?"

Fuck, Joey thought.

"Of course not, boss. I'm at a pay phone. The number, though. It's all scratched out."

"Joey. If you're lying to me, it's going to be on the records that I'm just about to go get for you. You know that, right?"

"I'm sorry, boss. I'm at the apartment. I wasn't thinking."

Mazzucchelli muttered something that Joey couldn't make out, but the tone of voice alone was enough to make him wince a little.

"Call me back in an hour. I'll let you know what I find."

"Okay. Sorry, boss."

Mazzucchelli sighed. "You're a good guy, Joey. Just stop being such a fuck-up, all right?"

Gina snuck out a little before eleven. Father Henry watched from the cottage as she slipped out the sacristy door and started down the street. She'd picked out an old black Navy jacket, but she had the same blue wrap-around skirt and a weathered black purse. With her hair pulled back and no makeup, she looked totally different than the young whore he'd taken in off the street.

He watched as she strode calmly to the street, heading north. Once she was out of sight, he leaned back, took off his glasses and pressed the bridge of his nose. Eyes closed, he waited for a moment, giving the Lord one last chance to come to him with the sign or insight he'd prayed for most of last night and a fair part of the morning. All he saw was the dark back of his eyelids.

He sighed, finished his sandwich in two quick bites, and headed over to the church. A flock of pigeons took wing as he walked past. She'd left the door unlocked, and he closed it carefully before going down the stairs.

The cot was neatly made. A towel hung in the bathroom, still wet from her shower. He felt like a nosey parent sneaking into a child's room to go through her dresser. And if it seemed like a betrayal of trust, well, she wasn't playing perfectly straight with him either.

He found her bags stowed under the cot. Now there was a question. She'd been borrowing clothes from the donations, so that couldn't be what she'd brought with her. With a sinking feeling in his belly, Father Henry pulled out the blue athletic duffel bag, its slick plasticized cloth hissing against the concrete of the floor. He crossed himself and undid the zipper.

The money was in rolls a little bigger than his fist—worn hundred dollar bills wrapped by thick red or beige rubber bands. At a guess, there were maybe seventy or a hundred rolls. He sat on the floor and hefted one, trying to estimate the sum, even just roughly, but his mind rebelled. When he put it back and closed the bag, he noticed the black-red stain on the cloth.

So that's why they call it blood money, he thought, and had to stifle giggles even though he knew it wasn't really funny.

The little suitcase had a cheap lock, and Father Henry forced it with a penknife. Inside were nineteen small packages with a space where the twentieth had clearly been. They were white powder in carefully taped cellophane bags. Father Henry had seen enough movies to know that this was where he was supposed to poke his knife into one and taste the contents from the blade, and he even felt a slightly disembodied urge to go through the motions. Not that he had the first damn idea what drugs tasted like, but it was what they always did.

Still, it was pretty clear that Gina wasn't carrying around baking soda. The rolled up bills were drug money, and these right here were the drugs— cocaine or heroin or something else. He couldn't see as the exact chemistry mattered all that much. The question was still the same—what to do.

He crossed his legs uncomfortably and considered the packages. The obvious thing to do was call the police. ("I'm a Jokertown whore and the police, won't help me," she'd said. Well it was clear enough now why that was, and it wasn't about someone being an informant.) Yes, that was the right thing. There was no call for a simple man like him to go getting involved with this kind of thing. The police would know best what to do.

But it would mean that Gina went to prison, at the very least. Or maybe she'd get killed. It didn't sit right. She was only seventeen, after all.

When he was her age, he'd been on a permanent drunk, so adept with his wild card talent that he could turn the water to wine when it touched his lips and the backwash wouldn't even pink what was still in the glass. He'd been kicked out of school for being drunk in class, kicked out of the house to live in the apartment over Uncle Elmore's garage.

He'd branched out a little after that—a few light narcotics and such, Valium especially being in fashion. If someone had come to him then with cocaine or heroin, Father Henry knew he would never have made it to twenty alive. He'd been at the age when you were supposed to be stupid and self-destructive. And with as low as he'd been, it was hard to say that Gina deserved a tougher break just because she was young and foolish here and now instead of thirty-odd years ago in Alabama.

Hard enough, in fact, that he couldn't do it. *Let he who is without sin,* and he'd racked up a lot of mileage sinning when he'd been young and addicted.

His right leg was falling asleep, tingles shooting down his thigh to the foot. He shifted his weight, but it only hurt worse so he stood.

Something had to be done though. Whatever else, nothing right or good would come from the drugs. And so maybe that was why God had sent Gina to him.

He pressed his lips together, leaned down, and closed the suitcase.

"Well, Lord," he said aloud as he walked to the bathroom. "I hope this was more or less what you were aiming for."

It took longer than he'd expected to flush all the powder down the toilet, but he managed it.

The west end of the park butted up against the New York Public Library, the north end against 42nd Street. Just about where the two met, there was a small building—a walk-in public restroom. They left the corpse of the British guy there, sitting in one of the stalls with a surprised expression and his jeans around his ankles.

The day was cold with low scudding clouds that seemed barely higher than the skyscrapers, but the foot traffic down 42nd was still thick. Demise sat in a chair on the brown, winterkilled grass conspicuously wearing an Aerosmith t-shirt and reading the *Wall Street Journal.* He had gooseflesh up and down his arms, and the chill would have been uncomfortable if the sick pain of his death hadn't dwarfed it. The t-shirt, on the other hand, couldn't be forgiven. He looked like a fucking idiot.

The girl showed up at noon. She cleaned up pretty nice—long black hair pulled back from her sharp features, a blue skirt that swirled a little around her ankles. She looked better without makeup. She was walking across the park toward him with a studied casualness that was about as subtle as blood on a wedding dress. An amateur.

He folded his newspaper and stood just as Phan and his cheap sunglasses sidled up behind her. The shifting emotions on her face were a joy to watch—confusion, recognition, fear, despair, calm all within a half second. Bitch should have been an actress.

"You know who we are," Demise said as Phan—gun pressed discreetly in the small of her back—steered her toward him.

The girl nodded.

"You know why we're here."

She nodded again.

"Good. Let's go someplace a little more private and talk."

The whore didn't fight, didn't make a break for it. She just walked with them down to 41st where they had a limo with a Shadow Fist driver waiting in a loading zone and climbed in with them. Demise pulled a jacket over the idiot t-shirt as soon as he got in. He sat in the jump seat, facing her. Phan was beside her, gun no longer concealed and not particularly pointing at her. The driver pulled out into traffic.

"Okay," the girl said. "So you going to kill me or what?"

Phan slammed the butt of the pistol into her face. The scream was short and high.

"We might, we might not. It depends," Demise said. "You have the sample."

She pulled a cellophane packet out of her pocket. Phan took it, turned it over in his hand, and nodded. Demise smiled. The girl's cheek was puffing out where Phan had hit her, and she was sniffing back blood.

"Where's the rest?" he asked.

She shook her head.

"I tell you that and you don't need me," she said. "Here's the deal. You can have all the shit, but I keep ten percent of that cash as a finder's fee."

Demise leaned forward. She knew about him, and she tried not to meet his eyes. He waited. The limo hit a pothole and they all lurched a little. Phan sighed uncomfortably. Demise kept waiting, staring at her dark brown eyes and willing them up toward his. He got her when she glanced over to see whether he was still looking. He took her almost to the point of no return—farther than he'd taken Randy—before he looked away.

The driver looked back and Phan waved the pistol in a *keep your eyes on the road* gesture. It was almost fifteen blocks before she stopped crying.

"You understand the stakes?" Demise asked.

She nodded. The bravado was gone. She had stopped worrying about the bloody nose Phan had given her. Her mouth and chin were crimson, her eyes wide and empty. When she wiped her mouth on the black sleeve of her jacket, the blood smeared.

"We get all of it back by tomorrow at noon," Demise said slowly. "The money and the smack both. You do it like a nice girl, and you can live."

"Tomorrow," she agreed.

"You can meet us in the same place. Just like today. You bring everything."

"Everything," she echoed. Tears ran down her face, but her expression stayed blank. He wasn't sure she was taking in what they were saying, but then she went on. "I'll have all of it for you, just don't kill me, okay? That's the deal. You don't kill me."

Phan smiled and holstered the gun. Demise leaned back and spoke to the driver over his shoulder.

"Jokertown. We'll drop her there."

The rest of the ride was in silence. The girl looked out the window, eyes vacant with fear. Phan leaned back. The ponytail really did look pretty sharp on him. Demise tried to picture the guy with a mustache, just thinking how the two would go together. Maybe he'd try it.

At the bleeding edge of Jokertown, the limo pulled over and Demise popped the door open for her.

"Tomorrow. Noon," he said. "And wash your face. You look like someone beat the shit out of you."

She scrambled out of the car and strode off down the street her head down. Phan leaned forward, watching her. The first flakes of snow pearled the windshield.

"Go ahead of her about three blocks and turn right," Demise said to the driver. "You can drop us there."

"Now what?" Phan asked as the limo forced its way out into traffic.

"Follow her," Demise said. "She's not thinking straight. She'll head straight for the stuff. We get the money, get the drugs, and snuff the bitch."

"Sounds good," Phan said. "But I get to kill her."

Demise raised an eyebrow.

"You enjoy it too much, man," Phan said. "It's not healthy."

Joey stood on the street outside Our Lady of Perpetual Misery shifting his weight from one leg to the other. Mazzucchelli had been pretty clear—the only calls coming into the apartment in the last few days that looked off were from the church. It only made sense to check it out.

Just take a look around, Mazzucchelli had said. *If it looks like that's where they're working from, call me and we'll send in a team.*

The stone building loomed across the street, grey and impassive. He didn't see any Shadow Fist operatives walking in or out. Didn't see any heroin blowing down the street with the snow. It occurred to Joey for the first time that he wasn't sure exactly what it was he was looking *for*.

Since when did the Fist work with jokers anyway? Fuck, since when did they work with Catholics? The whole thing didn't make sense. The confusion nauseated him a little. He should have worked with Lapierre. This was a job for someone smart.

The urge hit him to take another pill like he was hungry and the pills were food. He took the bottle out and considered it. His arms didn't really hurt—hell, they hadn't really hurt in weeks—but the pills made him feel better. Some part of him knew that wasn't good—even felt guilty about it. But that didn't make him want the stuff any less.

Something huge and bright blue swooped overhead, shrilling like a flock of birds. Joey shrugged deeper into his jacket, pushing the drugs away. He hated Jokertown.

"Just go in and look around," he muttered to himself. "Like you were just gonna go light a candle for some dead joker mother-fucker. That's the thing."

Joey squared his shoulders, crossed the street and walked up the steps. He held the door open for a nice little piece of ass—definitely not a joker—who was heading in right after him. Dark eyes, dark hair. She would have been really pretty if someone hadn't been beating the crap out of her.

Of course he expected her to be upset. He'd have been naive to think she wouldn't. But he'd rehearsed what he'd say, some of it standing in front of the bathroom mirror so he could try out the facial expressions too.

He'd planned to start by scaring her. Then he'd take the moral high ground—she'd misled him, lied to him even, betrayed his trust in her. If she didn't walk out on him right then, he could forgive her and explain why he'd gotten rid of the drugs and that the church would still protect her.

He'd also hidden the money, figuring it made it more likely that Gina'd be in the mind to hear him out.

"You get it back!" she screamed, leaning over him. "You crawl in the fucking sewer and get it back, you fat fucking sonofabitch!"

He lay on his back, his arms up to protect his face. Gina knelt on his chest, her weight making it difficult to take a breath. The cot was on its side where she'd thrown it, and his left ear hurt pretty bad where she'd hit him.

"Now, you . . . my trust . . ." he tried.

"You shit-sucker! You fuckbrained joker asshole! That was my fucking *life!*"

She swung at him again, her hands in claws. Then she stood and kicked him in the small of the back—she didn't quite get his kidney, but it still smarted pretty good—and started pacing the length of the small room, shaking her head, arms crossed. Carefully, Father Henry raised himself up to sitting and picked his glasses back up from the floor.

"Now, Gina," he said. "I think you need to just calm down a mite."

"Shut up before I kill you."

He rose slowly to his feet. That kick was going to leave a bruise. He could already feel it. He straightened his shirt.

"I didn't do what you'd have wanted, maybe," he said, "but it was right. You can try beating on me if you want, but that won't make keeping folks hooked on drugs a good thing. And these people you're messing with, now, they're not the sort of folks a girl like you should be . . . you know . . . messing with."

Since she didn't respond, he figured he'd gotten the moral high ground after all. It didn't seem to have all the weight he'd hoped for. She muttered something, paused at the foot of the stairs, her eyes narrowed and calculating.

"I need the money," she said. "I've got a few hours to make a run for it."

"You've accepted the protection of the church," he said, feeling a little better for being back on-script. "We'll take care of you, but that means no more lying and playing fast and loose with the truth. I didn't go to the police and you should see . . ."

"If you'd gone to the cops, I'd be dead already. I need the money, Father."

She was looking at him now with a deathly calm. Her face was bruised, her mouth thin and bloodless. She'd never looked less like a child.

"Come on, then," he sighed and walked up the stairs.

Quasiman was sweeping the aisles and between the pews, his hunched back moving irregularly as bits of him vanished and reappeared. Father Henry nodded to him as he walked up the pulpit and took out the duffel bag. Gina snatched it from him and slung it over her shoulder.

"Thanks," she said and strode for the main doors. Father Henry sat down and watched her go, rubbing his sore ear.

It wasn't how he'd seen things going. He'd had a scenario in mind where Gina would have been safe, where maybe he'd bring a little light into her life. A little hope. A chance, maybe, for salvation. Instead, the most he could really hope for was the existential appreciation of a city's worth of drug addicts thanking him for thinning down the supply. He was out of his depths in Jokertown. That was all.

"Father Henry?"

Quasiman stood before him, broom in hand. He wore an expression of concern.

"Yes?"

Quasiman beamed.

"I thought I remembered you," he said, and vanished. Father Henry shook his head and levered himself back up to his feet just as Gina came back down the aisle. Her face was ashen, her footsteps unsteady.

A blocky man in a black coat walked beside her, carrying the duffel bag full of money. He also had a gun to her neck.

The priest stood up with a wobble, his face going paler. Joey felt something like pleasure and dug the barrel into the girl's neck. She flinched.

"Well now," the priest said, tugging at his collar. "And how can I help you, son?"

"Get in the back. Now!"

The priest grinned nervously like Joey'd said something clever, turned and trotted toward the back. Joey pushed the girl ahead of him, enjoying the way she stumbled. Joey really felt like he was getting back his stride.

The priest led the way down a flight of stairs to a little kitchen. Joey kept his back to the wall, his gun trained on the two of them. Without letting the barrel waver, he threw the duffel bag on the table.

"That's the money," he said. "So that's a good start. Now all you gotta do to keep breathing is give me the shit."

"Well now," the priest began, "you see that might could pose a bit of . . ."

"It's not here," the girl snapped.

"Okay. So where is it?" Joey demanded, moving a step toward them. The priest flushed pink and looked away, shaking his head like he was talking to himself. The girl kept her eyes locked on his.

"It's coming. My partner Jade, she's supposed to be here with it any minute."

The priest shot a look at her, eyebrows raised.

"Then I guess we'll wait for Jade," Joey said, grinning cruelly. He stepped close to them now. The priest was already flinching away in expectation of a blow. "If there ain't no one here soon, though, I'm gonna start getting bored. And then I'm gonna start cutting off fingers."

He walked backward slowly, a deep satisfaction flowing through him. He was back. For the first time since the fucking arrow, he was really back. It was like riding a bicycle. Just get a couple civilians shitting themselves scared, and it was like his body knew what to do. He had the money, it looked like he could maybe get the drugs. That'd show Mazzucchelli. Shit, that'd show all of them.

Close enough to start celebrating, he figured. He took the bottle out from his pocket and opened it one-handed. The priest raised his eyebrows.

"Good trick, opening them child-proof things like that," the priest said. "Takes some practice."

"You shut the fuck up," Joey said.

"No offense. No offense."

Joey glared as he sidestepped to the sink and tapped out two bright pink pills onto the counter. The priest was watching with an odd expression as he poured a glass of water with his left hand. Joey scowled, radiating menace as he popped the fag-pink pills into his mouth. He had to take his eyes off the pair for a second when he drank.

As the water washed the pills down, a strange warmth spread in his throat. Panic hit him and he was across to the priest, the barrel of the gun pressed between the fat man's eyes, before he knew he'd moved.

"What the fuck's wrong with the fucking water?" he demanded.

The priest managed a wan smile and shook his head.

"It's got something in it. I can feel it. Like taking a drink."

"Oh," the priest said. "That's not the water, son. That'll happen sometimes with narcotics. Pain killers especially. The capsule cracks a little on the way down. That is Darvon, isn't it? I always though it was a lovely color."

"Shut the fuck up!" Joey said. The pills were warm in his gut, and the pleasant, loose sensation spreading to his arms and legs. He took another cautious sip of the water. It didn't taste weird at all, didn't make his throat feel hot.

"Try it, if you'd like," the priest said. "You can just crack one open and wash down a touch of the powder. It does the same."

"If you're fucking with me . . ." Joey said, but he took out another pill, cracking it between his fingertips, and popped it into his mouth. It was viciously bitter, but when he drank the water, the warm feeling came again. It had an aftertaste like grapes. He licked his lips. The priest smiled and seemed to relax.

"Shit," Joey said. "How'd you know about that?"

"My friends and I were known to sample some narcotics in our younger days. Before I took the cloth. Since then I've spent a certain amount of my time ministering to folks who shared my peculiar form of weakness. I'm Father Henry Obst, by the way. I'm filling in for Father Squid for a couple weeks while he's away. This here's Gina. She's accepted the protection of the Church."

"Yeah," Joey said, sarcastically. "And how's that going for her?"

"I recall the first time I took codeine," Father Henry said. He was leaning back now, the air of fear almost entirely gone. "I was just a young thing back then. Grade school. Before I drew . . . well, anyway. My mama gave it to me in cough syrup. That was legal back when I was a pup."

"Oh yeah?"

"It was a lovely feeling. Now I do have to say that you don't seem the sort of fella to indulge, though. Not when you're on the job as it were. I assume it's for medical needs?"

Joey nodded. His tongue felt a little thick, but the warmth in his gut was relaxing and calm. He was in a perfectly calm place. He was in control. He was good. Hell, he was perfect. "Fucker shot me with an arrow," he said. "Months ago. Scar tissue's all messed up with the nerves."

"Ah," Father Henry said, nodding sympathetically. "Must be a trial for you."

"Yeah."

They were silent for a few minutes—Joey wasn't sure exactly how many. Time seemed to be doing something weird.

"I recall when I myself was in terrible pain," the priest said, reflectively. "It wasn't physical, mostly, but terrible all the same. I could turn . . . that is . . . well, wine was a staple of my diet as a young man. Anyway, it took me some time before I understood I was an addict. I'd lost a great deal that was very dear to me."

Joey laughed, and waved his gun languidly at the two of them. His hand seemed oddly far away.

"You were an addict?"

"Still am, son," the priest said gravely. "Will be until the day I die. It's just a disease, and no shame in it. You just need to get right with yourself and the Lord. You know, God takes care of his own. If you just let Him."

"It's not like I'm hooked or anything," Joey said. "I just need them, you know? I mean it's not like I take 'em for fun. It's just . . . if I don't . . . I just gotta get through the day. I just gotta show the guys I'm not . . . shit, I'm not making sense."

"Yes, you are, son. You most certainly are."

Joey nodded. The priest seemed like he was the center of the world. Everything else was narrowing around the thick, pasty face with its calm, accepting expression. Tears filled Joey's eyes. The little kitchen was swimming.

All the weeks of being laughed at, the shame of his cravings, the nightmares of watching arrows piercing his guys, of being the only one left while his friends died around him—it all bubbled up at once. He lost track of where he was, where the floor was, whether he was standing up.

"Father," he choked out as the darkness and sorrow enfolded him, "I think I've got a problem."

Father Henry stood over the collapsed thug who lay snoring gently on the floor. The relief mixed pleasantly with what he imagined was a somewhat prideful smugness at Gina's open-mouthed wonder.

"Now you let that be a lesson to you," he said. "Always read the warning labels when you get a prescription. Lot of times you mix alcohol with 'em, it's a very bad idea."

"Damn," Gina said. "I mean that's . . . pathetic."

"Well now, give him a little benefit. He didn't know no better. Gina, if . . . well now, if you're going to be going, I think you might best be at it. This fine young man is only going to be asleep for so long."

The girl looked at him, nodded, and picked the duffel from the table. She hesitated for a moment, then leaned over and kissed him briefly on the lips.

"Thank you," she said, and was gone up the stairs.

Father Henry sighed and slowly dragged the unconscious thug to the cot, rolled him onto it and covered him with the blanket Gina had been using. It was odd the way God put things together and took them apart. But then he supposed that was what they meant by ineffable. The question of what to do with his new ward, now, was an interesting problem. He didn't imagine there was a Hired Thugs Anonymous, but given his last few days, he wasn't going to rule it out either.

When he lumbered up the stairs, he was surprised to find Gina sitting in the front pew, her head in her hands.

"He's here," she said. "Out on the street."

"Who's here?"

"Demise," she said, and it came out like she was already dead. "And the other one's out back. I'm fucked."

She dropped the duffel bag and sat on the front pew, her head in her hands. She was weeping.

"Now you just tough back up there, miss," Father Henry said. "It's like I told you. You accepted the protection of the church, and that means me. I took care of things with that last gentleman, and I'll take care of this one too."

"Don't be a shithead. That guy was some pill-popping dumbfuck. Demise is an ace."

"Watch your language," he said, picking up the bag and stowing it back behind the pulpit. "You go downstairs and wash yourself up. I'll find us a way to settle this thing out."

She looked up at him with a mixture of hope and disbelief on her face. He only raised his eyebrows—one of the expressions he'd practiced, so he had a pretty clear idea how it looked on him—and pointed to the stairs. She didn't have much faith in him; that was clear enough from the way she moved. She went, though.

Once she was gone, Father Henry rolled up his sleeves and rubbed his hands together. "Quasi! Come over here, boy. I need to talk with you. Who exactly is this Demise fella?"

Demise stood in a doorway across the street from the Church of Jesus Christ, Joker, where he could watch the front doors and the side. Phan was somewhere on the other side, keeping an eye on the other side and the back. The whore hadn't come out, though he'd seen her poke her head out the door once. It didn't seem likely that she'd actually stashed the shit in the church, but the longer she stayed in there, the more he was willing to consider it.

The snow was changing to sleet, freezing where it struck. He checked his watch. Fifteen more minutes, he figured, and they'd have to go in after her. He wondered how Danny Mao and the other bosses of Shadow Fist would feel about killing people in a church.

"Mr. Spector?" a distant voice shouted over the noise of traffic.

He looked up. A short, pear-shaped man with a clerical collar stood before the doors of the cathedral, waving over at him with a goofy grin. Demise tilted his head. "Now what the fuck is this?" he muttered.

"No call to be shy now, sir," the pear-shaped priest shouted, a thick southern accent drawing out his words. "Come on over and let's talk this here thing out."

He hesitated for a minute, but then stepped out across the street, dodging cars, until he reached the opposite sidewalk. "Who the fuck are you?" he called.

"Father Henry Obst," the priest said, beaming. "Lately of Selma. I'm taking over for Father Squid for a mite while he's traveling the world. Come along inside now, sir. We've got a little matter of business to discuss, I think."

"Do you know who I am?"

"Rumor has you're a hired killer for some sort of Asian mob," the priest said pleasantly.

"Well. Yeah," Demise said. "Where's the whore?"

"Oh, she's in here," the priest said. "I think we can get this whole thing taken care of to everybody's satisfaction. Come on along, now sir. No reason to do this out in the weather."

The priest turned and trundled back into the cathedral. Demise stood looking at the open door, then, shaking his head walked up and entered the church. The space was bigger than he'd remembered, and almost empty. The twisted, two-headed Christ impaled upon a double-helix cross seemed to writhe as Demise walked down the aisle, his footsteps echoing. The scent of car exhaust and snow mixed with ghost-faint incense.

The whore was there, sitting in the first pew with her head bowed. The little priest was still smiling and leaning against the altar rail.

"Now then, sir," the priest said. "I understand there was something you were looking for."

"The bitch stole something," Demise said. "I've come to collect it."

"Well now, you see that's the issue that we need to look at, you and me.

The drugs and the money—I presume that's what you had in mind? Yes, well, they are no longer in this fine young woman's care. I've taken them myself in the name of the church."

"Okay," Demise said. "So I should kill you instead?"

"It's one of life's little ironies that you and I should be the ones having this conversation," the priest said, sticking his hands in his pockets and looking out over the pews. His round, puffy face had taken on a philosophical cast that looked like he'd rehearsed it in the mirror. "The virus has given me the ability to recreate Our Lord's first miracle from the marriage at Cana, and you his final one in rising from his tomb. We represent the alpha and the omega, you and I. Not that it's done either of us much good. I have a sermon I'll be delivering on the subject come Sunday. You should come hear it."

"Whatever," Demise said. "How about we get back to business. Give me the shit and I'll walk out of here. Nobody gets killed."

"You forget sir that you are in the house of the Lord. You have no power here."

Demise laughed, a little disbelieving cough, and locked his eyes into the watery blue of the priest's. Father Henry met his gaze placidly. Demise pressed the pain along where the channel should have been, but nothing happened. He could see the priest considering him, could look into the black of the little man's eyes, but there was no connection, no lock.

"God is stronger than a virus, sir," Father Henry intoned, and for almost half a second, Demise got nervous. Then he noticed the red marks on the bridge of Father Henry's nose.

"You're fucking nearsighted," Demise said.

Father Henry's expression froze and the whore gave out a little moan. "I knew this wouldn't work," she said.

"You thought you could fuck with my head by taking off your glasses?" Demise said, almost laughing. "Christ, what a fucking hick."

"The power . . . the power of God protects me. You just stand your ground there." The priest's voice was wobbling like his neck fat.

Demise stepped forward, took the little man's chin in his hand, and lifted. Father Henry, eyes pressed closed, took his hands out of his pockets. Demise didn't see the little black cylinder until it hissed, a stream of pepper mace already scalding his eyes and nose. The pain was nothing compared to the constant pain of death he carried with him, but the stuff did make his eyes water. The little priest pulled away, falling loudly over the rail, while Demise wiped at the tears and roared.

He never saw the whore coming up behind him.

The first jolt of the stun gun hardly stopped him—the pain was negligible. He spun, reaching out for the bitch, but she danced back and then swung in low, catching him just under the ribs. By the fourth shock, his muscles were going weak, and it was getting hard to breathe. The fifth one—a lucky shot on the back of his neck—made his whole right side go numb.

Demise gave out before the batteries did.

Father Henry sat at the altar, wiping his forehead with a handkerchief. With his glasses back on, the assassin turned from a muddy man-shaped blur into an actual man, hog-tied in the aisle before the altar. Gina, smart girl that she was, had gagged him with a sock and a strip of cloth and covered his head with a pastel pink pillowcase. She'd moved fast, and it was a good thing. The man had never quite lost consciousness.

"So what do we do now?" Gina asked softly.

"Well, we have this gentleman here, the other one back in the kitchen," he whispered back. "Seems like hitmen are what you might call thick on the ground just now."

"There's still the other one out back. The other one from the car."

"Well that's all well and good," Father Henry snapped, "but I don't think I'm much up for doing this a third time today. A man has limits."

"I wasn't saying that," Gina said. "But we've got to do *something.*"

"All right. Here, you keep an eye on this here miscreant and I'll see whether I can't work something out with our friend downstairs."

Demise shifted, straining against his bonds, and tried to shout something, but Father Henry was damned if could tell what.

Friday, February 6, 1987

"THE WHOLE THING WAS a setup," Joey said. "I'm telling you, boss. I was lucky I got out of there at all."

The restaurant was almost exactly the way he'd imagined it, except that he was empty-handed, Mazzucchelli was frowning, and Lapierre was over by the bar chatting up a waitress. Joey shook his head.

"And this priest got you out?"

"He woke me up after those four Fist guys jumped me and got me outta there."

"Four guys?"

"Maybe five," Joey said, trying not to wince with the lie. But it wasn't like he could tell Mazzucchelli he'd passed out.

"The cops were coming, and he was thinking the Fist might try to kill me. They'd went in there and *forced* him to help them out. I'm telling you, the guy's a fucking hero going against them like he did."

Mazzucchelli took a bite of his pasta and shook his head. Joey scratched at the scars on his left hand.

"Sounds like bullshit," Mazzuchelli said.

"There was a Fist hanging just outside the back door," Joey said. "And the cops—they picked up Demise there, didn't they?"

Mazzucchelli took the starched white napkin off his knee and dabbed the corner of his mouth.

"Yeah," he said with a long, slow, sigh. "Yeah, they did."

"If I'd have jumped the gun and called in backup, they'd have ambushed us, boss. Demise was just the bait."

"So how'd this hero priest get the drop on Demise?"

Joey grinned. "Yeah, he told about that too, when he was helping me get my feet. It went like this, see . . ."

Demise walked out of the detention center in the late afternoon, pissed off. He still had on the fucking Aerosmith t-shirt. The car waited for him at the curb, Phan Lo at the wheel. Demise climbed in and slammed the door.

"What the fuck took you people so long?" he demanded as Phan pulled out into traffic. "I was in there overnight. How hard is it to post a little bail?"

"Gambiones," Phan said. "They hit back yesterday."

"No shit?"

"They torched five of our places. We lost twenty, maybe thirty men. Word on the street is they were trying for Danny Mao."

"Still doesn't explain why I had to spend a night in the lockup."

"You weren't the top priority," Phan said.

They drove in silence. The day was clearer, but cold. Phan turned toward Chinatown.

"Did you, ah, mention to anyone . . ." Demise began, but the sentence trailed off.

"They know you got your ass kicked by a deuce priest and a Jokertown whore," Phan said. "They laughed about it a little and got back to business."

"Shit."

"The whole thing was a setup. I saw one of the Gambione guys coming out the back right before the cops showed up. So we got suckered. Let it go, man. No one's going to remember *how* they did it. You want to get another shirt?"

"Yeah," Demise said. "You know, that attitude is just like you. It's just exactly like all of you. It's not about who's going to remember what. It's about principle. If you let people fuck with you, pretty soon everyone's going to think they can get away with shit."

When Phan spoke, his voice was measured and careful. "I don't think that someone who fucking kills people by looking at them is going to have a lot of trouble with people taking him lightly."

"You don't get it. The priest has to die. And I know where he's going to be on Sunday morning. I'll kill the little shit in the middle of Mass."

"Hardcore," Phan said, sounding unimpressed.

Sunday, February 8, 1987

DAWN THREATENED IN THE east, the light from the snow-covered trees making the kitchen window glow. Father Henry put the telephone handset back in its cradle just as Gina emerged from her room wrapped in a thick wool robe two sizes too big for her.

"Coffee smells great," she said, then "It's so quiet out here."

"That's what we call the country. Haven't you ever been out of the city?"

"Nah. I was born in Queens."

"You take cream or anything?"

"No. Black and bitter does just fine."

Father Henry poured the coffee into a couple of Marriage Encounter cups and took them over to the table.

"The Archbishop says he'll have tickets to Rome ready for us down in Albuquerque by Monday morning."

"I thought there was a month wait for passports."

"Vatican passports," Father Henry said, blowing on his coffee. "There are certain advantages to being a sovereign nation, after all. And a quarter million dollars is a pretty sizable donation. Exerts a kind of influence."

"That was my money."

"It was blood money and only the grace of Christ shall make it clean."

"And the other quarter million?"

"I'm a man of Christ. It'll be just fine right where it is. You need any—like maybe for tuition or something?—you just come see your Uncle Henry."

"Tuition? Give me a break," she said, laughing. Her face didn't look so sharp, he thought. "I'll go down on you for a hundred thousand, though."

"I was thinking about cooking up some eggs," he said, ignoring her. "Care for any?"

"Sure," she said. "Over hard."

He tried the still-scalding coffee and reached up for a good copper frying pan. Gina stood, her hands deep in the robe's pockets, went to the window and looked out into the woods. He wondered what it would be like, seeing a pine forest at dawn for the very first time.

Just another little miracle, he figured.

Age of Wonders

SEVEN
January 2005

SHE FOUND HIM. FATHER Henry was now working as a mid-level bureaucrat at the Vatican. She managed to get him on the phone by claiming to be the secretary of a small parish society raising funds for widows and orphans who suspected embezzlement by the treasurer and wanting to know who to report the problem to.

"Yes, how can I help you?"

"Hi, Father Henry? My name is Raleigh Jackson, I'm a reporter and I'm tracking down some leads about criminal syndicates working in Jokertown in the nineteen-eighties—"

"So you aren't with the Widows and Orphans Society from the parish of St. Patrick's in La Junta, Colorado?" He had a pleasant Southern accent. Soothing.

"Um. No, sir."

"You lied?"

Yeah, this wasn't a great way to start an interview with a Catholic priest. "Your secretary wouldn't take a message otherwise."

"Hmm," he murmured skeptically.

"I wanted to talk to you about the time you served at Our Lady of Perpetual Misery in Jokertown—"

"I'm afraid I don't talk about that time. At all. Now you have a nice afternoon—"

"Please, no one wants to talk about it. It was almost twenty years ago, it's history. Don't you think people have a right to know their own history?"

"Look here, the Shadow Fists might be gone and the Mafia a pale imitation of its former self. But some of these people are still out there."

"James Spector—Demise—is dead. He's been dead for years."

"You sure about that, miss?"

Dr. Tachyon had given a sworn affidavit that the man had been cremated, that nothing remained of him. But Tachyon was a thousand light-years away, on Takis. No way could she interview him.

She didn't answer.

"You have a nice day now, Miss Jackson," he said, and hung up.

Another dead end.

After tracking down comedians and boy bands, the criminal underworld was heady and overwhelming. Raleigh dug up harrowing crime scene photos and depositions. Police flow charts showed networks of gangs that had formed back in the sixties, broke up, and re-formed as something else, usually in control of one of a number of criminal syndicates. All of them made use of wild cards as enforcers, assassins, couriers, informants, and sex workers. It didn't matter that wild card powers and expressions were unique and made the people involved instantly identifiable. Most of them thought of themselves as above the law. The various threads led back to some of the worst incidents of violence in New York City over the last thirty years, Raleigh's whole lifetime. The battle at the Cloisters, the Astronomer, the Rox Campaign. The Immaculate Egrets, the Demon Princes, the Werewolves, the Shadow Fists, the JJS, the Twisted Fists.

Tracking all this was still easier than figuring out who her father was.

Aurora had only been able to give her the first names of the two anonymous partygoers she'd found so enticing: Jimmy and E. Maybe not even real names, but the handles they went by at clubs and parties. Aurora had been unapologetic about not even knowing their last names. Nevertheless, Raleigh managed to learn something about them. James Duffey was still in Manhattan and ran an art gallery in the Village specializing in Caribbean artists. He was the one with the lizard tail, one of those intriguing rather than difficult physical changes. It had made him really popular at parties when he was young. Now, he wore tailored suits. That was how she'd tracked him down. A handful of tailors in Manhattan specialized in alterations for jokers. Duffey's tailor talked. She'd stopped by the gallery once, but he wasn't in. She was almost relieved—she didn't know if she wanted to talk to him. All the time she'd spent thinking about finding her father, and she still didn't know what she would say.

The other, Eli Winters, had moved to Los Angeles and taught music at a private high school. He was married with a young son. Potential half brother? Raleigh just didn't know. And apart from demanding paternity tests in person, she wasn't sure what the next step was.

So she went back to unraveling the criminal underworld.

A number of third-tier Shadow Fist lieutenants had re-formed into new, competing gangs to try to keep their criminal operations going. Russian mobsters had moved in. By making her lists, tracking the lines of associations between them, she uncovered a few relationships she was pretty sure hadn't yet been noticed by the police. Asta Lenser—the ace known as Fantasy—had never been formally connected to the Shadow Fists and other criminal organizations, but her presence in many reports spoke to a deep involvement. Was she the secret power behind the reorganization of these crime networks? The mysterious ace known as Croyd Crenson, who woke in a new form every time he slept, was at the top of just about every agency's "person of interest" list. How did you find someone who completely changed every few weeks? The thrill of the hunt grew. If Raleigh could get just one big scoop—

She blogged about it, speculating. Who was public, who was secret, how did they connect, what happened to the figures who had vanished. She was careful—she only said anything publicly when she had ironclad proof. No one would get her for libel or defamation. Maybe she was secretly hoping someone would come forward with one solid lead.

Her mother would have told her, *Take it easy, relax, this is too much, this is too stressful.* But the files—it was all here. If she could just find the right connection and make the right phone call, she could make a difference.

Raleigh didn't notice the car following her. Later, she would think about how naive she'd been, how totally unprepared. She must have thought that the work would protect her. Her name on the byline made her a semipublic figure. She was only looking for the truth. Only telling stories. Dragging details that shouldn't have been forgotten into the light. She wasn't hurting anything.

The car stopped at the curb maybe twenty feet behind her. She was aware of it at the edges of her vision, the way you always had to be aware of traffic while walking in the city. It might have just been parking, just a cab letting someone out. Then someone yelled, "Gun!"

There was screaming and running, and like an idiot Raleigh turned to look, scanning the crowd. And seeing the man with the gun pointed right at her. She remembered thinking, *Well, that can't be right.* All she felt was disbelief. She didn't even move.

Someone tackled her out of the way. Someone else tackled the gunman. New Yorkers, doing what they did best, banding together and Not Putting Up With This Shit.

Somehow, she ended up shoved against the wall of the adjacent building. The would-be shooter was at the bottom of a dog pile, and a pair of cops was already running toward them, barking orders to the crowd. Someone had a hand on her shoulder.

"You all right?"

"I . . . I'm not sure?" It hit her at once, what had happened, how close she came. She started shaking.

"Hey, can we get paramedics here?" Sirens already hollered down the street. "Who'd you piss off?"

"I don't know—" No, she knew exactly what it was. She'd been poking at the scattered remains of the Shadow Fists like a kid poking at a wasp nest, and she must have been getting close. But the story was a decade old, it shouldn't have been relevant—unless it was.

The guy who'd tackled her knelt on the pavement with her. He glanced around nervously, especially when the cops arrived and started questioning people.

Before he could flee, she demanded, "Who are you?"

He seemed normal enough, if gaunt, and he had maybe something weird going on around the eyes. One hand was tapping at his thigh. "Name's Croyd," he answered after a moment's hesitation. "Next time someone points a gun at you, you duck, okay?"

"Okay—wait a minute, Croyd Crenson? Are you Croyd Crenson?"

He winked. Then got to his feet and jogged off, into the crowd. She never saw him again.

She wanted to throw up. She put her head in her hands and shut her eyes, but couldn't get that image, that black mouth of the gun, out of her mind.

"Hey, miss—was it you had the gun pointed at you? Can you ID him?" Now a uniformed cop was kneeling beside her. He gestured back to the gun-man, facedown on the concrete, hands cuffed behind him.

Raleigh was shocked that she didn't recognize him. She'd seen a man, maybe tall, maybe wearing a suit. She realized now she couldn't remember. All she saw in her mind's eye was the gun. "Yeah, maybe."

More cops had arrived. They were talking to people, witnesses. Sirens and flashing lights abounded. Then the paramedics. "Are you hurt?"

"I don't think so," she said. "I don't—"

"Miss, you need to breathe. Take a deep breath. You're going into shock."

"No, you don't understand, I'm latent, I'm positive for the virus but my card hasn't turned." Everyone drew back, as if she might explode. Maybe she would. She felt so light-headed . . .

Someone put an oxygen mask over her mouth. Told her to breathe. She did. A few more moments, or hours, or maybe just seconds, passed.

"I think you're okay. You're having a panic attack. It's just shock. Your card isn't turning."

"What?"

"We should take you in and check you out to be sure. But I think you're going to be fine. You ready to stand up?"

Was it weird that she called Gavin before she called her mother? "I'm at the hospital. I'm fine. Or I will be. I'm sorry, it's been a rough morning."

"I'll be right there," he said, before asking for a single detail.

First thing she did when he got to the emergency room was hug him as tight as she could, and he kept asking, "You're okay, you're really okay?" And she kept nodding though she wasn't entirely sure it was true.

He took her home. She argued about it—she was fine, she could get her-self home. But he insisted, and she realized that she should let him. That if their places had been reversed she would want to make sure he got home. Home this time meant Aurora's apartment. They'd had to have a discussion, what home actually meant for her, and they decided she'd be more comfort-able with her mother, in the more familiar surroundings. She called ahead to let Aurora know, then had to talk her down when her mother realized what exactly had happened.

The pair of them fussed, stuffing blankets around her and making tea. It was almost adorable, and Raleigh was too tired to argue.

Then Margot Dempsey from *Aces!* called the apartment.

Aurora picked up. "Oh, hello Margot. Yes, she's here, but I'm not sure she's in any shape—"

"Mom, I'll talk to her. I need to talk to her." She took the phone while Aurora and Gavin both watched her closely.

"Raleigh," Margot said sternly as a greeting. "I heard what happened. No story is worth dying for. Especially not for a gossip rag that people pick up in the checkout line while they're buying ice cream and Doritos."

But I can do more, so much more. "I'm so close to breaking this wide open—"

"Yes, I know, that's why someone's just sent you a very loud message."

She said, "If they wanted to kill me there are easier ways to do it, not out in the open in broad daylight where they'd get caught—"

"Raleigh my dear, they do it in broad daylight because they *want* to be seen. They're sending a warning. The clown who did it won't even be charged. He's probably already out on bail, want to bet?"

That pulled Raleigh up short. She really didn't understand, did she?

"Go back to feel-good features," Dempsey ordered. "This isn't worth getting hurt over. Maybe it's time to do that retrospective on your mother. What do you think?"

"I think I should maybe think about this tomorrow." Gavin handed her a fresh mug of tea. She smiled a thanks. He just looked worried.

"Take a couple of days off," Dempsey said. "Rest up and we'll see you soon."

She hung up and put her hands over her eyes. She was developing an amazing headache.

"Honey, are you sure you're okay?" Aurora asked. She was perched on one side of her, Gavin on the other. She was being smothered and took a deep breath to let that feeling go.

"I just need a good night's sleep," she said softly.

Gavin met her gaze, and she looked away, because he could see. He knew her. Knew that she was already thinking about the next piece of the puzzle. And he also knew better than to say a word about it. Just kissed her on the head and told her he'd see her tomorrow.

◆

Raleigh could go back in time. Far enough back that there wouldn't be any danger involved. History, this was all just history if you waited long enough.

Out of all the folders, all those lost archives, one of them was the oldest. The oldest dates, the earliest events. Surely this one would be safe. The label read CASH MITCHELL. At first she didn't know if this was a person or a gambling scheme.

Turned out, it was a person. And the more she read into the story, the less she believed it.

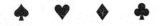

Storming Space

by Michael Cassutt

"**WOULD THAT BE MR.** Cash?" the voice behind me said, surprising the hell out of me. I was in Haugen's Bakery on Highway 14 getting my morning cup of coffee, though that's not why I stopped there. I didn't even like coffee much; it made me jittery, and made my heavy lifting tricky at best, almost impossible. The owner, a joker of indeterminate gender named "Fran," was hard on the eyes and nerves.

But Haugen's had this waitress named Evelyn. Well, her name was *pronounced* Evelyn: on her nametag it was written, no fooling, "Eva-Lynne." She was tall and slim and blond and about 25 years old, and my purpose in life, that unseasonably hot day in October 1968, was to find out what mistake she made in a past life that dumped her into a bakery in Mojave, California. Until then I, like the truckers passing through, continued to come by for some really bad coffee, questionable pastries, and just a whiff of her perfume. Perhaps a throaty, "Thanks for coming in. Good to see you again." (She always seemed on the verge of remembering my name.)

You certainly didn't come to Haugen's to have strange foreign men loom up behind you without warning.

"Hmm?" I said, or something equally articulate.

"Mr. Cash Mitchell?" The speaker was a man about forty, thin, dark. Indian, I judged, from the lilt to his voice. Not a joker, either.

"Speaking," I said, foolishly, as if we were on the telephone. (I was moving closer to my encounter with Eva-Lynne.)

"Ah, good. I am Tominbang. I wish to speak with you on, a matter of great urgency." He shook my hand a bit too enthusiastically.

And I took another step forward. The customer in front of the customer in front of me—a busy-looking woman of 35, almost certainly a real estate professional—suddenly launched a complicated series of orders at Eva-Lynne, no doubt nosh for some morning meeting. I was trapped.

"I'm listening," I said to Tominbang. If you saw me, medium height, overweight, glasses, you would not be intimidated. But I had had a good couple of months lifting various items for Mr. Warren Skalko of Lancaster, Las Vegas, and other municipalities, so I felt smug. I could not imagine why this foreign man would be talking to me; more precisely, I suspected that any association between us was not going to make me rich. (This turned out to be painfully true.)

"Mr. Warren Skalko recommends you to me," Tominbang said.

I lost probably a third of my attitude at the mention of my mentor. "I'm always happy to meet a friend of Mr. Skalko's," I said, summoning as much enthusiasm as I could. Just to be safe. "Where do you know him from?" Mr. Skalko had several sorts of associates, some from his noted (and legitimate) charity work, others from his country club, and a few from being what that same popular press called "the crime lord of the southwest."

"We were introduced on the first tee at Riviera," Tominbang said, naming Mr. Skalko's Los Angeles country club, and nicely slipping into the second category of Skalko associates. "He mentioned your specific abilities as a mass transporter—"

He was interrupted by a commotion not five feet away. Real Estate Woman was giving my beloved Eva-Lynne a hard time. "What the hell do you expect me to do? Carry it all by myself?"

The customer in front of me, sensing a longer-than-usual wait for bad coffee, shook his head and departed. At that moment I caught Eva-Lynne's eye-and was struck by something I'd never seen there before.

Panic.

She was trying to maneuver a heavy, unbalanced load of hot coffees and pastry—enough food for a group of a dozen longshoreman, I judged—while behind her a coffee machine somehow managed to boil over and one of the bakers chattered in her ear. Big bad Fran was busy elsewhere. "I'm sorry," she was saying, "Just give me a—"

"Let me help," I said, surprising myself as I edged past the annoying Real Estate Woman and placed a hand on Eva-Lynne's shoulder. This is how my lifting works: physical touch, with mass-to-be-moved proportional to the strength of my grip. The trigger is emotion, and anger or even general annoyance (my usual state), is the most reliable.

You can bet I was gentle. I didn't want hot coffee spewing all over us. Sure enough, the load lightened just enough so that Eva-Lynne didn't have to worry about it. One lovely eyebrow arched in surprise. "Out to your car?" I said to the Annoying Real Estate Woman.

"No, why don't you just carry it over to Joshua Street for me." Ordinarily I have little patience for sarcasm, but being in actual physical contact with Eva-Lynne had a mellowing effect.

"Let me help," I whispered to Eva-Lynne, since I had to remain in physical contact to keep lifting. And we glided outside into the gravel parking like a Kern County version of Fred and Ginger.

"Thank you," Eva-Lynne told me, once the order was safely deposited on the front seat of a new 1969 Ford LTD, and Annoying Real Estate Woman had departed. "I really appreciate it." Her nose sort of crinkled, and she smiled. "Your name is Cash, isn't it?"

At last! I'd made it across the barrier, from vaguely familiar five-day-a-week morning customer to friend-with-a-name! Who knew where this could lead! I was just about to extend my hand when Fran appeared in the doorway. "Eva-Lynne, we have *customers!*"

"Back to the grind," she said, heading back inside. I followed.

In those brief-but-glorious moments of personal contact, I had forgotten about Tominbang. "You are a gentleman, Mr. Mitchell."

"Not really," I said, and I wasn't just being modest. "What was it you wanted to talk to me about?"

"Ah, my project," he said, lighting up like a Mojave dawn. "I am thinking of making a flight to the Moon."

Nothing less could have torn me away from Eva-Lynne. (And even then, it was close.)

Mr. Tominbang's late model El Dorado was parked outside, right next to my '66 Mustang (the fruit of my first lifting jobs for Mr. Skalko, a shipment of color televisions that somehow fell off their truck). There was some discussion as to whether I would ride with Tominbang ("Where are we going, exactly?") or he with me, until we compromised on having me follow him. That was a relief: if I'd left the Mustang for, say, two hours, the next place I would have seen it would have been as pieces in one of Mr. Skalko's other subsidiaries, the Palmdale chop shop.

Tominbang headed north, then west on Highway 58, toward the nether reaches of greater Mojave. This was strange territory for me: I live south of Palmdale, which is itself south of Mojave, in my little rat shack on the slope above Pearblossom Highway. I only found myself frequenting Haugen's Bakery on Highway 14 thanks to visits to one of Mr. Skalko's hideouts—excuse me, residences.

No sooner had we cleared the collection of shacks, trailers and used auto parts lots that is Mojave than I developed second thoughts. Maybe it was the wind, which was blowing hard enough to nudge the Mustang off the centerline. (Did you know that Tehachapi is the windiest municipality in the continental US?) Maybe it was hearing Scott McKenzie singing, "If You're Going to Jokertown" for the hundredth time in a week, with its lyrics about taking that longshot when you see it. (A guy like me doesn't have many opportunities with a girl like Eva-Lynne.)

Maybe it was thinking about what Mr. Tominbang said. A flight to the *Moon?*

I was seven years old when the wild card turned, so aliens from another planet were as real to me as Rin Tin Tin or my Fourth grade teacher. My older brother, Brad, used to force me to play Buck Rogers with him—the times we weren't playing Wake Island, that is. We fought marsh creatures on Venus, dust dragons on Mars, and even some weird rock beings on the Moon.

Brad wanted to explore space when he grew up. Who cared that the Takisians had been there first? Human beings would go further, faster! He read all the Tak World novels, which he then passed down to me. (I read them, too, but under duress.)

More practically, he went to college at Purdue, got his engineering degree in '61, then joined the Air Force. This was not long after the X-11A fiasco; I remember him telling me that the US was edging back into the space business—but in secret. He had heard rumors of new students being recruited out of Purdue.

Brad went off to Vietnam and disappeared over Haiphong in January 1964. He was still listed as Missing in Action. And America's "secret" space program? For all I knew that day, we could have had a fleet of flying saucers bombing Haiphong, maybe, or spying on all the freaks in Berkeley.

They sure weren't flying to the Moon.

We were now so far into the wilderness that my radio reception was fading: there was mention of a riot at some rock concert in California. There were always riots in the news that year. I wouldn't have bothered to pay attention, but it said the Hell's Angels were involved. I knew the local Angels: they also did some jobs for Mr. Skalko. When I changed channels, all I got was country and western crap, or preachers, so I switched it off.

Besides, Tominbang's car was turning onto a dirt road leading to a pair of distant hangars at Tehachapi-Kern Regional Airport. We had passed up a perfectly good asphalt road that led to a perfectly good administration building and tower. I made a note to send Tominbang a bill for any damage to the Mustang's undercarriage.

The wind was still blowing when we got out. Tominbang's tie flapped noisily. I wedged dust out of the corner of my eye as my guide fumbled a key out of his pocket and spent an unnecessary amount of time trying to open a padlock.

I looked at the two big hangars and what I couldn't see from the road—a set of fuel tanks and other mechanical structures behind them, along with a much better road that led back to the airport proper. No other cars present, except one battered blue Scout. "Here we are," Tominbang said proudly, wrenching the door open.

We had to pass through an anteroom of sorts to enter the hangar itself. Actually, a room and a hallway, with Tominbang flipping on lights as we went. "Please excuse," he said. "I have just acquired this property and have yet to staff it completely."

"How many, uh, staff, are you going to have?" I asked, smelling mildew and seeing rust and dirt wherever I looked.

"Perhaps three dozen. Perhaps more."

Were forty people enough to build a spaceship that could fly to the Moon? I doubted that.

"Before we proceed, I must ask . . ." His voice trailed off as he pulled a two-paged typed document out of the drawer of a battered metal desk. "This is a non-disclosure agreement certifying that you will keep what you are about to see confidential, until such time as it becomes public."

I looked around at the cold, unused office with its peeling paint, and tried "not" to laugh. And signed. "How much is this all costing?" I said, handing the document back to Tominbang.

"The final price tag will be close to ten million dollars US," he said casually, as if he were disclosing the price of a new suit of clothes.

He opened one last door, and we emerged into a rather different space: a huge space probably three stories tall. Bing, bing, bing, on went the lights.

And sitting in the middle of this space was a strange vehicle I can only describe as stubby-winged and shaped like a pumpkinseed. "This is Quicksilver," Tominbang said, proudly waving me toward it. "A prototype space plane developed at Tomlin four years ago."

Not the X-11A. "Never heard of it."

"It was secret."

"Then what's it doing here?" And in the hands of a shady foreign national?

"The Quicksilver program was cancelled last year. It proved to be technically feasible to fly it from the surface of the earth into orbit and return, but at a much higher cost than the Pentagon was willing to pay. Especially with a war going on. *This* Quicksilver is supposedly being stored until the day it can be displayed in the Air Force Museum."

"How the hell did you even *hear* about it?"

"Ah," Tominbang said, very pleased with himself, "my business is computers and telecommunications. One of my subsidiaries had the contract for the Quicksilver ground stations."

So he knew about it legitimately. Well, semi-legitimately.

Up close Quicksilver looked used: the paint was faded. There were what appeared to be scorch marks on its skin. Of course, those were just the superficial details. "It was flown into orbit," Tominbang said.

"Earth orbit is a long way from the Moon."

"That's where *you* come in," a new voice said.

Out of the shadows lurched a slim, weathered man of sixty. Or, once he stepped into the light, a hard forty. His hair was gray and ragged, like a military crewcut gone to weed. His eyes were pale blue. It was the web of lines around them that made him seem old.

"Al!" Tominbang said, with the sort of enthusiasm I used to have for Christmas morning, "Commander Al Dearborn, I have found Mr. Cash Mitchell." Tominbang turned to me. "Commander Dearborn is a Quicksilver pilot."

We shook hands. His grip was surprisingly limp. "Call me Al. All my ex wives do." He smiled. "Though they usually add 'that cheating son of a bitch.'"

"I'll skip that part until I know you better."

Dearborn laughed, perhaps a bit too hard. "That's good. You're gonna need a sense of humor on this thing."

That statement alarmed me, and Tominbang noted my reaction. "Commander Dearborn is a noted humorist," he said. *And drunkard,* I wanted to add. "He was the primary test pilot for Quicksilver."

"Actually, I was a Navy exchange test pilot for the bird at Tomlin. The Air Force project pilot was a buddy of mine, Mike Sampson."

I didn't like Dearborn's smell and boozy appearance, so my normal sociability was strained. "So why don't we have Sampson here?"

"Major Sampson is still on active duty at Tomlin," Tominbang said, quickly, and with a nervous glance at Dearborn. Obviously this was a delicate subject.

Dearborn peered at me as if we had not just been introduced. "I can't decide whether I'm gonna like you or want to kill you."

Ultimately, he did neither. What he did was throw up on my feet.

I'm not a fastidious man; I generally wear T-shirts and jeans, to the annoyance of Mr. Skalko, who clings to the sport coat look and seems to want a "team uniform" for his associates. I also wear sandals, generally a wise choice in the desert heat.

It was not wise on that day. Having my bare feet splashed with vomit violated even my loose standards of hygiene. I practically screamed in disgust. Then, with Tominbang's help, I found a men's room and managed to rinse off. Repeatedly. The sickening odor, combined with the ancient fetor of the men's room, almost made me pass out.

Tominbang was more upset than I was. He kept apologizing for Dearborn. "He has a drinking problem. But he is very capable. He has been logged two hundred hours of Quicksilver test time, and made three orbital flights."

"Can he stay sober long enough to do the job?"

"It was my impression that he only drinks when he doesn't have a mission."

"You'd better get him to work, faster," I said. "If he throws up on me again, I'm walking out."

If I expected an apology from Dearborn, it would have to wait. He was passed out—let's say sleeping—on a pile of canvas formerly used to protect the Quicksilver vehicle. This gave me my chance to pin Tominbang down. "So, what exactly is the plan here? Can you really fly a spaceplane to the Moon?"

"Oh, yes. With your assistance, Mr. Mitchell."

"You're losing me."

"Since Quicksilver is capable of orbital flight, it only requires minor modifications for landing on the Moon. A landing gear must be added. Communications gear has to be beefed up. We need to obtain suitable space suits. And the life support fittings need to be changed to accommodate a crew of three."

Everything was making sense up to the last point. "Why do you need three people? Isn't this a one-man vehicle?"

Tominbang looked at the floor, as if he were embarrassed. "We will need the pilot—Dearborn. We will need a spacecraft specialist. And I wish to go along."

That was alarming. "You're spending all this money just so *you* can fly to the Moon?"

"No, Mr. Mitchell, that would be crazy," he said, meaning nothing of the sort. "I have a practical reason. I have made a fortune in allowing certain electronic financial transactions to pass through the off-shore offices of my communications firm. But governments have been making that sort of work more difficult, and it will soon be impossible. I hope to set up the ultimate offshore data recording and retransmitting station."

I was about to say that that idea sounded crazier than simply spending $10 million for a ride to the Moon. But Tominbang leaned close again. "*This is the information you must keep confidential.*"

"No problem," I said, wondering just what subject I could bring up that would lead to my immediate departure from the hangar. I might even be able to stop at Haugen's and resume that interrupted flirtation with Eva-Lynne. "You were about to explain why you needed me."

"Because of your unique lifting ability, Mr. Mitchell. Quicksilver's power plant can't blast it out of earth orbit, or off the surface of the Moon. Unless, at a key moment, we can somehow reduce its mass to a fraction."

I opened my mouth to laugh, then closed it. The biggest object I had ever lifted was a semi-trailer full of Johnny Walker and other fine beverages. (Mr. Skalko was unhappy with certain tariffs due him from the passage of this truck through his territory.) That semi dwarfed Quicksilver.

So the gig seemed possible, in theory. Which is all I've ever had. (As my father used to say, "Cash, you violate the laws of gravitation." To which I usually answered: "I never studied law.") Nevertheless, the very idea of performing a lift while in space and sitting on a rocket—well, it made me feel as faint as when I was washing Dearborn's vomit off my flesh.

"I don't know about this," I said, perhaps more than once. It was one thing to fantasize about kicking up the dust of Mars with your boots. It was quite another to entrust your life to a crazy foreign man with more money than sense, and a drunken pilot. Oh, yes, on a flight to the Moon!

"The compensation would be of the highest degree," Tominbang was saying, perhaps more than once and in different ways.

I have many faults, among them slovenliness and laziness, but the greatest of these is greed. So I said, "How much?"

And then he mentioned a figure that would not only buy my cooperation, but my silence and enthusiasm and that of everyone I know for at least a year. "Mr. Tominbang," I said. "You've got a deal."

(If you're thinking that I thought I would find Eva-Lynne easier to impress if were a moderately richer man, you would be correct.)

Dearborn uttered a snort at this point, forcing me to look his way. "And what about him?"

"He has already agreed to the terms." He shook his head. "He really just wants to fly Quicksilver again."

I said, "Oh," or something equally helpful, then added, "Are we going to dry him out? Seeing as how we'll be a quarter of a million miles from home and depending on his sobriety?"

"I am searching for a way. I would take him into my own residence, but my travel schedule does not permit it."

"What about Dearborn's situation? Does he have a wife?"

"Sadly, Commander Dearborn needs a place to stay."

I don't want to recount the rest of the conversation. I must have been weakened by dollar signs, because I agreed to take him in.

Temporarily.

"Doreen threw me out when I told her I had spent the weekend with Tominbang." Dearborn and I were headed back down Highway 14 toward Palmdale. It was midafternoon, but he had awakened from his nap as fresh and perky as a teenager on a Sunday morning. If he had any reservations about going off to live with a man he had just met, not to mention vomited on, he hid them. "She thought that was some kind of code name for a Thai hooker, and that was it."

"Doreen sounds as though she's a bit suspicious."

"Well," he said. "I may have given her reason to be. On other occasions." And he laughed. "Hey, does this thing go faster than 55?"

"Not when I'm driving it," I said. That was one of the hard lessons I had learned in my association with Mr. Skalko: keep a low profile and avoid even the *appearance* of breaking the law.

Dearborn laughed and sat back, his feet up on the dash. "You know, they've got this new invention called 'air conditioning.'"

"Never saw the need," I said. The high desert gets hot at midday, but one of the side effects of my wild card is a lower body temperature. Except when I'm lifting. And I generally don't lift when driving.

"You're a deuce, huh?"

"Yeah. Want to get out and walk?"

He pointed to himself. "I've got a touch of it myself," he said, surprising me for the second time that day. I wondered what his power was? But he offered nothing. "Besides, I've worked with many a joker in my day." He pointed to the south and east, the general direction of Tomlin Air Force Base. "Right over there."

"I didn't know we were allowed in the Air Force."

"Well, Crash, there's allowed, and then there's "allowed." The policy was certainly against it. But some got in. Stranger things have happened."

"Like Tominbang getting hold of Quicksilver."

Dearborn started laughing. "Yeah, ain't that unusual? It's not as though we have a lot of them sitting around. They built two, and broke one. There was also some kind of ground spare, but that's it."

"So right now, nobody's missing the Quicksilver."

"Nope. She's all ours, Crash." He slapped me on the back so hard I almost drove off the road. "Hey," he said, suddenly serious, "what the hell kind of name is Crash? For a flight project, that is."

"Don't tell me you're superstitious."

"Son, there isn't a pilot alive who isn't superstitious."

"Don't worry," I said. "The name is 'Cash,' not 'Crash.'"

I was spared the indignity of adding "cook" to my new role as "host" when Dearborn suggested we make a stop in Lancaster for an early dinner. Naturally, he knew a little place just off the Sierra Highway on Avenue 1. I was reluctant, at first, until Dearborn offered to pay. "Just because I'm homeless don't mean I'm broke."

Well, given the fee Tominbang offered, I was far from broke, too, though my riches were still theoretical—which is to say, non-existent. "Besides," Dearborn added, "I owe you."

The restaurant was called Casa Carlos; it was a cinder block structure surrounded by a pitted gravel parking lot. (Actually, that description fits almost any structure in the area.) The jumble of cars spilling beyond the nominal border of the lot testified to the joint's reputation for fine Mexican cuisine, or possibly the lack of other dining options.

It was dark, smoky and loud when we walked in. The floor was sawdust. The clientele a mixture of agro workers in stained shirts and cowboy hats, and the local gentry in short-sleeved white shirts and undone ties.

At first I expected one of those tiresome displays of familiarity, in which Dearborn, the Anglo regular, would embrace Carlos, the Latino owner, exchanging a few laughs and phrases in Spanish. At which point Carlos would snap his fingers at a waitress and order her to bring "Senior Al" the *chimichanga* special or whatever. It was the sort of arrival staged by Mr. Skalko across the width of the LA basin.

Nothing of the kind occurred. We slunk into the restaurant like two tourists from Wisconsin, quietly finding a table off in one corner.

Dearborn did take the seat that would keep his back to the wall, and his eyes on the entrance. I'd seen that maneuver with Mr. Skalko, too. "Expecting someone?"

"As a matter of fact, I am. An old buddy who eats here about four times a week."

I let the subject drop as a waiter arrived. We ordered a beer each, then, when the plates arrived almost instantaneously, started in on the food. I should say, I ate; Dearborn devoured a double combination that seemed to consist of a heap of refried beans and cheese the size of a football. At one point he slowed down long enough to say, "Don't watch too close now, Cash. I only had one meal in the past twenty-four hours, and, as you will recall, I was unable to retain that for long."

The beer had mellowed me to the point where I was able to smile at the memory. I got Dearborn talking about himself, partly to avoid having to talk about myself, but also to hear the standard military shit-kicker war story bio. I was surprised, then, when Dearborn told me he was from Chicago and had grown up in a privileged North Shore family. His father had been a senior executive at Sears prior to the wild card, at which point he had been turned, losing his job and his money. Dearborn was lucky enough to win an appointment to the naval academy at Annapolis. After graduating in 1951, he became a naval aviator.

He won his wings of gold too late to shoot it out over Korea, but served with the fleet in the Mediterranean, then did a year of graduate work in nuclear engineering, before coming to Tomlin in 1958 to attend the test pilot school as a navy exchange pilot. "I had just graduated and joined the project when they had the accident."

He meant the X-11A disaster, the spectacular mid-air collision between a prototype space plane and its mother ship that killed pilots Enloe and Guinan, and sparked a wild card hunt that destroyed the home-grown American space program. Or so I'd heard.

"That was a bad scene, for a long time after. I stayed at Tomlin flying chase and pace on a few other programs. They sure weren't eager to let the X-ll guys get their hands on new aircraft. We were jinxed." He smiled. "I missed out on three other accidents. There was quite a bad string there around 1961, '62.

"But when General Schriever became head of Systems Command, he rammed through the Quicksilver program. I was the only X-11 pilot around, and being in the right place at the right time, got in on the ground floor." He smiled. "Ruined my Navy career, of course."

"Ruined? Being one of the first Americans to fly into orbit? Even if it was secret, you should have had it made!"

"You don't know much about the military, do you, Cash? When I joined Quicksilver, I had already spent four years here at Tomlin, which meant I was working for the Air Force, not the Navy. I needed to do a tour at the Pentagon and in 'Nam, then command a ship. If I ever wanted to command a carrier, which is the whole *reason* you become a navy aviator.

"I stayed at Tomlin through the first year of test flights. Me and the prime Air Force guy, my old buddy, Mike Sampson. Then the program got cut back, and both of us were left twisting in the wind. Sampson made out better than me: he went off to drive 105s out of Cam Ranh Bay, and wound up getting a Purple Heart.

"I was too old to go back to the fleet. Why waste time re-qualifying me for carrier ops? I'd be eligible for retirement before I finished a tour like that. So they assigned me to a missile test squadron at China Lake." He smiled bitterly. "That's when I started drinking. And drank myself right out of the cockpit, right out of the Navy, and out of marriage number two."

In spite of that, he had ordered a beer, though, to be fair, he had barely sipped it. "I'm guessing Doreen is number three?"

"Correct. I came back to southern California to work for Lockheed as a civilian, since they had the support contract for Quicksilver. She was my first secretary . . ." He laughed at the memory. "Guess I wasn't cut out to work in an office. Too much opportunity for mischief."

I must have been feeling brave. I pointed at the beer on the table. "Are you cut out for Tominbang's project?"

Dearborn smiled, picked up the beer and poured it on the sawdust floor. "Being the first human on the Moon? I can give up drinking for *that*, no problem!"

His voice trailed off and his expression grew tense. I realized he was looking over my shoulder. "Well, well, well," he said, softly.

I turned and looked: all I could see was another man about Dearborn's age, though smaller and less weathered, smiling and chatting with the hostess. "Is that the guy you were expecting?"

"Yes. Major Mike Sampson! Hey, 'Wrong Way!'" He started his phrase in a conversational tone, but by the time he reached "Wrong Way" he was shouting.

"Wrong Way" Sampson—the compact man at the entrance turned with the deliberation of a gunfighter being challenged. Then he recognized Dearborn, and his face lit up like a harvest moon. Working his way to our table, he knocked over other patrons like tenpins, stopping short of actually hugging Dearborn. Instead, he punched him in the shoulder. "You lucky son of a bitch!" he said.

"How much luck can I have, if you found me!" They exchanged similar sentiments for several minutes. Eventually I was introduced; Sampson wound up joining us.

It turned out that he had recently returned to Tomlin after recovering from wounds received in combat. He was now head of something called a "joint test force" at the flight test center. "Why didn't you just take disability?" Dearborn said.

"Because I *wasn't* disabled," Sampson snapped. "Yeager fought his way back into the cockpit after getting burned in that crash, and he was much worse off than me." He hesitated, glancing in my direction, but some invisible gesture from Dearborn cleared him for further revelation. "Besides, the Air Force has some very interesting stuff cooking. I want to be part of it."

"Nothing as interesting as what we're doing," Dearborn said, shooting me an all-too-visible shit-eating grin. He then proceeded to violate every clause in Tominbang's confidentiality agreement, telling Sampson every detail of the project!

Sampson absorbed the information silently, but appreciatively, nodding with growing enthusiasm. "I should have known," he said. "Everybody was saying, 'Poor Al, he really screwed the pooch at China Lake.' But I knew better. I said, 'It only means there's something great coming along for him.'"

Sampson would go far in politics, because he almost had me believing him. Dearborn chose to do the same. "Thanks, buddy. But I really pushed the envelope on luck this time, let me tell you."

"We're older, Al. Like pro athletes, the power isn't what it was."

"We've both got enough juice for one last caper, especially something like this. Are you in?"

"Hell, yes!" They shook on it. "Obviously, it will all be on the Q.T. Vacation time or evenings."

"You already know the vehicle, so you shouldn't need more than that."

After confirming various phone numbers and some personal catchup—there was fond mention of a woman named Peggy, a name which meant nothing to me—Sampson went off to meet his original dinner companions, who must have been furious by that time.

I was a little furious myself. "What do you think you're doing? You told him about the project and signed him up as what? Your alternate?"

"Look, Tominbang's putting out a lot of his own money in this. And, let's face it, Cash, I'm not the most reliable individual. I'm thinking of the program at large: Sampson's good. Weird, but good. He'll be there only if we need him."

"Do you think we will?"

"The one thing I learned from flight test is this: nothing ever goes as planned. I don't care if you're a nat, a joker or a deuce. Always, always, *always* have a backup."

My apartment had two bedrooms, and came already furnished, so I was easily able to make up a place for Dearborn to sleep. Or, to be more precise, to live.

Before turning in, he said, "Days on the flight line start early, Co-pilot." Somehow, between the pouring of the beer on the floor, and my announcement that I had made up his bed, "Co-pilot" had become Dearborn's name for me. "I usually wanted to be at ops by six A.M. Since we aren't flying yet, I want to be back at Tehachapi by seven."

Which is why Haugen's Bakery appeared to be closed when we pulled in the next morning. It was six-twenty—mid-morning by bakery hours. Seeing lights and activity within, I got out of the car and rapped on the front door. Dearborn got out to stand looking across the high desert to where the sun was already up, shining down on the vastness that was Tomlin.

As I waited for Eva-Lynne, I wondered idly where she lived—a trailer out back, perhaps? Or one of the grim little brick bungalows scattered in half-assed developments among the Joshua trees?

And did she live *with* anyone? She wore no ring. And in all the hours I had spent in her company, however remotely, I had never seen her with a boyfriend, or seen her give any sign of having one.

A key rattled in the door: Eva-Lynne, brushing a stray wisp of blond hair away from her face. "Oh, hi!" A pause. "Cash!" She lowered her voice . . . flirtatiously? "My hero. We're just opening. The usual?"

"Yes, thank you."

I followed her in. "You're early today," she said, slipping behind the counter, though not without giving me a memorable retreating vision. "New job?"

"How did you know?" The door opened and closed behind me.

"Just a guess. You've always looked a little—at odds," she said, handing me a cup and my bag of Danish, and waving away my money. "My treat, as a thanks for yesterday."

I was so pleased by the mere knowledge that Eva-Lynne had actually given me some thought that I almost missed what happened next:

Dearborn stepped up to the counter. He made no overt sign that he found Eva-Lynne attractive. In fact, he was painfully polite, as he asked for a large cup of black coffee.

She spilled it. "Oh, God," she said, reddening, "what's the matter with me?"

Dearborn quickly righted the cup and sopped up the pool of coffee with a napkin before Eva-Lynne could deploy her counter rag.

It was only a moment, but it made me sick. Dearborn's mere *presence* had unnerved Eva-Lynne.

I had to keep him away from her.

We said nothing about the events at the bakery as we drove the last few miles up to Tehachapi-Kern Airport. What, indeed, could I have said? *Commander Dearborn, please don't have any contact with a woman I worship from afar?*

He would have laughed at me. I would have laughed at me.

Then we reached Tominbang's hangar, and the subject no longer seemed as critical.

In the hours since Dearborn and I had driven off, the Quicksilver team had gained a number of new members. First off, a pair of steely-eyed security guards in khaki and sunglasses quizzed us before we could get close.

There were at least thirty cars of varying age and make in the lot. The lights were on in the hangar. People were scurrying around, apparently to great purpose. Tominbang was the center of attention, introducing people to each other, signing various pieces of paper, smiling and nodding the whole time.

Many of the new hires, I realized, were deuces. Possibly all of them. "I guess Tominbang's the only nat in the place," I said to Dearborn.

"Think again, Co-pilot."

I hadn't spotted Tominbang as a deuce, but, then, I often fail to detect them. It made all the sense in the world, though. Who else would have come up with the idea of a flight to the Moon as a solution to a financial problem?

Sure enough, spotting us, Tominbang broke away from the fluid horde. "Greetings, crew mates!" He was smiling so broadly that he seemed deranged, an unfortunate image. Certainly he was, now that I had been alerted to it, clearly a deuce. "We are really rolling now!"

Paralyzed by the troubling sight of Tominbang's smile, I could not respond. Fortunately, Dearborn was more resilient. "Where the hell did all these people come from, T?"

"I have been hiring them in Los Angeles for the past three weeks. Today was the day they were to report."

I finally found my voice. "What are they supposed to be doing?"

Tominbang was like a car salesman showing off the features of a new model Buick. "That group," he said, indicating a group of five examining the undercarriage of Quicksilver, "will perform mechanical modifications to the exterior of the vehicle."

"Landing gear," Dearborn added, helpfully. Obviously he had had more extensive conversations with Tominbang than I.

A smaller clump was busy looking into the open cockpit. "That team will modify the life support systems, and also the space suits." I hadn't thought about space suits. Obviously we couldn't walk on the Moon in our street clothes!

There were other groups in discussion—legal, security and public relations, Tominbang said. I gave those issues zero thought at that time.

The smallest group—a pair of jokers, one an honest-to-God human-sized cockroach, the other apparently related, since he looked like a giant bee—stood nearby, watching us with what I took to be unnecessary interest. "And what do they want?"

"Ah," Tominbang said, as Dearborn chuckled, "our trajectory team. These are specialists from Cal Tech who will program the maneuvers Commander Dearborn will make with the Quicksilver."

"The nav system is primitive, but workable. Propulsion is the big question mark."

"I thought propulsion was my responsibility," I said, foolishly.

"Absolutely!" Tominbang said. "These two are your instructors!"

I have never done well in school. I have done spectacularly poorly with nat tutors. I could not imagine myself working happily with teachers who were *jokers*.

Before I could protest, however, Dearborn slapped me on the back. "You better get started, Co-pilot. We launch in sixty days."

Before that day was out, I was introduced to Bacchus, the bee-like joker, who claimed to have been a professor at Cal Tech in an earlier life. The roach was named Kafka, and he made sure I knew he had no degrees of any kind. "I'm just a homegrown genius," he said, without a trace of humility.

Bacchus took the lead in my education, hissing and wheezing his way through my first my first lessons in astro-navigation, making it clear that I, who could barely find the North Pole in the night sky, would need to learn the locations of twenty "guide" stars. (Navigation and propulsion—which is to say, my lifting—were linked, since the lifts had to occur at precise locations in space.)

It just got worse from that point on.

The only bright spot in that first two weeks was that I was able to keep Dearborn away from Eva-Lynne. Well, it was not so much a deliberate action on my part as deliberate inaction. Even though I hated being locked in a room with Bacchus and Kafka I began to prolong my lessons as late as I dared, and within the first week Dearborn was so frustrated that he went to Tominbang and said he needed a car of his own.

Tominbang obtained a 1959 Cadillac convertible with fins more suited to an airliner. It was painted pink. Dearborn, ever practical and obviously secure in his image, took it happily. He even went so far as to apologize to me. "Sorry, Co-pilot, but for the next few weeks, I'm flying solo. You've won your wings." Sure enough, I saw less and less of him at my apartment, though he did actually make it home every night—sober. Now all I had to do was be sure to arrive at Haugen's by six-thirty every morning, and linger there until I saw Dearborn's pink beast flash past.

While the extra time spent at the bakery caused me to gain weight (I was now averaging two pieces of Danish per morning), it also allowed me to approach Eva-Lynne.

It was slow going; she had to work the counter, and she was, it seemed, immensely popular. But over the course of a week I learned the following: she was 24. She lived with a cousin in Rosamond, the tiny community to the south of Mojave, at the entrance to Tomlin. Her favorite musician was not, as I had feared, one of the Monkees or possibly Simon and/or Garfunkel, but "all those Motown singers."

And, a big surprise, she was not a refugee from a bad experience in Hollywood. She had, in fact, never been to Hollywood, and didn't know if she wanted to go. "*Everybody* keeps asking me about it, so maybe I should."

While she was beautiful enough to compete in that brutal environment, I could not, in good conscience, advise her to try. "You're the only reason people come to Mojave."

"Stop!" she said, blushing with what I hoped was pleasure.

What I didn't learn was whether or not she would go out with me. Part of it was due to my own inability to utter an invitation. The sheer amount of foot traffic also made such a delicate conversation difficult.

It was on a Friday morning in early June, however, less than three weeks after Mr. Tominbang first approached me, that I felt I had my opening. I had arrived, as usual, at six-twenty, only to find Eva-Lynne with her eyes red-rimmed. I immediately asked if she was all right, but got no answer, because Fran was already yelling at her, a more frequent occurrence. "Hey, beauty queen, get your ass over here!"

I got my coffee and Danish and sat down at one of the small tables by the window, and witnessed no further outbursts. Imagine my surprise when, during a quiet moment, Eva-Lynne suddenly sat down with me. "Cash, do you mind if I ask you a question?"

Only if I can ask you one in return. The words appeared in my brain, but stayed there, stuck amidst the numbers. "Sure," I said, pathetically.

"This new job you got—could they use a secretary or something? A girl to answer the phones, maybe?"

I had no idea of Tominbang's staffing requirements. But at that moment, in a fit of arrogance, I decided I would pay Eva-Lynne's salary, if necessary. He was paying me enough. "We sure do," I heard myself say. "It's only a temporary job, though."

"Anything to get me out of here now."

"What time do you get off work?" I was able to ask her a question like that as long as the next phrase had nothing to do with a date.

"Two."

"Can you get a ride to the airport in Tehachapi?"

She got a look on her face that suggested a hidden power, one having more ancient roots than the wild card. "*That* won't be a problem."

I described Tominbang's hangar, then told her I would alert our guards to be looking for her around 2:30.

She leaned forward, kissed me on the forehead, and said, "You're a doll."

I drove to Tehachapi wrapped in a golden cloud.

It wasn't until that afternoon, after Eva-Lynne, eyes alive and happy, arrived for her appointment, after I had spent the day in a tedious session with Kafka concerning retrograde impulses of the Quicksilver propulsion system, that I realized I had made a terrible mistake:

I had brought Eva-Lynne into daily contact with Al Dearborn.

It was only a gradual realization. Tominbang would have hired Eva-Lynne on sight (as my father used to say, he seemed to have an eye for the ladies), though he was not too proud to accept my offer to underwrite her salary. "I think she will prove to be an excellent addition to the team," he said. "If you find any more like her, please bring them to me." For a variety of reasons, I was not tempted. (Besides, there was only one Eva-Lynne.)

She was immediately assigned to general office help, with special duty as my part-time assistant. (Bacchus and Kafka were burying me in technical documents that required filing and organizing.)

Only then, once she had signed the now-familiar non-disclosure agreement, did she learn what we were doing. "To the what?"

"The Moon," I said, the first time I had ever actually said such a thing aloud.

"Who? How?" She was genuinely astonished and, I think, a little frightened. (As if this were nothing but a cover story for some much more mundane, but very illegal activity.)

I showed her our Quicksilver, then introduced her to several members of the team. She soon came to be comfortable with the idea of flying to the Moon. More comfortable, I noted, than she seemed with the number and variety of jokers and deuces.

It wasn't until the end of the workday, as I was preparing to offer Eva-Lynne a ride back to Rosamond (after all, it was on my way), that Dearborn appeared.

Three weeks without drink—three weeks with the job of a lifetime—had improved his looks and his energy; not to mention his manner. (No more vomiting on feet.) He gave Eva-Lynne a wave, as if she had worked there all along, and turned to me. "We're going to take our bird out for a test hop tonight. What do you say, Co-pilot?"

"Would a simple, 'No, thank you,' be sufficient?"

"We're not going into space, Cash. Just a little proficiency run around the neighborhood. Uh, no 'heavy lifting.'" He laughed at his own joke, and turned to Eva-Lynne. "Will we have the honor of your presence?"

"What time do you want me?" she said, forthrightly, eyes blazing, using exactly those words, and breaking my heart.

Our small group moved into the hangar proper, where Tominbang and the rest of the team gathered, and I lost track of Eva-Lynne. I confess I got angry—at Tominbang, for disrupting my life and dragging me into this stupid project; at Dearborn, for being everything I was not.

Even, I must admit, at Eva-Lynne.

Darkness fell, and a huge orange Moon rose in the east—like a giant jack o'lantern rising from the desert. I had barely begun to study lunar geography, but I could already recognize the dark smear that was the Sea of Storms—Quicksilver's landing site.

Our landing site, if I had the stomach to turn around and face my fears. (And I don't mean fears of death.)

So I did.

Quicksilver was towed to the runway apron by a tractor with a sputtering motor.

"You'd think they could afford a new tractor," Eva-Lynne said behind me.

I was feeling mildly heroic, proud of a chance to show off for Eva-Lynne, when Bacchus appeared suddenly out of the shadows, handing me two ring binders filled with paper. I glanced at the pages. "I had to pencil in some figures, position of the Moon at launch time, stuff like that. But it should give you a good sense of when to do your mass transfer."

"To what end?" I wasn't worried about doing the lifts. All I had to do was glance at the orientation of Quicksilver, its velocity, its reported position in three axes, and wait for Dearborn to tap me on the shoulder.

"For a proper simulation," he said, clearly disgusted with my lack of professionalism.

I turned, hoping to re-connect with Eva-Lynne, but Commander Dearborn chose this moment to emerge from the hangar.

He was wearing a heavy, silvery garment like a diving suit, complete with a neck ring. Under one arm he carried white helmet. He seemed completely focused on the task ahead of him, like a bullfighter I had once seen in Tijuana.

Tominbang was a step behind him, but compared to Dearborn's glittering presence, might as well have been invisible.

(I noticed one strange face in the crowd, not far behind Dearborn: Sampson, his backup pilot.)

Dearborn stopped and looked up at Quicksilver, which had now been towed to a distance of fifty yards from the hangar door. He raised his helmet, lowered it over his head, locked it into place.

Some of the team members *applauded*. I felt an unfamiliar surge of pride. From what I could see of Tominbang's face, so did he.

And, for a moment, so did I. I was part of that crew!

The next half hour raced past. Dressed in street clothes (but carrying a crash helmet handed to me by Kafka), I joined Dearborn and Tominbang aboard Quicksilver. I had never been inside the vehicle before, and had to be helped down through the top hatch into the newly-installed airlock by Sampson. ("This is where the weapons bay used to be.") Then I crawled forward into the cabin and wrenched myself to the left-hand seat. (There were three, one forward, and two behind.)

"I hope I don't have to get out of this thing in a hurry," I said, half-joking.

"The pilot can blow the canopy for emergency egress," Sampson said, his eyes bland and almost sleepy. I decided right then that I didn't much like him. Maybe it was the air of truly unpredictable strangeness he radiated—his "wrong way" wild card, no doubt.

As the team cleared out, my helmet radio squawked. "Pilot to Co-pilot," Dearborn said, "that pistol grip tiller close to your right hand is your lifting mechanism. It is finely calibrated to connect with the center of mass of this vehicle. Touch it only when you do your lifting."

"Uh, roger," I said, trying to sound astronautical.

There was some chatter on the radio that did not directly concern me. Next to me, Tominbang practically bounced up and down like a restless child.

Dearborn counted down to ignition, and pressed the start button. Flame shot out of the back of Quicksilver. In a cloud of debris, the pumpkin-seed vehicle started rolling down the runway. It rotated almost immediately, then headed straight up into the night sky . . .

I felt some pressure, but not much more than on an airplane.

For the first few moments, that is. The pressure kept building and building, and to my extreme discomfort, we rolled to our left and over on our backs. "Why are we doing this?" I said between clenched teeth.

"Aerodynamics don't apply here," Dearborn said, almost cackling with glee. "It just lets our radio antennas communicate with the ground."

Then he said, "First waypoint, Co-pilot. Give her a little lift."

As I've said, annoyance is my perpetual state, and it quickly transitions to anger.

We made a good test lift.

Twenty minutes later we were back on the ground, hatch opened. As I walked away, weak in the knees, I looked back to see Quicksilver glowing like a campfire coal on the runway.

A crowd surged toward us. Dearborn removed his helmet, he handed it to me. "Flies great, doesn't she, Co-Pilot?"

I couldn't help agreeing.

My elation was so profound that it wasn't until an hour later, as the crowd finally thinned, as Quicksilver was towed back into the hangar, that I realized Dearborn was gone.

And so was Eva-Lynne.

He didn't come home that night. I know, because I sat up until three.

Maybe that's why, when the phone rang at six A.M., I was willing to face—no, to welcome—my next challenge. "Yes, Mr. Skalko."

Mr. Warren Skalko gave no overt sign of his power or his wealth. No flashy car. No expensive suits. No gold pinkie rings or necklaces. No thick-necked sideboys. (They were around, but you never saw them, unless you happened to realize that the occasional passing motorcyclist was probably one of them.) His golf game was average, and his bets were small—five-dollar Nassaus. Even his physical person was nondescript: at 50 he was of medium height, a little overweight, balding, his eyes swimming behind thick glasses. If you met him without knowing who he was, you would have thought yourself in the company of an accountant, and not one who handled large accounts.

At one point, early in our relationship, I was silly enough to ask him why he did what he did, when he seemed to live so modestly.

"I can't help myself," was his reply.

He always made his own calls, too. "Cash, Warren Skalko here," he chirped. "Sorry about the early hour. Wondering if you'd have time to get together later this morning, around eight, at the usual place."

Eight it was, at the driving range of a ratty municipal par-three in Lancaster. It was October now, and the desert nights were cold enough to leave frost on the fairways and greens. So the crowd at the driving range was sparse.

Only Mr. Warren Skalko taking some swings with a seven-iron. "Tominbang tested his plane last night," he announced the instant I was within earshot. (That was another Skalko trait: getting directly to the point.)

I think my heart stopped for a good five seconds. Obviously Tominbang had a distant connection to Mr. Skalko. Less obvious was why Mr. Skalko would have any interest in his activities. Equally less obvious, but of much greater concern to me was whether Mr. Skalko was angry about my involvement. "Yes."

"Think it's gonna work? This flying to the Moon?"

I couldn't help a reflexive smile. "I *hope* so." It was, after all, my life.

"Oh, you'd be all right. That Dearborn fella, he's got the luck." *Swish.* Mr. Skalko launched a shot down the range. "But I'm not sure I like this deal," he said.

This was not code for a stronger emotion. Mr. Skalko was a direct man: if he really hated Tominbang's project, he would have said exactly that.

"I'm not sure of the value, either," I said.

"Why are you doing it? The money?" Mr. Skalko knew everything he needed to know about my money problems.

"Yes," I said, then adding, because he would know, anyway, "And a girl."

"Ah. That's even worse." *Swish* went the dub. "When is the big day?"

"We're scheduled to take off in two weeks."

Mr. Skalko examined the seven iron, and then, apparently deciding, he had had enough fun at the driving range, slid it back into his golf bag. "Tell you what," he said, "give me a call when it looks as though you're ready to go. No later than the day before, at the usual number." He sighed and looked around at the countryside. "I need to think about what this means."

There was never any doubt that I would agree to do whatever Mr. Skalko wanted.

It was only after putting miles between my car and Mr. Skalko that I began to feel troubled by my new status as a spy inside Tominbang's project. My heart began to beat faster, my breathing grew ragged. It was as if I had just run a mile.

I would have been alarmed, but I had learned to expect this reaction. All I could do was pull off at the first auto salvage yard I came to.

Here were hundreds of Fords, Chevys, Buicks, complete with tailfins and chrome, all suitable for my brand of lifting.

I started at the end of one row and lifted seven in a row, flipping each car onto its hood with a loud bang! Not only was it noisy, it was dusty. But by the time I had reached the end of the row, my heart rate had returned to normal. And my emotions were spent.

I drove past Haugen's Bakery (I no longer had reason to stop), then directly to the hangar, where I almost welcomed the sight of Eva-Lynne tottering in, giggling, wearing yesterday's dress, and on Dearborn's arm.

My father used to tell me I had no spine, an unfortunate phrase, given that it literally applied to at least two of my joker playmates. Perhaps that's why I gave his judgment so little credence for so long.

But various mistakes in my life, beginning with flunking out of Harvey Mudd followed closely by a disastrous marriage, which led to excessive gambling and debts, and thence an unsolicited association with Mr. Warren Skalko, had convinced me of the truth of my father's evaluation.

I had been a coward. Or, if you find that too harsh, I had never faced a challenge, either professionally or personally. Case number one, Eva-Lynne, now lost to a man who embraced challenges, or, if necessary, *created* them.

Case number two—the flight to the Moon. Some time between Dearborn's walkout in his silver suit, and my "workout" at the auto salvage yard, I decided that this was the one challenge I had to face.

When I reached Tehachapi-Kern, I avoided any chance of contact with Eva-Lynne, and immediately searched out a technician named Sobel, who had left messages for me for at least a week.

He turned out to be some sort of aquatic joker who actually had to wear a bowl-like helmet filled with water, as well as a bubbling device which regularly uttered a disturbing noise like a baby's cry. "Wouldn't you be happier in the sea?" I asked him.

"Never learned to swim," he said, completely deadpan. (Well, they do call them jokers.) "Actually, I signed up when Tominbang hired a friend of mine. Who wouldn't want to be part of the first flight to the Moon?"

Which made me feel bad that I had ignored his messages. When I learned that he was the specialist in charge of space suits, that he had wanted me to come in for fit checks for a suit of my own, I felt even worse.

Fortunately, we got to work, and within two hours I learned more about the operational aspects of the flight to the Moon than I had in three weeks. The silver suit, made mostly of heavy rubber, was one of half a dozen originally developed for the X-11A program a decade past, acquired, no doubt, through some shady contact of Tominbang's. "We're adding special boots, a white coverall and a special helmet visor for use on the lunar surface."

"I'll be out on the surface?"

"At the moment, only Dearborn and Tominbang are scheduled to walk on the Moon. They will erect the relay station. But if they have trouble, you will have to help them." Somewhat ashamedly, I found myself hoping they would: why go all the way to the Moon and not walk on it?

I bent myself into various shapes in order to get my head through the helmet ring. Then I was zipped tight, and immediately began to perspire. I could not stand up straight, either. "You'll be sitting most of the time," Sobel said, taking some measurements, like a tailor, then helping me out of the garment. "You'll either be hooked up to Quicksilver's cooling system, or to a backpack."

Then a more practical question arose. "What about sanitary facilities?"

Sobel smiled and held up a metal bottle and tube. "Standard USAF catheter."

"And what about . . . other functions?"

"You'll be on a low residue diet for the last few days prior to the flight."

"How long will I be in this thing?"

"Two days, tops."

That was some relief.

When I returned to my office, I found Bacchus leering all over an alarmed Eva-Lynne. (I couldn't help noticing that she had, indeed, changed clothes from the previous night.) "I'll be with you in a minute, Doctor," I told this sex-crazed joker. "Eva-Lynne, I need to talk to you in private."

As I closed the door, she said, "Thank God. I've met some aggressive men in my life—" I could only imagine. "—but he is by far the worst. I don't even like having him *breathe* on me."

"Sorry. I should have warned you."

"I'm not sure a warning would have done much good. I probably wouldn't have believed you." She favored me with the same smile that had so bewitched me that first time I saw her. "But it's very sweet of you to protect me."

Seeing that she was about to leave, I cleared my throat and prepared to subject myself to bad news. "Speaking of protection, did you get home all right last night?"

She whirled to face me, and I saw a look on her lovely face that I had never seen before. One lovely golden eyebrow rose slightly. The effect was far more womanly, if that's the word. Knowing. "Let's just say, I got where I was supposed to get."

I must have blushed. I certainly had no idea what to say. And I never, in fact, got the chance to respond, because Eva-Lynne prevented it. She took me by the hand and said, "You know, Cash, I think you and I need to have a picnic."

My protest was truly feeble. "There's nowhere to eat." Most of Tominbang's team packed lunches, or ate the offerings of the tiny cafeteria over at the airport.

"Don't be silly, Cash. It's not about food."

"I hope you weren't under the impression I was a virgin," she said, once we'd reached our picnic grounds, a flat area halfway up the hill a hundred yards beyond the fence which ringed Tominbang's hangar complex. In one last stab at being a masculine provider, I had bought two bottles of Dr Pepper from the building's vending machine as we walked out.

"No," I said, telling the truth. This was, after all, 1968. Virginity had ceased to be in fashion about the time of my sophomore year at Harvey Mudd some years earlier. I had been married, and had been in several shorter sexual relationships myself, so I should have been beyond the adolescent fear that my sexual skills would not measure up, so to speak.

"But you were hoping I wasn't a slut," Eva-Lynne said, articulating my next thought before I could. My blush confirmed her statement.

She exhaled. "Have you ever heard of Diamond Butte, Arizona?" she said.

"Should I?"

"No reason. When I get through telling you about it, you'll probably wish you still hadn't of heard it." Diamond Butte, she explained, was a tiny town in the northwestern corner of Arizona a few miles south of Utah. "It's cut off from the rest of Arizona by the Grand Canyon, but technically not in Utah. It's kind of like—what's that television show? *The Twilight Zone.* Nobody knows which set of laws to apply, because no one's there to enforce them."

"Let me guess," I said. "Nobody enforces either set."

"Right." She grimaced. "Which is why, for years, most of the people in the area were polygamists. My family, for example. My mother was my father's seventh wife. I had twenty brothers and sisters. And I was literally sold to a man—my future husband—when I was fourteen. I became his eleventh wife when I was sixteen."

"And that's what you ran away from?" I said, hoping that was the end of the story.

Eva-Lynne ignored me. "It was bad. Polygamy may work for some. I think my family generally got along. But Roderick, my husband, was a bastard. I think he would rather have beaten us rather than slept with us.

"All of us tried to run off at one time or another. We all got caught and taken back, and it would be even worse.

"Finally one of the other men in the town heard what was going on, and challenged Roderick. But Roderick killed him and took his wives for his own.

"Which left him free to get rid of us. He sold us to the Gambiones, Cash. They dragged us off to New York, Jokertown, where they had a brothel just for jokers." Her voice had grown quieter as she spoke. By this time there were tears rolling down her cheeks. For her sake and mine, I wanted her to stop. But no. "I spent three years there." Now her smile was savage. "I was very popular with the clientele.

"Eventually one of the girls died; a joker killed her. The Gambiones had to lie low for a few weeks; they shipped most of us to San Francisco.

"I'd saved a little money." She hesitated for a moment, then said, in the smallest possible voice, "I used my charms. And I got out. You wanted to know how someone who looks like me winds up in Mojave? That's why."

"I had no idea."

"I'm glad. But now you know. And now you have good reason not to fall in love with me."

I mumbled something. "What was that?" she said.

"My mother used to say, even after the wild card: 'love trumps all.'"

Eva-Lynne gave a short, sharp laugh. "I'll tell you what—"

She was interrupted by the blare of a warning siren, the same one used the night of the flight test. We both jumped at the sound, and she said, "We'd better get back."

As we started down the hill, I let Eva-Lynne lead the way, thrilling to her every step and sway. In spite of the revelation of her sordid or, at least, troubling past, I loved her more hopelessly than ever.

As we reached the hangar, we saw that Quicksilver had been rolled into the open. Eva-Lynne took my hand and said, "I can't believe you're going to ride that thing all the way to the Moon."

"And, hopefully, back again," I said. She laughed. For a moment, everything seemed possible.

Then Kakfa scuttled up to us. "Need to talk," he hissed. Or perhaps spat would be a better word. He looked directly at Eva-Lynne. "Alone."

She took her dismissal with grace, and headed back to the office.

"We're launching tonight," Kafka said.

"Tonight? Since when?"

When Kafka got agitated, he began to scuttle back and forth, like a roach in a jar. "Tominbang's orders. He says there are 'problems.'"

"What kind of problems?"

"I don't *know*," Kafka hissed. "But we go tonight!"

I had prepared myself to make the call to Mr. Skalko. I had not expected to do it so soon.

"Tominbang's in a lot of trouble," Al Dearborn told me a few moments later. Tominbang had failed to appear for a lunch meeting. Instead he had telephoned, and wound up telling Dearborn his sad story: he had not been using his own money for the Quicksilver-to-the-Moon program. Instead, he had dipped into funds belonging to others, apparently in the hopes that profits from the first Moon flight would allow him to pay back his unwitting "investors" before they realized they'd been robbed.

But one of the parties found out. "Some guy named Warren Skalko. Ever heard of him?"

"Yes," I said. In order to keep Dearborn from pressing further (since I doubted I could lie to him), I added, "he's the local godfather. Bad news."

The bad news explained the flurry of activity in the hangar. Jokers and deuces were shredding papers; a bum barrel out back was aflame. Every few moments, a car would launch itself out of the parking lot in a spray of gravel. "You'd think we were about to be bombed," I said to Dearborn.

"From what Tominbang said, that's a distinct possibility."

"How can we launch tonight if he's not here?"

"He's not making the trip."

"Given the situation, I'm not sure I'm making the trip." In fact, I was, at that moment, quite sure I wasn't. I was two minutes away from making a hasty departure from Tehachapi-Kern.

"Well, Cash, as you know: without you, there is no flight to the Moon." He smiled to take the edge off what was clearly a threat: "I'd hate to have to kidnap you."

"In that case," I said, "when do we leave?"

Dearborn clapped me on the shoulder. "That's the spirit!"

Seeing one last opportunity to put an end to this madness, I said, "Can we operate Quicksilver with a crew of two?"

"Operate, yes. But the mass properties have been very finely calibrated to your talents, Co-pilot. We've *got* to have a certain amount of mass in that right-hand seat. And, given that we can probably use the extra hands on the Moon, I'd rather not just fill it with a sack of cement."

Just then, Bacchus walked in, brought by Eva-Lynne. "You wanted to see me?" the joker physicist said.

"Yeah, how much do you weigh?"

"In the mornings I mass 185 pounds," Bacchus said, his voice like a hiccup. "By evening that decreases to around 182, depending on my fluid intake—"

Dearborn held up his hand. I could have told him that with Bacchus, there was no such thing as a short answer to a direct question. "Sorry. That puts us over our weight limit—"

Before I could even *think* it, much less say it, Eva-Lynne announced, "One hundred and twenty pounds."

"What's that?" Dearborn said.

"How much I weigh."

Bacchus snorted. Dearborn and I looked at each other.

"Do you know what we're talking about?" I said.

"Going to the Moon, Cash." As if she were talking about a drive to Barstow, or possibly as far as Las Vegas.

"Can we take a girl to the Moon?" I asked.

"I don't know about you, Co-pilot, but I can't think of anyone I'd *rather* have along." He grinned at me and Eva-Lynne. "Let's kick the tires and light this candle."

It was the evening of Friday, December 20. I realized that Christmas was only a few days away, and I had bought nothing for anyone—not even Eva-Lynne.

Dearborn and I struggled into our pressure suits. Eva-Lynne, after spending several precious moments wrapping her blond tresses into some kind of braid, wore hers as if she were born to it. I said as much as we walked toward Quicksilver.

"This suit is nothing, compared to a girdle."

Thinking of women's undergarments triggered another worry: "Uh, what are you doing to do about . . . sanitary matters?"

Eva-Lynne stifled a laugh, and motioned me close. "I helped raise a dozen babies, Cash. I know how to make a diaper!" My curiosity more than satisfied, I was about to climb into Quicksilver's cockpit when she added, too loudly for my taste, "What are you guys using? Can-o-pees?"

Dearborn was already in the forward seat as I strapped into the left rear position. Then Eva-Lynne wedged herself into the one to my right—Tominbang's former seat.

Sobel was about to close the airlock hatch when he leaned in, agitated. "Bikers are storming the gates!" he said. "What should I do?"

"Lock the damned door and take cover," Dearborn growled. He had already started the engine.

Sobel froze with indecision for a long moment. Then, apparently deciding that Dearborn's order made sense, gave me his hand. "Good luck! Bring back some green cheese!"

He wiggled out of sight and closed the hatch behind him. We heard several clicks as the latches fired, and we were sealed in. "One minute," Dearborn said. "Hold on, people. You're going to take the ride of your lives!"

Eva-Lynne reached back to take my hand. I felt no fear: I was too convinced of Dearborn's luck to think I could be killed in his presence. But I felt trapped in the pressure suit, my movements hampered.

Spang! Something struck Quicksilver! "What was that?" Eva-Lynn said.

"I think the SOBs are shooting at us," Dearborn said. "Hang on, we're go." And go we were—

For perhaps a hundred yards down the runway. Even with my limited visibility, I could see the flashes of bullets striking the pavement in front of us. Then one of them struck home, making the cockpit ring. Then I heard hissing.

Red warning lights erupted on Dearborn's console. A bell sounded. "Goddammit," he snapped. With inhuman—or joker—calm, he tried to stop our rollout. The whole vehicle shook as we skidded off the runway. Only then did I realize just how fast we'd been going.

Quicksilver slewed to the left and slammed into something immobile. Eva-Lynne and I were thrown to the left; I hit the bulkhead, though my harness and suit protected me from injury. Eva-Lynne seemed to be fine.

Not so Dearborn. Perhaps his harness had been loose. In any case, he had hit the instrument panel. He was breathing hard, waving weakly at the two of us with a free hand, "Get out!"

I obeyed, hitting the emergency egress switch on the canopy. It flew off with a muffled *thump!* The next few moments were chaotic as I unstrapped, helped Eva-Lynne, and got both of us out of Quicksilver.

Lights blinded us. Shadowy figures boiled out of the darkness, swarming over Quicksilver and Dearborn like insects.

Eva-Lynne and I were hustled to our feet, and half-dragged to the hangar building. I still had my helmet on, so sounds were muffled and vision was impaired. I saw some of the Quicksilver team members lined up against the wall, hands (or, in the case of Kafka, pincers) in the air, as beefy nats and jokers in the black leathers of Hell's Angels held them at gunpoint.

I saw Sobel lying face-down on the ground just outside the hangar, a trail of blood marking the path of his death crawl.

We were shoved into the same equipment room where poor Sobel had helped us into our suits not an hour earlier. We barely had time to catch our breath when Mr. Skalko entered, accompanied by several of his thugs. "You," he said, pointing to me. "Out."

I was hauled to my feet and essentially stripped of my suit. Then, wearing nothing but a T-shirt and shorts, I was marched out of the hangar. Dearborn and Eva-Lynne remained behind.

"You cut it a little close," Mr. Skalko said.

"Tominbang moved up the launch." I'm sure I sounded angry, because I was. I had assumed that Skalko would take action once he knew the Quicksilver launch was imminent. I hadn't expected that action to be a mob shootout.

"I know that now. Good thing for you." I'm sure Skalko knew all about Tominbang's plans. For one thing, he had surely interrogated the poor man. For another, I doubt I was his only spy inside the program. "Kind of a shame," he said. He actually sighed. "I was still thinking about it when you called."

"Why did you stop it? The money?"

Mr. Skalko looked at me with amusement. "You mean, what he stole?"

"Yes."

"I deal with stuff like that all the time. No, I had to kill this whole idea. Going to the Moon."

Now I was as intrigued as I was angry. "Why would you care?"

"One flight means nothing. It's what happens after the flight." He looked at me as if weighing my worthiness. Apparently I was found worthy. "Once you've proven you can do this, other people will follow. They'll build a little outpost up there. Then a bigger one. Then a whole damn city.

"And to service that city, they will have a regular system of transportation that *I can't control*." He stood there, in the darkness of a desert night, looking at the stars. "Things will come into this country that I can't stop. That would be bad for my business."

I saw the point. Not that I cared. "What's going to happen to them?" I said, meaning Dearborn and Eva-Lynne.

"I don't know yet." He saw that I was ready to go back into the hangar. "I want you to go home."

He tossed me my car keys. I don't know if he found them with my clothes, or whether he had his own set, which would have been a typical Skalko touch. "Oh, by the way," he said, "we're ending our association."

In spite of the fact that I wanted our association to end—better yet, to *have ended* some time prior to this—I started to protest. Mr. Skalko held up his hand. "You've done good work. You've been paid well. But I know people, and this one is going to haunt you. Keep your mouth shut and you don't need to see me again."

I had just stepped out of the shower, having taken inventory of a new set of bruises, when I heard wheels crunching on the gravel drive. By the time I was dressed, there was a knock at my door.

Dearborn and Eva-Lynne. He was limping, and Eva-Lynne was supporting him.

Skalko's men had let them go. After all, the purpose of the attack had been to stop the flight to the Moon. Tominbang had already been punished.

I wanted both to spend the night, but Dearborn shook his head. "Co-pilot, we're not out of the game yet. We need your car."

The drive to Los Angeles took two hours, perhaps because it was Friday night, with the holidays approaching. South from my place in Lancaster, through the Antelope Valley into the San Fernando Valley. Then down the new freeway into western Los Angeles. I asked Dearborn several times where I was heading, but he just smiled (or grimaced; he was clearly in pain). All he would tell me was my next turn.

Eva-Lynne dozed in the back seat.

Eventually we arrived at Douglas Field, a small airport in Santa Monica bordering the plant where so many aircraft had been built over the decades. The Douglas Company had moved its manufacturing elsewhere, leaving behind a number of huge, empty buildings. I was directed to drive up to one of them.

Eva-Lynne woke as the car stopped. "What are we doing here?" she said.

Dearborn postponed his answer until he had unlocked a side door.

We walked into a hangar much like the one at Tehachapi-Kern. Even more strangely, a Quicksilver vehicle sat in this middle of this one, too. And my old friend, Kafka, was busy in the cockpit!

"*Here* is where we're going to launch the first flight to the Moon," Dearborn said, looking pale but satisfied. As Eva-Lynne and I stared in wonder—and began to recognize other members of the team from Tehachapi-Kern—he explained that Tominbang had always felt that Mr. Skalko would eventually learn of his plans, and strike at him. So he had paid for modifications to a second Quicksilver vehicle, the "ground spare" originally ticketed for the museum!

That was astounding enough. But then Eva-Lynne asked another question: "You've got another vehicle. Great. But you can't possibly fly it."

"I know," Dearborn said. "Mike!" he called.

A vaguely familiar figured emerged from the other side of Quicksilver. Major Sampson, Dearborn's old X-11A colleague, his alternate.

"Remember what I told you, Cash. Always, always, *always* have a backup."

The preparations resumed, almost as if the horrifying incident at Tehachapi-Kern had been nothing more than a fouled-up dress rehearsal for some high school drama. Dearborn assured Eva-Lynne and me that Sampson was perfectly capable of flying the mission. Better yet, that he knew all about my lifting power and just how that integrated into the flight plans.

As the sun rose over the mountains to the east, on the cold morning of Saturday, December 21, 1968, Sampson, Eva-Lynne and I once again donned our suits (brought here from Tehachapi-Kern by Kafka) and boarded Quicksilver.

We were much more business-like this time, due, I think, to our improved realization of the seriousness of what we were attempting, and also to Sampson's more disciplined methods.

At 6:51 a.m., the main rocket kicked in, and we started down the runway. On Sampson's order, I grasped the tiller, and we lifted.

Even though the test hop had prepared me for the experience of flying into orbit upside down, I was startled by the sight of Douglas Field, then downtown Santa Monica and the Pacific, all of Southern California and finally the blue earth itself growing smaller while rising to the top of the window.

We were feeling heavy, of course. Kafka had told me we would endure at least 6 Gs. But we were strapped in so tightly that it was merely a mildly unpleasant feeling, not something truly stressful.

What *was* unnerving was being able feel every burp and pop of our rocket motor. "A little instability there," Sampson said, far too casually, following one particularly wrenching example.

Our flight on the rocket lasted less than three minutes, and ended with an abrupt shutdown which flung us forward in our harnesses. (This was, for me, the single most disquieting sensation of the whole voyage. I felt as though I would fly right through the forward windows.)

"Everybody okay back there?" Sampson asked, in that peculiar, fatherly tone of his.

"Fine!" Eva-Lynne answered brightly. I glanced over at her, and was rewarded with her best smile.

"We're going to loop around the earth once," Sampson explained, for Eva-Lynne's benefit, "then let Cash do his thing. That will send us toward the Moon. In the meantime, enjoy the view. I plan to."

Of course, being forward, Sampson actually *had* a view. Though shortly even he didn't have much to see, as we flew over the nightside of the earth. Below us was darkness punctuated by a surprising number of lightning flashes. Hundreds, in fact.

Eva-Lynne and I removed our helmets and watched this display with enthusiasm, as Sampson tended to the business of orienting Quicksilver. Rolling the vehicle tended to change our view, and, ultimately, made me ill.

In fact, as we neared the completion of our first orbit, and Sampson gave me warning that I would be lifting in ten minutes, I realized I was too sick to do anything. I opened my mouth to say so, and promptly repeated Al Dearborn's greeting to met that first day at Tehachapi-Kern—I threw up.

"Oh, dear," Eva-Lynne said. Fortunately, she had noticed that I was turning green, and had a paper towel and airsickness bag ready. The mess was blessedly minor, and within minutes I was feeling better.

Better—but nowhere near capable of doing a lift. "Two minutes," Sampson said. "Are you ready back there?"

"I don't know."

He twisted and faced me. "Eva-Lynne, seal your helmet."

With a speed that astonished me, Eva-Lynne did as she was ordered. Then Sampson turned halfway toward me and began speaking in a voice so low I could barely hear him without my helmet open. "I know all about your phone call and your friend, Skalko. But she doesn't. Want to see the look on her face when she hears you sold us all out?"

I felt a sudden, and all-too familiar, surge of anger.

"Now!" Sampson said.

My hand found the tiller, and we lifted.

Because we had taken off earlier than planned, we sailed toward a Moon we couldn't see. With his telescope, Sampson claimed to be able to see a dull sliver limning the nightside, but I couldn't. "Don't worry," he said. "It's out there."

"I'll just have to take your word for it," I told him.

The day-long flight would have been intolerable if we'd had to stay strapped in. Fortunately, the airlock behind the two rear seats provided a certain amount of room—and privacy.

We all needed it, especially Eva-Lynne. But I also crawled inside the lock, primarily to get away from Sampson. I understood the rationale for his nastiness in forcing me to lift. He must have known that I needed a strong emotional charge, however brief, to channel. But I didn't like him for it. Perhaps it was his general air of smug superiority; perhaps it was just knowing he had a tool he could use against me again.

Perhaps it was the nagging feeling that we were doomed because the lucky Commander Dearborn had somehow managed to miss the trip, and we were left with the man who would always be in the right place at the wrong time. I spent the entire flight from the Earth to the Moon feeling like a man who has just been told he has months to live.

I dozed for a fitful couple of hours, and woke to find the Moon not only visible, but growing in size.

"Looks like we're here," Eva-Lynne said.

I had no difficulty getting in the proper mood to make the braking lift: the sheer spectacle of seeing the lunar landscape provided all the adrenaline I needed. To my mind, we were falling lower and lower, going faster and faster, about to crash into a bleak world of mountains, craters and rocks. The craters themselves were filled with smaller craters as well as giant boulders—

I made the braking lift; Sampson followed with a series of bursts from the main engine, and we began our descent.

I wish I could say I saw it, but with Quicksilver in a wings-level, nose forward position, only Sampson could see the lunar surface. Eva-Lynne and I saw nothing but the black sky of lunar night, until, at that last instant, the sunlit peaks of the dark gray mountains appeared. "Thirty seconds," Sampson told us. (He was giving us—not to mention Dearborn and the rest of poor Tominbang's team back on Earth—a terse commentary the whole way down.)

At the last moment, it seemed that we were traveling far too fast. Sampson announced, "Contact!"

And we scraped to a stop, rocking for a moment, as if on the edge of a cliff, then settling gently.

We had reached the Sea of Storms. "Please be advised," Sampson radioed, "we have arrived." I realized that Eva-Lynne had been clutching my hand the entire time.

No warning lights glared on Sampson's console. We heard no unusual sounds. So we stayed, our time on the lunar surface necessarily limited. After all, in Tominbang's vision, we were merely pathfinders demonstrating that it was possible to reach the Moon—and return safely. Sampson had the simple task of erecting Tominbang's communications array, whether or not our unfortunate backer ever used it.

In the original plans, Dearborn would have done the work, with Tominbang's assistance. Now it was up to Sampson and me.

Within an hour, Sampson emerged from the airlock, stepping onto the surface and uttering one simple word: "Wow."

He went for a short scout while, with Eva-Lynne's help, I repressurized the airlock and moved inside with the array package. "Sure you don't want to come out?" I said.

"Very sure. This is close enough for me."

Mission rules dictated that one of us had to remain inside Quicksilver. Eva-Lynne had volunteered: I don't believe she had a great deal of faith in her hastily modified pressure suit. (In fact, once she landed, she unzipped it, and eventually shed the whole thing.)

She gave me a kiss, then closed the inner hatch.

Once the air pressure had bled down, I opened the outer hatch and hauled myself out. Moving was incredibly difficult, not because of lunar gravity (which, thanks to the heavy suit, felt the same as Earth gravity to me). I slid rather than climbed down the side of Quicksilver, and fell to my knees in the lunar soil. I saw the slightest puff of gray dust, which settled instantly.

"Oh, beautiful," Sampson said, sarcastically.

I thought at first he was referring to my inelegant first steps, but instead he was looking at the undercarriage of Quicksilver:

A shiny gash ran from back to front. The cause was obvious . . . a small, rounded rock that rose about a foot higher than the otherwise flat, soft lunar soil around it. "Did that do any damage?"

"Hard to tell," Sampson said, getting on his hands and knees and trying to look under the vehicle. "There's a stain on the skin of the ship, but that could have been there before landing, or even before we took off."

Sampson's attitude suggested a man who was confronted with, at worst, a flat tire. I envied that, as I stared at what could only be a fuel leak, knowing we needed to fire the main engine before I could perform a lift that would send us flying back to Earth. "What do we do?" I said, trying not to sound as terrified as I felt.

He was back on his feet, bouncing toward the array package I had dropped. "Complete the mission. We'll deal with the other problem in its turn."

"It's too bad this had to happen," Sampson said abruptly, about halfway through the construction of Tominbang's array. Just when I thought he was going to address our problem, he continued: "If the damn Takisians hadn't arrived, this would be the biggest story on the planet! 'Man on the Moon!' Can you imagine? Thousands of people would be listening on the radio. We might even have television here.

"And we would just be the first. There would be other landings, too. Scientists would come up here. Even tourists. Once the human race proved it could do something like this, it would never turn back!"

I could have argued with him: I wasn't too sure that the human race "would never turn back!" We'd "turned back" every chance we got.

Or I could have told Sampson that a certain mobster in southern California agreed with him completely. But all I said was, "If the Takisians hadn't come, *neither* of us would be here."

So we completed our mission, performing an hour of pointless work under the glare of a naked sun. Only when we were starting back toward

Quicksilver did I pause to attempt to appreciate the fact that I could die in a place no humans had ever visited. I remember thinking it was an honor I would rather have done without.

Eva-Lynne would die, too, which made it even worse.

As Sampson loped ahead of me, I stopped and, using my boot, wrote the following in the soil: "Cash + Eva-Lynne." I wondered how long it would be before human eyes saw it. If they ever saw it.

Sampson was already back at his controls when I emerged from the air-lock. He acted as if everything were fine. "Strap in, gang. No sense hanging around longer than we have to."

As I finished removing my suit (it was covered with dust, and my oxygen tanks were empty), I put my head close to Eva-Lynne's. "Did he—?"

"I was listening," she said, finishing my question. We had no time for further conversation, because Sampson snapped, "Let's go back there!"

I was angry, but I strapped in. In fact, I tried to reassure Eva-Lynne. "It might be nothing," I said, whispering.

Sampson finished his checklist, and with twenty seconds' warning, punched the engine start button. With a dull drone, it started up—

Then died. Now the warning lights flashed. "Dammit." It was the first time I had heard Sampson use profanity. "We've got fuel, but we've got a leak in the line that runs to the main engine." Which meant we didn't have enough energy to get off the surface of the Moon.

I looked at Eva-Lynne; it was her turn to see panic in my face. For a moment she seemed lost. Then that disturbing, yet attractive knowing look appeared on her face, and she leaned close to me. Her hair, stirred by small breezes from the ventilation fans, surrounded me, caressing me. I forgot about the stale odor of the Quicksilver interior as I inhaled perfume.

And felt her warm breath on my neck and her hand on my chest. Her lips brushed my ear. I think I mumbled a syllable of protest. "Sshh," she said. Then: "Colonel, why don't you step inside the airlock."

Sampson didn't hesitate. With a look on his face that combined disgust and hope, he crawled past us and into the chamber, dogging the hatch.

My straps seemed to unbuckle themselves. Eva-Lynne's undergarment removed itself, as did mine. I took her in my arms, feeling her breasts against me, her mouth on mine.

Moments later, I fumbled for the tiller, and faster than any rocket, we fired off the Sea of Storms.

That is the inside story of the first human flight to another world. This is, as far as I know, the only record of it. None of the support team talked. I don't believe many of them knew what our true destination was.

I never saw or heard from Tominbang again, though the relay station was fully operational. Did he survive to make his transactions?

Sampson is now a major general, first chief of the new Space Command.

Age of Wonders

EIGHT

February 2005

RALEIGH WORKED AT GAVIN'S apartment, the TV on in the background playing a talking-heads news show, her files and notes spread out over his tiny kitchen table. His place was a studio, small and utilitarian, but the thrift-store shelves full of books made it seem warm. His mother made quilts, and two of those dressed up his threadbare sofa. He'd only told her his mother had made them *after* they'd had sex on them multiple times, which was weird and then funny. He had his volunteer shift at the literacy center after work, so she'd picked up dinner and had it warming in the oven for when he got home.

She lined up a series of clippings on everyone from the Tominbang moon shot, building up a timeline of what had happened after. She'd tried tracking down the few surviving participants and for her trouble received a cryptic cease-and-desist warning on the letterhead of a high-powered South Carolina law firm. She was still trying to figure that one out.

The door opened, and Gavin called, "Hey!"

"Hey!"

He came over for a kiss before he even set down his bag. Like they were an old married couple or something. Sometimes she stepped back and marveled at how comfortable she was with him. Hadn't they just met yesterday?

"Everything okay?" he asked.

"Everything's fine," she said, knowing there was more to the question, that he, and everyone, was still worried after the attack. Dempsey had been right, the gunman was out on bail and it looked like the DA would offer a plea deal that would keep him out of jail. Margot insisted on vetting all her blog posts now. Nothing of any seriousness at all would go live. Raleigh chafed. But maybe there were other outlets, other ways of getting these stories out in the world. She had so much material.

She went to get the food from the oven, and he started gathering up her files to clear the table. He paused, and she glanced at him over her shoulder.

"What's this?" he asked, reading. He skimmed one sheet, then the next.

He'll never talk, at least not until he's safely retired. He was mortified at witnessing my love-making with Eva-Lynne. (He wouldn't meet our eyes on the flight home.) An association with our highly illegal operation would also be bad for his military career, which is going great. He took the lessons he learned from Quicksilver and applied them to a revamped vehicle called the Hornet, which flies into orbit without the need of an assist from a horny deuce.

Nor will you find Eva-Lynne or Cash Mitchell on *Peregrine's Perch* telling tales of that first flight to the Moon. Not as long as Warren Skalko lives. Skalko never forgets.

Nevertheless, I am forever grateful for my small role in a secret history. I not only found Eva-Lynne, I learned the truth of her lifelong lesson, the one she almost imparted to me on the hillside above Tehachapi-Kern Airport:

Sex trumps all.

Then another, a printout of a fifty-year-old newspaper article with the head-line Local Landlord Ducks Fraud Charge.

"Just a story I'm working on," she said neutrally.

"And who is Warren Skalko?"

"Nothing. No one." He glared, and she sighed. "He was this two-bit gangster from Nevada, active in the fifties and sixties. You guys don't want me working current events so I'm a historian now."

"And he's dead?"

"Very dead."

"No heirs or followers or anything who might have picked up where he left off?"

"Not that I've found."

"But it's crime stuff? Gang stuff? After what happened you're still look-ing into these mob connections?"

"This was fifty years ago, everybody involved is dead."

"Do you know that?"

"Well no, but the odds are—"

"The wild card virus fucks with the odds! You of all people should know that!" His hands squeezed, crumpling the pages he held.

"Gavin, it's fine—"

"These people will kill over these secrets."

"And if I stop . . . then they win. I can't let them intimidate me. What kind of journalist would that make me?"

"An alive one?"

"I'll be careful—"

He set down the pages on the table, on top of other pages he'd gathered up. Pressed his hands flat. She'd never seen him this angry—never seen him angry at all—and it took a moment to realize what was happening.

"Gavin!" she shouted, storming to the table.

All the paper lying there was blank. Every newspaper clipping, microfilm printout, file folder, her notes, Digger Downs' notes. All of it. Just a ream of blank paper scattered across the table now.

"Oh shit," he said softly, backing away.

He meant to do it, she knew he did. But his eyes grew wide, anguished. As if he'd fully intended to erase her work but hadn't realized exactly what that meant until it was done. Maybe he hadn't thought he could do it all in one go. She stared at all that blank paper. Her breath caught, and her voice died.

"Raleigh. I'm really sorry."

She couldn't even look at him right now. She gathered up the pages—they were blank, but they were still hers, and this seemed weird and irrational but she did it anyway, scooped them up and shoved them in her backpack and grabbed her coat and scarf off the back of the chair.

He kept his distance, pleading. "I'm sorry." She headed for the door, her jaw clenched, moving lightly so she wouldn't scream. He said, "I just . . . I want you stay safe. I want to keep you safe."

She turned on him. Faced him, but kept her gaze on the floor. Looking at him hurt. "That's not your job. This is my decision and you don't get to take that away from me."

"Raleigh. I lost my temper. Please."

She left the apartment.

She walked back to her mother's place, half expecting Gavin to follow, but he didn't, which was probably for the best. Cried part of the way, badly enough that a guy at a newsstand asked her if she was okay. She smiled as best she could, noticed the new issue of *Aces!* was out, with her cover profile about a new German ace named Lohengrin, who had visions of medieval glory and a conjured set of shining armor to match. Seeing the issues she worked on in the wild usually gave her a thrill, but this time she didn't feel a thing.

When she got home, she thought she might try to sneak back to her room so she wouldn't have to talk to her mother. But Aurora was curled up on the sofa, a giant glass of wine in hand and a box of tissues in her lap. She was crying even more than Raleigh wanted to.

"Mom, what's the matter?" Her own angst forgotten, she dropped everything and sat on the other end of the sofa.

Aurora sniffed, shook her head. "Oh, I thought you were staying at Gavin's tonight. I wouldn't have let myself go like this if I knew you were coming home."

"Mom, it's okay, I just want to know what's wrong. Can I help?"

Aurora wiped her nose with a tissue, took a long drink. Shook her head. "My agent won't return my calls. I haven't had a job in months. I know I've been hanging on by my fingernails for years, but something always came along. I just thought . . . something would always come along. Now I'm not sure. I guess I'm really finished."

"Oh, Mom."

Aurora was years past her peak stardom, sure. But Raleigh had never seen her despair like this. Her shimmering lights seemed muted, sticking close to her hair and shoulders instead of radiating out.

"Where's that wine, I think I need some of that too."

"It's right here, you'll have to get a glass—Raleigh, have you been crying, too? Tell me."

Her lips pursed, her eyes squinted. She fully intended on holding it together so she could comfort her mother. But she couldn't do it. "I think Gavin and I just broke up."

"Oh, honey." She opened her arms, and Raleigh fell into them.

They ended up finishing the whole bottle together, and Aurora put in the DVD of *Hello, Dolly!*, which had been both their favorites when she was little, and they just didn't think about anything for a while.

♦

Graham Carter, the entertainment lawyer Aurora had dated briefly in the year before Raleigh's birth, worked at a firm with swanky offices in a building on Avenue of the Americas. Raleigh sat outside the main doors. A little park area, with stone planters and concrete benches, had been set up here. With a book and cup of coffee in hand, she pretended like she belonged. She schemed. Maybe she could accidentally run into him as he walked out of the building after work. Somehow contrive to give him a paper cut and then take the blood sample for a paternity test. And he would sue her ass off for invasion of privacy or something. Maybe she shouldn't be here at all. Instead, she should write a letter on *Aces!* letterhead and make it sound like she was working on a story, like she had some journalistic integrity.

This might have been the problem: was this quest personal or had it turned into a job? She was so intent on solving the mystery, digging up this detail as if she were tracking down crime lords and ace astronauts, that she hadn't much thought about what happened after. So she found her father. Then what? What did she expect to happen?

She wasn't sure what she wanted to happen.

The big glass doors at the front of the building opened, a handful of people in expensive business suits and flapping overcoats walked out, some of them heading for the taxi stand on the corner, others walking down the street to the subway station. *He* was there. Graham Carter had gained weight, and his close-cropped black hair was dusted with gray. He wore wire-rimmed glasses and an intent expression, not looking around, certainly not noticing the twenty-something with the ratty backpack and giant cup of coffee sitting nearby. His hand that gripped his briefcase was scaled and clawed, like a bird's. Raleigh wouldn't have noticed if she hadn't looked twice. In the old photo, that arm had been hidden from view, tucked behind Aurora's back.

She could trip him, maybe. Apologize profusely. Use a handkerchief to wipe up the blood from any scrapes and use that for a paternity test—

That was an insane idea. She was nuts. And Carter climbed into the next cab and was already gone while she sat and dithered. Her coffee had gone cold in the meantime, and she threw the whole thing out.

Gavin left voice mails both at Aurora's place and at work. Raleigh didn't erase them, but she couldn't bear to listen to them, either.

She reconstructed her notes about Warren Skalko, trying to work out what had happened to him. He had disappeared under mysterious circumstances in Las Vegas in 1971. That sparked her instincts. She read a lot of old newspaper articles, called a lot of bureaucrats, and got the police reports of witnesses who had been the last ones to see him alive. A couple of names kept showing up. She followed leads, just as far as she could.

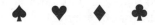

Dry to the Touch

by Caroline Spector

Las Vegas, 1963

JOE FELT COOL THAT afternoon. The air was cool. The breeze on his face was cool. He'd been cool when he talked to Dorothy Webster, the prettiest girl in school. He grinned happily. The nebbishy guy he'd been was gone and in his place was this new Joe. This cool Joe. It was March and he could see nothing but cool times ahead.

He passed Klein's meat market, then Sylvia's flower shop—called A Floral Affair—and was almost to his folks' dry cleaner's when he heard shots coming from inside the store. He dropped his books and ran to the front door. There was blood on it, a bright red splatter so shockingly out of place that it stopped him short for a moment. Then he rushed inside.

On the floor lay his father. A tall, thin man stood over the body, nonchalantly holding a revolver. Joe screamed, then dropped to his knees, grabbing for his father's body. Instead, he slipped on the bloody floor and flopped onto his father's chest. As he shoved himself into a kneeling position, his hand slid across the gunshot wound. It was slick and hot.

He heard the click of a gun hammer. It sounded remarkably like it did on TV. Joe looked up. The tall man was pointing the gun at him. This was how he was going to die, and it wasn't going to be cool at all. He would be groveling on his knees.

He raised his bloody hands and said, "Why? *Why?*"

The tall man shrugged. "You don't skim from Mr. Skalko."

"But, but Pop only worked for Mr. Skalko a little while. He'd never do something like that!"

"Kid, I don't make the rules."

Joe closed his eyes and a horrible sensation ran through him. He was only fifteen. Dying was stupid.

Nothing happened.

He opened his eyes. The tall man was looking at him speculatively. Joe observed that the tall man had dirty-blond hair and then was appalled that this was what he noticed in that moment.

"Ahhhhhh!" he exclaimed with a heavy exhale. This made the dust fly off his hands into a sunbeam pouring through the front window. The motes danced there, and it was pretty and horrible.

The tall man gave a thin smile. He thumbed off the gun hammer. In one quick stride, he grabbed Joe's hands and slammed them into the wet blood. The blood turned to dust and Joe jerked away. The tall man grinned.

"This is your lucky day, kid." The tall man grinned. "You're going to be a real help to me and Mr. Skalko. Better that than dead. Yeah?"

Joe shook his head. "I can't do anything! There's nothing I can do!"

"Oh, kid, you'll find out. Now help me with this body."

Joe recoiled. "That's Pop! Are you crazy?!"

The tall man brandished the gun again. "Kid, I don't give a shit who it is. You *had* a dad. I bet you got a mom at home."

Joe's eyes widened with fear. "She couldn't have anything to do with this!"

"Let's keep it that way."

Las Vegas, 1971

"**WILL YOU COME FOR** Passover?" Susie asked. She was dressed in full showgirl regalia: fishnet stockings, four-inch heels, and a leotard cut up to *there*. She was also balancing a ten-pound jewel-encrusted, ostrich-feather-topped headdress as if it were the most natural thing in the world. Her real name was Sarah Goldstein, but she went by Susie Barber. She'd explained to Joe that Susie Barber was a better stage name than Sarah Goldstein. Joe didn't agree, but he didn't tell her so.

"Probably not," he replied softly. He'd suddenly stopped growing at fifteen and was now short and squat with dark brown hair and eyes of an indeterminate color. The perpetually anxious expression etched on his face made him appear older than his twenty-three years. He wasn't cool now at all.

They were backstage in the dancers' dressing area. It was lined with makeup tables facing light-bulb-ringed mirrors. The muffled sound of the orchestra and band starting and stopping "This Guy's in Love with You" filtered through the upstage wall. It was a rocky dress rehearsal by the sound of it. Doing a decent Burt Bacharach tribute wasn't easy, but he was Skalko's favorite composer and what the boss wanted, the boss got. *Like he does with everything else,* Joe thought with a shudder.

"Mom wants me to come to her house," he continued, trying to look anywhere other than directly at her. He knew it was rude, but sometimes direct eye contact made him panicky.

"But Passover hasn't been the same since Pop died," he continued. "It doesn't mean that much to me now anyway." March was bad for Joe. When Passover fell in March, as it often did, it was worse. Too many memories of when and how his card had turned. Thinking about it made him even more anxious and jittery. He patted the bottle of Valium in his pocket, just to be sure it was still there.

Susie gave him a bright smile. There were so many things he wanted to tell her. Things he never could. And he thought she was only kind to him because he was a useless wreck. He was a safe man.

"Maybe your mother and Harriet might come, too?" she asked. She was nothing if not persistent. "Rabbi Menken—he's Reform—likes to 'perform' the Haggadah. He's a frustrated singer and likes to feel as if he's part of the whole showbiz thing. It's always a production. But fun. My boyfriend isn't coming because, well, he's *very* not one of us."

Joe didn't know anything about Susie's new boyfriend. She'd been very quiet about him. Joe figured that he wasn't Jewish. And since she'd never dated a man who wasn't Jewish—as far as Joe knew—he wondered what was going on.

Joe caught himself staring at her. It was difficult not to. She reminded him of Julie Newmar—statuesque and gorgeous. Her hair was coppery, and she was so sweet it made him ache. Susie was everything he wanted—and couldn't have. And he felt safe with her. She always made him want to tell her things about himself. And that was dangerous for both of them.

"Please ask," Susie continued. "Really, I can make room. There will be interesting people, I promise. A friend of mine who dances at Circus Circus is coming. I think the two of you will hit it off. She's Jewish, too. Your mother will love her." The last bit she said in the Brooklyn accent she'd spent months and hundreds of dollars losing but could still put on in a snap.

Joe smiled wanly. Susie loved to set him up. Her success rate was abysmal. Once the girls discovered he was just a janitor, they fled. And if they'd known what he did for Skalko, they would have been horrified. Joe was horrified himself. Thinking about it made him shake and he wanted a Valium—*now*.

"You should stop trying to fix me up," he said, sweeping up the glitter, spangles, and feathers that molted off the dancers. "You have a terrible track record and I'm not looking for anyone right now."

It was a lie.

He already knew what he wanted, but it was impossible. Susie treated him like a human being. He wasn't used to that, except from his sister and mother. They worshipped the ground he walked on.

His heart began rabbiting. It wasn't pleasant and it wasn't just out of love. It was out of fear and embarrassment. And when he thought about his father, it made everything worse. The only thing he could do to feel better was to concentrate on getting the floor perfectly clean. That and his Mother's Little Helpers. The Rolling Stones were right, you could take shelter in them. The bottle of Valium moved a little in his pocket as he swept. It was comforting.

"Well, tell your mother and Harriet they're invited. And be sure to tell them the rabbi is coming—that might convince them. I promise not to push Connie at you."

"Connie?"

"Connie Bird. She used to be Doris Epstein. My friend. Showbiz, right?"

"Right," he replied.

She gave him a quick smile, and then her body was encased by a golden neon glow that slowly changed colors. Joe started getting sweaty immediately. It was her deuce. She glowed neon, and everyone around her began sweating. That's why she was the centerpiece of the show. The audience loved the neon, the dancers glistening with sweat, and Susie looking like a young Greek goddess. It was what sold the show.

She was the total Vegas package.

"Susie, you're fabulous," the stage director yelled. Even though the director wasn't mic'd, Joe could hear him as if he were in the dressing room. The director clapped his hands. "The rest of you girls pay attention to what and how she's doing the routine. I swear, it's like none of you have ever danced before!"

"Hey! You try dancing next to Little Miss Easy-Bake Oven," snapped one of the other dancers. Joe was pretty sure it was Lizzy Perkins. She had a mild joker. Medusa-like snakes covered her head. Except hers were rubber with sequined scales. They were sparkly and made her look "exotic," according to the other dancers. In more uncharitable moments, Joe thought she looked like a four-year-old's art project.

"Just get back to work! Sweating is your job!"

The band resumed playing "This Guy's in Love with You" with more Sousa than Bacharach.

"Hey, Joe," Lovey Dovey said. "There's a job for you out front."

Joe sighed. It was the end of his shift and he was tired.

"What and where?" he asked, resigned to his fate.

"Puke," she replied. Her hands looked like birds' feet, the wicked-looking talons painted a lurid salmon pink. It was her signature color. Skalko's club had a surprising number of jokers and deuces, but only if they were pretty like Susie or appealingly odd—and beautiful—like Lovey Dovey. Joe knew Skalko also had aces on the payroll, and he avoided them as much as he could.

"In that far corner by the blackjack tables," Lovey Dovey continued, gesturing her claw in the general direction of the main room. "At least he didn't do it on the table. But no one's too upset. He lost a stack of dough and he tipped me well. Anyway, you cool with dealing with that? I know you're the best at taking care of this sort of thing."

Joe nodded, trying to seem normal and not blitzed out of his head. He was grateful that Dr. Henman, the casino doctor, was happy to keep his prescriptions filled. Uppers or downers, it didn't matter what he wanted. The doc made sure he had it. The doctor took care of everyone. Joe had heard

Dr. Henman had once been a surgeon, but Joe couldn't believe it because his right hand was missing its thumb.

Lovey Dovey had a fabulous Afro and skin the color of burnt umber. Like all the waitresses, she wore platform shoes, and a geometric-patterned miniskirt so short that occasionally her panties peeped out. Atomic Ace, the name of the casino, was emblazoned across the butt. The skirt pattern was a smaller version of the pattern on the carpet. A crimson long-sleeve shirt was knotted under her breasts, showing an expanse of firm but softly rounded belly. Joe was surprised she wasn't in the show. She certainly hit all the right physical notes, but she'd pointed out to him once that her talons made her less than the showgirl type.

"C'mon," she said, and led him to the puke.

When they got there, Joe saw it had started soaking into the carpet. It smelled like partially digested sweet liquor and too much free steak.

"I'll take it from here," he said. "You go on."

"Thanks, Joe," she said with a smile.

"No problem. Don't worry about it."

She glided off. Joe waited until she was down by the end of the blackjack tables before he put his cleaning caddy down and squatted next to the puke. He glanced around. Aside from the usual eye-in-the-sky cameras and the aces Skalko used to catch cheaters, no one was around to see him. He turned his back to the camera and the aces, then touched the puke with the tip of his finger. It vanished, leaving only dust. He swept it into his dustpan, knowing he'd have to come back with the vacuum to get all of it out of the carpet. There was still a faint smell of vomit, so he gave a quick spray of potpourri Glade. He preferred it over the janitorial spray that smelled like rotten lemons.

He checked the walls and saw some splatter, turned that to dust as well, then wiped down the wall.

Joe the Janitor to the rescue, he thought. And then he wanted to puke, too.

It was 6:00 P.M. Joe was changing into his street clothes when Mike "Skinny T" Thomas sauntered into the men's locker room. Every time Joe saw Skinny T it was like a kick to the gut. Joe loathed him. This time of year made the loathing burn even hotter. Skinny T looked almost the same as he had that afternoon in March when he'd killed Joe's father.

"We have a job for tonight," Skinny T said. He wore a blue polyester suit with wide lapels and belled pants. It was paired with a dark orange paisley-patterned shirt. He looked like an advertisement for Howard Johnson's.

Joe tried to keep the hatred off his face. It rarely worked. Skinny T disliked being called that and expected everyone except Mr. Skalko to call him Mr. Thomas. Joe had had numerous elaborate fantasies about killing Skinny T over the years, and they never involved calling him Mr. Thomas.

"Another one? Is it a Mr. Skalko job or a you job?" Joe asked. He was tired and immediately knew he shouldn't have asked. Skinny T wasn't supposed to be using Joe without Mr. Skalko's say-so, but he did it anyway. Skinny T had a temper, and Joe had been on the receiving end of it more than once. Except for the constant threat from both Mr. Skalko and Skinny T toward his mother and his sister, Joe would have killed both of them. At least he liked to think he would have.

"Yeah, but that wouldn't matter now—would it?" Skinny T asked.

"No," Joe replied, defeated.

"Be ready at eight. I'll come and get you like always."

As Skinny T left the room, Joe quickly popped another Valium. The bottle was getting low, and he missed the soft cha-cha-cha sound it made when full.

Joe was ready at 8:00. Earlier, he'd called his mother to tell her he had to work late and wasn't coming for Shabbat dinner. Like Susie, his mother and Harriet were somewhat observant. Since his father had been murdered, his mother had become more religious. But not in a Billy-Graham-Evangelical sort of way.

She did Shabbat dinner and refused to cook or clean or do any chores from Friday sundown to Saturday sundown. She read mysteries and ate leftovers instead. Harriet still went to work—she didn't have the luxury of taking time off. The family dry cleaning business wouldn't take care of itself. Joe would have been happy to work there, but every time he went into the store, he started shaking. He'd tried to get jobs at other casinos, but Skinny T had put out the word that Joe belonged to Skalko. Joe was stuck working—and *working*—for them.

Joe waited outside his tiny apartment for Skinny T and tried not to nod off. He'd begun supplementing his Valium with Quaaludes. The doc said they would help him sleep. The 'ludes took the edge off even better than Valium and left him feeling filled with a golden glow he didn't get anywhere else. Except maybe around Susie, but that might have been her deuce. He giggled dopily to himself. It was March and things cooled off considerably after sundown. Away from the Strip and all that concrete and asphalt, the cold still had a winter bite. He could see the neon glow from the Strip and wondered if there would be a time he wouldn't be able to see it anymore.

Skinny T never showed.

Joe waited until 9:00, then went back inside his apartment. It was little more than one room and a hot plate. Skinny T not showing broke through the golden Quaalude glow and Joe contemplated taking another one, but decided against it. Skinny T had never missed getting Joe to a job before.

There were no good options far as he was concerned. He definitely didn't want to be the one to tell Skalko about Skinny T. *Fuck you, Mr. Thomas,* he thought. Off in the glow, he could be as bold as he wanted, but Skinny T vanishing was bad. There was no choice but to go back to the casino and tell Skalko that his top hit man was missing.

It had taken one and a half black beauties (swallowing the half capsule had been nasty as usual) to get Joe sober enough that he felt able to talk to Skalko. He was just pulling his apartment door shut when his phone rang. Only a handful of people had his number and no one except his mother ever called anyway. The phone—a pink Princess number he'd found in the trash and repaired—was across the room. It took four steps to reach it.

"Hello?" he answered, trying to sound somewhat straight.

"Joe? Joe? Is that you?"

It was Susie. Joe was stunned and felt a little dizzy.

"Joe. It's Susie." Her voice was strangely monotone and devoid of her usual cheerfulness. "Joe?"

"Yes, Susie," he replied, glad that he sounded pretty normal. "Uhm, why are you calling?"

He thought it sounded as if he was interrogating her. But he was still pretty high and couldn't be sure.

"Joe, I need your help."

How Susie could need him for anything was beyond Joe. But that didn't matter. He knew he was going to help her.

"Of course," he tried not to slur. "What do you need? Something about Passover?"

"No. I just . . . I need you to come to my house right away."

"Uh . . . okay. Where do you live?"

She gave him her new address and he wrote it down in his neat hand. There were some things he still retained from what little school he'd attended.

"I'll be there as soon as I can." He was higher than he'd realized earlier and wasn't sure how fast he could safely drive his rickety VW Bug to her house.

"Hurry." She hung up and Joe stared at the peony-colored receiver for a moment, then dropped it into its cradle and hustled out the door, but not before he grabbed another black beauty and dry-swallowed it.

Joe saw Susie's new copper-colored Thunderbird—it matched her hair, she'd exclaimed when she bought it—parked in the driveway of her house. The house was small, squat, and made of adobe. The front door was painted aqua, and there were matching tiles surrounding the wooden front door-frame. A speakeasy grille was at eye height.

He knocked. For a moment, he wondered if he'd just made the whole thing up in some drugged-out stupor, and now he was going to seem like a creepy stalker.

The little door behind the grille opened a crack.

"That you, Joe?" Susie whispered.

"Yeah, it's me," he replied, bouncing on his toes a little. The speed had hit on the way over. It was always faster on an empty stomach.

The door opened about a foot, and she reached out and grabbed his wrist. She opened the door just enough to pull him inside, then she shut it behind him. It was then he saw that she was dressed in baby-blue pajamas covered in a tiny rose print, and that they were covered in blood. She was barefoot and her feet and hands were covered in blood, too.

There were many things he'd fantasized while thinking about Susie Barber. But even while he desired her with a terrible ache, he also dreamt about going out together like a real couple, having kids, having a life with her.

Susie Barber in blood-soaked pajamas hadn't been one of those fantasies.

He stared at her and she stared back.

"Holy shit," he said.

"Yes," she replied dully.

"Are you okay? Are you cut or something? Do I need to get you to a doctor?"

She laughed, and it was scary.

"No. No. No. No. I just—" She waved her hands and then turned on her heel. Her bloody footprints patterned the living room.

"Follow me." She looked over her shoulder and gave him one of her bright smiles, but her eyes were blank.

She led him through the small living room. A couple of low-slung chairs and a loveseat upholstered in neutral tones fought with a shockingly bright-green shag area rug on the floor. On the arm of one of the chairs was a hand-crocheted afghan. A sliding glass door leading to a patio took up most of one wall. An adobe fireplace jutted out into the room on the left side, and there were two doors opposite it. It was a little larger than the apartment where she'd held a seder two years ago. Skalko must have given her a big raise. It was tough to afford a house in the shitty economy.

Susie opened the door nearest to the sliding glass door.

"Come in," she said, holding the door open for him.

Joe really didn't want to go through that doorway. He already had a lifetime of going through certain kinds of doorways.

But he did anyway.

Lying on the floor, blood spreading under him, was Skinny T. Dead as the day was long. He was wearing a black shirt and black jeans. A vicious joy surged through Joe, then monumental disappointment and rage. Killing Skinny T had occupied an enormous amount of Joe's fantasy life during the last decade. Then he twigged and it was awful. Skinny T was Susie's secret, not-so-Jewish, boyfriend.

"Skinny T," he blurted out. Joe half expected Skinny T to pop up and beat the shit out of him for saying it.

"He hated being called that," Susie said. Her voice wasn't as flat now. "He just hated that. You know, hated it so much . . ."

"Yeah," Joe replied, and she stopped talking. He surveyed the remains of a terrible struggle. A broken lamp was on the floor, its shade crushed. The bedcovers were pulled halfway off and smeared with blood. A chunk of bloody mirror was caught in one corner of them. There was an over-turned armchair. Shards of the shattered mirror from the Art Deco vanity were scattered across the floor. Skinny T lay in the wreckage, a single ragged wound to his neck.

"Did you do that?" Joe asked.

She shook her head. "I don't . . . I guess . . . We were fighting, and he started pushing me around, and I was trying to get away, and then he fell against the mirror. It fell over and smashed . . . He knocked me to the floor, and then he kicked me in the stomach and said he wasn't going to mark up my face, that I needed to be pretty. My hand got tangled up in the sheets and I grabbed a piece of that mirror. He laughed like hell when he saw I had it. Then he yanked me off the floor and slapped me hard in the face anyway. I guess he couldn't help it. That's when I reached up . . ." She made a quick cutting motion. "And now he's . . ." She waved a hand at Skinny T. "It was so easy. I never thought it would be so easy. He died so fast . . . I tried to stop the bleeding, but . . ." Her hands shook.

Joe wished he'd been the one to kill Skinny T. He wished it more than anything. But he'd make do with the corpse on the floor.

And then Susie started crying, but it wasn't hysterical. It was angry cry-ing. Her face was red with tears. She wiped her nose with the sleeve of her pajamas and left a smudge of blood on her cheek.

"Why did you call me? What can I do?" Joe asked. *Does she know?* he wondered frantically.

"I don't know." Her shoulders drooped. "You just seem so solid. You al-ways take care of everything at the casino. You're the first person anyone goes to when there's something that's a mess. And . . . you're my friend." Her eyes were downturned, and then she said, "And I didn't know who else to call. I couldn't call the police. This looks so bad, you know? Because it is. And most of the cops are on the payroll of the mobbed-up guys. And do you really think Skalko would believe me? Or even care that I was trying to pro-tect myself? That I tried to stop the blood?"

Joe squatted next to Skinny T's body. *That's right,* he thought. His over-whelming rage made him light-headed for a moment. *You're dead and I can call you anything I want. You fucker.*

"You did okay," he said, reaching out and touching the blood on the floor. It turned to powder. "I'll take care of it."

Susie didn't say anything, just stared at him as he systematically toured the room, touching everything with blood on it. Then he turned to her.

"I need to touch your pajamas," he said.

"Why?"

"Because you're covered in blood," he said, figuring she'd understand. "As it is, you were lucky this floor is tile and everything is still kinda wet."

Susie looked at him, then down at her pajamas, and then ran to the little bathroom off the bedroom. She didn't close the door, and Joe could see her back arch as she vomited.

Then she closed the toilet lid and flushed. She lay down on the tile and rested her head there for a moment. Her palm was covered in blood.

"Let me see your hand," he said, walking slowly toward her. She lifted her hand and stared at the blood.

"In a second," she said, pushing herself to her feet. "I'm going to take a shower."

"You can't," he said sharply. Joe wasn't wild about who he was when he was just Joe the Janitor, but he really didn't like Joe the Cleaner. "We have to put the body in there. And I have to see about your hand."

He stepped forward and grabbed her hand. Then he touched the blood on her palm, dusting it. There wasn't a cut, much to his surprise, it was only Skinny T's blood.

Susie just stared at him for a moment. "The sheet," she said, looking at her palm. "I had my hand in the sheet when I grabbed the piece of mirror. That makes it look worse, doesn't it? Looks like I meant to do it."

"Do you have any other cuts?"

She shook her head. "I don't know. I don't think so . . ."

"It's okay," Joe said patiently. The black beauties made the wonderful golden glow fade to a jittery grey. "I've done this before . . . a lot. You got a first aid kit? I'll need it, just in case you do get cut while we clean this up."

She nodded. "In the closet."

Joe rooted around in her closet. It smelled like her. Spicy, warm, and safe. He knew he was being creepy, and he didn't care. He found the kit in the back of the closet under a shoebox. There was a pair of slippers on the floor and he grabbed them. When he backed out of the closet, she was sitting on the edge of the bed staring at him. He knelt down and dusted the blood on her feet, then he slid the slippers on her.

"Jesus, Joe, who are you?"

"I'm a cleaner," he replied. He flashed back to the dry cleaner's and Skinny T. His hands started shaking. "It's what I do for Skalko. I take care of messes he has Skinny T make." He was getting shaky now and it wasn't all the speed. This was the first time he'd ever told anyone about his power or how he used it. Only Skalko and Skinny T had known until now.

"It's my real job . . . I do this." He gestured to Skinny T's body, and then around the room. "I've been doing this for years."

"Joe . . ." Susie was freaking, he could tell.

"Look, don't get upset." He grabbed the hem of her pj's and the blood there powdered and fell to the floor.

Joe began dragging Skinny T's body to the bathroom. Susie—her legs wobbly—grimaced as she grabbed Skinny T's ankles and helped Joe maneuver the body to the tub. It was a tight fit. They rolled him in, and he landed on his side, face against the side of the tub, ass halfway in the air.

They were close enough that Joe could smell her perfume under the fear sweat. Half the women in the show wore the same fragrance. It was Charlie. Bottles of it dotted the makeup tables backstage at the casino.

What's wrong with you? he thought. *Stop sniffing her and her stuff.*

Susie stared down at Skinny T's body. Then she hauled back and punched him in the butt.

"You bastard," she growled. Then she slumped as if all her energy was gone. "Do you want to know why we were fighting?"

Joe didn't care. At least, not right now. The body had to be dealt with ASAP, and they needed to figure out how to cover the whole thing up.

Skalko might have looked like an accountant, and he acted like a devoted family man—but he was as vicious as any other mobster on the strip.

Vegas was changing. It was casting off those things that had made it alive with danger and glamour. So Skalko had changed Atomic Ace into a hipper version of itself over the last few years . . . but he himself was unchanging.

"Do you have a saw?" Joe asked. "Electric knife? Anything we can cut him up with?"

Susie shook her head. *Is she losing it?* he worried. But then she looked at him, and he saw she was deep inside what was happening. And the sudden realization of what he was asking for, and why, turned her pale as paper. Without a word, she shook her head.

"Shit," Joe said. Skinny T usually brought all the materials they needed for their jobs. "Is his car anywhere around?"

"No," Susie said softly. "He's been borrowing mine. Said his was in the shop."

"Gimme the keys." He followed her into the living room.

"You have an ace power," she said, rummaging in her fringe-trimmed suede hobo bag. She pulled out a set of keys with a Taurus astrological charm dangling off it.

"No," he replied, marveling that she only had three keys. "Deuce."

"Blood to dust? That's scary." Susie was prattling. "I mean, you could kill anyone with that."

Joe shook his head. "Doesn't work that way. I can only powder bodily fluids once they're out of the body. But I can powder *all* the bodily fluids. It's disgusting. Do you know how often I've had to clean up vomit because everyone thinks I'm so good at it?"

"Oh."

"Stay here," he commanded. Joe the Janitor would never have spoken to Susie this way, but he wasn't Joe the Janitor at the moment. After tonight, he wasn't sure he could be Joe the Janitor ever again. He headed out to her car, leaving the front door slightly ajar. There was no one to see him, and he unlocked the trunk. Inside were the tools of his trade: hacksaw, electric slicing knife, rope, plastic sheets, a rubber tube with big needle attached, and a shovel.

With another glance around, Joe grabbed as much as he could for one trip. He spotted a spool of duct tape in a corner of the trunk, put it on his wrist like a bracelet, and took that as well. He hustled back to the house and slipped inside.

Susie wasn't in the living room. The sliding glass patio door was open with bloody slipper prints leading to it.

Dammit, he thought, putting the tools on the loveseat. *She's bolted.*

Then he saw her on the patio, smoking.

"Didn't know you smoked," he said, stepping through the door.

"Not usually," she replied. She held the cigarette out. Her hand trembled. "You want a drag?"

Joe shook his head. "I'm going to get the rest of the stuff out of the trunk. Then I'll start working on him. You should make sure all the windows are covered, and that the doors are shut and locked."

"I know. I'll be in to help in a minute."

"No."

She took a deep draw on the cigarette and blew smoke out. Then she coughed. "Like I said, I don't do this often." She waved the cigarette around for a moment. "I should help, if not for me . . ."

Joe sighed. The window of opportunity was quickly closing. It took time to cut up a body and dispose of it properly.

"I have to start working on . . . things now. Please come inside and close the drapes." He went and lifted her slipper, drying the blood there, then touched where she'd walked. Cleaning the house was going to be a bitch.

Susie nodded and stubbed her cigarette out in a blue pot next to the door, and then came inside.

Joe went to the bathroom and began stripping the body, powdering the blood on the clothes as he went. Skinny T's pants weren't cooperating because the angle of his body was awkward. Joe grunted trying to move it into position.

"Let me help," Susie said. Her voice was choked. "I've undone his pants before."

Having her say it so bluntly made Joe blush. She was about his age, so he shouldn't have been surprised. And then he thought about too much. His joy at Skinny T's death was drowned for a moment, then surged back, hotter than before.

Joe shoved the body around until the buckle appeared. With shaking hands, Susie quickly undid it. Together, they stripped off the pants.

"You know," Susie said, dropping Skinny T's arm back into the bathtub where it made a soft thud. "I always thought you were this sweet Jewish guy who needed my help to get a nice Jewish girl. But now . . . it turns out you're this."

"This part is pretty gross," Joe said, pulling the exsanguination gear out of his pocket. He didn't want to talk to her. Not right now.

He jammed the needle into Skinny T's neck and started draining the rest of the blood from the body.

"When did your card turn?" Susie asked, as if they weren't getting ready to cut Skinny T into pieces.

Joe had been wondering when she was going to ask. Every time he thought about it, the world slanted sideways.

"In '63. I'd just turned fifteen." He wanted a Valium. Or a 'lude. Maybe a Dilaudid, though those made him useless for hours. Anything so he didn't have to rub up against that memory.

"Mine turned when I was thirteen," she said. "Our neighbor made a pass at me as he was walking me home from babysitting. Can you believe it? I was just a kid." She shook her head. "Sorry, that sounds so dumb right now. I lit up neon, and he started sweating. Mom came out—it was a mess. What happened to you?"

He put his hand under the blood draining from the rubber tube. "I've never told anyone," he said, his mouth going cottony. "Not Mom. Not my sister Harriet. They can't ever know." His hands started shaking again and this time it wasn't from the black beauties. "I'll tell you later," he said.

It didn't take long to get the blood drained. Skinny T was almost dry. And when that was done, he took up the electric knife. It was the Scovill brand that was advertised as a new way to cut up turkeys. *Like a regular knife wouldn't work just fine,* he thought. However, it did a bang-up job on human flesh. *The marketing on that would be something to see,* he thought.

He turned the knife on, and it shook and made a *rnnnnnn-rnnnnnnn* noise. It was a new one because he'd burned the old one out during the last job.

"This is going to get messy. Please, just let me do this alone."

"Joe . . ."

"Fine." He started cutting into the fleshy part of Skinny T's thigh. He looked up, and Susie was as pale as if she'd been the one drained. Then she fainted and hit her head on the sink as she went down.

"Oh, shit!" Joe dropped the electric knife and knelt beside her. There was a moment when he thought she was dead. Then she opened her eyes and said, "I don't think I can do this."

"Of course you can't! I've been doing it for years and the only way I can get through it is to be high. Just go lie down, or watch TV, or do something—anything—else. It's going to take me a while." He helped her up, then led her out the door. "Is your head okay?"

She touched it and winced. He was worried she might have a concussion, but there were more immediate matters at hand. He went back into the bathroom.

A few minutes later, he could hear Frank Sinatra singing "Will You Love Me If My Card Turns?" He started working on Skinny T's thigh again, and the music got louder.

◆

Susie was wrapped in the afghan and sleeping on the sofa when Joe was fin-ished with Skinny T. He'd stacked the neatly wrapped packages of the re-mains in the bedroom. It was midnight and he still had to drive out to the desert to bury the body parts. It was going to be a difficult trip, because his car was crap. Then he wished Skinny T had brought some acid for the finger-tips the way he usually did, but there was nothing to be done for that now.

He shook Susie awake.

She opened her eyes and stared up at him. "Crap," she said. "I thought for a minute . . . never mind." She sat up. "I guess you're done? If I'd never dated him, none of this would have happened. People make mistakes, but he was something else entirely." Anger swept over her face, and she shook her head. "At first, it was exciting to be around him. I guess that's why I started seeing him. He was so different from the other men I've dated. Well, all two of them. But then we had to keep everything secret . . . I didn't like that. Yesterday, I found out what they were up to."

"What who were up to?" Joe asked. He was impatient to get going.

"Mr. Skalko and Mike—you know, Skinny T. That was his real name: Mike Thomas. Anyway, I heard them on the phone. You know how you can listen to people talking on the phone if you're careful picking up the other receiver on the other end of the line?" Joe nodded. "I was curious. Mike had never told me what he did. I knew he worked for Mr. Skalko, and I wanted to know." She smiled bitterly. "They were talking about me and some of the other girls at the casino. Mr. Skalko wanted to make some of us girls . . . make us do things with certain customers."

The chorus girls talked about how Skalko ran hookers. For some stupid reason, he'd thought the wild card girls who worked the casino were special. Atomic Ace was supposed to be a safe place for them to work. That's what he had told himself.

"Oh, we weren't going to be farmed out to just anyone. Only *special* cus-tomers would get girls like me. You know—'high end' girls with a wild card." She looked lost. "Why us? You can go *anywhere* in Vegas and get a joker or deuce who'll screw you for money!" She pulled the afghan tighter and hugged her knees to her chest. "Mike—Skinny T—was only too happy to oblige. He called me a great piece of ass."

Susie started crying, but this time it wasn't angry crying, it was something-broken-inside crying. Joe didn't know what to do, so he awkwardly patted her head. She winced.

"Ouch," she said. "That's where I hit the sink."

"Skinny T killed my father," Joe blurted out, trying hard not to reach for a Valium. He still needed to be sharp, and the black beauties would be fading soon.

"What? *What!*"

Joe nodded, and a sick expression crossed his face. "I was fifteen. We had, have, a family business—a dry cleaning and laundry business. Mom ran that. Harriet and I helped out after school. Dad would run the store on Tuesdays so Mom could play mah-jongg. Dad also worked part-time for Skalko doing counting, but they thought he was skimming. But I don't think he was. I think they got it wrong."

Susie reached out to touch his arm, but he shied away. He couldn't bear to have her touch him now. Not after he'd been cleaning. "Skinny T had just shot Dad when I showed up. I don't remember much of anything else about that day except finding Skinny T standing over Pop."

He paused. He did remember. He remembered everything. What he was wearing. (Dark blue trousers and a white button-down shirt. Over that, a red corduroy jacket because it was spring and still cold sometimes.) What he'd had for lunch. (Bologna and that yellow, waxy American cheese. It wasn't kosher, but he traded with a friend who liked corned beef.) How he did on his math quiz. (B+.) Clowning it up with his friends until the teacher scolded them that class had already started. And how he'd felt so good that day. It was a special day. He had been cool. It was going to be a day where he changed into someone different. And then he'd found Pop and Skinny T and then he was different.

"I slipped and landed on Pop. My hand landed on his wound and the blood was so hot and sticky. I was holding him, I think I was. Skinny T was about to shoot me when my card turned. All of Dad's blood turned to powder and blew away. Then Skinny T grabbed my hand and hit the blood on the floor under Dad, and it dusted too." He remembered there were daisies on the counter—his mother's favorite flowers. It was a stupid thing to remember.

"But he didn't kill me." Joe felt himself slipping into Joe the Janitor, and that was bad. But he couldn't stop himself. "Skinny T was clever, and he realized I could be useful. That I could make his life easier. He is . . . he was . . . Skalko's top hit man. The one who always takes, I mean, took, care of important . . . things. And that's why he took me to Skalko."

"That's sick." Susie hunkered down again, bringing the afghan back up under her chin.

Joe nodded. The whole thing seemed so far away, as if he were looking through the wrong end of a telescope.

"Skinny T made me clean up the shop while he dumped Pop's body into the trunk of his car." Joe wanted to swallow, but his mouth was too dry for it.

"At some point, he dropped me off near school and I walked home." Tears ran down his cheeks. "I knew Mom and Harriet were going to ask me about Pop and about the store and I had no idea what I was going to say. I'd become something terrible."

"Jesus! I can't even begin . . ." Susie stopped. Then she took a slow breath and said, "That's beyond awful."

"I guess the cops got paid off," Joe said, wiping his hands across his face. "There was never any real investigation. Pop just disappeared. No bodies. No witnesses. And Skalko and Skinny T made it clear I was to be like the Three Wise Monkeys."

"Joe," Susie said. It sounded as if she was going to cry.

"That was eight years ago," he said, almost dreamily.

Joe remembered being terrified as he waited in the antechamber of Skalko's office. He figured they weren't going to kill him. That would have happened already—at least it's what he'd hoped. Part of him knew he must be in shock because he wasn't screaming. It occurred to him that a normal person would be screaming. Eventually, the secretary sent him into Skalko's office. There was a glossy sheen to the furniture, and the carpet was immaculate. Skalko sat behind a large wooden desk. Unlike the other, streamlined furniture in the room, it was heavy and looked as if it came off the set of *Love Finds Andy Hardy*. Skalko looked Joe over, then explained what he expected Joe to do.

"Skinny T—that's Mr. Thomas to you—is your immediate boss. You do what he says."

"I should have gone to the police," Joe continued. "But I was just a kid. There was Mom and Harriet to consider. After Pop was killed, I couldn't go back to school." He hunched over, as if he was expecting to be hit. "I started working at Atomic Ace because I couldn't get another job. Skalko made sure of that. He's very big on keeping track of his assets. They started feeding me Valium so I could get through the cleanings. And for after. That was pretty much it for me."

Susie got up, folded the afghan neatly, and hung it on the loveseat. "I should change."

"Why?"

"Because I'm going to come with you to get rid of . . . you know."

Joe wanted to shake her. Apparently, she hadn't been paying attention to his story. "You need to stay here."

"Nope." She shook her head.

"Why are you being so stubborn?" he asked. Joe the Cleaner was back in full force now and he was exasperated with her.

"Just stop arguing with me," she said. Then she went into the bedroom, and he heard her gasp. Those packets of Skinny T had no doubt been a shock. Joe was grimly pleased.

He heard her rummaging through drawers. Moments later, she came out wearing a pair of men's jeans and a dark Henley tee. Her hair was pulled back into a ponytail. In her hand, she carried waffle-stomper boots with socks tucked inside them.

"My father was a kosher butcher," she began as she sat down and pulled on her socks. "We lived in Brooklyn. Needless to say, things were strict kosher in my family." She put on her boots. "Occasionally, he'd let me help out in the shop, but it was on the down low. Mom would have been meshuggah if she'd found out. Anyway, I've handled a lot of meat." She pointed to the bedroom. "That's all he is now."

Impressive bullshitting, he thought. But she wasn't going to keep it together for the whole job. He was pretty sure of that. Joe went into the bedroom and grabbed a bundle of Skinny T. If she insisted on coming, she was getting Joe the Cleaner.

"How did you end up in Vegas?" he asked, as if they were chatting backstage like normal. He cradled the thigh like a baby.

"I wanted to be a dancer," she replied nonchalantly, clearly understanding what he was up to. "I tried out for the Rockettes, but I didn't make the cut. One of the other girls said I might do well here." She went into the bedroom.

"My father didn't want me in Vegas," she continued. "See, one side of the family had worked for Cousin Benny at the Flamingo. And no, I never met him. Died in '61 before I got here. The other side was deeply involved with the Jewish community." He heard her yanking the sheets off the bed.

"Anyway, Skalko was the last of their 'Angels.' In the fifties and sixties a lot of casino owners helped keep the Jewish community afloat. So, my aunt made a call for me. Skalko saw something he liked and now here I am."

He heard her grunt, and then she appeared at the doorway with one of the smaller packages in her arms. It looked to be Skinny T's feet.

"You know, the Jewish community here is very pro–wild carders. Because they remember . . . you know . . . what was happening before Wild Card Day."

Joe nodded. The entire German side of his family was gone. Once he'd heard his father say he was almost glad that there were wild carders because now there were people more hated than the Jews.

"Let's get on with it," Susie said.

Methodically, they loaded the trunk with the packages of Skinny T and then put Joe's tools in, too. It didn't take long. Joe dusted the little blood that was left on the floor of the bedroom. Then Susie locked up her house and got in the driver's side of her car.

"You shouldn't be driving," Joe said, holding the passenger-side door open.

"My car," she said simply. "Get your car and put it in there." She pointed at the little detached garage toward the back of the house.

Susie backed her car out and pulled behind his VW bug. He was used to cleaning alone. And he wasn't sure what to make of Susie anymore. *But then,* he thought, *she might not know what to make of me.*

"What do we do now?" Susie asked.

It was 3:00 A.M. and they'd just finished burying the last of Skinny T. Joe had thought he'd be elated, but all he felt was a dull satisfaction. Nothing would bring his father back. Or any of the people Joe had cleaned.

They sped along the dark stretch of highway leading back to Vegas and Skalko. Joe glanced at the speedometer and saw they were doing 90 mph.

"You want to slow down?" he asked. The black beauties had completely

worn off and so had his Quaalude haze. He popped a Valium and was dis-
mayed that there were only a couple left. There had been a lot more when he
came over to Susie's, he was sure of it.

"I'm going this fast so we can get back before sunrise. You need to get
home, too. And don't take another one of those."

He popped it in his mouth like a Tic Tac and dry-swallowed. Sliding back
into Joe the Janitor was going to be easy. "Well, we have to account for some
time," he mused. "Skinny T was supposed to be at my house by eight P.M. You
called me at nine P.M., so hopefully Skalko will think something happened
to him between your house and mine."

"Okay," she said, nodding. "What about the job you were supposed to do?"

Joe cracked the window a little. The whistling, cold wind blew across
his face. "He never told me. Never does . . . did . . . Just picked me up and
took me to whatever job they needed done." The headlights illuminated
the scrubby brush and sandy earth passing by. The white striping down the
middle of the road was hypnotic.

"I'll go in early," Joe said. "I'll go see Skalko and tell him what happened.
That I waited until nine, then went inside and passed out until this morning. He'll believe I passed out. You go to rehearsal at the usual time. Act like
normal. If they come and talk to you, just tell them he left around quarter
to eight."

Her face was grim in the green dashboard light.

"If Skalko finds out I killed him and that you helped me get rid of the
body," she said. "Jesus, Joe, we might as well be dead now."

He nodded and turned on the radio. There was static, and then "Cher-
ish" by the Association came on, cutting in and out until Susie reached over
and snapped the radio off.

Joe stood outside Skalko's office, shaking. He'd driven home, showered, then
booked it down to Atomic Ace. It was just before 6:00 A.M. He knew Skalko
often got in early. Or just stayed all night at the casino.

He knocked tentatively on the door, hoping no one was there. A moment
later, Skalko's secretary unlocked the door and stuck her head out. It reminded him of the Gatekeeper from *The Wizard of Oz*. And he had to stifle a
giggle that would have ended in hysterical laughing.

"It's early," she said, keeping the door slightly ajar. "What do you want?"

"I'm Joe Belenky. Mr. Skalko knows me." Before he drove over, Joe had
taken a Valium. But just one. He needed to be sharp. "I need to talk to him.
Is he in?"

"He just got here. Hasn't even had his coffee yet. And that means he
won't be happy to see anyone."

Great, Joe thought.

"Give me a moment."

She shut the door and Joe heard her locking it. He shoved his hands into his pockets because they started feeling itchy. From the lack of his usual dose of Valium or having to see Skalko, he wasn't sure. All he knew was that things could go sideways very fast if he wasn't careful.

Suddenly, the door opened, and the secretary glared at him with narrowed eyes. "Come in," she said in a clipped voice. "I'm going to get his coffee now. I wouldn't tell him anything bad."

Panic sweat broke out all over Joe's body. He lightly touched it, drying himself instantly. The powdery residue was transparent. It wouldn't cool him. He knew that from experience. He just wouldn't be as sweaty. Sweaty would be very bad. Sweaty would make him look guilty. The secretary waved her hand in the direction of Skalko's office. Then she slipped out the door.

He swallowed hard, and then knocked.

"Come in," Skalko said crisply.

Joe obeyed.

It was always a surprise to see Skalko in the flesh. He was wearing a sports jacket and looked more like a Little League coach than a mobster. Like Joe, his features were unremarkable. Perhaps that was the reason he'd flown under the radar. Or maybe there were just more attractive targets out there.

Skalko gave Joe an appraising look.

"What can I do for you, Joe?" Had Skalko yelled, it wouldn't be as terrifying. But Joe was already terrified, so he was no judge. It felt as if there were no air in the room. He couldn't speak. He couldn't move. If he didn't say something, it was going to seem super weird.

"Uhm, I think there may be something wrong with Mr. Thomas," he said. His voice was a little shaky, but not near as bad as he'd expected. "He said he'd pick me up last night at eight P.M., but he never showed."

Skalko got very still. "Did he call? Anything?"

Joe shook his head. "No, sir," he replied, hoping he looked his normal doped-up self. "I was at the end of my shift and he told me I was going to do a job. Said he'd pick me up at eight o'clock. I waited outside until nine o'clock, then I figured he was running late, so I went inside 'cause it was getting cold. I crashed, I dunno, around ten. I guess."

"And you didn't find this whole thing strange? Perhaps out of the ordinary? Why didn't you contact casino security? They can always reach me."

"I'm sorry, sir," Joe replied. "Like I said, I crashed pretty hard." He slipped his hand into his pocket. He knew there were two Valiums and half of a Quaalude left in the bottle. It was his just-in-case stash bottle.

"You junkies," Skalko said with a sigh. "Always nodding off." Joe didn't say anything and became very interested in his shoes. "Go do your shift," Skalko said dismissively. "If I need you, I'll let you know."

Joe turned to go, relieved he wasn't dead.

"And, Joe," Skalko said.

Shit, Joe thought. *Shit. Shit. Shit.*

"If there's any mischief involved in this, it's going to get ugly. Skinny T is my best employee. He does his job and I like him. Like he was my own kid."

Joe nodded, then glanced back at Skalko. "Yes, sir," he replied. It was the only safe answer.

Susie was late getting to rehearsal. Joe made sure he was backstage as much as he could be. Backstage was part of his assigned area, and he was there so much that he was treated as if he were part of the furniture. But today he was constantly having to deal with messes in the main casino and attendant areas.

There were messes he could use his power on and ones he couldn't. And then there were things too gross for even him to touch that he still needed to deal with. *People are disgusting,* he thought.

He'd finally finished up in the main room and hurried backstage just as Susie came striding in. The color was high on her cheeks and her eyes were red and puffy. She had her rehearsal clothes on under her wrap dress, which she untied and tossed off just before running onstage.

Toward the end of Joe's shift, Susie found him mopping next to the backstage toilets.

"We have to be careful," she said softly. "I got a call from Mr. Skalko's office telling me to come in early. I just got out of there. He asked me all kinds of questions and I told him what you said to. That Skinny T left around a quarter to eight. He told me Skinny T was missing and I started crying because I was so scared. So I tried to pretend it was because Skinny T was missing, and I was worried. I told Skalko to let me know if there was anything I could do."

One of the other dancers ran down the backstage steps and dashed up to them. "You got a tampon?" she asked Susie. "Sorry, Joe. I don't mean to embarrass you."

"It's okay," he replied while Susie went to her dressing table and fished one out of her purse. "I have a mother and a sister. I know what a tampon is."

"Susie find you a girl yet?" the other dancer asked.

"Uh, uhm, I . . ." He blushed.

"Stop bugging Joe," Susie said as she handed over the tampon. "His love life is none of your business."

"But it's yours? Admit it, you're a big yenta." She turned and hurried to the bathroom.

"It's a good thing you're always trying to fix me up," Joe said. "It's not going to seem as weird for us to be talking."

"How did it go with you?" she asked.

He shook his head. "I'm not sure. Skinny T vanishing is bad. But I'm a junkie." He shrugged his shoulders. "Of course, I get all the drugs I need from Dr. Henman. Legit. He's never turned me down. But I think he may be on pills, too. Besides, what motive do I have?"

"All the motive in the world," she whispered. "And Skalko knows that."

"We'll be careful. Do things like always. I'll come for seder. That'll look normal. I've gone before and everyone knows you keep trying to set me up. You can always tell him you feel sorry for me. He'll believe that."

Nervously, she started mucking with her hair. "I better be convincing the next time." She made the universal jazz-hands gesture. "And I wanted to be in showbiz." She smiled wanly. "Not funny? Hmmmmm? Well, the first seder is on the twenty-ninth."

His shoulders slumped. "Which of your friends will be there?"

"Just Connie. She's a nice girl."

He slumped down even more. "I'm not a nice boy," he said softly.

"Susie! Get your ass onstage," the director yelled, loud enough that his voice came through the upstage wall.

The dancer Susie had given the tampon exited the backstage bathroom and then grabbed Susie by the arm, pulling her toward the stage entrance. "C'mon! You can talk to your boyfriend later."

"I'm not her . . ." Joe began, but they were already gone.

He slipped his hand into his pocket, but he already knew what he'd find there. Nothing.

"I can't believe you didn't want to come," Joe's mother said with mild indignation. Joe could smell the chocolate on her breath. She claimed to have low blood sugar and that made him laugh. She just liked chocolate. A lot.

"Got into the Whitman's Sampler again?" he asked, chiding her gently.

"Mom." Harriet put on her long-suffering voice. It fooled no one. "Why have you been eating chocolate? There are always hors d'oeuvres. You're acting like we haven't been to Susie's for Passover before."

His mother adjusted her best dress—a blue and gold brocade that Joe thought made her look like she was wearing a couch slipcover—and gave Harriet a stern look.

"It's different this time," she snapped. "There's a rabbi running the seder."

"Yeah," Harriet sighed. "It'll be longer."

Joe was as relaxed as he could be. He'd laid off the 'ludes and had only popped a few Mother's Little Helpers. He'd added half a black beauty and was now almost normal. Except somehow the word had gotten out that Skinny T was missing, and that made him want to blow through his prescriptions.

Two days before Passover, Susie had called.

"Mr. Skalko brought me into his office again," she said. Her voice was high and fluttery. "He was asking more questions about Skinny T. And I don't know what I'm going to do about the seder." Then she was crying. "What a stupid thing to think about now! But I haven't started the baking. Or any of the cooking. You said things should look normal. Thank goodness, your mother said she'd bring her brisket."

"You talked to my mother!"

"Joe, you said to keep things normal. Your mom called and asked what she could bring. The last time your family came, she brought brisket."

"My mother makes terrible brisket."

"I know, but what was I supposed to say?"

"Okay, so what can *I* do to help?" he asked. And then he smiled—there was something he did well.

"I can clean your house," he said. "No one will think it's too weird. And I can check to make sure everything is spotless—just to be sure. That's one less thing for you to worry about."

There was silence on the other end.

"Susie?" He heard her exhale and then snuffle.

"I will not ask you to clean my house, Joe. That would be . . . weird and awful. You've done so much . . . Too much already. . . . I can't even begin . . ."

"I know," he replied. "I'm offering. Let me help."

There was resignation in her voice when she replied. "Okay, Joe. Okay."

A cool, fresh breeze came in through the patio door. Joe had left it open while he cleaned for that very reason, but he didn't want the house chilly when Susie got home, so he shut it.

He'd just finished moving the furniture around Susie's small house. There was just enough room to set up the table and chairs she'd rented. He was rather pleased with the arrangement.

There was a *snick* in the front door lock and then he heard Susie let herself in. "Hey, honey," she said, using a singsong voice. "I'm hooooome."

"Ward," he replied, playing along. "I'm worried about the Beaver."

She stopped in the living room and admired what he'd done.

"I think it's that Eddie Haskell," he continued. "You should talk to him about spending too much time with Eddie."

She laughed, and his heart soared. "You've done wonders," she said with a smile. "Nice June Cleaver, too."

He shrugged. "It's what I do. I cleaned everything, moved your furniture around, and also, as you now know, I do an excellent Mrs. Cleaver."

"Okay, but where are your pearls and heels?" she asked as she dropped her purse on the table. "I can't believe you got everything set up perfectly."

She looked tired, and that worried him.

"Are you okay?" he asked, suspecting he already knew the answer.

"Sure, it's just—" She paused, and a guilty expression crossed her face. "Michael was a murderer. A horrible person. . . . But I killed him. *I'm* a killer."

"You're not a killer!" Before he could think about it, he grabbed her hands. "What you did, you did in self-defense. We have to hide it because he was one of Skalko's men. Skalko wouldn't care that it was in self-defense."

He dropped her hands, face reddening, embarrassed that he had grabbed them in the first place, and started putting the last of his cleaning materials into his caddy. It belonged to the casino—it even had Atomic Ace stamped on the side—but no one checked on that sort of thing.

"Joe, I haven't been able to sleep."

He wasn't surprised. Since working for Skalko, the only sleep he had gotten was under the influence. So he slid his hand into his pocket and pulled out his bottle of Valium.

"Try these," he said softly. "They work." *At least for a while.*

She looked at it as if he'd offered her a cockroach on toast. "I don't use," she said. "I mean, I don't disapprove—to each their own—but it's not for me."

"This isn't using. It's a prescription. Look, Dr. Henman prescribed them. You're just trying to get some sleep."

Gingerly, she took the bottle from his hand. There were five 10 mg tablets inside. He knew. He usually knew how many he had. It would wipe him out of his Valium prescription, but that wouldn't be a problem. He had refills. And there were always the 'ludes.

"Cut those in half," he said. "And if you feel like you need more than that, take the other half. Don't take more than one whole one at a time." He didn't want to tell her how many he took in a day.

He took the bottle from her, opened it, and snapped one of the pills in half. Then he held it out to her. Reluctantly, she took it from him. Then he went into her kitchen and returned with a glass of water. He watched until she'd taken it. Then gave her the bottle back.

"You know I don't think any less of you because of this," Susie said. She shook the bottle. His mouth watered. "Seriously now. We were friends before this . . . thing. You've done more for me than anyone in my life ever has—than anyone will ever do. I could never think of you as anything other than my closest friend. Not to mention your great *Leave It to Beaver* impression. I'm assuming there's more than one?"

"How are you, Mrs. Cleaver?" he asked in his best Eddie Haskell imitation. Then he straightened the already straight table and fiddled with one of the chairs. "I'd pretend to have buck teeth and a flat tail, but that's a little difficult to pull off."

"Should I be feeling anything?" she asked.

He smiled wanly. Amateurs. "No," he replied. "Not for a little while." He shoved his hands into his pockets and rocked back and forth for a moment. "Okay, well, I'll see you tomorrow."

And then he fled.

Susie opened the front door, beamed with neon brilliance, and said, "Mrs. Belenky! Harriet! Joe! It's so good to see you! Thank you for coming." It was a bit effusive. Joe thought she looked nervous and hoped it was just from getting ready for the seder.

"I thought I told you to call me Marian the last time we saw each other,"

Joe's mother said. She held out the pan of brisket. "Here you go! There's gravy, too. Harriet has that." Harriet held up the aluminum-foil-covered gravy boat.

"Yep," Harriet said with just a hint of resignation. "Lots of gravy. And it will be needed."

Joe's mother gave Harriet a stern look as Susie ushered them inside. Susie was glowing neon, and the three of them began looking more than a little moist.

Susie's living room was filled. Joe was surprised to see Lovey Dovey and a couple of other jokers. There was a pretty, dark-haired girl talking animatedly to Lovey Dovey. She had to be the setup. Even had he been interested, she was way out of his league.

"Harriet, Mrs. Bele—I mean, Marian, why don't you head on in? I think you know the rabbi and a couple of my friends from the last seder."

His mother beamed at Susie and said, "I do indeed! Thank you so much for inviting us." Happily, she headed for the rabbi.

Joe stepped closer to Susie. "I didn't know Lovey Dovey was going to be here. Is she . . . you know, Jewish?"

Susie shook her head. "No, but I like her. She was interested in what a seder was like. And she was one of the girls Skalko mentioned in his conversation with . . . you know who. I wanted to be certain she's okay. I was careful what I said to her."

Joe's stomach felt like he was on a roller coaster during a long downhill part. She shouldn't have told anyone anything.

Susie went into her tiny kitchen—which was crammed with plates, bowls, and pans—and slid the brisket into the already crowded oven.

"What have the two of you been whispering about?" Harriet asked handing the gravy boat to Susie. "Can I help? I mean with the canapés." She shot Joe a knowing look and then waggled her eyebrows at him. He gave her a please-don't-do-this-now look. She grinned at him.

"So," Harriet continued. "Who are you setting Joe up with this time?"

Susie glanced at Harriet, then grabbed a tray of chopped liver on matzoh topped with tiny pickles and held it out to her. "Would you pass this around? It's Connie. You should go interrogate her now, so Joe is as embarrassed as possible when he meets her. She's wearing a maxi-dress."

"Ooooo, is she very pretty?" Harriet asked conspiratorially. Joe was heartily sick of this conversation.

"She's very pretty. And a dancer."

Harriet grinned wickedly, then she saluted Susie. "Okay. Canapés and embarrassing anecdotes, ahoy." She sauntered out of the kitchen with a low chuckle.

"You should go out there and chat," Susie said as she started chopping walnuts to add to the charoset. She leaned close. "You have to at least pretend to be interested in Connie. It'll look . . . Oh, dammit!" She dropped the knife and grabbed her hand. "I just cut myself."

"Let me see," Joe said, taking her hand into his. Her hands had a fresh manicure. The red nails were filed into wicked-looking points. But the cut wasn't bad, and he held his hand on her wound and kept drying the blood until the flow stopped. But it didn't. Dust just kept running through his fingers. He tried to press down harder on her wound, but it just made things worse.

"Joe," she said. The anxiety in her voice had made it higher, almost squeaky. "Joe, what's happening?"

"I don't know," he replied. He yanked his hand away and the blood came out scarlet again and started to slow. "I've never had this happen before."

"Well, have you ever tried it on a person before?" she snapped. "You know, a living one?"

He shook his head. "No, no, never. Oh! Oh! Pop, I put my hand on his chest. It must have . . ." He looked at Susie and saw mirrored there his own horror.

"Joe, no," she said. "You can't think like that."

"He's the only other person I've touched like that. I fell on him. I touched his wound. I dusted his blood. Oh, God," he said, his stomach feeling as if it were plunging down, never to stop. But then the nausea hit and he felt acrid puke start to slide up his throat.

He turned to run to the bathroom, and found Harriet standing in the doorway. "This is an interesting development," Harriet said quietly. "You and Susie holding hands. And it also appears as if you can turn blood to dust."

"Uhm, no, you've misunderstood," Joe began. "You see . . ."

Harriet waved him off. "Nope. Saw what I saw. You have a wild card. Why didn't you tell me?"

"All I can do is turn bodily fluids into dust. Like, once they've been . . . er, expelled. It's gross." He hoped he could keep the vomit down and seem normal. "That's why I work as a janitor. It's the only thing I can do."

"All this stuff happening," Harriet continued. "You and Susie. You and Connie, maybe. Though why Susie would set you up is a whole other story. Your wild card, as gross as you say it is, is super interesting. Joe, you've been keeping secrets."

"It's getting to be sundown," the rabbi called from the living room. "We should get started soon. Is the seder plate ready?"

"Almost!" Susie called out. She spared a quick glance at Harriet, then took a taste of the charoset, added a few tablespoons more of chopped-up apple, and nodded as if pleased. Joe would have given anything if they could erase that night and she could look that way again. It had only been a week, but the time felt longer, stretched out to a breaking point. She put a scoop of the charoset on the plate with the maror, egg, roasted chicken neck, potato, and salt water. Then she handed it to Harriet.

Joe glared at Harriet. "This isn't the time to talk about it," he said. Joe the Janitor had taken his leave for a moment. "And don't tell Mom or anyone else."

"Are you kidding? I'd never tell Mom, and you shouldn't either. But I have a lot of questions. And you know I can keep a secret."

"Sure." There was a deeply annoyed tone in Joe's voice. Harriet gave him a smile, and it reminded him of when they were kids. But the memory was like a faded Polaroid. From before Pop and everything else that had happened.

Susie was pretending not to hear them, a ridiculous pretense in the tiny kitchen, and checked on what was in the oven.

"And don't think I'm done with you, either," Harriet said to her. Face flushed from the oven, Susie unfolded to her whole height and looked down at Harriet imperiously. This had no effect on Harriet.

"No, we're not done," Harriet said, looking at them with narrowed eyes. "Not by a long shot."

"It was Skalko on the phone."

Joe just nodded and started drying the salad plates. "What'd he want?"

"Joe, he pretended like he forgot I had the night off from the show. He knows all about the holidays. He takes care of our community. He's one of our Angels. Why would he be calling today? Unless . . ."

"He's only had a week to figure out what happened to Skinny T," Joe replied, trying to keep his voice calm. "If he asks you again, just keep to the story. He doesn't know anything."

She nodded. "I'm so scared."

"It'll be okay," he said, gently squeezing her wrist. "We'll figure something out."

When Joe wanted to think, he came down to the Strip in the morning and walked from the Flamingo down to Atomic Ace. At 8:30 A.M. it was empty, for the most part. Its neon signs were just a collection of colored tubes held in place by ugly brackets. A few hookers were out, and they looked tired. There was nothing glamorous about the Strip right then. Nothing to hide what was real.

Skalko was Old Vegas. The Vegas where Joe got stuck being a criminal and an addict. And Skalko ran his business old boss-style. Problems were taken care of by people like Skinny T and Joe. A lot of problems got buried in the desert.

Old Vegas didn't realize what was happening until it was too late. They should have realized when Circus Circus went up. The owner didn't care who was gambling or how elegant the place was. It wasn't even on the Strip.

Atomic Ace might have been one of the casinos with "classy" jokers, but at Circus Circus it was a freak show run by a mysterious backer rumored to be a wealthy joker. All anyone knew about him was that he wore a gold death's-head mask. And he was happy to have families. In fact, the casino catered to them.

Leave Junior with our babysitters and go hit the slots! There were peanut butter and jelly sandwiches for the kids on the buffet and special areas for families to eat. There were jokers peppered throughout the casino, but only the ones who didn't shock the trade. The really ugly ones worked in the kitchen.

After that, corporations started buying out the casinos. There were still a couple of holdouts like Skalko, but things had changed forever.

Joe was no closer to a solution than he'd been when he'd started his walk. For ten years he'd been complicit in covering up murders. In the pill fog, he'd pretended he wasn't a monster, divorced himself from the bodies and graves. He'd been cleaning for so long he hadn't realized it was part of him. Just like being a junkie.

He reached Atomic Ace and went in the employees' entrance, then changed into his uniform just like usual.

"Mr. Skalko wants to see you," Lovey Dovey said. "He's in his office."

Joe snapped off the vacuum. He'd been cleaning in the blackjack area. There was one player at the hundred-dollar table desperately trying to make up his losses.

"Know why he wants to see me?" he asked, trying to remain calm. It could be nothing. Maybe another job.

She stopped and shrugged. "I don't know, and I know better than to ask. And now I need to get this drink to the poor bastard at that table who's losing the family nest egg."

Joe's hands shook as he started winding the power cord to the vacuum. He tried to look as innocent as possible. After all, the eye in the sky and Skalko's aces were watching everything.

Skalko's secretary wasn't in the antechamber to Skalko's office, so Joe went and tentatively knocked on the office door. He wrapped his arms around his body to dry his sweat, then realized that might make him look guilty, so he let them hang limply by his sides. The only thing that gave him a ray of hope was that if it was really bad, one of Skalko's aces would have summoned him. At least, that was how Joe figured it. But he was pretty high and a lot of weird shit was making sense.

He heard Skalko's muffled voice telling him to enter. The doorknob was a little slippery in Joe's hand, despite him powdering his sweat just a moment before. He held his breath and stepped inside.

"You wanted me, Mr. Skalko?" Joe decided playing dumb junkie who was obsequious as fuck was the way to go. It wasn't a reach.

Skalko didn't look up from his papers, just waved his hand to the chairs in front of the desk. "Sit down."

Relief sweat started rolling down Joe's armpits. He sat, then jammed his hands under his pits to dry them. If Skalko wanted him dead, Joe knew he'd never see it coming. As Joe sat, there was another knock on the door.

"Come in," Skalko said sharply. Joe looked over his shoulder, and as he did he saw Susie stepping inside. And he knew that the look of horror on her face when she saw him was mirrored by his own.

"Susie," Skalko said quietly, looking up from his papers. "I believe you know Joe."

The same smile she used onstage crossed her face. "Of course I know Joe. I've been trying to set him up for years, haven't I, Joe?"

Joe turned back to Skalko. "Yes, sir," he said. The only thing missing was a salute. "Yes, sir. She's very bad at it."

Skalko chuckled and Joe exhaled with a little too much relief. Maybe this wasn't something bad. Maybe it wasn't about Skinny T after all. But Joe knew that was bullshit. There was no other reason for them to be in Skalko's office together.

"I think you both know why you're here," Skalko said with a friendly smile. "Please, Susie. Sit."

When she did, he could see her legs trembling. Joe was glad that he was just sweating; at least he could do something about that. "I'm very sorry, Mr. Skalko, but I really *don't* know why we're here," Susie said politely. She even sounded like she was puzzled. Joe had to admire her. She was going to brazen it out.

"You know," Skalko began, his voice still light, "I've figured out the who and when. Pretty sure I know the where. But the why, now that puzzles me. You want to tell me why you killed Skinny T, Susie? I know it wasn't Joe because if he was going to kill Skinny T, it would have been years ago."

Susie looked indignant. "Mr. Skalko! He was my boyfriend!"

Skalko shook his head and then cocked it to one side. "Well, I guess we'll have to talk about it at length," he replied. "Both of you, come with me."

Skalko led them out of the office. His secretary was still absent. There was no one to see them as they got into Skalko's private elevator and were whisked to the underground garage.

The garage stank of oil and car exhaust. A row of black Lincoln Continentals were parked across from the elevator. A single Cadillac was parked in the middle. Joe knew it belonged to Skalko. He only drove Caddies.

"Here," Skalko said as he tossed a set of car keys to Joe, who fumbled and dropped them. Skalko looked at Joe with disgust. "You're driving," he said coldly. Joe squatted and picked up the keys.

"Driving where?" Susie asked. She sounded baffled, as if everything happening was a mystery to her.

"Just get in the car, Susie," Skalko said as he opened the front passenger-side door. She put her hands on her hips, and as she did so she said, "Mr. Skalko, I don't know what you have in mind, but I'm not getting into that car."

"I'd be happy to put you in," Skalko said impatiently. "But you wouldn't like it. Now get in." Susie walked slowly toward Skalko. When she got close, he grabbed her by the arm, then pushed her into the car. She hit her head on the doorframe with a hard thud. Skalko thumbed the lock, then shut the door. Through the rear window Joe saw Susie holding her head.

"Now you," Skalko said. He pulled a revolver out of his pocket and gestured. Skalko waited for Joe to get behind the wheel. Then he got into the backseat. Inside it smelled like new leather.

Joe looked into the rearview mirror and met Skalko's eyes.

"She doesn't know anything, Mr. Skalko," Joe said quietly. "She doesn't need to be part of this. It's all on me."

"I'd like to believe you, Joe. I really would. But she's the last person to see him, and you're the one who came and told me he'd never shown up. Skinny T had many failings, but he was never late. Let's go."

The Caddy's ride was smooth on its cushy shocks. It didn't matter what the road was like, though most of them were in decent shape, it just floated along. And it handled great compared to the VW Bug Joe had—anything would—and then he realized it would likely be the last car he ever drove.

"Just keep going straight into the desert, Joe," Skalko said. "You know the way." In the rearview mirror, he saw Skalko lifting a bowling bag onto the backseat. A box labeled MR. SKALKO: SHIRTS was on the seat next to him.

"Here's an interesting fact that I imagine Joe knows, but you don't, Susie." Joe didn't like where this was going. He saw Susie stiffen and her right knee begin to jiggle. "The human head weighs about ten to eleven pounds."

Skalko unzipped the case. He reached in and took out something swathed in Saran Wrap, then held it over the front seat and let the plastic wrap unroll. Joe glanced down, but didn't need to look to see that it was Skinny T's head. He was still recognizable, though much the worse for wear. Joe wondered how the fuck Skalko had found it. The head dropped into Susie's lap. She stifled a scream.

"Do you miss him?" Skalko asked her. "I know you were together. Did he tell you about our plans? I'm guessing he did. And I bet you didn't want to go along with it. Nice Jewish girl like you."

Susie picked up the head with just the tips of her fingers and dropped it on the seat between her and Joe. Delicately, she wiped her fingertips on the skirt of her black rehearsal dress.

"Mr. Skalko, I don't know why we're here. And I certainly don't know why you just dropped someone's severed head on my lap," she began. Joe was astonished by her cool tone. "But I don't have anything to do with that head. And I'm certain that Joe doesn't either, no matter what he says. I don't know where Mike is, and I haven't seen him in over a week."

"Mike's staring at you, Susie," Skalko chortled. "And I'm impressed with how well you're keeping it together. Normally, I could use someone like you, Susie. Someone who can handle a situation, but the two of you killed Skinny T. And he was special to me. Weren't you, Skinny?" He reached over the seat and gave the head a pat on the cheek. "He was like a son to me. Also, you're a broad and you're more useful with your legs open. How'd you kill him?"

Joe wanted to hurl with fear for her and he gagged a little.

"What's that?" Skalko said, taking the head in his hands and facing it toward himself. "Joe has the pukes? After all this time, you'd think he would be used to it."

"What Mike? You miss her?" Skalko said, turning the head toward Susie. She stared straight ahead. They hit a pothole and Skalko tightened his grip on it. "I say she's an ungrateful bitch."

"Mr. Ska—" she began.

"Shut up," Skalko said almost cheerfully. "Shut up, or I'll blow your brains out all over my nice, new Caddy. And I don't want to do that.

"Bet you're wondering how I knew it was Joe here involved in all this." He cocked the head to one side. "Joe here, like the junkie he is, has a habit. Mike kept me informed where you liked to bury things. The whole fucking desert and you go the same places. Fucking junkies."

Joe glanced at Susie and she darted her eyes at him, too. A great act is a great act, but Susie had no more act in her. Joe could tell she was done and that her fear had taken over.

"It *could* have been someone from another gang," Skalko said, as if he were puzzled. "But I got no beef going on with anyone, right now. Killing Skinny T would just create a situation. So, what happened to him? Started backtracking and it all led to you, Susie. I just want to know why? You had to know this is where it would end." He leaned the head in close to her. "C'mon, why not tell me? You want to."

Susie shook her head, pursed her lips, and didn't answer.

"Susie, tsk . . . tsk . . . tsk." The cheerful voice was still there, but now it was laced with malice. It sounded like a precarious balance between the tenor of two friends chatting and one of them red-faced screaming at the other. Joe had never seen Skalko scream, or even heard of it happening, but he knew rage when he heard it.

"Pull over here," Skalko said. "Now!"

Joe yanked the wheel right and drove off into the sand. Scrubby plants scraped the bottom of the Caddy, and it slowed noticeably. "The car can't handle this," Joe choked out. "We're going to get stuck."

"We're not going far," Skalko replied. Joe glanced in the rearview again. Skalko met his eyes. Joe had known since they got into the private elevator that they were as good as dead.

Instead of running, or trying to do *anything*, Joe had just waited for the inevitable to happen. He hated the person he saw mirrored in Skalko's eyes.

The highway had vanished in the rearview mirror when Skalko told him to stop. The Caddy was clearly unhappy with the now sandy terrain.

"Get out," Skalko said, dropping Skinny T's head back into Susie's lap. "Bring him along."

As she slid out of the car, she took the edges of her skirt and cradled Skinny T's head. Joe got out, too. It was hot, but not unbearable. In Joe's experience, it was a pretty good time to get rid of bodies. Fairly late in the afternoon.

"Open the trunk," Skalko said to Joe, who obeyed. "Get out that shovel. You're going to dig. You know the routine, Joe."

"No sir, I don't. I only cut up people after they're dead. Not my usual."

"You're really going to have us dig our own graves?" Susie walked toward the back of the car. Skalko smiled at her. Joe noticed that she'd taken her shoes off.

Skalko laughed. "Give the girl a pony," he said. He waved the gun in their general direction. "Too bad this is it for you." He lowered the gun and shot Susie. Or at least he tried to. He missed her, and then she hurled Skinny T's head at him. It caught him off-guard and knocked his hand to one side. Another round fired.

"Joe," she cried. "Run!"

She started off, zigzagging as she went. She didn't get far. This time, Skalko didn't miss. There was a grunt and she dropped.

Joe hadn't followed her. He hadn't run away. He moved toward Skalko. "I wouldn't do that," Skalko said. Joe gave serious contemplation to just letting Skalko shoot him and making him dig their graves himself. But there was still a flicker of desire to live in him. He couldn't do anything about Susie, but he could do something for himself. "I still need you to dig that grave."

Joe backed away. He reached into the trunk for the shovel.

"Do that slowly," Skalko said, gesturing with the revolver. Joe obeyed. Doing what someone told him to do was a natural reflex for him. Joe the Cleaner was going to vanish forever. He'd certainly stepped out during all of this and he'd left Joe the Janitor behind.

"Just turn around. You're going to do what you do best, Joe." Joe heard the rattle of a tool bag and knew what Skalko was going to make him do. It would be as bad as Pop, maybe worse.

Joe dragged the shovel behind him, stopping when he got to Susie's body. Her shirt was bloody, but not as much as Joe expected. Skalko threw the bag of tools and it hit Joe in the back. He tripped over Susie's body, dropped to his knees, then he threw up. He puked until there was nothing left, then he dry-heaved. His throat and chest burned and ached.

"Are you done?" Skalko asked as Joe turned to face him. He stood next to Susie's head now. Joe was sure he saw her hand twitch.

"Why?" Joe asked. He was certain he'd imagined her hand move. "Why not have someone else just kill us?"

"Oh, Joe, you don't get it? This really *isn't* business. It really *is* personal. I wanted to do this myself. I didn't think it would be so easy to find Skinny T's body. Well, his head. With a whole desert out here. You go to the same places." Skalko waved the gun. "Jesus, you're an idiot." Skalko shook his head.

"The only thing I regret is missing her the first time. Throwing Mike's head at me, pretty smart, though. But I'm also out of practice. You gotta keep the skills up." He pointed the revolver at Joe's foot, then, at the last minute, moved it slightly to the right. He fired and Joe felt a harsh spray of sand on his feet and ankles. "See, that's better. I wasn't trying to hit you."

Of all the crazy shit Skalko had done that day, for some reason, this was the thing that pissed Joe off. He thought about rushing Skalko, but Skalko wiggled the gun at him and said, "I know what you're thinking, Joe. You're debating if you can get to the gun before I kill you. Probably not. We're at pretty close range."

Joe saw Susie slowly turn her head over. Now she was facing Skalko's shoes. She dragged her hand up her side, and then quickly slid it under the hem of his pants and raked her long, knife-edge nails down his shin.

"You bitch!" Skalko shouted, pointing his gun at her. But Joe was already lunging for him. A bullet clipped Joe's shoulder and, as he started to fall, he grabbed Skalko's hand. Another bullet went off, powdering sand up between them.

"You fucking idiot!" Skalko shrieked, and slammed his gun into Joe's face. Joe saw nothing but red for a moment.

"You're out of bullets," he giggled.

"I don't need a gun to kill you," Skalko said, tossing it aside.

"Joe, his ankle," Susie whispered. He could see her trying to push herself up to her knees. She was oozing blood, but nothing terrifying. Joe was glad Skalko had depended on Skinny T for this sort of thing. He'd hit her in the side, through the fleshy part. He really was a lousy shot.

"Goddammit, Joe," she gasped. "His fucking ankle."

It took a moment for him to understand what she was saying, then he dropped to his knees and grabbed Skalko's shin where Susie had gouged him. She'd clawed him good and deep, and blood was starting to flow. Joe squeezed with all his might. Dust began flowing through his fingers.

Skalko looked baffled, then amused. "You really are pathetic, Joe. What are you going to do? Make sure my loafers don't get stained? Now let go of me." He shook his leg, and Joe squeezed even tighter. Susie struggled to her feet.

"And what do you think you're doing?" Skalko asked her, laughing. "You'll bleed out slowly. And you know, I like that idea. But I really wanted him to chop you up like he did with his father. But, so it goes."

The dust was running fast through Joe's fingers now. Susie staggered at Skalko, who just laughed.

"Seriously, wha—"

She tripped over Joe and fell into Skalko. He caught her, then quickly tried to drop her, but she'd wrapped her arms around him. Together they went to the sand.

Joe was yanked hard and almost lost his grip, but he held tight. He hoped Skalko was distracted enough that Joe would have enough time . . .

Susie screamed as Skalko jabbed her wound, but she held on fast to him. Finally, he bucked her off and she rolled, curling into a ball, holding her side.

The dust was still running through Joe's fingers. A breeze kicked up and blew the dust away. Skalko sat up and tried again to get his ankle away from Joe.

"What are you up to there, Joe?" he asked. His voice was a little wobbly, as if he'd had a couple of drinks. "There's no reason to dust anything now. It's over."

Joe looked up at Skalko and gave him a bloody-toothed smile. "It's a surprise."

Skalko's eyes grew wide as he realized what was happening. "You little prick," he said as he passed out. Joe held on until nothing ran through his fingers.

Joe got to his feet and staggered to Susie. There was a moment when he was afraid she really *had* died, but then she looked up at him, glassy-eyed.

"Can you make it to the car?" Joe asked. He wasn't sure he could carry her.

She nodded. "Think so," she said wearily. "If you help. So, I guess he's dead. What are we going to do?"

"Well, we're not dead, yet. We both need a doctor and I bet Dr. Henman will help. And Harriet, she'll definitely help us out. There's a gas station up the road. I can call them from there."

As Susie rolled onto her hands and knees, some blood dripped onto the sand. It was dark and Joe had a moment when he wanted to dust it, but realized that was habit. They held each other and stumbled to the car. Joe eased Susie into the passenger side. He got his stash bottle out and offered her a Percocet. She took it, and then dry-swallowed it. He shook another out, then did the same.

There was a gas can in the trunk and he used it to drench Skalko's body. He lit it. The flames licked up blue and red. He was free from Skinny T and Skalko, but he still felt dead inside. He turned and walked back to the car.

They were silent as the road slipped by. The sky was fading to indigo. Susie leaned forward and turned on the radio. David Cassidy was singing "I Think I Love You" through the static crackle. Joe reached over and snapped it off.

"When we get through this . . ." he began.

"If," she said dreamily. The Percocet had kicked in. "If."

"*When*," he continued. "Where do you want to go? We can't stay in Vegas. At least not now."

He glanced over and she gave him a blitzed smile. "East. I'd go east. Back home," she replied. "I just want to go home now."

A mile sped by, and then he said, "I think I'll go west. West to Los Angeles."

He looked at her, and saw she'd passed out. His heart ached and his dreams were dying hard. There was nothing between them now except blood, death, and dust.

Skalko's car was found the next afternoon. There was some shock; no one knew who he had pissed off enough to get whacked.

Atomic Ace was suddenly in play, but it didn't really matter to Joe or Susie. Harriet and Dr. Henman *had* saved them. Harriet by coming to get them on the highway. And the doctor had been only too happy to help patch them up after Joe explained what had happened.

Joe left for L.A. a few days later. It was a bitch packing his VW Bug with his shoulder stitched up, but the doctor had told him he was lucky. Both of them had been. He didn't feel lucky.

He went by his mother's house to say goodbye to her and Harriet. It was predictably tearful. Now that he knew where he was going, he wanted to be gone. He had bottles of pills that Dr. Henman had provided and the road to L.A. was straight through the desert. That drive wouldn't bother him. He knew the desert well.

One clear day, a few years later, news got back to him via Harriet that Susie had moved to New York with Lovey Dovey. Eventually, she'd married a Broadway producer and had had a kid. When Joe heard that, he popped a 'lude and went back to vacuuming the floor at Hyatt House.

Age of Wonders

NINE

March 2006

JOE BELENKY HAD DIED of a drug overdose in Los Angeles in 1995. He had been positive for the wild card, but there were no definitive records of how his card had expressed, or if any wild card powers had been involved with Skalko's death. But he *had* been the last person to see Skalko alive, by all reports. He, Skalko, and Susie Barber had all been seen leaving the casino together on the day of his disappearance. The police hadn't investigated too much. He'd been a gangster, finally pissed off the wrong person, and that was that. A lowly janitor and showgirl couldn't possibly have anything to do with it. Could they?

Shortly after Skalko's death, Susie Barber had fled to New York. And if that didn't look suspicious . . . She was still here. Raleigh tracked her down through a back channel, looking at tax records for the area. She had a phone number, an address. She could show up at the woman's front door and ask about Skalko and all the dirt she had on him.

It was history, she kept telling herself. It didn't matter. Raleigh wouldn't be bringing up bad memories, and she certainly wouldn't be putting Susie Barber in danger. Except she didn't know that for certain.

In the end, she couldn't write the story. On the one hand, it sounded like a triumphant against-all-odds—cute Vegas reference there—story of underdogs sticking it to the evil crime lord. Skalko didn't seem to have any relatives or henchmen or anyone left who would want revenge. Then again, he might. Or someone else might decide to harass them for no reason in particular. Putting herself in danger was one thing. Putting someone else?

At long last, she decided this wasn't her story to tell.

Not right now, anyway. She put her remaining notes back in the file, the file back in the box, and the box back in the dark, dusty corner of the archives.

People kept secrets for good reasons. Because the world might blow up if the secrets got out. Because they were protecting themselves or others.

Because they were afraid.

She kept telling herself she was too young to be burned out, but she went into the archives now and instead of seeing possibilities, she saw a big pile of dusty paper that maybe ought to be left to rot. She had her career—more than a foot in the door, she was making a name for herself. Did it matter?

So many people, so many lives, filed away in these boxes. She'd pulled a chair into the archives room and flipped through folders, waiting for a fresh story to jump out at her. But it had gotten to a point where they all seemed the same. Sex, drugs, violence, secrets. She'd gotten a long way from Carlotta DeSoto and didn't know how to get back there.

"Knock knock." Digger Downs stood at the doorway.

"Who's there?" she answered tiredly.

"You know what? I'm sorry, I thought I had a good knock-knock joke but I guess I don't. I didn't even laugh at those when I was a kid."

She leaned back and looked up at him. The middle-aged man was leaning against the door frame, arms crossed, studying her. How had he gotten through all these years without burning out? "What do you want, Downs?"

"Just wanted to tell you in person, I'm taking a leave of absence from the magazine."

That got her to sit up. "But . . . you've been here for decades. Why?"

"Trying something a little different. It's very hush hush, but if it works out you'll be hearing about it, trust me." He had a suspicious gleam in his eye, and Raleigh wanted to put her hands around his obnoxious little throat.

"What is it?"

"Not gonna tell."

"Fine, don't." She slumped back down to the box at her feet, and stared at files without really seeing them.

"Wow, gave up quick there." She didn't answer and hoped he'd go away. But he didn't. "Margot says you're late on your next feature."

"Ran out of steam, I guess."

"You've gotten too close to this," he said, gesturing to the room, the boxes. "You started taking it personally."

"Why the hell would I take any of this personally?" she said, laughing a little. The minute she used these files to look for her father, it got personal.

"You tell me."

She looked at him. "If it's because my mom is an ace—"

"She's technically a deuce, but that's only part of it. Isn't it?" He let the question hang.

"I don't know what—"

"Here's *my* secret. I'm an ace. I can smell people with the wild card. They smell different to me. Sweeter, like some weird perfume. It's hard to explain. You know how many secret aces I've uncovered in my time? Why do you think I started these files? So I'm asking you now, flat out: what are you hiding? Is it telepathy? You have some kind of secret charm field like the Envoy? What's your power?"

"I'm not anything, I don't have powers—"

"Then you're a joker? You have a mouth where your navel's supposed to be? Out with it, kid. I can smell it on you."

She very much wanted to scream. Hit something. *How dare he, this nosy, creepy busybody* . . . "I'm latent," she said. "I don't have anything except bad odds."

He hesitated, then said, "I'm sorry."

"Yeah, everybody is. Doesn't do me any good, does it?"

"I don't know," he said. "You ever tried?"

"Can you leave me alone, please?" she muttered.

"Okay, I confess, I'm disappointed, I had sort of hoped I could uncover at least one more secret ace before I waltz out of here. But this will do. So I'm telling you—you're latent. Use that. You're writing all these stories, digging into these secrets, telling stories about actual people and not sensationalist wild cards fireworks. And this whole time you've had your feet on both sides. You've got credibility."

"I don't—"

"Yeah, you do. Think about it. But you know, if you don't go there—your secret is safe with me. I trust you to return the favor. See you around."

He gave a mock salute and walked out of the room. And she thought about it, until Eddie came back to see if she was okay. She realized she needed coffee, and she was just about to do something she hated: admit that Digger Downs was right.

Raleigh went to the blog, to write it all down before she could chicken out. The only person she ran the post by was Margot Dempsey, who studied her for a moment. Her boss didn't get that hangdog look of pity on her face. Just nodded and said, "Run with it." So Raleigh did.

I want to talk about the fifth card in this game.

In Texas Hold'em, the dealer places five community cards in the middle of the table. The first three, the flop, land faceup, and the players who haven't folded right at the start use them, along with their two personal cards, to build a hand. They bet on what the last two cards, still facedown, might be. The fourth card, the turn, and the fifth, the river. Ace, joker, black queen. Those are the three cards everyone talks about when they talk about the virus. The ones that are always faceup. In some rounds of Hold'em, those last two cards might never get turned over, if one player is able to drive the others to fold with their betting and their bluffing.

A lot about the wild card virus and its consequences stays hidden. We stare at the backs of the cards and wonder what might happen if we turned them over.

Deuces, like the runner-up at the beauty pageant no one ever remembers. And latents, waiting for the card to turn. To see if we win or go bust.

I've been waiting my whole life to see if I win or go bust. I'm latent, right there on the river, watching life go past me and trying to figure out where I'm going to land. I've been looking for answers in the whole sordid sensational history of the wild card world. I keep thinking I find them—that everyone has secrets, that secrets blow up, that we all have regrets. And then I'm not so sure it means anything at all.

When people find out about me, they usually look at me like I'm about to keel over right there. And somehow I just keep going. I think a lot about the first time I interviewed the great Peregrine and she told me something that sounded wise and marvelous and almost too simple to share: We're all just getting by. And, we have to use what we've got.

It has been suggested by the peanut gallery here at the office that my status has given me insight. I'm not sure about that. But I'm writing this in the hopes that it might give you insight. Now that you know where I'm coming from, maybe my stories will mean a little more.

Meanwhile, I'm just going to keep putting my chips on the table, and keep playing this game as long as I can.

Her email inbox blew up the same day. She tried her best to go through it, but ended up skimming and putting off the rest to deal with later. Most of the messages were positive, thanking her for her confession. Many of those were from people who said they were latents—how glad they were to know they weren't alone. A few from crackpots describing to her how she was destined to die in agony, as all those inflicted with the virus were.

One of the names jumped out. It sounded familiar, but she couldn't remember from where. "Eddie, remind me, who is Gary Bushorn?" she called across the room.

"He's the charter pilot who got Gregg Hartmann out of the country in '94. He was supposed to be up on criminal charges but the island in BFE Ireland he ended up at refused the extradition order."

She remembered now. The sensationalist footnote to Senator Hartmann's fall had only taken up a few minutes or so of the news cycle at the time, and the man had dropped out of sight. "Any reason the guy would be sending me email?"

That earned a pause in the office, as Eddie and a couple of the other staff writers looked over. "What's he want?"

She opened the email and read to herself.

"I just wanted to tell you how much I appreciated what you wrote about being a latent. I know what that is like. Not myself, but someone very close to me. And you're right, these stories aren't as flashy and are maybe a side of the wild card most of us don't want to think about. But for those of us in the middle of it . . . it will never get easier. Anyway, thank you for putting some of that into words and sharing something so personal."

Eddie prompted, "Raleigh, geez, what'd he say, you look like you're about to pounce."

"It's fan mail," she said, a little breathlessly. "And maybe a story. Hold on." She immediately wrote back. "Would you be willing to talk to me?"

Bushorn wouldn't leave Rathlin Island, and Raleigh didn't want to do this over the phone. These days she had enough standing at the magazine to ask for a trip, and wonder of wonders Dempsey gave it to her. She went to Ireland.

The ferry from Ballycastle to Rathlin eased up to the dock. The sky overhead was roiling, storm clouds churning, shades of gray tumbling over each other, promising rain and reneging on that promise when a flash of sun came through. The wind smelled of salt and stone, and the waves chipped at the island's rocky shore. Part of the island had been set aside as a bird sanctuary. Thousands of graceful slim-winged seabirds nested on the bare rock of vertical cliffs, perched in cracks and crevices in the unshaken faith that their eggs and chicks would stay safe. Their only predators out there, hundreds of feet over the water, were each other.

The tall black man waiting at the end of the dock, in shirtsleeves and sweating despite the brisk wind, had to be Gary Bushorn. She approached, smiling a greeting.

"You're Raleigh Jackson," he said.

"I must stand out in a crowd."

"Not a lot of black folk in this part of the world," he said, chuckling.

Rathlin Island was four by two and a half miles of windswept land off the northeast coast of Ireland, indistinguishable from other islands except for how it had intersected with history. In the 1950s the British government had instituted a policy of isolating victims of the wild card virus. At least, the ones who weren't immediately useful. The quarantine hadn't held long, but for a time, the island had been something of a leper colony. A Jokertown, but instead of growing organically, it had been propped up. Not many of the original exiles remained, but over the years a handful of others arrived, wanting the privacy the island afforded. The safety of the tight-knit community that still held on here.

"Let me show you around," Gary said, and brought her to an aging Fiat parked past the docks area.

The population of the island fluctuated between one and two hundred, he explained. Tourism was becoming a thing, though. The islanders weren't quite so suspicious of outsiders as they used to be. A couple of B and Bs had opened, and birdwatching tours were on offer. Gary made some cash as a taxi driver and tour guide. For all that he had only arrived here a decade ago, he'd made the place home.

"Anything specific you want to know?" he asked, as he eased onto a dirt road. A small cottage, whitewashed with a thatched roof that looked like it should exist in a different century, came into view.

"I'm not sure," she said, hesitating. "I'm writing a book. That is, I'm thinking of writing a book. I've just found so many stories and so many people
who've just been living their lives with all these obstacles and no one knows
anything about it, and maybe they should. I don't know. It might not work."

"Or maybe it will," he said.

He parked the car, and she climbed out. An instant peace settled over
her. The grassy hill sloping down toward wave-wracked cliffs. The distant
calls of seabirds, the salty wind. The rich smell of a peat fire. Time seemed to
slow. Gary, wearing a contented smile, watched her taking it all in.

"This place means a lot to you," Raleigh said. "Can you tell me about it?"

"Yeah, I think I can," he said softly. "Come on, let me show you the
cottage."

Promises

by Stephen Leigh

THE SQUALL ROARED AND threw horizontal rain, coming in from the northeast off the North Channel and the Waters of Moyle. The storm had developed unexpectedly an hour ago. The fierce wind rattled the shutters, howled through the cracks in the stone walls and stretched wispy, persistent fingers down the chimney. Rain hissed and beat on the stones, and streams of cold water fell from the ends of the roof's thatching.

"Shit!" Caitlyn cursed as a gust blew out the match she'd placed to the newspaper under the peat in the hearth. There were only two matches left in the pack, and she'd been trying to get the damned fire going for the last fifteen minutes, since they'd gotten back from Church Bay.

"Mathair?" Moira, Caitlyn's daughter, shivered in the chair, her knees up to her chest and a woolen blanket wrapped around herself. They'd both been soaked just running the dozen steps from the car to the cottage. The storm had blown down the lines somewhere on the island, which made the electric heaters useless, and the small, three room house had seemed as icy and damp as the sleet outside. Moira's face was illuminated in the orange-gold light of the oil lamps, her round features emerging from darkness like a Vermeer painting. "I'm awful cold."

"I know, darling. It's just that the peat's gotten soaked, and this damned wind . . ." Caitlyn struck another match. Her movements were clumsy and stiff, but she managed to light a corner of the paper. The crumpled sheet blackened and curled, the flame leaping blue and yellow as it crackled, but the flame hissed wetly and guttered out once it reached the sod, and Caitlyn cursed again. The shutters banged in a renewed gust, and a rivulet of water trickled down the inside of the chimney.

The noise of the storm lifted to a wild roar: the door to the cottage opened. A man's form filled the doorway. Moira screamed at the dark apparition, like a banshee in the midst of a tempest, startling enough that Caitlyn wouldn't have been surprised to hear a keening death-wail. Caitlyn rose—slowly, the only way she could move—to Moira's side. She patted her daughter's shoulder with an unbending hand. "Hush," she told her, though her eyes were on the stranger. "There's nothing to be frightened about."

"Where the hell am I?" he asked.

"You don't know?" Green shook his head slowly. Caitlyn waited to see if he would say more; he didn't. "You're on Rathlin Island," she told him finally, "just off the coast of Northern Ireland. And I'm curious how 'tis that you came to be on Rathlin, seeing as you don't know where you are. I take it you didn't come over on the ferry. You don't know about Rathlin, do you?"

She saw his hesitation again. "No, I don't. I . . . I was on a ship, a pleasure craft, just me and a few friends I was visiting, coming out from Scotland. The storm . . . I guess it was too much for the boat . . ."

"And your friends? What happened to them?"

"Gone," Green answered. "Lost."

Caitlyn gave him slow nod. "I have soup on. You look strong enough to dress yourself. There's a chamberpot under the bed if you would be needing it, or you can use the bathroom just off the kitchen. I'll let you get yourself ready while I put the bowls on the table. You can come on in and eat with the two of us, or I can bring it in here."

"I'll be out," he said. "Just give me a few moments."

Another nod. Caitlyn left the bedroom, feeling his gaze on her as she walked out with the stiff-legged gait of a marionette.

The man emerged from the bedroom by the time Caitlyn, with Moira's help, got the soup to the trestle table. He sat, wearily, and she ladled out a bowl for him, passing it across. She could feel the heat radiating from him. "Would you be wanting some milk with that, Gary?" she asked.

"Sure. Sounds good. I—" He stopped. At the end of the table, Moira giggled.

"'Tis Gary, not John, isn't it?" Caitlyn asked.

Muscles clenching in his jaw, he nodded. The spoon in his hand reddened like the glowing filament on an electric stove. "You knew all along?"

"The radio," she told him. "I was listening to the BBC. There was a news reports about a plane fleeing from the authorities in the States that had come over Ireland and gone down not a dozen miles out from here. The man said the passengers might have parachuted out of the plane, and were dangerous folk: a man who claimed to be former U.S. Senator Gregg Hartmann, who looked like a great yellow caterpillar, and a nat woman with blond hair named Hannah Davis. The pilot, they said, was a black man." Caitlyn paused. "They gave his name, too, and you don't look to be a yellow caterpillar or a woman." She glanced at the bowl in front of him. "I'd tell you your soup's getting cold, but I doubt that's a problem for you."

"What are you going to do now?"

Caitlyn would have shrugged, but it wasn't something her body could do. "I'm going to eat my soup, and make certain my daughter eats hers. Then I'm going to wash the dishes."

"That's not what I meant."

She hoped she was right.

He hadn't moved. He swayed from side to side, as if it were only an effort of will that kept him standing. With just under two hundred people on the island, Caitlyn knew them all by face and name, and this man was a stranger: tall, with skin the color of dark chocolate. He wore a leather jacket and there were straps and harness about him that looked as if he'd cut something from around him with a knife. He was drenched, the short, wiry black hair beaded with the rain; he steamed, wisps of vapor rising from him. She supposed he might have come over on the Calmac Ferry, maybe one of the rare visitors that came over from Belfast or Dublin to see one of the island's archeological sites and who had been surprised by the storm. Strange, though, that no one down in Church Bay had mentioned a visitor.

"I saw you through the window," he said, and the accent was decidedly American. His eyes closed, then he opened them again with an effort. "I can help . . ." He took a step into the room, almost falling, then another and another, walking past them toward the fireplace as Caitlyn hugged Moira to her, watching and wondering what she would do. *I haven't checked the phones; they may be down too, and besides it would take Constable MacEnnis forever to get here in this weather . . .*

The stranger crouched in front of the fireplace. He reached out a hand toward the small stack of peat. Caitlyn cried out with mingled wonder and fear.

Flame surged around his fingers, the peat hissing in the blazing heat of it and finally catching fire. He left his hand there, in the dancing blue flames, and Caitlyn saw the flesh blistering and charred to gray-white.

He collapsed.

Caitlyn saw his eyelids flutter. She waited, and when the man's gaze found her, she brought the glass of water to his cracked, dry lips. He drank gratefully, muscles moving in his long throat. "Better?" Caitlyn asked. He nodded. "What's your name?" she asked then.

He hesitated, and she saw his eyes narrow. "John," he said. "John Green." His head lifted up, looking around the small room. His hand brushed the bed underneath him with a metallic rattle.

"Sheet metal," Caitlyn told. "I doubt it's very comfortable for you, but you scorched my best sheets, and I was afraid you'd actually set the bedding on fire, as impossible as that seems. But maybe not for you, eh?" She kept her voice carefully neutral. "When I first felt your skin, I thought you were burning up with the worst fever I'd ever seen. You were sweating terribly. I was sure you'd die. But then I saw your hand healing as I watched, and your breathing was quiet. You slept easily, yet the fever never left you. And you're still sweating, though there's a chill in the air. So you're an ace, are you, John Green?"

"I'm nothing like an ace. That's for damn sure." The man gave a hoarse

chuckle, grimacing as he pushed himself up. The blanket—actually an old horse blanket Caitlyn kept in the car; she wasn't about to risk her good comforter on the man—fell around his waist. He seemed to realize for the first time that he was naked under the blanket, and he pulled the edge of it back up around himself. "My clothes?"

"Washed and ready for you." She cocked her head at him with a faint smile. "Soaked through and muddy, they were. You didn't want me to leave them on, did you?" He was staring at her, and she knew what he saw. The face that looked back at her every morning from the mirror was striking: flawless milky skin under curls of bright red hair, wide and round eyes that were the green of rich summer grass, full lips that seemed to easily smile. *"You're a rare beauty, Caitlyn Farrell, that you are,"* her father had told her, years ago, and she'd blushed at the words even as she'd hoped desperately that they were true. *"The image of your mathair, when she was young . . ."* Her father had died during the '62 Infection, or at least that's what they'd been told—one of the thousands who had drawn the black queen. He'd been at work and neither he nor his body had ever returned home. And her mother . . . she'd been with her mother the night the virus spread over Belfast, and she'd watched in terror as the virus tore her mother's body apart, as the woman screamed in terror and pain. Her mother had always loved knitting and sewing; the virus had drawn needle-sharp spines from her bones, lancing through her flesh at all angles, tearing and ripping, leaving her snared everywhere in a nest of hundreds of ivory porcupine quills that stabbed at her own flesh and that of those who would try to care for her. For twenty more agonizing years, she would live that way.*

Caitlyn had first thought that the virus had somehow left her unaffected. She'd been wrong . . .

"Mathair!" Moira called from the other room, and she heard her daughter's running footsteps. "Is the burning man awake yet?"

Caitlyn rose from her chair as her daughter burst into the bedroom. She could feel his gaze on her: the way her head would not turn without the entire body moving with it, the creaking protest of her knees, the slow-motion change of the expression in that perfect face, the awkward way she hugged her daughter, bending from the waist with her back impossibly straight: a doll with frozen joints. "You can see him in a little bit. Go on with you, now." Moira stared at the man in the bed for a moment, then laughed and ran from the room.

"She's cute. Looks like you. Your sister?"

Caitlyn turned—slowly, carefully, her whole body making the motion—to find Green regarding her curiously. "Her mathair. Mother."

She saw him blink in genuine astonishment. "I'm not just saying this, but you sure don't look old enough to have a child that age. What is she? Nine? Ten?"

"Ten in another month." She couldn't keep the sadness from coloring her voice. Whatever the man might be thinking, looking at her, he kept it to himself.

"I know. But that's all that's going to happen." She paused. "You're not a danger to me or my daughter, Gary. I can see that, just looking at you. And you *are* on Rathlin."

"You don't know me."

"I know enough." A faint smile touched the corners of her lips and vanished. "Eat your soup," she said.

"You really should," Moira interjected, her voice serious and earnest as only a child's can be. "Mathair makes *very* good soup."

The man nodded.

"You're sweating," Moira told him.

He touched his sleeve to his forehead. "It's a bit warm in here for me," he said. The spoon sizzled as it touched the broth.

After lunch, Caitlyn went outside and stood in the sunlight, her eyes half-closed. She could hear the sea pounding relentlessly against the cliffs; to the northwest where the ruins of Robert the Bruce's Castle were hung in moss and vines. Gulls swung overheard in the rare blue sky, calling in harsh voices. A few minutes later, she heard the door to the cottage open and shut again, and footsteps crunching over the gravel walk. "What did you mean, that I was on Rathlin?"

Caitlyn swiveled her entire body to turn to him. "You don't know about Rathlin? The Belfast Infection of '62?"

He lifted his shoulders. "I heard something about Belfast, I think. Not a lot."

Caitlyn nodded. "I suppose it wasn't much compared to what happened in New York the first time. Still, the outbreak was a nasty one. No one knows where it started or why, only that most of Belfast was affected. Five thousand or more people drew the black queen and died in the first day; people fled the city in droves during the panic. Afterward, the government decided that they if they wanted to bring the people back to the city, they had to show Belfast was clean and safe. They didn't want the jokers staying around to create yet another Jokertown—that wouldn't look good.

"One of the politicians got the bright idea that maybe they should just move the jokers out. Relocate the resulting Jokertown to an island. And, oh yes, make sure that they were sterile and couldn't produce more monsters. So they moved the hundred or so inhabitants who once lived here on Rathlin and brought in the jokers, and of course the relocation and sterilizations were all 'voluntary' . . ."

Caitlyn tried to give her smile a sardonic twist. "They brought maybe three or four hundred of us in before they were stopped—too many protests from the United Nations, Jokers Amnesty International, the JJS, and nearly every human rights organization. But they also didn't move us back. To make it look better, they gave us some limited self-government." She laughed, a sound with an edge of bitterness. "You Yanks did the same thing with your Native Americans, putting them on reservations. Officially, we're part of the UK. Unofficially, they leave us alone and try to forget us. Eventually, Belfast got its Jokertown anyway. Most of us already here on Rathlin—the Relocated—stayed. Why not? This is our island now. There are less than two hundred of us left; we've gained a few people over the years who came here, but we've lost far more." She paused. "Not many left. Most just died."

"You must have come here later."

She shook her head. "I was with the initial group. I was sixteen, then."

The man was staring at her, and she could see him doing the calculations behind his eyes. "Thirty-three years ago . . . You can't possibly be forty-nine."

"Touch me," she said to him. When his eyes widened, she laughed. "Go on: my face, or my arms."

His hand reached out to her cheek. She nearly flinched, expecting his skin to be hot, but it felt nearly cool. He stroked her cheek, pressing once. She knew what he saw, what he felt: a slickness like hard rubber that would not easily yield to the press of his fingertip. Like touching a doll's face.

The touch, though, was nice, and his hands were gentle and his chocolate eyes sad, and the baritone of his voice was rich and deep like a cello. *Almost ten years, it's been. An entire decade since you've been held and kissed and loved . . .* She tore the thought away as Gary's fingers dropped from her face. *You can't think that way. You can't.*

"That's what the virus did to me. It left me a permanent sixteen. I suppose I'll always look this way. My body's slowly hardening, calcifying. I came here because my mother was one of the Relocated; they knew I might have been infected, but no one was quite sure at first. I know now—and I don't need the blood test to tell me. It's moving through the rest of me now, faster and faster. I can't turn my neck, can't bend over easily, can't bend my knees or my elbows all the way. And it's spreading inside, or so the doctors tell me. Sometime soon . . ." She continued to smile; she had no choice. But twin tears trickled down the ceramic gloss of her cheeks.

"I'm sorry," he told her. It was the same thing *he* had told her, the man who'd been Moira's father.

"Don't be sorry for me," she said. "Be sorry for *her*."

The man glanced back at the cottage. His gaze moved across drystone walls, erected over a century ago. Stones that would still be there long after she was gone. "Your daughter carries the virus too." There was no question in his voice. Caitlyn nodded in reply.

"Aye. She does. When they came out with the blood test, I had her checked."

"You said they sterilized the Relocated . . ."

"They did. Maybe they botched my surgery. Maybe my tubes grew back. Maybe the virus wouldn't allow it. Who knows? Maybe I should never have left the island." She took a deep breath, feeling the pain in her chest as muscles resisted expanding. "And maybe I should never have come back here after I did." Caitlyn lifted her arm and daubed at the tears with the sleeve of her cotton sweater. Her arm moved like a clumsy stick. "Have you ever done something you felt was right, but you knew at the same time was incredibly stupid, something you knew would end up possibly hurting you more than you could bear?"

"Yeah," Gary answered, his voice no more than a whisper. "I know that feeling real well. Real fucking well."

Inside the cottage, Moira turned on one of the cassette tapes Caitlyn had bought her at the store in Churchill Bay. Her high, little-girl voice sang along with a bright, cheery children's tunc. "She carries the virus, aye," Caitlyn said, smiling at the sound. "It's in her blood, from me and from her father who had a minor ace, and if she's like almost all who carry it as a latent, it will manifest itself when she hits puberty. When that time comes, I have a 99% chance of watching her either die in agony or becoming horribly disfigured for the rest of her life." She turned back to Gary, feeling her face still trapped in the eerie smile. "I could have had an abortion. But I was scared, and I was still in love, and I was stupid. I *should* have had an abortion. Instead, I listened to him, the father who said he'd love me forever and who told me that after all the chance that the virus would get passed on to her was just one in four and that I should have the baby. I promised him I would. I kept my promise. And I found out that for him 'forever' was only until he fell in lust with some nat woman he met in the pub. By then I was so big with Moira that it was too late to do anything but carry her to term. Now I have to look at her every day and know that I'll lose her soon . . . or worse. I have to look at the eyes of the people here on Rathlin with me, who stare at me and wonder what kind of monster would condemn her child to that."

Caitlyn took a deep, sobbing breath. "That's something I wonder myself, every day."

Someone was pounding on the door. "Caitlyn!" a man's voice called. "Are ye in there?"

"I'm here, Duncan," Caitlyn called back. She saw Moira sitting up in her bed alongside. The clock on the nightstand said 7:00 AM and the sun was barely up. "Go on, girl, and let Constable MacEnnis in. Start the coffeemaker going. I'll be right there."

"What about the black man, mama?" she asked, a bit wide-eyed.

"He'll have heard Constable MacEnnis, I'm sure. *If* he's still here . . ."

Moira jumped from the bed and padded away. It took Caitlyn several seconds to roll stiffly from the bed and get to her feet. Pulling her nightgown close around her, she walked lock-jointed into the front room. The couch where the stranger had lain the night before was empty, the blanket on the floor. Moira was at the door, holding it open just a crack. "Constable MacEnnis says for you to come outside, mam," Moira said, with a tone of awe in her voice. "There's another man with him."

"I'm coming, Duncan," Caitlyn called. She patted Moira on the head as she reached her. "Why don't you stay here, darling? Get yourself some cereal . . ."

The sunrise had left a damp and heavy morning fog in its wake. Two figures stood in the mist. Duncan MacEnnis was, like all the residents of Rathlin except Moira, a joker. Caitlyn knew his story—everyone on Rathlin knew everyone else's story. MacEnnis had been a constable with the *garda*, the police force in Belfast. He'd been called to investigate the report of a man acting strangely in an alley between dreary brownstones. As MacEnnis approached the suspect, who was gibbering madly and pounding at the brick wall of the nearest house as if he could smash his way through it, the man exploded in a gory fountain of flesh and blood. The virus wasn't carried in the blood and gore that spattered MacEnnis, but it was in the air that night, carried on the breeze moving down the valley of the River Lagan. Nothing had happened then, not until after MacEnnis had cleaned up after his shift and stopped in at Crown Liquor Saloon on Great Victoria Street. There, he'd lifted a glass of stout and watched as his hand melted around the glass, the flesh running like hot wax down his arm, his shoulder, his chest, his face, puddling then hardening again as he screamed in agony and terror, as patrons shouted and scurried away from him . . .

The Melted Man, with runneled flesh and eyes popping garishly from a hairless, pitted skull.

The man behind MacEnnis was a giant. He stood head and shoulder above the garda, and his face and hands seemed to be carved of gray and shiny stone, all the edges hard and sharp. She knew him—she'd seen his pictures many times in the papers: Brigadier Kenneth Foxworthy; the man they called "Captain Flint," whose hands were razor-edged knives, whose voice was as soft as his body was hard. An ace, not a joker.

"I see that you know who I am," the man said, the voice so low a whisper that Caitlyn had to lean forward to hear it at all. *"You don't seem too surprised. Would that mean you know why I'm here?"*

Caitlyn glanced at MacEnnis; the skull-face was impressive, teeth gritted behind a lipless mouth, but the constable gave a nearly imperceptible shrug. "I assume you're going to tell me—" Caitlyn began, when two other people came from behind the cottage: a man with a bulging, domed forehead holding a blue steel revolver as he herded Gary toward the group. A sheen of perspiration covered Gary's face and hands.

"He was halfway across the field, Brigadier," the man called. "Must've slid out the back when he heard us coming. A bit of a hard run, the way he's sweating, but he stopped when I showed him the gun."

"Excellent work, Radar," Flint whispered. He turned back to Caitlyn. One eyebrow raised slowly in question; otherwise, the face remained entirely impassive.

"He's a friend of mine," she told the stone giant. "He's been here a few days now. He told me he was going for a walk around the island. I don't believe we have a law on Rathlin against that."

MacEnnis was staring at her with his bulging eyes, though he said nothing. Flint merely snorted. *"Odd, then, that he doesn't appear in the Jerry's register or in the Ballycastle visitor's log. How did he get here? Fly?"* He turned to the black man. *"That is how you came here, isn't it, Mr Bushorn?"*

Gary shrugged. "You tell me."

The expression—or rather, the lack of one—on Flint's face remained undisturbed. *"Where are your friends?"*

"They weren't friends."

"You expect me to believe that blatant falsehood about being 'kidnapped' and forced to fly Senator Hartmann and Ms. Davis here?"

"I expect you'll believe whatever you want."

"Tell me where they are."

"I don't know. They parachuted out of the plane near Dublin."

"Then why didn't you broadcast that immediately and land there or in Belfast?"

"Hartmann had already shot out the radio so I couldn't call. It was night, I didn't know the area, and I was flying by sight on a stormy night. I figured by the time I got to Scotland, it would be dawn and I could see better. I didn't make it."

"You've been here a day and half and have made no attempt to contact the authorities. Hardly a 'victim's' response."

"I wanted to avoid being your victim, too. Do you blame me?"

Flint seemed to sigh. *"Handcuff him and put him in the car,"* he said to Radar. *"He's under arrest. There are agents from the States coming over for him."*

"No." Caitlyn moved toward Gary as Radar pulled the cuffs from a back pocket. "Duncan, he's asked to stay here. He's one of us."

"Shite." The curse was audible to everyone, and MacEnnis's face became even more skull-like with the rictus of a grimace. "Is that true? You're a joker?" MacEnnis glanced at Gary, who looked first at Caitlyn.

"Yeah," Gary said finally. "I guess it is. Or maybe a deuce." He lifted his hand, his eyes tightening in concentration. A moment later, a small blue flame flickered from his fingertip and swept down the entire index finger. Gary grimaced in pain as the flame licked at his flesh. "That's it. That's the extent of my great powers. Get a Bic lighter, and you can do the same. Otherwise, I have a body that runs way too hot, and it fucking hurts. I'm good at scorching bedsheets, too." They could all see the finger's skin bubbling as the flame guttered out. The dark flesh had gone an ugly white as great blisters rose. Gary cradled the damaged hand to his belly. Perspiration was rolling down the side of his face. "I ain't no goddamn ace. Right now, asylum sounds good."

"Got any other skills?"

"I'm a fair mechanic."

"You're in luck, then. Things break here, all too often." With a sigh, MacEnnis turned back to Flint. "Sorry," he told the Brigadier. "I can't let you to take this man."

Flint almost, *almost* laughed. *"I don't think you understand, Constable,"* he husked. *"I'm taking him back to Scotland. He aided two extremely dangerous fugitives in escaping from the authorities in New York City, and this is now an international matter. Rathlin is still part of the UK, the last time I checked. He comes with me."*

"Rathlin might be UK, but odd how I don't see nats here at all. Odd how we get almost no money from Belfast or London. Strange how the only businesses here are those we've made ourselves," MacEnnis answered. He waddled forward until he was standing in front of Flint, his horrible face tipped back to stare up at the man. "This isn't Northern Ireland, this isn't the Scotland or Wales or England. 'Tis Rathlin, and you can squawk all you like about the law, but 'tis me that's the law here, and I'm thinking that I'd rather have me a mechanic on the island than an arrest on my books."

Flint leaned over the much smaller man. One of his fingertips, almost casually, touched the tip of the nightstick in its loop on MacEnnis's uniform belt. A sliver of ash curled away, falling to the ground. *"You are interfering,"* he said, *"in a greater matter than you can realize."*

"Ace matters?" MacEnnis asked. "That has nothing to do with Rathlin. Rathlin is for nasty jokers." He glanced at Gary. "You, mister. You want to go with Cap'n Flint here?"

Gary shook his head. MacEnnis turned back to Flint. "You see, he already likes it here, and he's a mechanic. I say he can stay. If you take him by force, you'll do so without my cooperation. We'll protest to every authority and every human rights organization, including the UN."

Flint hissed, a sound like steam. *"You are making a mistake here, Constable, one that may harm everyone infected by the virus. And you are subject to UK law, despite the lax and indulgent attitude Rathlin has enjoyed in the past."*

"The mistake, Brigadier, is the arrogance of you aces. This is Rathlin. I wonder how it will look when taking this man results in an extremely visible demonstration down in Church Bay, with every joker here putting themselves between you and your ship. Sure, you're stronger than us and you have the law on your side, and you can demonstrate that, all in full view of the cameras." MacEnnis tapped the radio on his belt with a hand of bubbled flesh. "You want me to make that call to the Mayor? You said you came here looking for a dangerous ace. I say I don't see one."

Flint glared at MacEnnis, who stared placidly back. Finally, Flint's searing gaze moved to Gary. *"I now know where you are,"* he said. *"Consider yourself already in custody, because the instant you leave this miserable little flea speck in the ocean, you will be arrested and prosecuted. There is nowhere you can hide. You've just given yourself a life sentence to Rathlin."*

With that, Flint gave a nod to Radar and stalked back toward the constable's open jeep. MacEnnis gave an audible exhalation. "I hope you know what you're doing," he said to Caitiyn, "because your track record so far isn't very good." Appraising eyes stared at Gary below the rim of his *garda's* cap. "Welcome to Rathlin, Mister Mechanic. I hope you like your new home."

She asked him no questions. She simply let him stay with her.

It had been a week. There'd been no other visitors. No new word at all, not from MacEnnis or the embassy, or anyone. It certainly didn't surprise Caitlyn that no one came up to the house, that they'd been left entirely alone after the first flurry of activity. She wondered what Gary thought.

Caitlyn was standing at the cliffs at the northeast curve of the island, a painful three-quarter-mile walk from the cottage, but she forced herself to do it, not wanting to give in to the encroaching slow paralysis of her body. Her small herd of black-faced sheep grazed in the heather nearby, with Moira cavorting through the field with the one lamb that had been dropped that spring, her high-pitched giggle making Caitlyn's smile genuine. She didn't hear Gary come up behind her, only felt the touch of his warm hand on her shoulder. She would have jumped, startled, had her body been capable of it, but she simply stood there, gazing down at the waves pounding the cliffs two hundred feet below like a statue erected there.

"That's pretty," he said.

"Aye." His hand left her, but the sense of the touch remained. She enjoyed the sensation. She could hear him coming around to her left, then saw him. He was looking down curiously.

"See the cave there?" she asked. She pointed, her arm slowly raising; he nodded. "That's Bruce's Cave. The tale is that Robert the Bruce stayed there in 1306 after he was defeated in the Battle of Methven and fled Scotland. 'Tis said that while he was hiding in the cave, he watched a spider trying to build its web by leaping from one rock to another. The spider tried and failed dozen of times, but every time it climbed back up and made the attempt again, until finally it succeeded. The Bruce was so inspired by the spider's courage and perseverance that he resolved to go back to Scotland and continue his fight against the English."

"I guess I should have studied my history more back in school. I kinda remember the name, I think, but not much else."

"There's lots of history here on Rathlin. There were stone age axe factories here 3000-2500 BC. The island's been ruled by Firbolgs, Celts, English, Scots, and Irish. There have been battles and massacres. Out there—" she pointed to the gray ranks of waves stretching to the misted horizon, "there's Sloghnamorra, the swallow hole of the sea, a maelstrom. Under Church Bay, there's the hulk of *HMS Drake*, torpedoed in 1917 by a German submarine; there are a dozen more shipwrecks in and around the island. And the views: you should see the sea stacks by the West Lighthouse, or the cliffs by Slieveacarn."

"You'd make a fine tour guide, I'm sure."

I'm just saying that for eight square miles or so of land, there's much to see and learn here, if you must stay."

"*You* left."

Caitlyn could feel the color rise in her hard cheeks. "Aye, I did. I thought it would be better out there." She turned to face him. He was watching her: soft brown eyes, a slow smile that crinkled his face. "I was wrong," she said. "I belong here."

He nodded, and she was relieved he asked no more questions. "Yeah. Sometimes you find that place."

"And New York City is that place for you."

He shrugged, then nodded. "Yeah. That's where my family is." Caitlyn waited, and he continued after a moment. "God, I need to get back there. My family . . . My mom's getting up there and isn't well, my little brother Arnie and his wife own half the business with me, and without a plane or a pilot . . ." Another pause.

"No wife yourself? No family?"

A shake of his head. "I had myself fixed when I was in the army; you know, snip-snip." His fingers made a scissoring motion, and he gave her a rueful, almost angry smile. "Didn't want to father no wild card babies. Guess we ain't so different, the people here and me."

He drew a long breath, his nostrils flaring. A wave splashed spray on the rocks below. Gary bent down. She watched him pick up a gray, limestone rock and heave it over the cliff edge. They both listened; there was no sound against the crash of the surf and soughing of the salt wind. "I appreciate everything you've done for me," he said.

"'Twas nothing," she said automatically.

Moira bounced over toward them, laughing.

"To me, it was. You didn't have to go out of your way, and you did." Moira put her arm around Caitlyn's waist. "I just hope—"

"What?"

He shook his head. "I was returning a favor, that's all. That's what got me into this mess. I believe you have to pay back what's given to you, and that's how I got into this. I owed Hartmann for what he did for me. I promised him I'd do him a favor, any favor. All he had to do was ask. So when he did . . ."

"You're saying that Captain Flint was right?"

A nod. "Yeah. I don't know why Hartmann and that woman wanted to come to Ireland, but I brought them. Now"—he picked up another rock and threw it—"it looks like I stay." There was pain in his eyes, and Caitlyn would have frowned. Instead, the smile lessened.

"I'm sorry."

"So am I." Another grimace. "If I'm going to be a mechanic, then I need to set up a place of my own. You said the population was down to a few hundred from five? Bet that means there's lots of vacant houses around. Guess I can find one that'll do."

"Stay with us," Moira interrupted. "I like you. You're the Burning Man. Do you know math?"

"I used to be pretty good at it."

"Then you can help me. School starts next week." Her voice dropped to a conspiratorial stage whisper. "Mathair's just *awful* with math."

Gary's eyes drifted upward from Moira to Caitlyn's face. "I think your mother's smarter than you think."

She didn't know what she saw in his face then. MacEnnis's words came back to her: "*. . . your track record so far isn't very good.*" She hadn't felt the impact of a person's gaze since . . . *How much of it is because he looks so normal, compared to the others on the island? Are you still that shallow, girl?*

She said it anyway.

"You can stay with us. If you like."

She expected him to balk and refuse. At the very least, she expected him to question what that meant even though she wasn't sure herself.

He didn't. He stared at Caitlyn for long seconds, then looked down again at Moira, smiling at her. "I'd like that," he said to Moira rather than Caitlyn. "And we'll work on that math."

". . . right, I understand, Arnie, but I've given the accountant permission to liquidate my 401k—use that to get through the next few months, at least, even though taxes are gonna chew up a lot of it . . . No, the plane's a total loss. I had to ditch in the ocean . . . You need to hire another plane and pilot . . . I know, man. I know. But I called the embassy in Belfast, and they told me that there are indictments out for me for attempted murder, assault, illegal flight and dozen other things down to littering, and that if I leave this island, not only will the UK have my ass but the good ole USA will be filing immediate extradition papers . . . All right, man. I'll keep trying . . . Right. Hartmann's office gave me the name of a lawyer, some guy named Dr. Praetorius; he's supposed to start working on that end . . . Give my love to Mom and tell her not to worry. I'm fine at the moment, but I miss everyone. Tell Serena the two of you will make it through this, and kiss little Keisha for me too, and let her know that her uncle loves her . . . Make sure you take care of Mom. Call her every day and check on her; you know how she is about taking her pills . . . Yeah, goodbye."

Caitlyn heard the click of the receiver in its cradle, and when she glanced up, Gary was staring at her. "I'll find a way to pay you back. I know all these calls have been expensive. Arnie doesn't think the business is going to make it, and they found a blood clot in Mom's leg . . ." Gary ran a hand over tight-curled black hair.

"What did Mayor Carrick say when you spoke with him?"

Gary nodded. "There's nothing he can do either—he was the one who suggested calling the U.S. Embassy. I've tried to get hold of Senator Hartmann's offices, too; no one will talk to me there; all they could suggest was some J-Town lawyer—Hartmann's the one guy who might be able to get me out of this, and no one knows where the hell he is. No one else seems to be able to do anything. If I leave, I'll be tossed in jail. That's the bottom line."

"I'm sorry."

"Not as fucking sorry as I am," he answered, then grimaced, looking in the direction of Moira's room. "Sorry," he apologized, pacing the length of the room and back.

"She's asleep. You must be tired, too."

He responded as if he hadn't heard her. "I need to get back. Everything and everyone I know is back in New York." He looked at her with stricken eyes. "I should never have done what I did, but I promised the man. I promised."

"Promises are important." She managed to say it without bitterness.

"Yeah. And this is one I wish I hadn't kept." He blinked. Walking over to the chair where she sat, he crouched down, touching her arm. His fingers radiated heat. "Sorry. I don't mean to sound ungrateful. You've taken huge chances with me, someone you don't know at all—all of you here have. It's just . . ."

"I know," she said. "You want to go home."

He laughed, bitterly. "You got that right."

November, 1995

GARY SAT WITH MOIRA at the desk near the front door. He huddled with her over her open textbook. Caitlyn watched the two of them, wondering.

He'd already become more a part of her life than she'd ever expected. He and Moira . . . her daughter had bonded immediately and unquestioningly to her 'Burning Man,' and he responded to her with a teasing seriousness that made Caitlyn sometimes feel clumsy in her own relations with Moira.

And yet. . . . He kept his distance with Caitlyn, careful not to say or do anything that might be construed as an advance. At first, she'd found that comforting . . .

"Look," he said to Moira, his baritone voice warm in the cool air of the room. "Remember when you introduced me to Codman Cody at the West Lighthouse? How many fingers does he have?"

Caitlyn could see Moira squeeze her eyes shut in concentration. "Six," she said at last. "Four on his right hand, two on his left."

"OK. And if he held his left hand over his right, that'd be two over four—like a fraction. What if he took away half the fingers on each hand? What would that look like? Think about Codman Cody's hands . . ."

Again, the eyes closed, then opened. "That would be one on one hand and two on the other," she said.

"Would he look silly then, with only three fingers?"

Moira giggled. "Aye, he would." They both laughed, then Gary drew a two-fingered hand and a four-fingered hand on the paper in front of them. "So you can divide the number of fingers on both hands by two, right? Which means two over four can be reduced to what fraction? Look at the hands."

"One over two!" Moira roared. "One half."

Gary applauded softly. "Hey, you got it! What if he had six fingers on his right? Could you reduce two over six?"

A pause. Then: "One over three." Moira giggled. "I understand. Thanks, Gary."

"You're welcome. Now . . . why don't you get to bed? Your mom and I gotta talk . . ." He kissed her forehead and Moira flung her arms around his neck. She ran over to Caitlyn and did the same, then scurried off to her room. Caitlyn watched Gary straighten the desk and put Moira's notebooks in her backpack.

"You're good with her," she said into the silence, and his deep brown eyes glanced back at her.

"She's a great kid. I like her a lot." His gaze turned away as he tucked Moira's math book in and closed the flap. His dark, long fingers tapped the blue cloth. He pushed back the chair. "I'm going for a walk. Wanna come?"

She hesitated. "I don't know . . . Moira . . ."

"Just tell her we're going. She'll be fine."

"All right," she said finally. "Let me get my shawl . . ."

The night was cool but dry, a strong, high wind draping shreds of cloud over a half-moon and ripping them away again, though only a faint breeze stirred the dry leaves of the hawthorn in the yard. She envied the ease with which Gary moved in the darkness, contrasting with her own clumsy, stiff-legged gait. He slowed his own pace to hers, walking alongside her down the narrow asphalt road winding westward. He was careful not to touch her, always keeping a distance between them. They said nothing, listening to the night birds, the soughing of the wind, and the faint sound of the water. They passed Abigail Scanlon's cottage, a quarter mile down the road—"Wide Abby," they called her. The old woman was out on her porch: Caitlyn could see the outline of the misshapen body, like someone laying on their side, the legs at either end of the stretched frame, the head a bump in the middle of a log, the hand waving at either end, unable to reach each other across the huge girth between them. Caitlyn remembered how they'd had to alter her cottage, the door hinged sideways, all the furniture low and wide. Caitlyn waved to her. "A beautiful night, 'tis it not, Abby?" she called out. There was no answer, only a faint wave from one of the hands.

They walked on. She could feel Gary glancing from her to Abigail. "Moira goes to 'school' every day, but she's the only one there," he said finally. "She seems to know everyone on the island, and half the time she's over at someone's house. But y'know, in two months I've never seen anyone at all ever come to your house. I notice that you don't go to the grocery yourself, that the person who delivers them leaves the box on the stoop and never knocks or rings the bell to say hello. I notice that your neighbors don't say much to you." He stopped, and she knew he was waiting for an answer. When she remained silent, walking on, he continued. "Is it me? Is it because I'm there?"

She smiled, because she must. "No," she answered. "It's not you. It's . . . complicated."

"I'm listening."

"I don't know if I can explain it to you. This isn't your home; you weren't sent here. You didn't have to make the choice we made." He said nothing; after a moment, she continued. "I came here with a mother who looked as deformed and disfigured as anyone here, who was in the same kind of pain. She lived for two decades that way, in daily pain and torment, and I took care of her. I took care of some of the others, too. That was nothing special. That was something *we all* did, those of us who could. And then . . . she died. And I left—because I could; because as far as I knew then, all the wild card had done to me was keep me forever young; because—unlike the rest of them here on Rathlin—I could get by in the normal society out there. I wasn't ugly or horribly changed. I didn't ooze slime or have spines or drag myself around like a slug. I was *pretty* and normal. Back then, when you looked at me or saw, you wouldn't notice *anything* unless you watched me very carefully. I left. I left *them* behind. At the time, I didn't think I'd ever come back."

They'd reached the point where the road curved away north to Church Bay. The west side of the island around Church Bay slid gently into the water, unlike the steep cliffs that lined most of the island's perimeter. They stood on a rise, the bay glittering below, while away over the channel, the lights of Ballycastle in Northern Ireland gleamed six miles away, tantalizingly close and impossibly far away.

"They're jealous of you," Gary said, "because you look like a nat, because you could blend in."

"That's part of it, aye. Then there's Moira. They love her, Gary, they do. She's Rathlin's only child, and they all feel like they're her aunt or uncle. But at the same time, she . . . She's a slap in their faces. All of them made the decision to stay here. They made the decision that they wouldn't bring any more children into the world to be like them, to suffer the way they've suffered. I left them, and I came back with Moira . . ."

"So they hate you."

Caitlyn tried to shake her head. It would turn only slowly. "Hate's an awfully strong word, and too simple. It's . . . it's more that they're terribly disappointed in me. I've shamed them, and along with that they can't quite ever forget that I selfishly abandoned them, and they can't forget that I've almost certainly condemned Moira to die young and in horrible pain because of the virus she carries. What I did *was* selfish and it *was* abandonment, and it *was* cruel. I did it purely for me."

"Sometimes you have to think about yourself first."

"Maybe," she answered. "But then you have to live with everybody else afterward."

He gave her a contemplative *hmm*, leaning on the stone fence that bordered the roadway. She saw his gaze catch on the Ballycastle lights and remain there. "You really want to go home, don't you?" she asked him.

A nod. "Yeah. I do. Arnie called earlier today, while you were bringing back the sheep. Mom's getting worse, and their finances . . . My savings are gone; I can't afford that lawyer anymore. I done everything I can think of to do. I even talked to Codman Cody about trying to sneak off the island at night in his boat, have him land me somewhere on the coast and see what happens . . ." She saw his hand form a fist and slowly loosen again. "I left without saying goodbye to anyone. I miss my family, I miss my friends, I miss walking around the city, all the people and the sights and the food . . . But I ain't going back as a prisoner." He looked at her over his shoulder with a wry smile. "I guess there are all kinds of prisons, aren't there?"

There was such gentle sympathy in his face, such compassion in his eyes . . . She wanted more than anything to lean toward that mouth, to kiss him and to feel him respond. She stared back at him, the eternal smile on her face, holding her breath. She could not move.

But he did. His head turned, he bent toward her so close that she could feel his warmth. He stopped. Pulled back, his expression stricken and guilty. "I'm sorry," he said. "I shouldn't have . . . I'm really sorry."

"Don't apologize," she told him.

He shook his head. "It ain't right, not when I'd leave here tomorrow if I could. Not after you took me in, let me stay with you. I'm really sorry, Caitlyn. I don't want to make you feel threatened or bothered or—"

"Stop it," she told him. "It's fine. It's . . ." . . . *what I want too. I'm just so afraid of it and I don't know if I can anymore, and . . .* There were a dozen other things to say, but she couldn't say any of them. ". . . forgotten," she finished.

But she didn't forget it. She remembered. It haunted her dreams for a long time.

"I hope you find your way home," she told him.

Rathlin's lone lawyer was also Rathlin's Mayor, an elderly gentleman with long white hair that covered most of his body. His snouted face and prominent front teeth made him look like a large rodent; the delicate eyeglasses perched there, the wire rims tucked behind his ear flaps, magnified the tiny black eyes, and the suit he wore made him look like a cartoon character. His hands were pink and wrinkled and folded on top of the newspaper that covered his desk.

Joseph Carrick: "The Rat of Rathlin," as he'd been dubbed by the *Sun* and other tabloids.

DISASTER AVERTED! the headline trumpeted. Then, in smaller, type: BLACK TRUMP DESTROYED IN JERUSALEM. SENATOR GREGG HARTMANN AMONG DEAD.

"I thought . . . I thought that since Senator Hartmann was dead that the charges against me might be dropped," Gary told Carrick.

Carrick's whiskered nose twitched. "I'm afraid they haven't. I've made the inquiries you requested: the charges against you stand, and I've been told by the authorities in Northern Ireland, Great Britain and your own country that nothing has changed—you will be arrested the moment you step foot off Rathlin." Carrick traced the headlines with a slow forefinger. "I am sorry, Mr. Bushorn. There's nothing I can do."

"Mayor," Gary said, a tone of desperation in his voice, "Look, Hartmann was just about my last hope. I gotta get back—you don't understand."

"Joseph, surely there's *something* else you can do?" Caitlyn's voice drew Carrick's attention away from the paper. His tiny lips, in the shadow of the snout, pursed in a tight moue of annoyance. Joseph Carrick had once openly courted Caitlyn, in the months after her mother's death and before her flight from Rathlin. Caitlyn knew he'd considered her departure a personal insult—she'd heard him say it to others: *"She think she's too perfect to be touched by the likes of a joker . . ."*

"I've done all I can," he answered tartly. "Surely you're not totally disappointed in the news, Miss Farrell, since that means your 'house guest' will be staying." Caitlyn's cheeks went hot—she started to answer, but Gary had already risen from his chair. His forefinger stabbed the paper in front of Carrick.

Around the finger, white smoke curled away. "You," Gary said, "will apologize to Caitlyn. I don't care if you're the fucking Mayor, I don't care if you call Constable McEnnis and have him drag me off the island as a result." His hand went down flat on the newspaper. The smell of ash and burning paper rose. Tiny flames leapt around his hand. "You know *nothing* about her, or you would have kept your mouth shut just now." Fire crackled around his wrist. "Do I make myself clear?"

Carrick's tiny eyes widened more than Caitlyn thought possible. He nearly squeaked as he pushed his chair back from his desk. "Aye, I understand," he said hurriedly. "Caitlyn, I apologize. I certainly didn't mean to imply . . ."

Gary swept the paper onto the wooden floor and stamped out the fire. The photo of the crater in the midst of Jerusalem was now a smoking hole. "I believe Caitlyn asked you a question just now."

Carrick was staring at the ruins of the newspaper alongside his desk. His head jerked back to Gary, then Caitlyn. "I suppose I could contact a few people I know in your state department. Perhaps some sort of amnesty could be arranged now that the Senator is dead and the crisis over. Why don't you come back in a few weeks or so . . ."

He did come back. Every week. And every time the answer was the same. "I'm sorry, Mr. Bushorn . . ."

December, 1995

THERE WAS WRAPPING PAPER strewn over the front room of the cottage, and Moira was sitting happily near the fire playing with a rag doll and a chess set. Caitlyn had given Gary a short-sleeved shirt woven from the wool of their sheep. "You don't exactly seem to need a sweater," she told him. "So I thought . . ."

"It's lovely," he told her, and the way he looked at her made the smile widen on her face. "Here," he said, handing her a package. "This is for you."

He set the small box on her lap. Awkwardly, she opened it—her elbows had tightened severely since the onset of winter, and she could barely move them. She stripped away the bow and the paper, and opened the lid. She could feel him watching her.

Inside, in a nest of tissue paper, was a pockct watch. She could hear it ticking. She stared at the watch, shimmering through sudden mist in her eyes. "Where did you get this?" she asked. It was all she dared to say.

"I found it, out in the back shed when I was looking for some tools. I cleaned it up, took it apart. I traded Motormouth down in Church Bay some work on his cycle in exchange for ordering the parts I needed from a repair shop in Dublin. They said it was an expensive watch, an old one—Gold over silver on the casing, and well worth the time and money to fix it. The inscription said 'To Patrick, Love Shannon.' I showed it to Moira; she said she'd never seen the watch before, but that you'd told her that Shannon and Patrick were the names of her grandparents. So I thought . . ." He paused. His head cocked inquiringly toward her. "Did I do something wrong?"

Caitlyn tried to shake her head. It moved slowly left, then right. "I'm sorry," she said. "It's . . ." She stopped. She still hadn't touched the watch. She didn't dare. "It's a long story."

"I'm not going anywhere." He sat cross-legged on the floor in front of her. "Is it your watch?"

Another slow nod. "Aye. Patrick was my da; he drew the black queen and died in '62; Mathair gave him the watch on their first anniversary. The watch came with us to Rathlin after . . . after the Relocation. Funny, it worked fine in Belfast, but once we got here, it never did. Something broke inside it, I guess, jostled loose."

"The mainspring," Gary said. "It snapped. Probably wound too tight, or it had gotten rusty over the years."

Caitlyn reached down and touched the face of the watch. "I took the watch with me when I left Rathlin, after she died. He . . . Moira's father, that is—"

"Does this man have a name?"

"Robert," Caitlyn answered. It had been ten years since she'd spoken that name. It still hurt. The word was an incantation, summoning up all the pain and anger she'd felt, and she could feel muscles pulling uselessly at the smooth expanse of her face. She let out a breath, trying to exhale the poison within the memories. "The watch . . ." Another exhalation. "It was another broken promise in a long string of promises: the promise that he loved me, the promise that he'd stay faithful, the promise he wouldn't drink, the promise that he wouldn't hit me, the promise that he'd take care of our child, the promise she wouldn't have the virus . . ." She stopped, hearing the bitterness rising in her voice and hating the sound of it. "He had an ace, the ability to enchant with song, and when you heard his voice, you couldn't move or leave and he could twist your emotions about, make you cry or laugh or shout or fall in love. But the talent was wasted on him, lost in the drink, the temper, the skirt-chasing and the ego. He knew what the watch meant to me. I gave it to him, not long after we became lovers. He said 'Sure, Caitlyn, I'll be getting it fixed for you,' I kept asking him about it afterward, for weeks that turned into months, and he'd always tell me that, aye, he'd taken it to the jewelers, but that some part or another was on backorder and that he'd be going to check on it tomorrow . . .''

She laughed, a sound as bitter as her words. "After he left us for his pub floozy, I found the watch when I was packing to come back here. It was in one of his dresser drawers, still in the cardboard box in which I'd given it to him. He'd probably forgotten to take it with him that first time—it wasn't really important to him, just as I wasn't really important to him. And rather than tell me the truth, it was easier for him to make up the lies. Maybe he didn't even remember where the watch was anymore. When I came back here, I couldn't stand to look at it. It didn't remind me of my parents anymore; it reminded me of him." She wrapped the chain of the watch around one finger. She held it up to her ear, listening to the steady metronome of the mechanism inside.

"Thank you," she said. "Now it will remind me of my parents again."

She reached toward him; he leaned forward so that her hand touched his cheek, and he pressed it tight between head and shoulder, holding her. "You're welcome," he said. She was crying; she could feel the tears rolling hot down her cheeks, and he reached forward and blotted them away with a thumb. "Hey, it wasn't that much," he said.

"You can kiss her." That was Moira, bounding across the room and wrapping her arms around Gary's neck from behind as he sat in front of the couch. "She'd like that."

"Do you really think so?" Gary asked her, though his eyes were on Caitlyn. "I wouldn't want to do anything that you or your mom would regret."

"Oh, no," Moira answered. "You can. She *likes* you."

"Moira," Caitlyn said reflexively. Gary was still watching her, his hands on the cushions of the couch on either side of her. She could feel their heat on her legs.

"Well, you do," Moira answered. "I can tell. I'm not *stupid*."

"Moira, I think that the decision whether or not to kiss should be your mom's, not mine." He reached behind and pulled Moira around until she was sitting on his lap. "But I *will* kiss you," he told her, and gave her a comically sloppy kiss on the forehead as she squirmed and giggled on his lap.

"She's asleep?" Gary asked.

"Aye," Caitlyn said softly. He was standing near the fireplace. She'd placed the watch there on the mantel, where she could see it and hear it ticking. She limped over to stand in front of him. "She says what she thinks, I'm afraid."

"I never thought that was a bad thing. Keisha, my niece, she's the same way. Adults should do it more often." One corner of his mouth lifted. "I'd never make you a promise I wouldn't keep," he said. His head leaned down toward hers. His lips were soft fire against the slick ice of her skin, and she opened her mouth to him, the embrace suddenly urgent as his fingers tangled in her hair. His touch was a flame along her breast, a heat between her legs. "I don't know," she said, suddenly frightened. "It's been so long, and my body . . ."

"Hush," he'd told her. "I'm scared, too. Sometimes, the women I'm with, they say it's too hot, that they don't . . . and I . . ."

This time it was her touch that stopped his words. "We'll go slow. We'll help each other. We'll figure out what works. If you want."

"Caitlyn, the one promise I *can't* make to you is that I'll stay. I need you to understand that before anything happens. I'll be your friend and lover, I'll help you with Moira, I'll never try to deceive you. But if and when they let me go home, I'm gone that same day. If that changes things, then let's stop now. I don't want to ever hurt you."

"That's not a promise I'd ask you to make," she told him.

"Then this is what I want," he answered. "I want it very much."

March, 1996

"OH, GOD . . . ARNIE, NO, no . . ."

The sudden catch in Gary's voice made Caitlyn hold her breath. "Yeah, yeah, I understand . . . When did it happen? How? . . . Uhhuh . . . Wasn't there anything they could do, something . . . ? How's Serena and Keisha taking this? You called Uncle Carl yet? Is there anything I can do . . . Yeah . . . No, let me see if I can arrange . . . No, not a lot of hope for it . . . I'll call you back, and Arnie—I love you. Be strong, man . . . Yeah, see ya."

Gary stood there after he put the receiver down, staring vacantly. Moira, reading a book by the fireplace, looked over at him also. "Gary?" Caitlyn asked. "What's wrong?"

"My mom," he said. "She died." He blinked, and tears rolled from his eyes. They steamed and sizzled as they reached his cheeks. "She died and I wasn't there, and they're burying her on Saturday, and I'm here. I'm fucking *here*."

Moira's eyes widened at the profanity—Gary was always so careful around her, but he didn't seem to have noticed. "Oh, Gary . . ." Caitlyn started to rise—slowly, the only way she could—from the chair to go to him, but he waved her away.

"Just . . . just leave me alone. I need to take a walk." He strode out of the house, then, without looking at either of them, steam wreathing his face.

"Mathair," Moira said as the sound of the closing door seemed to echo through the room. "You should go with him. He needs you."

"I walk so slow, Moira," she protested.

"He needs you," Moira repeated, but Caitlyn was already rising, moving as quickly as she could to the door, taking her shawl from the peg as she left. The sun was setting in the west, obscured by driving gray clouds, and fine mist dampened Caitlyn's face. For a moment, she didn't see Gary, then she caught sight of a dark figure, walking over the rolling hills toward the cliffs. She hurried after him. "Gary!"

He turned. She saw him wave at her, gesturing her back. Then he turned again and continued to walk on. She hesitated, then followed.

He was standing near the edge of the cliffs above Bruce's Cave, staring out over the water. The sun had set, the edges of the clouds behind them tinted the color of blood, though ahead the sky was unrelenting black and dark gray, streaked with squall lines out over the water. Waves broke a startling phosphorescent white on the rocks far below. He hadn't turned as she approached, though she knew he had to have heard her. She put her arms around his waist from behind, pulling him into her; it was like embracing a wood stove, but she continued to hold him. "Gary, I'm so sorry . . ."

"Arnie said that she must have had the stroke some time in the morning. He came to check on her when he couldn't get hold of her on the phone, and found her unconscious. By the time they got her to the hospital, she was in arrest, and they couldn't bring her back." He spoke without looking at her; she felt more than heard his voice, her head on his back. "She wasn't real good about taking her meds. I used to call her every morning just to remind her."

"It's not your fault."

"Maybe not. Or maybe it was." He turned in her arms. "I'll never know, will I?" His eyes were narrowed, eyebrows lowering above like thunderheads. He pushed himself away from her. "I won't be there for the funeral, won't be able to grieve with the rest of my family. The business I spent most of my life trying to build is gone along with my savings, and what little I had left I've spent trying to get out of here. I've written or talked to every damn representative, to every paper from the *Times* to the goddamn *Jokertown Cry,* and I'm still on *Rathlin!*" The name was a shout as he flung his arms wide. "This isn't fucking jail; it's worse."

The words cut, lancing deep into Caitlyn's core. She was crying, unable to stop the tears, cold against her cheeks, salt mingling with the freshwater of the mist. "Gary . . ." She could say nothing, only stand there stricken and numb like the lifeless statue she was inevitably becoming, her arms still spread in the end of the embrace.

He was steaming in the mist, like a living cloud, and she couldn't tell whether he were also crying or not, his features half-obscured. The droplets hissed on his skin like water spilled on a hot griddle. "I have to get out of here," he said. "I've lost so much, and there's no way I can ever, ever get it back again . . ." He stopped then, looking at her. "Caitlyn," Her name was a sob. "Oh God, Caitlyn . . ."

His hands were on his head, his face lifted to the sky. She saw his chest swell in a long, ragged breath, then slowly relax again as he sighed. "It hurts," he said, simply.

"I know." Caitlyn took his hand, ignoring the heat. "Gary, I see you in pain and it makes me hurt, too. I wish there was something I could say or do to help. I'm so sorry for your loss, for the way you're trapped here . . ." She stopped. His fingers pressed hers.

"You're all that makes it bearable," he told her. "You, and Moira, too." His hand cooled; the rain no longer steamed as it touched him. "I never had the chance to tell her goodbye. Now I never will."

"I know. It's not fair."

He nodded. He pulled her to him. For a long time, they stood that way, until the light had left the sky and the hard rain began in earnest.

August, 1996

THE BOAT AND THE pier smelled of fish and Codman Cody.

"You shouldn't be going, Caitlyn," Gary told her. "If you fell in somehow . . ."

He didn't say the rest. He didn't need to. Caitlyn knew it all too well. In the last few months, the rigidity of her body had become worse. She couldn't sit at all anymore, and getting in and out of bed was difficult because she could barely bend from the waist. She could walk, albeit slowly and with a strange, lock-kneed gait like someone pretending they were a doll. Her shoulder and elbow joints still worked, but detail work with the hands was now impossible; she would never knit or sew again. She smiled at Gary—it hurt too much to frown. "I'll be fine. Codman has life jackets, and I can stand near the cabin, away from the side. Gary, I need to be there. Please don't argue."

His face softened. "All right," he told her. "But you wear a life jacket. Moira, you want to help your mom?"

Moira nodded. Cody blinked his round, wide-set fishy eyes, the scales on his skin glinting in the light from the lantern hung on the piling of the tiny pier at the western end of Church Bay. He tossed a life jacket to Moira with the shorter, two-fingered hand, webbing stretched between the wide-spread digits. "Hurry," he told them. "The tide's running out strong now."

Moira fastened the straps of the life jacket around Caitlyn, and then hugged her. "Be careful, Mathair," she said.

"I will. I'll see you soon. Remember, you're to go right over to Alice's house; I'll pick you up there." Moira nodded solemnly. She was blinking back tears, Caitlyn noticed, and she patted the girl's head. "Go tell Gary goodbye."

Caitlyn watched her run over to Gary, watched him effortlessly pick her up as Caitlyn once had and embrace her as Moira wrapped arms around his neck. "I wish you didn't have to go," Caitlyn heard her say to him.

"Part of me wants very much to stay," Gary told her, still hugging her. His gaze was on Caitlyn. "But I want to go home. You understand that, don't you? I want to go home."

"Mathair says they'll arrest you if they catch you. They'll put you in jail."

"Then I have to make sure they don't catch me, don't I?" He put her down. "I'll miss you so much, Moira. Give me a kiss?"

She kissed Gary, hugging him fiercely, and then turned and ran down the pier to the shore. Caitlyn could hear her crying as she ran, turning toward Codman Cody's small house, where his wife Alice waited.

"'Tis nothing," Caitlyn told Gary, who stood watching Moira's sudden flight. "She's just upset, but she'll be fine. Help me into the boat . . ."

A few minutes later, the *Ailteoir* ("That's 'joker' in Irish Gaelic," Caitlyn had told Gary when he asked) was grumbling its way toward the entrance to the harbor and out into the open waters of Church Bay. The night was moonless, the waves gentle as the small fishing vessel moved out into the open water, rolling softy. The light of Ballycastle shown directly ahead, and the line of the Irish coast was a blackness against the star-dappled sky. Cody steered the *Ailteoir* due south, following the line of Rathlin's southern arm. Once past the Rue Point and the South Lighthouse at the tip of Rathlin, he turned southeast, intending to land east of Ballycastle in the less-settled land between Fair Head and Torr Head. From there, Gary would try to make his way south to Belfast, where he could determine the best way to the States.

Caitlyn felt worry settle in her stomach. She'd helped him plan this escape, keeping to herself all the doubts and fears. She'd judiciously enlisted Duncan MacEnnis's help, and the Constable had recommended a local joker who could create the false IDs and passport Gary was now carrying, under the name he'd first given her: John Green. *It can't work,* she wanted to tell him. *A black man walking about in Ireland—how more conspicuous could you be? The first garda you come across will figure out who you are and place you under arrest.*

She clamped her lips shut, and concentrated on keeping her balance with the motion of the boat in the long swells. If he were going to leave, she wanted to be with him as long as she could. She wanted to see him on the shore. She wanted to watch him walk away into the night. She didn't think she could bear the pain of the loss if something went wrong and she hadn't been there.

"We're coming up on the two-mile mark," Cody said from his seat at the controls. He grinned at Gary and Caitlyn, exposing the twin rows of tiny triangular teeth that lined his mouth. "Another few minutes and you're technically off the island."

Gary nodded. He was standing alongside Caitlyn, his body a welcome warmth against the stiff sea breeze. He put his arm around her. Neither one of them said anything—it had all been said earlier that day, along with the tears, the kisses, a final few stolen moments of intimacy. His arm brought her close; she tried to bring her head down to lay against his chest and half-way succeeded. "Promise you'll be careful," she said, no more than a whisper. She wondered whether he would hear her, but she felt his lips on her hair and a kiss.

"I will," he answered.

"*Shite!*" The curse came from Cody, and Caitlyn felt Gary's body jerk and then move quickly away.

"What's the matter?"

"I have a blip on the sonar. Out there." He pointed to starboard, close to where Ballycastle glittered. Red and white lights blinked closer to them, sending wavering reflections chasing themselves over the water. They all heard the noise at the same time: the full-throttled roar of powerful engines. "Bleeding patrol boat. You'd best get in the cabin, Gary. Don't want them seeing you out on the deck . . ."

Gary ducked into the small cabin and closed the door behind him. A few moments later, the blue-white glare of a spotlight stabbed across the waves and settled on them. The patrol boats, a fast cruiser, pulled within hailing distance and shut its engines. "Hey, Cody!" someone yelled. "What the hell are you about in that rusting tub of yours, now?"

Cody blinked into the spotlight, shielding his eyes. "Cap'n Blane, is it? What's the problem? I'm still in Rathlin waters."

"You're a good half-mile outside, man."

"Not according to my instruments."

"Then your instruments are off or you've forgotten how to read them. And since when do you do your fishing at night? You know the regs, Cody—prepare to be boarded for inspection."

"Ah, now, Cap'n, you don't be needing to waste your time with that," Cody protested hurriedly. He clambered down from the top of the cabin to stand next to Caitlyn. The spotlight widened as he moved, then narrowed again. Caitlyn lifted her arm, squinting into the light. "The truth be, Cap'n, I'm *not* exactly fishing. I was taking Caitlyn here for a bit of a ride, and I suppose I wasn't paying as much attention to the instruments as I might be, if you take my drift. You're a married man too, are you not, Cap'n? So I expect you understand. Do you think I'd be trying to smuggle something over in this puttering slow thing?"

Cody's arm was around her, and she could smell the odor of rotting fish. But it was easy to smile . . . "I'd hate for something like this to get back to my missus," Cody said.

Caitlyn could hear conversation, then a burst of rough laughter and someone's voice saying audibly, "She's missing a nose if she's shagging the Codman . . ." The spotlight snapped off. After images danced purple and yellow in Caitlyn's vision. "Turn that rust bucket around, then," Blane's voice called loudly. "And next time, keep it closer to home."

Cody waved; the patrol boat's engines coughed and then roared as the prow lifted and the props churned the water to white froth. The lights receded, heading back toward Ballycastle. Cody went back to the wheel; Gary emerged from the cabin.

Cody spun the wheel, and the *Ailteoir* turned. The South lighthouse gleamed ahead of them. "They'll be watching now," Cody said. "I don't have a choice."

"I know," Gary said. "Maybe next time, eh?"

Cody sniffed. "Don't know about this 'next time,' either," he said. "The *Ailteoir* ain't much but she's all I have. I come out again like this, and Blane or whoever's out there waiting isn't going to be so accommodating. I lose the boat, and I lose everything. Doing this once is one thing, doing it again . . ." Codman gave a massive blink, his bulbous eyes seeming to vanish into his skull and them pop out again. "I'm sorry. I hope you understand."

Caitlyn thought Gary might be angry or upset. Instead, strangely, he shrugged and sighed. "I know, Codman. I have a plane rusting on the bottom north of Rathlin, that was *my* life, that I'd scraped and saved and borrowed to buy. And I threw it away for . . ." He shook his head. "I don't even know for what, but it sure as hell wasn't for me. So yeah, I understand."

He said nothing else on the way back. He held Caitlyn's hand, and he stared over the stern of the boat toward the lights of Ireland.

May, 1997

EACH WORD WAS A separate, labored breath of air. "Tell . . . them . . . to . . . come . . . in."

The doctor's eyestalks blinked, and he scuttled away crab-like, his brilliant orange and blue carapace leaving her vision. Caitlyn heard him talking softly with the two of them, and a few moments later, she heard Gary and Moira enter the bedroom. Their faces swam above her as they stood over the bed. Gary was trying to smile; Moira was openly crying.

Dying was suffocation by inches. Dying was slowly being turned to painted stone. Dying was forcing the muscles of lungs and heart to pump and knowing that it was a battle she had already lost, that she could continue fighting for only a few more minutes.

At least she would be a beautiful, smiling corpse.

"I . . . love . . . you," she told them. "I'm . . . sorry."

"You can just be quiet," Gary told her. "There's nothing to be sorry about." His hand stroked her face; she felt nothing of the caress—not the touch, not the heat. "We love you, too. I wish—" He stopped.

She would have nodded, would have smiled. She could only cry. "Moira?" she said.

"What do you want, Mathair?" She sniffed and scrubbed at her eyes with her sleeve. It hurt most to see her, to see how her face had lost its baby fat over the last few years, to see her shape changing to that of a young woman. To see the glimmer of the adult that she might become—and to know that because of the virus, she would never be that person.

Caitlyn had thought that the worst thing would be there to witness what the wild card virus would do to her daughter. Now she knew it was worse to leave and not know. "You . . . be . . . careful," she told Moira. "Every . . . one . . . will . . . watch . . . out . . . for . . . you."

"I know, Mathair." Then the tears came, and Moira hugged her desperately as Caitlyn strained uselessly to hug her in return, to move the arms frozen at her sides.

"Go . . . on . . . now," she told her. "Please."

Gary slowly, gently, pulled Moira away from Caitlyn. They started to walk away, but Caitlyn called out to him. "Gary . . ."

"Go on, Moira," she heard him tell her. "I'll be right out." Then his face returned, hovering over her. "Hey," he said. "Are you in pain, love? Maybe Doc Crab can—"

"No," she told him. "No . . . pain." She forced another breath through her lungs. She would have closed her eyes, but those muscles were no longer working, either. "You . . . kept . . . your . . . promises."

"It was easy. You made it easy."

"One . . . more."

"What?" She saw his face, his eyes narrowing. "Ah," he said, and the exhalation said more than words.

"No . . . you don't understand . . . Promise . . . that . . . if . . . you . . . get the chance to go home . . . you'll . . . still . . . go. Don't . . . worry . . . about . . . Moira. They . . . will . . . take . . . care . . . of . . . her . . . here."

"Caitlyn—"

"*No!*" The shout, though hardly more than a hoarse whisper, cost her. She had to struggle for the next breath and was afraid it wouldn't come. He waited, his hand stroking her hair. "Promise . . . it. That's all . . . I . . . can . . . give . . . you . . . now. It's . . . what . . . you . . . want."

"I know," he said. "But it's not going to happen."

". . . promise . . ."

Gary sighed. "All right. I promise. I'll go home."

January, 1998

". . . IT'S NOT SIMPLE, I know, but you can get it. First you have to isolate 'x' on one side of the equation, so . . ."

A knock on the door interrupted the algebra lesson. Moira shrugged at Gary and went to answer it. "Good evening to you, Moira," Constable MacEnnis said. The *garda* stood outside the door in a misting drizzle, beads of water running down his cap, the impossibly round, white eyes bright in the murky day. "This just came for Gary. I think he'll want to read it." He handed Moira an envelope. The ivory paper felt thick and heavy in his hand, spotted a bit with the rain. "It's from Mayor Carrick," MacEnnis added.

She could feel Gary behind her at the door. She handed him the envelope and stepped back. "Come on in," she said to MacEnnis. "No sense in standing out in the rain."

MacEnnis touched the crown of the cap with knobbed, scarred fingers. "I don't think so, Moira. I should get back . . ." He nodded to them and walked back to the Fiat parked at the side of the road. Moira shut the door, turning to find Gary still staring at the envelope in his hands. She knew then.

"Go on," she told him. "Open it."

He seemed to start, as if she'd shaken him from some reverie, then slipped his forefinger under the flap and slid it along the seal. He pulled out the paper—cream-colored legal bond—and unfolded it. She could see him reading the words, saw the tremble start in his hands and the eyes widen. Without a word, he handed it to her.

. . . granted a presidential pardon, effective immediately. Any and all charges pending against you have been dropped by the governments of the United States, the Republic of Ireland, and the United Kingdom . . .

She handed the paper back to him, then flung her arms around his neck, giggling as if she were nine again. "Oh, Gary! I'm so happy for you!"

He hugged her, but the embrace was half-hearted and he released her almost immediately. "Moira, I can't . . ."

She didn't answer. Instead, she went to the mantel, standing there for a moment as the heat from the peat fire warmed the front of her body, then turned, serious. "The night Mathair died, I listened to her talking to you."

He rattled the paper in his hand. "Moira, this doesn't mean that I have to go *now*. Or . . . we can *both* go. Would you like that? Would you like to go to New York City?"

She shook her head. "No. I wouldn't like that at all. I'm staying here. I'll be thirteen this year, Gary, and there's plenty of people here to look out for me. I'm Rathlin's only child, remember? They all know me."

"I should stay until—" He stopped. They both knew what he meant.

"I know my odds, Gary," she said. "I've known them for a long time. I also know that almost all latents express either at puberty or during some great emotional crisis. Well, the virus didn't show itself when Mathair died, and I doubt anything will be more traumatic than that, so . . ." She shrugged. "I don't want you to see me die, Gary. I don't want your last memory of me to be something awful. I'd rather stay that little girl you helped to learn her math."

"God, you sound like her."

Moira laughed at that, pleased, and with the laugh was a trace of the childish giggle. She came toward him. The paper with its words of release was smoldering in his grasp, and she took it from him. "This is what you always wanted, and Mathair knew that. I heard you make her a promise," Moira told him. "Now keep it."

He said nothing for a time, and she saw steam rise from the corners of his eyes. She went to the mantel and took Caitlyn's pocket watch from where is sat, bringing it over to him and pressing the round form into his hand. "Remember us," she said. "Remember us as we were."

"I will," he said finally.

The sound from the television set was tinny and the picture half lost in static. "Do you have any statement to make?" a reporter asked, shoving a microphone toward Gary, a darkness in a blizzard of transmitted snow and teeming rain from the storm flailing the island. She could see the curve of Church Bay behind him, gray in the downpour and besieged by a small invading squadron of press with cameras.

"I'm going home," he said simply. "That's all. I don't have anything else to say, and I'd like you all to just leave me alone." The press of reporters shouted a torrent of questions, but he ignored them, pushing through them. She heard some faint cries: "Damn, look out! He'll burn you if you touch him!" The cameras pursued him, but Gary pushed his way up the ramp and onto the ferry. The reporter who'd asked the question turned to face the camera. "This is the scene, live on Rathlin Island—"

Moira touched the remote and the television went dark. She stared at the glass tube for several minutes before getting up. She pulled on a sweater and her slicker and went outside to check on the sheep and open the gate to the pasture.

She had moved in with Wide Abby Scanlon, who'd agreed to be her guardian, but Moira told Mayor Carrick that she wanted to keep the old house and move into it herself when she was older. The man had wriggled his rat nose and she knew what he was thinking. *"Chances are that you won't be needing the house, dearie. Chances are you'll be dead . . ."* But he'd agreed, and every day she walked back to the old place. Every day she did the chores and pretended for a time that she was an adult and this was her house now, and that she was living here for the rest of her life.

That she would die here, as Mathair had, as her Gramma had.

She swept out the barn and laid down new straw, then walked out across the field to the cliffs and just stood there as the sheep grazed, watching the waves thunder into the rocks in cascades of white foam. After a few hours, she went back to the cottage to fix supper—she should get back to Abby's house, but she didn't want to. Not yet.

She crumbled newspaper and placed it on the grate, then put a few turves of peat on top. She reached up to the mantelpiece for the book of matches and crouched back down.

The pack was empty. She tossed the empty cardboard into the fireplace. The stillness of the house struck her then, the silence lurking inside even as the storm softly lashed the structure. She wanted to cry, hunkered there in front of the cold, dead fireplace, listening to the rain patter and splash against the windows and roof while the house itself was consumed with somber quiet.

She heard the door open, heard footsteps cross quickly toward her. A dark hand reached past her shoulder and touched the paper. A flame curled away, yellow fire spreading as the paper began to crackle and smoke curl away toward the flue. She could hear the ticking of a watch. "I knew I could find you here when you weren't at Abby's," he said.

He was smiling at her, uncertainly. She tried to frown sternly at him. "You broke your promise," Moira began, but Gary shook his head.

"I promised Caitlyn that if I could, I'd go home," he said. "I got as far the train for Belfast before I realized that I was going the wrong way."

"Gary . . ." She stopped. Took a breath and let it out again. She wasn't going to hug him, wasn't going to smile at him, because if she did either of those things, she'd be lost. "It's going to happen soon. I can feel it. You should have gone. I *want* you to go."

"Is that what you really want? To be alone? To be with Wide Abby when it happens and not me? If it is, tell me now and I'll go."

He cupped his large, dark hands around her cheeks, warm and soft and loving. He kissed her forehead, and she sank into his embrace, pulling herself tightly to him, a child again, sobbing into his chest. He simply held her, rocking back and forth as they sat on the floor in front of the fire. "I don't want to die, Gary," she said. "I'm so scared . . . so scared . . ."

"I know, I know," he crooned, whispering. "I'm scared, too. But whatever happens, I'll be with you. I promise you that. I'll be with you."

Age of Wonders

TEN

April 2005

RALEIGH AND HER MOTHER were like a mirror version of Caitlyn and Moira. But the wild card had been kinder to her and Aurora . . . so far. Raleigh felt the weight of it, of just how lucky she was. She didn't deserve it.

But deserve had nothing to do with the wild card.

She called her mother from Tomlin International as soon as she was off the plane. "I'm home. I'm going to splurge for a cab, so I should be there soonish."

"It's so good to hear your voice. How was the trip?"

"It gave me a lot to think about. A lot of material."

"As if you really need more to think about," Aurora said testily. "You're working way too much, and you haven't had any time off since you started this job, and—"

"Mom." But maybe Raleigh ought to take some time off. Especially if she was going to write this book she kept thinking about.

With a deep sigh, Aurora changed the subject. "How is your other project going?"

"What other project?"

"The search for the other half of your DNA."

Oh yeah. "I . . . decided to put that on hold for a while."

"Oh?" She sounded confused. "I thought this was really important to you."

"Yeah, so did I." But she had become suspicious of her motives. Was this for *her,* or did she just want to solve a mystery? Solving some mysteries created more problems than it fixed. "I've lived with ambiguity my whole life. I think maybe I kind of like it."

"Well. I'll open a bottle of wine to celebrate, right now. Better hurry home before I drink it all myself."

"Love you, Mom."

"Love you too, kiddo."

In the main terminal, she didn't even have a chance to look for the signs to the taxi stand before she saw Gavin standing there, right outside security, with flowers. Not ostentatious flowers. Red roses would have sent Raleigh walking in the opposite direction, because of the sheer presumption. But no, he just had a half dozen purple tulips wrapped in plastic, something he might have picked up at a corner florist on impulse. Her favorite color. Just an "I'm thinking of you," not a cry of desperation or overwrought apology.

She wasn't expecting this, and for a moment she just stopped and stared. "Hey," she said finally, approaching him.

"Hey."

"How did you know when I was getting in?"

He looked away, blushing. "You posted about it on your blog, right before you left Ireland. I just kind of worked out the timing. Don't be mad."

"That's kind of stalkery."

"Yeah. I'll leave if it's weird."

"And waste the flowers?" She took the bouquet and opened her arms for a quick, friendly hug. She had missed the shape of him, she discovered.

"Good trip?" he asked.

"Yeah. Yeah, it was."

"Feel like talking about it?"

She stopped. Regarded him. "I'm still mad at you. Like, if I can't trust you with a stack of my papers, how can I trust you about anything else?"

He frowned. "Yeah, I'm still kind of mad at myself about that one. Look, I'm not asking for a grand immediate gesture of forgiveness. I just wanted to see you. Maybe catch up on things. Can I get you a cup of coffee?"

"Mom's got a bottle of wine waiting at home. But . . . I'll need that coffee tomorrow to help me over the jet lag. That okay?"

"Perfect," he said, and smiled his amazing smile.

Age of Wonders

ELEVEN

One Year Later

"I HOPE SHE'S OKAY." Raleigh was at the door of Ramenrama, looking out to the street. Aurora was an hour late for the party.

"I'm sure she's fine," Gavin said, looking over her shoulder.

They'd taken over Ramenrama to celebrate Raleigh's book release. The official publication date wasn't until the following week, but then she'd be caught up in promotional tours and interviews, at the publisher's whim. So this party was for friends and family. And most of the staff of *Aces!*, who were celebrating as well: Digger Downs, in acknowledgment of his roots, had given them the scoop on his new gig, which had just gone public. He was a judge on a new reality TV show, *American Hero*. Peregrine was the host, and Raleigh had to hand it to the woman, she'd dropped all kinds of hints in the three interviews she'd done with her over the last year and Raleigh hadn't picked up on any of them. Peregrine knew how to work the press; she'd had a lot of practice, after all.

The publisher had sent over a case of the books, and they sat piled up on a table. There was her name, right on the cover. The cover art showed a shadowy hand starting to turn over a card in a spread of Texas Hold'em. Chips lay scattered on the background of green felt. And the title: *Waiting for the Turn*. Part memoir, part pop-history, part commentary. A combination of her blog posts and articles, expanded and given a shape. The world was three generations past the first Wild Card Day, but this wasn't about the big picture, the sweep of history and the grand analysis of how human history had veered into something new and strange. This was about the view on the ground.

"Hey, there she is," Raleigh said.

Aurora—her shimmering lights were on *fire*. A diamond-tinged halo of red and gold that made passersby stop and stare, even on the fringes of Jokertown. Aurora didn't seem to notice. She hugged her coat around her and hurried to the door, grinning.

"Mom!"

"Honey, hi there, can I crash your party?" She hugged Raleigh and kissed her cheek, waved at Gavin, greeted Margot Dempsey across the room. "You're looking lovely, dear."

"You say that to everyone," Dempsey shot back, gaze narrowed like a cat's.

"You are in a really good mood," Raleigh observed, and Aurora turned to her, eyes gleaming. Tears ready to spill over.

Aurora announced, "I got a show."

Raleigh laughed and hugged her. "That's fantastic! What is it? Can you talk about it?"

"Can everyone here plug their ears?" she called out to the room. "This hasn't hit *Variety* yet."

"No promises," Dempsey called back.

Aurora waved her off and talked anyway, fluttering, totally unlike herself. Gushing, even. "It came out of the blue, one of these kids' shows for Disney. I'm playing a grandmother, and while I don't think I'm quite old enough to play a grandmother I won't argue. It's about a family of witches, and they want my lights. Real-life magic, right? They wrote the part just for *me*! She's a great character, a comic foil, has all the best lines. Oh honey. *I got a show*." Then she pulled herself together, dabbing at her eyes and looking around the room with a proprietary air. "So, I'm very sorry about stealing your thunder but I'm crashing your party. Oh, hello Gavin, nice to see you."

"Ma'am," he said, amused, and offered a glass of champagne.

"Hmm, you are once again forgiven for pissing off Raleigh," she said, taking it, and swept off to take in the admiration of the rest of the party.

"I like this. I don't think I've been to enough parties in my life," he said, looking after her.

Raleigh eased up beside him, putting her arm around his middle. His arm came to rest over her shoulders like it was meant to be there. "Then we'll just have to throw a lot more of these things, won't we?"

"You're already working on another book, aren't you?"

"Yes," she said, grinning. "Yes I am."